Mindbend

MINDBEND

ROBIN COOK

G. P. Putnam's Sons /// New York

For Barbara

G. P. Putnam's Sons
Publishers Since 1838
200 Madison Avenue
New York, NY 10016

PROLOGUE

FETAL RESEARCH BANNED

New Regulations for Medical Research

By HAROLD BARLOW

Special to *The New York Times*

WASHINGTON, July 12, 1974—
President Richard M. Nixon signed
into law today the National Research
Act (Pub. L. 93–348). The law calls
for the creation of a National Com-
mission for the Protection of Human
Subjects in Biomedical and Behav-
ioral Research. There has been growing concern about the ethics of research involving children, retarded
persons, prisoners, the terminally ill,
and particularly fetuses.

It is hoped that by creating appro-

priate guidelines some of the shock-
ing abuses that have been exposed of
late can be obviated, such as the pur-
poseful infecting of a large number
of retarded children with hepatitis in
order to study the natural progres-
sion of the disease, or the discovery a
few months ago at a Boston hospital
of a dozen dismembered aborted fetuses.

The first phase of implementing
the law includes a moratorium on
"research in the United States on a
living human fetus, before or after
induced abortion, unless such research is done for the purpose of as-
suring the survival of such fetus."
Obviously the fetal issue is intimately
tied to the highly emotional abortion
issue.

Response to the new legislation in
scientific circles has been mixed. Dr.
George C. Marstons of Cornell Medical Center welcomed the new law,
stating that "guidelines for ethical
behavior in human experimentation
are long overdue. The competitive
economic pressure for research
breakthroughs creates an atmosphere where abuse is inevitable."

Dr. Clyde Harrison of Arolen
Pharmaceuticals disagreed with Dr.
Marstons, saying that "anti-abortion
politics are holding science hostage,
preventing needed health care research." Dr. Harrison went on to explain that fetal research has resulted
in many significant scientific gains.
Among the most important is a possi-

ble cure for diabetes. Fetal tissue injected into the pancreas has been proven to repopulate the islet cells that produce insulin. Equally important is the experimental use of fetal tissue to heal previously incurable paralysis resulting from spinal cord injuries. Injected into the site of the trauma, the tissue causes spontaneous healing by generating growth of new, healthy cells.

It is too early to judge the impact of this bill until the various commissions mandated by law make their recommendations to Secretary Caspar Weinberger. In the area of research the new law will have an immediate impact by severely limiting the supply of fetal tissue. Apparently planned abortions have been the primary source of such tissue, though it is not known whether or not this need played a role in doctors' decisions to abort.

Candice Harley felt the needle pierce the skin of her lower back, followed by a sharp burning sensation. It was like a bee sting, only the pain rapidly evaporated.

"I'm just putting in some local anesthetic, Candy," said Dr. Stephen Burnham, a swarthy, good-looking anesthesiologist, who had assured Candy that she was not going to feel a thing. The trouble was that she had already felt pain—not a lot but enough to make her lose a certain amount of faith in what Dr. Burnham had told her. She had wanted to be put to sleep. But Dr. Burnham had informed her that epidural anesthesia was safer and would leave her feeling better after the abortion and the sterilization procedure were over.

Candy bit her lower lip. There was another stab of pain. Again it wasn't severe, but she felt vulnerable and ill prepared for what was happening. At thirty-six, Candy had never been in a hospital, much less had an operation. She was terrified and had told Dr. Burnham as much. She felt the burning sensation again, and by reflex she straightened her back.

"Don't move now," admonished Dr. Burnham.

"I'm sorry," blurted Candy, afraid that if she didn't cooperate they would not take care of her properly. She was sitting on the side of a gurney in an alcove next to an operating room. A nurse was standing in front of her and to the right was a curtain which had been pulled to isolate the alcove from the busy OR corridor. Behind the curtain, Candy could hear muted voices and the sound of running water.

Directly ahead was a door with a small window through which she could see the operating room.

Candy's only covering was a flimsy hospital gown, open in the back where the doctor was busy doing whatever he was doing. He had elaborately explained to Candy what was going to happen, but her ability to concentrate was severely limited by the intimidating surroundings. Everything was new and frightening.

"Tuohy needle, please," said Dr. Burnham. Candy wondered what a Tuohy needle was. It sounded awful. She heard a cellophane package being torn open.

Dr. Burnham eyed the three-inch needle in his gloved hand, sliding the stylet up and down to make sure it moved freely. Stepping to the left so that he could make sure that Candy was sitting straight, he positioned the needle over the area he had injected with the local anesthetic.

Using both hands, he pushed the needle into Candy's back. His experienced fingers could feel the needle break through the skin and slide between the bony prominences of Candy's lumbar vertebrae. He stopped just short of the ligamentum flavum, the barrier covering the spinal canal. Epidural anesthesia was tricky and that was one reason Dr. Burnham liked to use it. He knew not everybody could do it as well as he could and that knowledge gave him satisfaction. With a flourish he pulled out the stylet. As expected, no cerebrospinal fluid came out. Replacing the stylet, he advanced the Tuohy needle another millimeter and felt it pop through the ligamentum flavum. A test dose of air went in easily. Perfect! Replacing the empty needle with one filled with tetracaine, Dr. Burnham gave Candy a small dose.

"I feel a strange sensation on the side of my leg," said Candy with concern.

"That just means we're where we are supposed to be," said Dr. Burnham. With deft hands he removed the syringe with the tetracaine and then threaded a small plastic catheter up through the Tuohy needle. Once the catheter was in place, he removed the needle. A piece of paper tape went over the puncture site.

"That's that," said Dr. Burnham, stripping off his sterile gloves and putting a hand on Candy's shoulder to urge her to lie down. "Now you can't say that hurt very much."

"But I don't feel the anesthetic," said Candy, fearful they would go ahead with the surgery even if the anesthetic wasn't working.

"That's because I haven't given you anything yet," said Dr. Burnham.

Candy allowed herself to be lowered to the gurney, the nurse helping by lifting her legs, then covering her with the thin cotton blanket. Candy clutched the cover to her chest as if it would afford some protection. Dr. Burnham fussed with a small plastic tube that snaked out from beneath her.

"Do you still feel as nervous?" questioned Dr. Burnham.

"Worse!" admitted Candy.

"I'll give you a little more sedative," said Dr. Burnham, squeezing Candy's shoulder reassuringly. While she watched, he injected something into her IV line.

"OK, let's go," said Dr. Burnham.

The gurney with Candy on it rolled silently into the OR, which was bustling with activity. Candy's eyes scanned the room. It was dazzlingly white with white tile walls and floor and white acoustical ceiling. X-ray view boxes lined one wall, futuristic electronic monitoring equipment another.

"OK, Candy," said the nurse who'd been helping Dr. Burnham. "We'd like you to scoot over here." She was on the other side of the operating table, which she patted encouragingly. For a moment Candy felt irritation at being ordered about. But the feeling passed quickly. She really had no choice. She was pregnant with an eighteen-week-old fetus. She preferred to use the word "fetus." It was easier to think about than "baby" or "child." Dutifully, Candy moved to the operating table.

Another nurse pulled up Candy's gown and attached minute electrodes to her chest. A beeping noise began, but it took Candy a while to realize that the sound corresponded to the beating of her heart.

"I'm going to tilt the table," said Dr. Burnham as Candy felt herself angle so that her feet were lower than her head. In that position she could feel the weight of her uterus in her pelvis. At the same time she felt a fluttering which she had noticed over the previous week and which she thought might be the fetus moving within her womb. Thankfully, it stopped quickly.

The next instant the door to the corridor burst open and Dr. Lawrence Foley backed in, holding up his dripping hands just like surgeons did in the movies. "Well," he said in his peculiarly inflectionless voice, "how's my girl?"

"I don't feel the anesthetic," said Candy anxiously. She was relieved to see Dr. Foley. He was a tall man with thin features and a long straight nose that sharply tented the front of his surgical mask. Soon all Candy could see of his face were his gray-green eyes. The rest was hidden, including his silver-white hair.

Candy had been seeing Dr. Foley on an infrequent basis for her routine gynecological care and had always liked and trusted the man. She had not had a checkup for eighteen months prior to her pregnancy, and when she had gone to his office a few weeks ago she had been surprised to see how much Dr. Foley had changed. She'd remembered him as being outgoing and not without a touch of dry humor. Candy wondered how much of his "new" personality was due to his disapproval of her unmarried pregnant state.

Dr. Foley looked at Dr. Burnham who cleared his throat: "I just gave her 8 milligrams of tetracaine. We're using continuous epidural." Stepping down to the end of the table, he lifted the blanket. Candy could see her feet, which appeared exceptionally pale in the bright fluorescent light from the X-ray view boxes. She could see Dr. Burnham touch her, but she felt nothing as he worked his way up her body until he was just under her breasts. Then she felt the prick of a needle and told him so. He smiled and said, "Perfect!"

For a moment Dr. Foley stood in the center of the room without moving. No one said anything; everyone just waited. Candy wondered what the man was thinking about, since he seemed to be looking directly at her. He'd done the same thing when she'd seen him in the clinic. Finally, he blinked and said, "You've got the best anesthesiologist in the house. I want you to relax now. We'll be finished before you know it."

Candy could hear some commotion behind her, then the snap of latex gloves as she watched Dr. Burnham fit a wire frame over her head. One of the nurses secured her left arm to her side with the sheet covering the OR table. Dr. Burnham taped her right arm securely to a board that stuck out from the table at right angles. That was the arm with the IV. Dr. Foley reappeared in Candy's sight, gowned and gloved, and helped one of the nurses spread large drapes over her, effectively blocking nine-tenths of her view.

Straight up she could see her IV bottles. Behind her, if she rolled her head back, she could see Dr. Burnham.

"Are we ready?" asked Dr. Foley.

"You're on," said Dr. Burnham. He looked down at Candy and winked. "You're doing fine," he reassured her. "You may feel a little pressure or some pulling, but you shouldn't feel any pain."

"Are you sure?" asked Candy.

"I'm sure."

Candy could not see Dr. Foley, but she could hear him, especially when he said, "Scalpel." She heard the sound of the scalpel slapping the rubber glove.

Closing her eyes, Candy waited for the pain. Thank God it didn't come. All she could feel was the sensation of people leaning over her. For the first time she allowed herself the luxury of thinking that this whole nightmare might actually pass.

It had all started about nine months previously when she had decided to go off the pill. She'd been living with David Kirkpatrick for five years. He had believed she was as devoted to her dancing career as he was to his writing, but sometime after her thirty-fourth birthday she had begun nagging David to marry her and start a family. When he refused, she decided to try getting pregnant, certain he would change his mind. But he had remained adamant when she had told him of her condition. If she continued the pregnancy, he would leave. After ten days of weeping and countless scenes she had finally agreed to this abortion.

"Oh!" gasped Candy as she felt a stab of white-hot pain somewhere deep in her being. It was akin to the feeling when a dentist finds a sensitive spot in a tooth. Thankfully, the stab didn't last long.

Dr. Burnham glanced up from his anesthesia chart, then stood to look over the ether screen at the operative site. "Are you guys pulling on the small bowel?"

"We just packed it away out of the operative field," admitted Dr. Foley.

Dr. Burnham sat back down and gazed directly into Candy's eyes. "You're doing just great. It's common for someone to feel pain when the small intestine is manipulated, but they're not going to do that anymore. OK?"

"OK," said Candy. It was a relief to be reassured that everything was going as it should. Yet she wasn't surprised. Although Lawrence

Foley's manner seemed to lack the old warmth, she still had every confidence in him as a doctor. He'd been wonderful to her from the start: understanding and supportive, especially in helping her decide about the abortion. He'd spent several sessions just talking to her, calmly pointing out the difficulties of raising a child as a single parent and underlining the ease of having an abortion, though Candy was already in her sixteenth week.

There was no doubt in Candy's mind that it had been Dr. Foley and the people at the Julian Clinic who had made it possible for her to go through with the abortion. The only thing that she had insisted upon was that she be sterilized. Dr. Foley had tried unsuccessfully to change her mind about the sterilization. She was thirty-six years old and she did not want to be tempted again to beat the biological clock by becoming pregnant, since it was obvious marriage was not in her immediate future.

"Kidney dish," ordered Dr. Foley, bringing Candy's attention back to the present. She heard the clank of metal against metal.

"Babcock clamp," demanded Dr. Foley.

Candy rolled her eyes back and glanced up at Dr. Burnham. All she could see were his eyes. The rest of his face was hidden by his surgical mask. But she could tell he was smiling down at her. She let herself drift and the next thing she heard was Dr. Burnham saying, "It's all over, Candy."

With some difficulty she blinked and tried to make sense of the scene slowly coming into focus before her eyes. It was like an old-fashioned TV warming up: first there were sounds and voices, then slowly the picture and meaning emerged. The door to the corridor opened, and an orderly pulled an empty gurney into the room.

"Where's Dr. Foley?" asked Candy.

"He'll see you in the recovery room," said Dr. Burnham. "Everything went perfectly." He moved Candy's IV bottle to the gurney.

Candy nodded as a tear ran down her cheek. Fortunately, before she could dwell on the fact that she would remain childless forever, one of the nurses took her hand and said, "Candy, we're going to move you over onto the gurney now."

In the adjoining auxiliary room, Dr. Foley directed his attention to the stainless-steel pan neatly covered by a white towel. To be certain that the specimen was unharmed, he lifted a corner of the towel.

Satisfied, he picked up the pan, walked down the corridor, and descended the stairs to the pathology department.

Ignoring the residents and technicians, though several of them spoke to him by name, he walked through the main surgical area and entered a long corridor. At the end he stopped in front of an unmarked door. Balancing the specimen pan in one hand, he got out his keys and opened the door. The room beyond was a small and windowless laboratory. Dr. Foley moved slowly but deliberately as he stepped into the room, closed the door behind him, and put down the pan.

For a few moments he stood paralyzed until a sharp pain in his temples made him stagger backward. He bumped the countertop and steadied himself. Glancing at the large institutional clock on the wall, he was surprised to notice that the minute hand seemed to have jumped five minutes.

Swiftly and silently Dr. Foley performed several tasks. Then he stepped over to a large wooden crate in the center of the room and opened it. Within was a second, insulated container. Releasing the latch, Dr. Foley raised its lid and looked in. Resting on a bed of dry ice were a number of other specimens. Dr. Foley carefully placed the newest addition on the ice and closed the lid.

Twenty minutes later, an orderly dressed in a white shirt and blue pants pushed a dolly into the small unmarked laboratory and picked up the ice chest and packed it in a wooden crate. Using the freight elevator, he took it down to the loading dock and put it into a van.

Forty minutes after that, the wooden crate was taken off the van and placed in the luggage section of a Gulf Stream jet at Teterboro Airport in New Jersey.

CHAPTER 1

Adam Schonberg's eyes blinked open and in the darkness of his bedroom he heard the undulating scream of a siren announcing yet another catastrophe. Gradually, the noise diminished as the police car or ambulance or fire truck or whatever it was receded into the distance. It was morning in New York City.

Snaking a hand out from beneath the warm blankets, Adam groped for his glasses and then turned the face of the clock radio toward him: 4:47 A.M. Relieved, he flipped off the alarm, which was scheduled to go off at 5:00, then pulled his hand back under the covers. He had fifteen more minutes before he had to haul himself out of bed and into the icy bathroom. Normally, he'd never take the chance of turning off the alarm for fear he'd oversleep. But as charged up as he was this morning that was not a possibility.

Rolling onto his left side, he pressed against the sleeping form of Jennifer, his twenty-three-year-old wife of one and a half years, feeling the rhythmical rise and fall of her chest as she breathed. Reaching down, Adam ran his hand lightly up her thigh, which was slim and firm from her daily dance workouts. Her skin was soft and remarkably smooth with hardly a freckle to mar its surface. It had a delicate olive tone that suggested southern European descent, but that was not the case. Jennifer insisted that her genealogy was English and

Irish on her father's side of the family, German and Polish on her mother's side.

Jennifer straightened out her legs, sighed, and rolled over onto her back, forcing Adam to move out of her way. He smiled; even in her sleep she had a forceful personality. Although her strong character could at times present itself to Adam as frustrating stubbornness, it was also one of the reasons Adam loved her so much.

Glancing at the clock, which now said 4:58, Adam forced himself out of bed. As he crossed the room to shower he stubbed his toe on an old Pullman trunk Jennifer had covered with a throw to serve as a table. Gritting his teeth to keep from crying out, he hobbled to the edge of the tub where he sat down to survey the damage. He had a remarkably low tolerance for pain.

The first time Adam had realized this was during his disastrously short high school football career. Because he was one of the larger boys, everyone including Adam himself had expected him to be on the team, especially since David, Adam's deceased older brother, had been one of the town stars. But such was not to be the case. Everything had gone well until Adam had been given the ball and told to run a play he had dutifully memorized. The instant he was tackled he had felt pain, and by the time everybody had gotten back on his feet, Adam had decided this was just another area where he could not compete with his brother's reputation.

Shaking off the memory, Adam quickly showered, shaved his heavy beard which would shadow his chin by five that afternoon, and brushed his thick black hair. He whipped on his clothes, barely glancing in the mirror, oblivious to his dark good looks.

Less than ten minutes after getting out of bed he was in the two-by-four kitchen, heating up his coffee. He glanced about the cramped, badly furnished apartment, vowing again that the minute he finished medical school he would find Jennifer a decent place to live. Then he went over to the desk in the living room and glanced at the material he'd been working on the night before.

A wave of anxiety passed through his body. In less than four hours he was going to be standing in front of the imposing Dr. Thayer Norton, chief of Internal Medicine. Grouped around would be the rest of the third-year medical students who were currently rotating on Internal Medicine with Adam. A few of the students, like Charles Hanson, might be rooting for him. But the rest would be more or less hoping that he'd make a fool of himself, which was a distinct possibility. Adam had never functioned well in front of a group, another disappointment for his father, who was a recognized and much-sought-after speaker. At the beginning of the rotation Adam had drawn a blank in the middle of presenting a case, and Dr. Norton had never let him forget it. Consequently, Adam had postponed his major case presentation until the end of this rotation, hoping that he'd grow more confident with time. He did, but not a lot. It was going to be tough and that was why he'd gotten up before the sun. He wanted to go over the material yet again.

Clearing his throat and trying to shut out the bustling noise of a New York morning, Adam began his presentation once again. He spoke out loud, pretending he was standing in front of Dr. Norton.

/ / /

Jennifer would have slept until ten if it hadn't been for two things: one, she had a doctor's appointment at nine, and two, by seven-fifteen the temperature in the bedroom had climbed to a tropical level. Perspiring, she kicked off the covers and lay still for a moment until the shock of yesterday's discovery had again settled in. Yesterday—after a month of trying to deny the possibility—Jennifer had finally gone out and bought a home pregnancy test. Not only had she missed two periods, she had developed morning sickness. It was the nausea more than anything else that had driven her to buy the test. She did not want to upset Adam, who had been irritable and tense for the last few months, until she was absolutely sure. The home pregnancy test had been positive, and today she was seeing her gynecologist.

Carefully she got out of bed, wondering if anyone realized that dancers, despite their limber grace on stage, were always stiff and sore in the morning. Stretching out her leg muscles, she felt the panic wash over her, obliterating the nausea.

"Oh, God," she moaned to herself. If she really was pregnant, how would they manage? The money she earned from the Jason Conrad Dancers was their only income, except for the money her mother sneaked to her behind her dad's and Adam's backs. How would they ever support a baby? Well, maybe the test was wrong. She was using an IUD, which was supposed to be the most effective contraceptive

device next to the pill. At least Dr. Vandermer would end the suspense. Jennifer knew that it was only because Adam was a medical
student that the doctor had agreed to fit her into his crowded schedule.

She turned to glance at the Sony clock radio her mother had given
her. She hadn't told Adam about the gift because Adam had become
touchy over her parents' generosity, or, as he termed it, their interference. Jennifer suspected this had become a sore spot with Adam
only because of his own father's stinginess. It was no secret to Jennifer that Dr. David Schonberg had been so set against Adam's marrying her that when Adam had willfully gone ahead and done it, he'd
been essentially disinherited. In one way Jennifer thought that she'd
get a bit of pleasure knowing how mad the old doctor would be if she
really was pregnant. Reluctantly, pulling her stiff joints into a steady
position, she brushed out her lustrous long brown hair and carefully
checked her face in the mirror to make sure its attractive oval planes
and clear blue eyes did not reveal her anxiety. No need to upset
Adam before she had to.

Forcing a cheerful smile, she sallied into the living room where
Adam was going over his speech for the tenth time.

"Isn't talking to oneself the first sign of dementia?" teased Jennifer.

"Clever!" acknowledged Adam. "Especially since I didn't think
Sleeping Beauty could cogitate before noon."

"How are you doing with the presentation?" she asked, putting her
arms around him and turning her face up for a kiss.

"I got it down to the required fifteen minutes. That's about all I can
say." He bent and kissed her.

"Oh, Adam. You'll do just fine. I tell you what: Why don't you give
the presentation to me?" She poured some coffee and then took a
seat in the living room. "What disease does the patient have?"

"Tardive dyskinesia is the current diagnosis."

"What on earth is that?" asked Jennifer.

"It's a neurological disorder involving all sorts of involuntary
movements. It's associated with certain drugs given for psychiatric
problems . . ."

Jennifer nodded, trying to appear interested, but Adam was only a
minute into his speech when her attention turned back to her possible pregnancy.

CHAPTER 2

Dr. Clark Vandermer's office was just off Park Avenue on Thirty-sixth Street. Jennifer got there by taking the Lexington Avenue subway to Thirty-third Street and walking north. The building was a large apartment house complete with awning and liveried doorman. Entrance to the professional suites was to the right of the building's main entrance. As Jennifer opened the front door, the slight smell of medicinal alcohol made her flinch. She had never enjoyed going to the gynecologist, and the idea that she might be pregnant made this particular visit especially upsetting.

Jennifer walked down a carpeted hallway, reading the names painted with gold leaf on the doors. She passed the entrances to the offices of two dentists and a pediatrician, and came to a door on which was written "GYN Associates." Below this was a list of names. The second name was Dr. Clark Vandermer's.

Jennifer took off the coat that she'd purchased secondhand in Soho for thirty-five dollars and draped it over her arm. Under the coat she was dressed quite well in a smart Calvin Klein shirtdress that her mother had recently bought for her at Bloomingdale's.

As she opened the door, Jennifer remembered the office from her previous visits. On the wall opposite the entrance was a sliding glass panel beyond which sat the receptionist.

There were a number of women in the waiting room. Jennifer didn't count but there had to be more than twelve. All were well dressed and most were either reading or doing needlepoint.

After checking in with the receptionist, who admitted that she had no idea how long the wait would be, Jennifer found a seat near the window. She picked up a recent copy of *The New Yorker* from the coffee table and tried to read, but all she could do was worry about Adam's reaction if she were really pregnant.

It was two hours and fifteen minutes before Jennifer was finally called. She followed the nurse to an examining room.

"Take off all your clothes and put this on," the woman said, handing Jennifer a paper cover-up. "I'll be back and then the doctor will be in."

Before Jennifer could ask any questions, the nurse was gone and the door closed.

The room was about ten feet square with a curtained window at one end, a second door to the right, and bare walls. The furniture included a scale, a wastepaper basket which was full to overflowing, an examination table with stirrups, an open locker, and a sink. It was hardly cozy, and Jennifer remembered that Dr. Vandermer was brusque to the point of rudeness. Adam had sent her to him because he was supposed to be the best, but "best" did not seem to include an evaluation of bedside manner.

Not knowing how soon the nurse would be back, Jennifer hurried. She deposited her large coat and bag on the floor and used the locker for her clothes. Once naked, she tried to figure out the cover-up. She couldn't tell if it should go on with the opening in the front or the back. She opted for the front. Then she tried to decide what she should do with herself. Should she lie down on the examination table or just stand? Her feet were getting cold from the tile floor. She lifted herself onto the examination table and sat on the edge.

A moment later the nurse returned in a rush.

"I'm so sorry for the long wait," she said in a pleasant but harried tone. "We seem to be getting busier and busier. Must be a new baby boom." She quickly began checking Jennifer's weight and blood pressure and then sent her to the bathroom for a urine specimen. When Jennifer returned, Dr. Vandermer was waiting.

Jennifer had always been leery of handsome gynecologists, and Dr. Vandermer evoked that old reservation. He looked more like an actor playing a role than a real doctor. He was tall with dark hair silvering on his temples. His face was square with a sharp chin line and a straight mouth. He wore a pair of reading glasses on the end of his nose and looked over them at Jennifer.

"Good morning," he said in a voice that did not invite conversation. His blue eyes swept over her, then her chart. The nurse shut the door behind them and then busied herself with the contents of a stainless-steel pan by the sink.

"Ah, yes. You're Mrs. Schonberg, the wife of Adam Schonberg the third-year medical student," Dr. Vandermer said.

Jennifer didn't know if it were a statement or a question, but she nodded and said that she was Adam's wife.

"I wouldn't think this was a good time for you to be having a baby, Mrs. Schonberg," said Dr. Vandermer.

Jennifer was shocked. If she hadn't been naked and vulnerable, she would have been angry. Instead she felt defensive.

"I hope I'm not pregnant," said Jennifer. "That's why you put in an IUD a year ago."

"What happened to the IUD?" asked Dr. Vandermer.

"I think it's still there," said Jennifer.

"What do you mean you think it is still there?" questioned Dr. Vandermer. "You don't know?"

"I checked just this morning. The strings are there."

Shaking his head, Dr. Vandermer indicated to Jennifer that he thought her less than responsible. He leaned over and quickly wrote something on the chart. Then he raised his eyes, took off his reading glasses. "On the history you filled out a year ago you indicated that you had a brother who'd only lived for several weeks."

"That's right," said Jennifer. "He was a mongoloid baby."

"How old was your mother at the time?" asked Dr. Vandermer.

"I think she was around thirty-six," said Jennifer.

"That's something you should know about," said Dr. Vandermer with thinly veiled exasperation. "Find out for sure. I want that information on the chart."

Putting down his pen, Vandermer took out his stethoscope and gave Jennifer a rapid but thorough physical examination, peering into her eyes and ears and listening to her chest and heart. He tapped her knees and ankles, scratched the bottoms of her feet, and inspected every inch of her body. He worked in total silence. Jennifer felt as if she were a piece of meat in the hands of a very competent butcher. She knew Dr. Vandermer was good, but she could have used some warmth.

When he finished, the doctor sat down and quickly wrote his findings on the chart. Then he asked Jennifer about her menstrual history and the date of her last period. Before she could ask any questions he motioned her into a prone position and began the pelvic.

"Just relax now," said Dr. Vandermer, finally remembering that his patient was probably anxious. Jennifer felt an object enter her. It was done smoothly and expertly. There was no pain, just an unpleasant fullness. She could hear Dr. Vandermer speak with the nurse. She heard the door open and saw the nurse leave.

Dr. Vandermer stood up so that Jennifer could see him. "The IUD is still in place, but it looks like it is low. I think it should be removed."

"Is that difficult?" asked Jennifer.

"Very simple," said Dr. Vandermer. "Nancy went to get me an instrument. It will only take a second."

Nancy returned with something that Jennifer could not see. She felt a fleeting twinge of pain. Dr. Vandermer stood up holding a coil of plastic in his gloved hand.

"You definitely are pregnant," he said, sitting down at the desk and writing anew on the chart.

Jennifer experienced a rush of panic similar to the one she had felt the moment she saw that the home pregnancy test was positive.

"Are you sure?" she managed with a quivering voice.

Dr. Vandermer did not look up. "We'll confirm it by laboratory tests, but I'm sure."

Nancy finished writing labels on the specimen tubes and came around to help Jennifer remove her feet from the stirrups. Jennifer swung around so that she was sitting on the side of the examination table.

"Is everything all right?" she asked.

"Everything is perfectly normal," assured Dr. Vandermer. He completed the chart, then spun around to face her. His expression was as neutral as when he'd first entered.

"Can you give me some idea of what to expect?" asked Jennifer. She folded her hands to steady them and put them on her lap.

"Of course. Nancy Guenther will be your nurse practitioner," Dr. Vandermer said, nodding at the nurse. "She'll go over things like that with you. I'll be seeing you for routine visits monthly for the first six months, then every two weeks until the last month. Then weekly unless there's a complication." Dr. Vandermer got up and prepared to leave.

"Will I be seeing you each time I come?" asked Jennifer.

"Generally," said Dr. Vandermer. "Occasionally I might have a delivery. Then you would be seen by one of my associates or Nancy. In either case they would report directly to me. Any other questions?"

Jennifer had so many questions she didn't know where to begin. She felt like her life was coming apart at the seams. She also had the feeling that Dr. Vandermer wanted to leave now that the exam was over. "What about when it comes time for my delivery?" she asked. "I don't mind seeing someone else for a routine visit, but when it comes to delivering, I feel differently. You're not planning a vacation around my due date, are you?"

"Mrs. Schonberg," began Dr. Vandermer. "I haven't taken a vacation in five years. I go to an occasional medical meeting and I'm planning to lecture at a cruise seminar in a couple of months. But that certainly will not conflict with your due date. Now if you have no more questions, I'll turn you over to Nancy."

"Just one more thing," said Jennifer. "You asked about my brother. Do you think it is significant that my mother gave birth to a defective child? Does it mean I might do the same?"

"I sincerely doubt it," said Dr. Vandermer, edging toward the door. "Leave the name of your mother's doctor with Nancy and we'll call and find out the details. Meanwhile, I plan to do a simple chromosomal study on you. But I don't think there is anything to worry about."

"What about an amniocentesis?" asked Jennifer.

"At this point I don't think there is any need for such a procedure, and even if there were, it couldn't be done before your sixteenth week. Now if you'll excuse me, we'll see you in a month."

"What about an abortion?" asked Jennifer anxiously. She didn't want Dr. Vandermer to leave. "If we decide not to have this child, is it difficult to arrange for an abortion?"

Dr. Vandermer, who'd had a hand on the door, stepped back in front of Jennifer, towering over her. "If you are interested in an abortion, I think that you are seeing the wrong doctor."

"I'm not saying that I want one," said Jennifer, cowering beneath his glare. "It's just that this isn't a good time for me to be pregnant, as you said yourself. I haven't told Adam yet and I don't know what his reaction will be. We depend on my income."

"I don't do abortions unless there's a medical reason for it," said Dr. Vandermer.

Jennifer nodded. The man obviously felt strongly about the issue. To change the subject she asked, "What about my working? I'm a dancer. How long will I be able to continue to work?"

"Nancy will discuss such questions with you," said Dr. Vandermer, glancing at his watch. "She knows more about that kind of stuff than I do. Now, if there is nothing else . . ." Dr. Vandermer moved away from the examination table.

"There is one other thing," said Jennifer. "I've been nauseous in the morning. Is that normal?"

"Yes," said Dr. Vandermer, opening the door to the corridor. "Such nausea is present in at least fifty percent of pregnancies. Nancy will give you some suggestions on handling it by altering your diet."

"Isn't there something I could take?" asked Jennifer.

"I don't believe in using medication for morning sickness unless it's interfering with the mother's nutrition. Now if you'll excuse me, I'll see you in a month."

Before Jennifer could say another word, Dr. Vandermer was out the door. He closed it behind him, leaving Jennifer with Nancy.

"Diet is a very important part of pregnancy," said Nancy, handing Jennifer several sheets of printed material.

Jennifer sighed and let her eyes drop from the closed door to the sheets of paper in her hands. Her mind was a whirl of conflicting thoughts and emotions.

CHAPTER 3

Adam turned west on Twelfth Street, heading directly into the wind and rain. It was pitch dark already, despite the fact that it was just seven-thirty. Only a half block to go. He had an umbrella, but it was in sad shape and he had to wrestle with it to keep the wind from inverting it. He was cold and damp, but worse, he was exhausted, mentally and physically. The all-important presentation had not gone well. Dr. Norton had stopped him not once but twice for grammatical errors, interrupting Adam's train of thought. Consequently, Adam had left out an important part of the case history. At the end Dr. Norton had merely nodded and asked the chief resident about another patient.

Then, to round out the day, Adam had been called down to the emergency room because it was understaffed and had been given the job of pumping out the stomach of a young attempted suicide. Inexperienced in such a procedure, Adam had made the girl vomit, and he'd caught it smack in the chest. And if that weren't bad enough, fifteen minutes before he was to be off duty, he got a complicated admission: a fifty-two-year-old man with pancreatitis. That was the reason he was so late coming home.

Passing the alley that communicated with the scenic airshaft outside their apartment, Adam saw the assortment of trash cans that the sanitation department noisily emptied three mornings a week. Today the cans were full to overflowing, and a couple of scrawny alley cats had braved the rain to investigate.

Adam backed through the front door to their building and closed the worthless umbrella. For a moment he stood in the ancient foyer and dripped onto the tiled floor. Then he unlocked the inner door and began mounting the three flights of stairs to their apartment.

To announce his arrival he pressed the doorbell as he pushed the key into the first of several locks. They'd been broken into twice during the year and a half they'd lived there. Nothing had been stolen, though. The thieves probably realized they'd made a mistake as soon as they saw the beat-up furniture.

"Jen!" called Adam as he opened the door.

"I'm in the kitchen. I'll be out in a second."

Adam raised his eyebrows. Since his hospital hours were so irregular, Jennifer usually waited until he was home to start dinner. Sniffing the savory aroma, he went into the bedroom and took off his jacket. When he walked back to the living room, Jennifer was waiting. Adam gasped. At first it appeared that she was only wearing an eyelet apron. Naked legs stretched from the bottom edge of the apron to high-heeled mules. Her hair was brushed straight but held back from her face with combs. Her oval face seemed to be illuminated from within.

Lifting her arms and positioning her fingers as if dancing a classical ballet, Jennifer slowly revolved. As she turned, Adam saw that under the apron she was wearing a lavender teddy edged in lace.

Adam smiled. Eagerly he reached out to lift the front edge of the apron.

"Oh, no!" teased Jennifer, avoiding his grasp. "Not so fast."

"What's going on?" laughed Adam.

"I'm practicing to be the Total Woman," quipped Jennifer.

"Where in heaven's name did you get that . . . thing?"

"This thing is called a teddy." Jennifer lifted the front of the apron and pirouetted again. "I bought it at Bonwit's this afternoon."

"What on earth for?" asked Adam, wondering how much it cost in spite of himself. He didn't want to deny Jennifer something she wanted, but they had to be careful on their budget.

Jennifer stopped dancing. "I bought it because I always want to be attractive and sexy for you."

"If you were any more attractive and sexy for me I'd never get through medical school. You don't have to dress up in frilly stuff to turn me on. You're plenty sexy the way you are."

"You don't like it." Jennifer's face clouded over.

"I like it," Adam stammered. "It's just that you don't need it."

"Do you really like it?" asked Jennifer.

Adam knew he was on thin ice. "I love it. You look like you belong in *Playboy*. No, *Penthouse*."

Jennifer's face brightened. "Perfect! I wanted it to be right on the border between sexy and raunchy. Now, I want you to march right back into the bathroom and take a shower. When you come out, we'll have a dinner that I hope will make you feel like a king. Go!"

Jennifer forcibly propelled Adam back into the bedroom. Before he could say anything, she shut the door in his face.

When he was finished showering, he discovered that the living room had been transformed. The card table had been brought from the kitchen and laid for dinner. Two empty wine bottles with candles stuck in them provided the only light. The silverware sparkled. They only had two place settings. Each had been a present from Jennifer's parents, one on their wedding day, the other on their first anniversary. They rarely used them, leaving the pieces wrapped in tinfoil and hidden in the freezer compartment.

Adam walked over to the kitchen and leaned against the door. Jennifer was working feverishly, in spite of the handicap afforded by her high-heeled slippers. Adam had to smile. This woman tottering around his kitchen did not look like the Jennifer he knew. If she noticed him, she gave no indication.

Adam cleared his throat. "Jennifer, I'd like to know what's going on."

Jennifer didn't respond. Instead she uncovered a pot and stirred the contents. Adam could see from the spoon when she placed it on the counter that it was wild rice. Adam wondered how much that cost. Then he spotted the roast duck cooling on the carving board.

"Jennifer!" called Adam a bit more forcibly.

Jennifer turned around and thrust a wine bottle and corkscrew into Adam's arms. He was forced to grab both lest they fall to the floor. "I'm making dinner," she said simply. "If you want to make yourself useful, open the wine."

Stunned, Adam carried the bottle into the living room and pulled out the cork. He poured a little wine into a glass, and held it up to the candlelight. It was a deep, rich ruby color. Before he could taste it, Jennifer called him into the kitchen.

"I need a surgeon in here," she said, handing him a large knife.

"What am I supposed to do with this?" he asked.

"Cut the duck in half."

Adam tried a few tentative thrusts with little success. Finally, he put all his strength behind the blow and sliced the duck in two.

"Now how about telling me what this is all about."

"I just want you to relax and enjoy a good dinner."

"Is there an ulterior motive for all this?"

"Well, I do have something to tell you, but I'm not going to do so until after we have this feast."

And feast it was. Although the snow peas were slightly overdone and the wild rice slightly underdone, the duck was sensational and so was the wine. As the meal progressed, Adam found himself growing sleepy. Jerking himself awake, he fastened his attention on his wife. Jennifer looked extraordinarily beautiful in the candlelight. She'd removed the eyelet apron and was now clothed only in the provocatively sheer lavender teddy. Her image blurred in Adam's mind, and for a brief moment he fell asleep sitting at the card table.

"Are you all right?" asked Jennifer, who was just beginning to describe the home pregnancy test.

"I'm fine," said Adam, unwilling to admit he'd been asleep.

"So," continued Jennifer, "I followed the directions. And guess what?"

"What?"

"It was positive."

"What was positive?" Adam knew that he must have missed some key phrase.

"Adam, haven't you been listening to me?"

"Of course I've been listening. I guess my mind wandered for a moment. I'm sorry. Maybe you'd better start again."

"Adam, I'm trying to tell you that I am pregnant. Yesterday I did one of those home pregnancy tests and this morning I went to Dr. Vandermer."

For a minute Adam was too shocked to speak.

"You're kidding," he said at last.

"I'm not kidding," said Jennifer, meeting his eyes. She could feel

her heart beating out a rapid rhythm. Involuntarily she'd clenched
her hands into fists.

"You're not kidding?" said Adam, uncertain whether he was about
to laugh or cry. "You're serious?"

"I'm serious. Believe me, I'm serious." Jennifer's voice shook. She'd
hoped that Adam would be happy, at least at first. Later they could
deal with the host of problems the pregnancy would bring. Jennifer
got up, walked around to Adam, and put her hands on his shoulders.

"Honey, I love you very much."

"I love you, too, Jennifer," said Adam. "But that is not the issue."
He stood up, shrugging off her hands.

"I think it is the issue," said Jennifer, watching him move away.
More than anything she wanted to be held and reassured that everything was going to be all right.

"What about your IUD?" asked Adam.

"It didn't work. I guess we should think of this baby as some sort of
miracle." Jennifer forced herself to smile.

Adam began to pace the small room. A baby! How could they have
a baby? They were just barely keeping their heads above water as it
was. They were already close to twenty thousand dollars in debt.

Jennifer watched Adam silently. From the moment she'd left Dr.
Vandermer's office she had feared Adam's reaction. That was why she
had dreamed up the idea of the celebration dinner. But now that the
meal was over she was left with the reality that she was pregnant and
her husband was not very pleased.

"You always wanted to have children," she said plaintively.

Stopping in the middle of the threadbare carpet, Adam looked at
his wife. "Whether I want to have children is also not the issue. Of
course I want children, but not now. I mean, how are we going to
live? You'll have to stop dancing immediately, right?"

"Soon," admitted Jennifer.

"Well, there you have it! What are we going to do for money? It's
not as if I can get a newspaper route after school. Oh God, what a
mess. I don't believe it."

"There's always my family," said Jennifer, fighting back tears.

Adam looked up. His lips had narrowed.

Jennifer saw his expression and quickly added, "I know how you
have felt about accepting support from my family, but if we have a
child it will be different. I know they would adore helping us."

"Oh, sure!" said Adam sarcastically.

"Really," said Jennifer. "I went home this afternoon and spoke to them. My father said that we are welcome to come and live in their house in Englewood. Goodness knows, it's big enough. Then as soon as I can get back to dancing or you start your residency, we can move out."

Adam closed his eyes and hit the top of his head with a closed fist. "I don't believe this is happening."

"My mother will enjoy having us," added Jennifer. "Because of the baby she lost, she's particularly concerned about me."

"There's no connection," snapped Adam. "She had a Down's baby because she was well into her thirties."

"She knows. It's just the way she feels. Oh, Adam! It wouldn't be so bad. We'll have plenty of space, and you could use the attic room as a study."

"No!" shouted Adam. "Thank you very much but we are not accepting charity from your parents. They already interfere in our life too much. Everything in this goddam dump is from your parents," he said, gesturing around the room.

In the midst of her anxiety Jennifer felt anger stirring. At times Adam could be so frustratingly obstinate, and certainly less than grateful. Right from the beginning of their relationship his rejection of her parents' generosity had been out of proportion. She'd gone along with it to a point, recognizing his special sensitivities, but now that she was pregnant it seemed unreasonably self-centered.

"My parents have not been interfering. I think it is time for you to control your pride or whatever it is that gets you so angry anytime my parents try to help us. The fact of the matter is we need help."

"You can call it what you will. I call it interfering. And I don't want it, today, tomorrow, ever! We're on our own and we'll handle this by ourselves."

"OK," said Jennifer. "If you can't accept help from my family, then ask your father for help. It's about time he did something."

Adam stopped pacing and stared at Jennifer. "I'll get a job," he said softly.

"How can you get a job?" asked Jennifer. "Every second you're awake you're either studying or at the hospital."

"I'll take a leave from school," said Adam.

Jennifer's mouth dropped open. "You can't leave school. I'll get another job."

"Sure," said Adam. "What kind of job? Cocktail waitress? Be serious, Jennifer. I don't want you working while you're pregnant."

"Then I'll get an abortion," said Jennifer defiantly.

Adam wheeled around so that he was facing his wife. Slowly he raised his hand and pointed his index finger at her nose. "You're not going to get an abortion. I don't even want to hear that word."

"Then go to your father," said Jennifer.

Adam clenched his teeth. "We wouldn't have to go to anybody if you just didn't get yourself pregnant."

The tears that Jennifer had been holding back all day ran down her cheeks. "It takes two, you know. I didn't do this by myself," she said, and broke into sobs.

"You told me not to worry about babies," snapped Adam, ignoring her tears. "You said that was your department. You did a great job!"

Jennifer didn't even try to answer. Choking, she ran into the bedroom and slammed the door.

For a moment Adam stared after her. He felt sick. His mouth was dry from all the wine he'd drunk. He looked at the cluttered table with the remains of their dinner spread out in front of him. He didn't have to look into the kitchen. He already knew what condition it was in. The apartment was a mess, and it seemed frighteningly symbolic of his life.

CHAPTER 4

Dr. Lawrence Foley pulled into his long winding driveway. The rambling stone mansion was still out of sight when he pressed the button that opened the garage door. Rounding the final group of elms, he could see the towers silhouetted against the night sky. The neo-Gothic castle in Greenwich had been built in the early twenties by an eccentric millionaire who'd lost everything in the crash of 1929 and blown his brains out with an elephant gun.

Laura Foley was in the upstairs sitting room when she heard the Jaguar enter the garage. At her feet, Ginger, their apricot toy poodle, lifted his head and growled as if he were a guard dog. Tossing aside the book she was reading, she looked up at the clock. It was quarter to ten and she was furious. She'd made dinner for eight o'clock, but Larry had never bothered to call to say he was going to be late. It was the sixth time he'd done that this month. If she'd told him once, she'd told him a hundred times to call. That was all she asked. She knew doctors had emergencies, but phoning only took a minute.

Sitting on the couch, Laura contemplated what she should do. She could stay where she was and let Larry fend for himself in the kitchen, though she'd tried that before with no results. Until recently, her husband had been sensitive to her moods. But for some reason, ever since he'd come back from his medical meeting four months ago, he'd been generally cold and inconsiderate.

Noises drifted up the back stairs from the kitchen, suggesting that Larry was already making himself something to eat. Not bothering to come and say hello added insult to injury. Laura lifted her legs off the hassock, wiggled her toes into her sandals, and stood up. Walking over to a gilt frame mirror, she peered at herself. For fifty-six she looked pretty darn good. But over the last eight weeks Larry had shown absolutely no sexual interest in her. Could that be the reason for his new burst of professional enthusiasm? It had taken Larry and Clark Vandermer twenty years to build their practice to the point where they could concentrate on gynecology rather than obstetrics. And then Larry had thrown it all away. After coming back from that medical meeting, he'd calmly announced that he'd quit GYN Associates and had accepted a salaried position at the Julian Clinic. At the time Laura had been so stupefied that she'd been unable to respond. And since joining the Julian Clinic, Larry had been taking on more obstetrical cases, even though he got the same salary no matter how hard he worked.

A crash interrupted Laura's thoughts. That was another problem. Larry had become clumsy of late, as well as having lapses of attention. Laura wondered if he were on the verge of some sort of breakdown.

Deciding that it was time to confront her husband, Laura straightened her robe and started down the back stairs. Ginger followed at her heels.

She found Larry at the kitchen counter, eating a large sandwich and reading a medical journal. He'd taken off his jacket and had thrown it over the back of a chair. When he heard her enter, he looked up. His face had that curious slackness it had developed in recent weeks.

"Hello, dear," he said in a flat tone.

Laura stood at the foot of the stairs, allowing her anger to build. Her husband looked at her for a moment, then went back to his journal.

"Why didn't you call?" snapped Laura, infuriated by his attempt to ignore her.

Larry raised his head slowly and turned to face his wife. He didn't speak.

"I asked you a question," said Laura. "I deserve an answer. I've asked you a dozen times to call me if you are going to be late."

Larry didn't move.

"Did you hear me?" Laura stepped closer and looked into her husband's eyes. The pupils were large, and he seemed to be looking right through her.

"Hey," said Laura, waving her hand in front of his face. "Remember me? I'm your wife."

Larry's pupils constricted and he blinked as if he had just noticed her.

"I'm sorry I didn't call," he said. "We decided to open an evening clinic for the neighborhood around the Julian and the response was better than we'd anticipated."

"Larry, what is wrong with you? You mean to tell me that you stayed until after nine o'clock to man a free clinic?"

"Nothing is wrong with me. I feel fine. I enjoyed myself. I picked up three cases of unsuspected VD."

"Wonderful," said Laura, throwing up her hands and sitting down in one of the kitchen chairs. She stared at Larry and took an exasperated breath. "We have to talk. Something weird is going on. Either you are going crazy or I am."

"I feel fine," said Larry.

"You might feel fine, but you are acting like a different person. You seem tired all the time, as if you hadn't slept in weeks. This whole idea of giving up your practice is insane. I'm sorry, but it is crazy to give up what has taken you a lifetime to build."

"I'm tired of fee-for-service private practice," said Larry. "The Julian Clinic is more exciting and I'm able to help more people."

"That's all well and good," said Laura, "but the problem is that you have a family. You have a son and daughter in college and a daughter in medical school. I don't have to tell you how much their tuition is. And keeping up this ridiculous house that you insisted on buying ten years ago costs a fortune. We don't need thirty rooms, particularly now that the children are gone. The salary you're on at the Julian Clinic barely keeps us in groceries, much less covers our commitments."

"We can sell the house," said Larry flatly.

"Yes, we can sell the house," repeated Laura. "But the kids are in

school and unfortunately we have little savings. Larry, you have to go
back to GYN Associates."

"I gave up my partnership," said Larry.

"Clark Vandermer will give it back," said Laura. "You've known
him long enough. Tell him you made a mistake. If you want to change
your professional circumstances, you should at least wait until after
the children's schooling is complete."

Laura stopped talking and watched her husband's face. It was as if
it were carved from stone. "Larry," she called. There was no response.

Laura got up and waved her hand in front of her husband's face.
He didn't move. He seemed to be in a trance. "Larry," she yelled as
she shook his shoulders. His body was strangely stiff. Then his eyes
blinked and looked into hers.

"Larry, are you aware that you seem to blank out?" She kept her
hands on his shoulders while she studied his face.

"No," said Larry. "I feel fine."

"I think that maybe you should see someone. Why don't we call
Clark Vandermer and have him come over and look at you. He only
lives three houses away, and I'm sure he wouldn't mind. We can talk
to him about getting back your practice at the same time."

Larry didn't respond. Instead, his eyes assumed the blank look
again while his pupils dilated. Laura stared at him for a moment, then
quickly walked over to the kitchen phone. Her irritation had become
concern. She looked up the Vandermers' number in the address book
that hung from the cork bulletin board and was about to dial when
Larry grabbed the phone from her hand. For the first time in months
the slackness had gone from his face. Instead, his teeth were bared in
an unnatural grimace.

Laura screamed. She didn't mean to, but she couldn't help it. She
backed up, knocking over one of the kitchen chairs. Ginger barked
and growled.

Despite the horrid expression on his face, Larry didn't respond to
Laura's scream. He hung up the phone, then turned. In agonized
slow motion he grasped the sides of his head with both hands while
an anguished wail escaped from his lips. Laura fled up the back stairs
in panic.

Reaching the top, she passed through the sitting room and ran
down the corridor. The huge house was built like the letter H with

the upper hallway traversing the crossbar. The master bedroom was over the living room in the wing opposite the kitchen.

Reaching the bedroom, Laura closed and locked its paneled door. She ran to their bed and sat on its edge, her breath coming in short gasps. On the night table was another address book. She flipped it open to the Vs. Keeping her finger on Vandermer's number, she lifted the princess phone to her ear and started dialing. But before the call could go through, one of the downstairs phones was picked up.

"Laura," said Larry in a cold, mechanical voice. "I want you to come downstairs immediately. I don't want you calling anybody."

A wave of terror swept over Laura, constricting her throat. Her hand holding the phone began to shake.

The connection went through and Laura could hear the Vandermers' phone ringing. But as soon as the phone was answered, the line went dead. Laura looked at the phone helplessly. Larry must have cut the wire.

"My God," she whispered. Slowly she replaced the receiver and tried to collect herself. Panicking was not going to solve anything. She had to think. It was obvious that she needed help; the question was how to get it. Turning her head, she looked out of the bedroom window. Lights were on at her neighbors'. If she raised the window and yelled would anybody hear, and if they did, would they respond?

Laura tried to convince herself she was overreacting. Perhaps she should just go downstairs as Larry suggested and tell him that he simply had to get help.

A thump on the door jolted her upright. She listened and was relieved when she heard a sharp bark. Going to the door, she pressed her ear against it. All she could hear was Ginger's whining. Hastily she undid the lock so the poodle could run inside.

The door slammed wide open, bruising her hand and crashing against the wall. To Laura's shock, Larry was in the doorway. Ginger rushed to Laura's feet and began to jump up and down, wanting to be picked up.

Laura screamed again. Larry's face was still grotesquely contorted. In his left hand was a Remington 12-gauge pump gun.

Spurred by utter panic, Laura turned and fled into the bathroom, slamming and bolting the door. Ginger had followed her and was trembling at her feet. She picked up the shaking dog and, backing up, watched the door. She knew that it was not much of a barrier.

A horrendous blast echoed around the tiled room as part of the door splintered and tore away. Flying debris stung Laura's face and the dog uttered a helpless yelp.

The bathroom had another door and, dropping Ginger, Laura struggled with its latch. She was dazed but got the door open and ran into a dressing room that led back into the bedroom. Glancing over her shoulder, she could see Larry's hand coming through the hole made by the shotgun blast.

As she raced through the bedroom, Laura caught a brief glimpse of Larry disappearing into the bathroom. Knowing she had only a few moments' head start, she dashed into the hall and half ran and half fell down the staircase. Ginger stayed at her heels.

Vainly she gave the front door a tug, but it was locked. The old man who had originally built the house had been so paranoid that he had equipped all the doors with locks that could be secured from both sides. There were keys somewhere in the bureau in the foyer, but Laura didn't have time to search for them. Her keys were in her purse in the kitchen. Hearing Larry start down the stairs, Laura ran down the gallery on the ground floor.

Normally, she put her purse on the desk beneath the kitchen phone, but it wasn't there. She tried the back door but, as she expected, it too was locked. With mounting panic, she tried to think of what to do. The fact that Larry had actually used the shotgun on the bathroom door made her heart pound. Ginger leaped into her arms, and she hugged him to her chest. Then she heard Larry's heels striking the marble of the gallery floor.

In desperation Laura opened the cellar door, flipped on the cellar lights, and pulled the door shut behind her. As quietly as she could, she descended the angled stairway. There was a way out of the cellar that was secured with an oak beam rather than a lock.

They had never used the basement because they had such an overabundance of space upstairs. Consequently, it was musty and filled with all sorts of junk from previous owners. It was a warren of little rooms, and poorly illuminated with infrequent light bulbs. Laura stumbled over debris in the hallway, clutching Ginger to herself as she navigated the strangely tortuous route. She was almost at the exit when the lights went out.

The darkness was sudden and complete. Laura froze in her tracks, disoriented. The terror consumed her. Desperately, she swung her left hand in front of her, searching for a wall. Her fingers hit rough wood. Stumblingly, she made her way along the wall until she came to a doorway. Behind her she heard Larry start down the cellar stairs. The sound of his footsteps was distinct, as if he were moving very slowly and deliberately. A flickering light indicated he was carrying a flashlight.

Knowing that she could never find the exit in the dark, Laura frantically realized that she'd have to hide. With all the rooms and junk that were there, she felt that she had a chance. She stepped through the doorway she'd found, and groped in the darkness. Almost at once her hands encountered window shutters leaning against the wall. Stepping around them, her foot hit a wooden object. It was a large barrel resting on its side.

After first checking to make sure that the barrel was empty, Laura got down on her hands and knees and backed into it, pulling Ginger after her. She didn't have long to worry if her hiding place were adequate. No sooner had she stopped moving than she heard Larry approach in the hallway. Although the barrel pointed away from the door opening, she could see dim evidence of his flashlight.

Larry's footsteps came closer and closer, and Laura struggled to breathe quietly. The flashlight beam entered the room and Laura held her breath. Then Ginger growled and barked. Laura's heart skipped a beat as she heard the pump action of the shotgun. She felt Larry kick the barrel, rolling her upside down. Ginger yelped and fled. Frantically, Laura struggled to right herself.

CHAPTER 5

The Eastern shuttle to Washington provided the first peace Adam had experienced since the previous night. After Jennifer had slammed the bedroom door, Adam tried lying down on the uncomfortable Victorian couch. He'd attempted to read about pancreatitis, but found it impossible to concentrate. There was no way he could stay in medical school if they lost Jennifer's income. At dawn, after only a couple of hours of restless sleep, he'd called the hospital and had a note left for his intern saying he wouldn't be in that day. One way or the other, Adam knew he had to come up with a solution.

Adam stared out the window at the tranquil New Jersey countryside. The captain announced that they were passing over the Delaware River and Adam estimated it was another twenty minutes to Washington. That would put him in the city at eight-thirty; he could be at his father's office at the Food and Drug Administration around nine.

Adam was not looking forward to the meeting, especially under the present conditions. He hadn't seen his father since the middle of his first year in medical school, and it had been a traumatic encounter. At that time Adam had informed the old man that he was definitely marrying Jennifer.

Adam was still trying to decide how to open the conversation as he walked through the revolving door of his father's building. As a child, Adam had not visited his father's office often, but had gone enough times to leave him with a feeling of distaste. His father had always acted as if the boy were an embarrassment.

Adam had been the middle child, sandwiched between an over-achieving older brother, David, and a younger sister, Ellen, the darling of the family. David had been the outgoing child and had decided as a youngster to become a doctor like his father. Adam had never been able to make up his mind what he wanted to be. For a long time he thought he wanted to be a farmer.

Adam got on the elevator and pushed the button for the eighth floor. He could remember going up in the elevator with David when David was in medical school. David was ten years older than Adam and, as far as Adam was concerned, seemed more like an adult than a brother. Adam used to be left in his father's waiting room while David was taken to meet doctor colleagues.

Adam got off at the eighth floor and turned to the right. As the offices became larger and more attractive, the secretaries got plainer. Adam could remember that it was David who had pointed that out to him.

Hesitating before the executive offices, Adam wondered what his relationship with his father would be like if David hadn't died in Vietnam. Not too many doctors had been killed over there, but David had managed it. He'd always been one to volunteer for anything. It had been the last year of the war and Adam had been fifteen at the time.

The event had crippled the family. Adam's mother had gone into a terrible depression that required shock therapy. She still wasn't her old self. Adam's father hadn't weathered the news much better. After several months of his withdrawn silence, Adam had gone to him and told him that he'd decided to become a doctor. Instead of being pleased, his father had cried and turned away.

Adam paused in front of his father's office, then screwing up his courage, walked up to Mrs. Margaret Weintrob's desk. She was an enormous woman who swamped her swivel chair. Her dress was a tentlike affair made from a flower-print cotton. Her upper arms had enormous rolls of fat, making her sizable forearms appear slender by comparison.

But, aside from her weight, she was exceptionally well groomed.

She smiled when she saw Adam and, without getting up, extended a hand in greeting.

Adam shook the slightly damp hand and returned the smile. They had always gotten along fine. She'd been Adam's father's secretary as far back as Adam could remember, and she'd always been sensitive to Adam's shyness.

"Where have you been?" she asked, pretending to be angry. "It's been ages since you've visited."

"Medical school doesn't allow for too much free time," said Adam. His father kept few secrets from Margaret, and Adam was sure she knew why he hadn't been around.

"As usual, your father's on the phone. He'll be off in a minute. Can I get you some coffee or tea?"

Adam shook his head no, and hung his coat on a brass coatrack. He sat down on a vinyl bleacher. He remembered that his father did not like to give the impression that the government was wasting the public's money on such frills as comfortable seating. In fact, the whole outer office had a utilitarian look. For Dr. Schonberg Senior it was a matter of principle. For the same reason, he refused the car and driver that came with his office.

Adam sat trying to marshal his arguments, but he wasn't very sanguine. When he had called early that morning to arrange the meeting, his father had been gruff, as if he knew that Adam was going to ask for money.

There was a buzz. Margaret smiled. "Your father's waiting for you."

As Adam grimly rose to his feet, she reached out and placed a hand on his forearm.

"He's still suffering from David's death," she said. "Try to understand. He does love you."

"David died nine years ago," said Adam.

Margaret nodded and patted Adam's arm. "I just wanted you to know what's going on in his mind."

Adam opened the door and went into his father's office. It was a large square room with tall windows that looked out onto a pleasant inner garden. The other walls were covered with bookcases and in the middle of the room was a large oak desk. Two good-sized library tables were spaced perpendicularly on either side of it, creating a spacious U-shaped work area. In its center sat Adam's father.

Adam resembled his father closely enough for people to guess their relationship. Dr. Schonberg, too, had thick curly hair, though his was graying at the temples. The greatest difference between the two men was size, the father being more than five inches shorter than his son.

As Adam came in and shut the door, Dr. Schonberg had a pen in his hand. Carefully he put it in its holder.

"Hello," said Adam. He noted that his father had aged since he'd last seen him. There were lots of new creases across his forehead.

Dr. Schonberg acknowledged Adam's greeting by nodding his head. He did not stand up.

Adam advanced to the desk, looking down into his father's heavily shadowed eyes. Adam didn't see any softening there.

"And to what do we owe this unexpected visit?" asked Dr. Schonberg.

"How is mother?" asked Adam, sensing that his fears had been correct. The meeting was already going poorly.

"Nice of you to ask. Actually, she's not too good. She had to have shock treatment again. But I don't want to trouble you with that news. Especially considering the fact that your marrying that girl had a lot to do with her condition."

"That girl's name is Jennifer. I would hope after a year and a half you could remember her name. Mother's condition started with David's death, not my marrying Jennifer."

"She was just recovering when you shocked her by marrying that girl."

"Jennifer!" corrected Adam. "And that was seven years after David's death."

"Seven years, ten years, what does it matter? You knew what marrying out of your religion would do to your mother. But did you care? And what about me? I told you not to marry so early in your medical career. But you've never had consideration for the family. It's always been what you wanted. Well, you got what you wanted."

Adam stared at his father. He didn't have the energy to argue in the face of such irrationality. He'd tried that on their last meeting one and a half years ago with no result whatsoever.

"Don't you care what is happening to me, how medical school is going?" asked Adam, almost pleading.

"Under the circumstances, no," said Dr. Schonberg.

"Well, then I made a mistake coming," said Adam. "We're in a financial bind and I thought that enough time had passed to make it possible for me to talk to you about it."

"So now he wants to talk finances!" said Dr. Schonberg, throwing up his hands. He glared at his son, his heavy-lidded eyes narrowed. "I warned you that if you willfully went ahead with the marriage to that girl I was going to cut you off. Did you think I was joking? Did you think I meant for a couple of years only?"

"Are there no circumstances that might make you reconsider your position?" asked Adam quietly. He knew the answer before he asked and decided not even to bother telling his father that Jennifer was pregnant.

"Adam, you're going to have to learn to take responsibility for your decisions. If you decide something, you have to stick to it. There is no latitude for shortcuts or compromises in medicine. Do you hear me?"

Adam started for the door. "Thanks for the lecture, Dad. It will come in handy."

Dr. Schonberg came around from behind his desk. "You've always been a smart aleck, Adam. But taking responsibility for your decisions is one lesson you have to learn. It's the way I run this department for the FDA."

Adam nodded and opened the door. Margaret backed up clumsily, not even bothering to pretend that she hadn't been listening. Adam went for his coat.

Dr. Schonberg followed his son into the waiting room. "And I run my personal life the same way. So did my father before me. And so should you."

"I'll keep it in mind, Dad. Say hello to Mom. Thanks for everything."

Adam turned down the corridor and walked to the elevator. After pushing the button, he looked back. In the distance Margaret was waving. Adam waved back. He never should have come. There was no way he was going to get money out of his father.

///

It wasn't raining when Jennifer stepped from their apartment building, but the skies looked threatening. In many ways she thought that March was the worst month in New York. Even though spring was officially about to begin, winter still held the city firmly in its grip.

Pulling her coat tighter around her body, she set off toward Seventh Avenue. Under the coat she was dressed for rehearsal in an old leotard, tights, leg-warmers, and an ancient gray sweater with the sleeves cut off. In truth, Jennifer didn't know if she would be dancing, since she was planning on telling Jason that she was pregnant. She hoped he would allow her to continue with the troupe for a couple of months. She and Adam needed the money so badly, and the thought of Adam dropping out of medical school terrified her. If only he weren't so stubborn about accepting help from her parents.

At Seventh Avenue Jennifer turned south, fighting the rush-hour crowds. Stopping at a light, she wondered what kind of reception Adam was getting from his father. When she'd gotten up that morning she'd found the note saying he was off to Washington. If only the old bastard would help, thought Jennifer, it would solve everything. In fact, if Dr. Schonberg offered support, Adam would probably be willing to accept help from her parents.

She crossed Seventh Avenue and headed into Greenwich Village proper. A few minutes later she turned into the entrance of the Cézanne Café, descended the three steps in a single bound, and pushed through the etched-glass door. Inside, the air was heavy with Gauloise cigarette smoke and the smell of coffee. As usual, the place was jammed.

On her toes, Jennifer tried to scan the crowd for a familiar face. Halfway down the narrow room she saw a figure waving at her. It was Candy Harley, who used to be one of the Jason Conrad dancers but who now did administrative work. Next to her was Cheryl Tedesco, the company secretary, looking paler than usual in a white jumpsuit. It was customary for the three of them to have coffee together before rehearsal.

Jennifer worked her way out of her coat, rolling it up in a large ball and depositing it on the floor next to the wall. On top she plopped her limp cloth bag. By the time she sat down, Peter, the Austrian waiter, was at the table, asking if she wanted the usual. She did. Cappuccino and croissant with butter and honey.

After she'd sat down, Candy leaned forward and said, "We have good news and bad news. What do you want to hear first?"

Jennifer looked back and forth between the two women. She

wasn't in the mood for joking, but Cheryl was staring into her espresso cup as if she'd lost her best friend. Jennifer knew her as a rather melancholy twenty-year-old with a weight problem which seemed of late to be getting worse. She had pixieish features with a small upturned nose and large eyes. Her disheveled hair was a dirty blond. In contrast, Candy was strikingly immaculate in her appearance, her blond hair twisted neatly into a French braid.

"Maybe you'd better tell me the good news first," said Jennifer uneasily.

"We've been offered a CBS special," said Candy. "The Jason Conrad Dancers are going big time."

Jennifer tried to act excited, although she realized she'd probably be too far along in her pregnancy for television. "That's terrific!" she forced herself to say with enthusiasm. "When is it scheduled for?"

"We're not sure of the exact date, but we're supposed to tape the show in a few months."

"So, what's the bad news?" asked Jennifer, eager to change the subject.

"The bad news is that Cheryl is four months pregnant and she has to have an abortion tomorrow," Candy stated in a rush.

Jennifer turned to Cheryl. "I'm sorry," she said awkwardly. "I didn't even know you were pregnant."

"No one did," added Candy. "Cheryl kept it a secret till she heard that I'd had an abortion. Then she confided in me, and it was a good thing she did. I sent her to my doctor, who suggested amniocentesis because Cheryl said she'd been doing drugs right through her second month. She hadn't realized she was pregnant."

"What did the test show?" asked Jennifer.

"That the baby is deformed. There's something wrong with its genes. That's what they look for when they do an amniocentesis."

Jennifer turned back to Cheryl, who was still staring into her espresso, trying not to cry.

"What does the father think?" asked Jennifer and then was sorry, for Cheryl put her hands over her face and began to sob bitterly. Candy put her arm about Cheryl as Jennifer glanced around at the nearby tables. No one was paying attention. Only in New York could you have such privacy in a public place. Cheryl took a tissue from her purse and blew her nose loudly.

"The father's name is Paul," she said sadly.

"How does he feel about your having an abortion?" asked Jennifer.

Cheryl wiped her eyes, examining a dark smudge of mascara on the tissue. "I don't know. He took off and left me."

"Well," said Candy, "that gives us a pretty good idea about how he feels. The bastard. I wish men could take on the burden of being pregnant, say every other year. I think they might be a little more responsible if that were the case."

Cheryl wiped her eyes again, and Jennifer suddenly realized how terribly young and vulnerable the girl was. It made the problem posed by her own pregnancy seem small in comparison.

"I'm so scared," Cheryl was saying. "I haven't told anyone because if my father finds out, he'll kill me."

"Well, I hope you're not going to the hospital by yourself," said Jennifer with alarm.

"It won't be so bad," said Candy with some assurance. "I'd been worried before my abortion, but it went smoothly. The people at the Julian Clinic are outstandingly warm and sensitive. Besides, Cheryl will have the world's best gynecologist."

"What's his name?" asked Jennifer, thinking that she could not say the same about Dr. Vandermer.

"Lawrence Foley," said Candy. "I'd been turned on to him by another girl who had to have an abortion."

"It seems like he's doing a lot of abortions," said Jennifer.

Candy nodded. "It's a big city."

Jennifer sipped her cappuccino, wondering how to tell her friends that she herself had just found out she was pregnant. She postponed the moment by turning back to Cheryl and saying, "Perhaps you'd like it if I went with you tomorrow. Seems to me you could use some company."

"I'd love that," said Cheryl, her face brightening.

"Not so fast, Mrs. Schonberg," said Candy. "We have rehearsal."

Jennifer raised her eyebrows and smiled. "Well, I have some news myself. I found out yesterday that I'm two and a half months pregnant myself."

"Oh, no!" exclaimed Candy.

"Oh, yes!" said Jennifer. "And when I tell Jason, he may not care whether I come to rehearsal or not."

Candy and Cheryl were too stunned to speak. In silence, the three finished their coffee, paid the bill, and set off for the studio.

Jason was not there when they arrived, and Jennifer felt relieved and disappointed at the same time. She removed her outer clothes and found a free area on the dance floor. Turning sideways, she lifted her sweatshirt so that she could see her profile. She had to admit that she already showed a little.

/ / /

Adam washed his hands in the men's room on the first floor of the hospital complex. Catching a glimpse of his haggard face in the mirror, he realized he looked exhausted. Well, maybe it would make the dean more sympathetic. After his disastrous meeting with his father, Adam had decided his only recourse was an additional student loan from the medical center. Straightening his frayed button-down collar, he thought he certainly looked poor and deserving, and that he should go directly to the dean's office before he lost his courage.

Bursting into the secretary's office to demand an appointment, Adam was almost dismayed when the woman said she thought the dean had a few moments between appointments. She went in to check. When she returned, she said Adam could go right in.

Dr. Markowitz stood as Adam crossed his office threshold. He was a short, stocky man with dark curly hair not unlike Adam's. He had a deep tan, even though it was just March. He approached Adam with his hand outstretched. When they shook hands, his other hand grasped the back of Adam's.

"Please, sit down." The dean gestured to a black academic chair in front of his desk.

From his chair Adam could see a manila folder with his name on the tab. Adam had met the dean only a few times, but each time Dr. Markowitz had acted as if he were intimately aware of Adam's situation. He had obviously pulled the file in the minute or two Adam had been kept waiting.

Adam cleared his throat. "Dr. Markowitz, I'm sorry to take your time, but I've got a problem."

"You've come to the right place," said Dr. Markowitz, although his smile relaxed an appreciable amount. Adam recognized that the dean was more politician than doctor. He had an unhappy feeling that this meeting would be no better than the one with his father. He crossed his legs and gripped his ankle to keep his hands from shaking.

"I just found out my wife is pregnant," he began, watching Dr. Markowitz's face for signs of disapproval. They weren't subtle. First, the dean's smile vanished. Then his eyes narrowed as he folded his arms guardedly across his chest.

"Needless to say," continued Adam, trying to keep up his courage, "this is going to put us in a financial bind. My wife and I depend on her income, and now with a child on the way . . ." Adam's voice trailed off. You didn't need to be a fortune-teller to know the rest.

"Well," said Dr. Markowitz with a forced laugh, "I'm an internist, not an obstetrician. Never was very good at delivering babies."

Some sense of humor, thought Adam.

"My wife sees Dr. Vandermer," said Adam.

"He's the best," offered Dr. Markowitz. "Can't get better obstetrical care than Dr. Vandermer. He delivered our two children."

There was an awkward pause. Adam became aware of the ticking of an antique Howard clock hanging on the wall to his left. Dr. Markowitz leaned forward and opened the folder on his desk. He read for a moment, then looked up.

"Adam, have you considered that this might not be a good time to start your family?"

"It was an accident," said Adam, wanting to avoid a lecture if that was what the dean had intended. "A birth control failure. A statistic. But now that it has happened, we have to deal with it. We need additional financial support or I have to drop out of school for a year or so. It's as simple as that."

"Have you thought about terminating this pregnancy?" asked Dr. Markowitz.

"We've thought about it, but neither one of us is willing to do so."

"What about family support?" questioned Dr. Markowitz. "I don't think that dropping out of school is a wise move. You have a lot invested in getting to where you are today. I'd hate to see that put in jeopardy."

"There's no chance of family support," said Adam. He didn't want to get into a conversation about his father's intransigence or his in-laws' interference. "My only hope is to borrow more money from the school. If not, I'll have to take a leave of absence."

"Unfortunately, you are already borrowing the maximum allowed," said Dr. Markowitz. "We have limited resources in regard to student loans. We have to spread around what we have so everyone who needs support has access to it. I'm sorry."

Adam stood up. "Well, I appreciate your time."

Dr. Markowitz got to his feet. His smile reappeared. "I wish I could be more help. I hate to see you leave us. You have an excellent record up until now. Maybe you should reconsider the advisability of allowing the pregnancy to go to term."

"We're going to have the child," said Adam. "In fact, now that the shock of it all is over, I'm looking forward to it."

"When would you start your leave?" asked Dr. Markowitz.

"I'm finishing Internal Medicine in a few days," said Adam. "As soon as it is over, I'll look for a job."

"I suppose if you're going to take a leave, it is as good a time as any. What do you plan to do?"

Adam shrugged. "I hadn't made any specific plans."

"I might be able to get you a research position here at the medical center."

"I appreciate the offer," said Adam, "but research doesn't pay the kind of money I'm going to need. I've got to get a job with a decent salary. I was thinking more about trying one of the big drug firms out in New Jersey. Arolen gave our class all those leather doctor bags. Maybe I'll give them a try."

Dr. Markowitz flinched as if he'd been struck. "That's where the money is," he said, sighing. "But I must say I feel as if you were deserting to the enemy. The pharmaceutical industry has been exerting more and more control over medical research recently, and I for one am legitimately concerned."

"I'm not wild about the idea," admitted Adam. "But they are the only people who might be seriously interested in a third-year medical student. If it doesn't work out, maybe I'll be back for that research position."

Dr. Markowitz opened the door. "I'm sorry we don't have more resources for financial aid. Best of luck, and let me know as soon as you can when you plan to get back to school."

Adam left, determined to call Arolen that afternoon. He would worry about pharmaceutical pressure on research once he had cashed his first paycheck.

///

"You're what!" shouted Jason Conrad, the head of the Jason Conrad Dancers. He threw up his hands in exaggerated despair.

For the four years that Jennifer had known him, Jason had always tended toward histrionics, whether he was ordering lunch or directing the dancers. Consequently, she had anticipated such a reaction.

"Now, let me get this straight," he moaned. "You're telling me that you're going to have a child. Is that right? No, tell me I'm wrong. Tell me that this is just a bad dream. Please!"

Jason looked at Jennifer with a pleading expression. He was a tall man—six feet three—who looked boyish despite his thirty-three years. Whether he was gay or not, Jennifer had no idea. Neither did any of the other dancers. Dance was Jason's life, and he was a genius at it.

"I'm going to have a baby," confirmed Jennifer.

"Oh, my God!" cried Jason, letting his head sink into his hands.

Jennifer exchanged glances with Candy, who had hung around for moral support.

"This is not happening to me," wailed Jason. "At the moment of our big break, one of the lead dancers gets herself pregnant. Oh, my God!"

Jason stopped pacing. Holding up his index finger, he looked at Jennifer. "What about an abortion? Surely this isn't a planned child."

"I'm sorry," said Jennifer.

"But you can always have another child," protested Jason.

Jennifer just shook her head.

"You won't listen to reason?" wailed Jason. He pressed a hand dramatically against his chest and began to take deep breaths as if he were experiencing severe chest pain. "You prefer to torture me like this, straining my heart. Oh God, the pain is awful."

Jennifer felt guilty about getting pregnant just when the troupe was receiving its big break. She hated to let anyone down. But Jason's response was a selfish one, and she resented his trying to manipulate her this way into something as serious as an abortion.

Candy took Jason's arm. "I hope you're kidding about this chest pain."

Jason opened one eye. "Me kidding? I never kid about something like this. This woman's driving me to an early grave and you ask if I'm kidding?"

"I can probably dance for another month or so," offered Jennifer.

"Oh, no, no, no!" said Jason, instantly forgetting his chest pain. He began pacing back and forth in front of the old ticket booth. "If you, Jennifer, are insensitive enough to abandon us at this juncture, we have to make an adjustment immediately." He stopped and pointed to Candy. "What about you? Could you dance Jennifer's part?"

Candy was caught off guard. "I don't know," she stammered.

Jason watched Jennifer out of the corner of his eye. He knew that Jennifer and Candy were friends. He thought that jealousy might accomplish what reason couldn't. He needed Jennifer at least until the TV show was taped, but Jennifer did not respond. She remained silent as Candy finally replied, "I guess I'm in good shape. I'll certainly try and give it my best."

"Hooray," said Jason. "It's good to hear that someone around here is willing to make some sacrifices." Then to Jennifer he said, "Maybe you should head into the office and have Cheryl take you off the payroll. We aren't a welfare organization."

Candy spoke up. "She should get her base salary for another two weeks. That's only fair."

Jason waved his hand as if he didn't care. He started back for the gym floor.

"Also," called Candy after him, "I think it would be easier for our accounting if we put her on maternity leave."

"Whatever," said Jason with little interest. He opened the door into the gym. They could hear the other dancers going through their routines. "Let's get to work, Candy," he called over his shoulder as he disappeared through the door.

The two women looked at each other. Both felt a little awkward. Candy shrugged. "I never guessed that he'd offer me a dance position."

"I'm happy for you," said Jennifer. "Really."

Together, they returned to the gym.

Jason's high-pitched voice reverberated around the large room. "OK, let's take dance variation number two from the top. Positions!" He clapped his hands and the echo sounded like the report of a gun. "Come on, Candy," he yelled.

For a few minutes Jennifer watched the rehearsal. Then, trying to shake off her feelings of regret, she headed down the hall to Cheryl's office.

Cheryl was leaning back, reading a paperback romance novel.

"You're supposed to put me on maternity leave," said Jennifer with resignation.

"I'm sorry," said Cheryl. "Did Jason throw a fit?" She put her book down. Jennifer could see the title: *The Flames of Passion*.

"One of his best," admitted Jennifer. "But I suppose it's understandable. This is a bad time for me to take a leave." She sank into the chair in front of the desk. "Jason agreed to let me draw base pay for another two weeks. Of course, I still get my percentages from past performances."

"What are you going to do?" asked Cheryl.

"I don't know," said Jennifer. "Maybe I can get a temporary job. Do you have any ideas? How did you find this position?"

"I went to an agency," said Cheryl. "But if you're looking for part-time work, try one of the temporary secretarial services. They always need people."

"I couldn't type to save my life," said Jennifer.

"Then try one of the big department stores. A lot of my girlfriends have done that."

Jennifer smiled. That sounded promising.

"Are you still going to come with me tomorrow?" asked Cheryl.

"Absolutely," said Jennifer. "I wouldn't think of letting you go by yourself. Were you alone when you had the amniocentesis?"

"Yup," said Cheryl proudly. "It was a breeze. Hardly hurt at all."

"Sounds like you have more courage than I," said Jennifer. Jennifer thought again about her mongoloid brother and wondered if she should ask to have the test.

Cheryl leaned forward, lowering her voice. "Like Candy said, I used to do a lot of drugs. Pot, acid, you name it. Dr. Foley said that I should have the test to check the chromosomes. But he made it easy. If you have to have it, don't worry. I was really nervous, but I'd do it again in a flash." She sat back, pleased with herself.

Jennifer stared at Cheryl, remembering Dr. Vandermer and his chauvinistic attitude. "And this Dr. Foley, you like him?"

Cheryl nodded her head. "Dr. Foley is the nicest doctor I've ever met. If it hadn't been for him, I wouldn't have done anything. And his nurses are nice, too. In fact, the whole Julian Clinic is just great. I'm sure Candy would call and make an appointment for you if you'd like."

Jennifer smiled. "Thanks, but my husband sent me to someone at the medical center. Now, to get back to business. What do I have to do to put myself on maternity leave?"

Cheryl wrinkled her nose. "I don't know, to tell you the truth. I'll have to ask Candy."

After making plans to meet Cheryl the following morning, Jennifer got her coat and bag and went out into the street. Walking to the subway, she struggled against an almost overwhelming depression. She had always expected pregnancy to be a wonderful experience, but now that she was bearing a child, instead of feeling happy, she was confused and angry. And worst of all she knew that she wasn't going to be able to share such feelings with anyone because she was certain no one would understand.

Biting her lower lip, Jennifer decided to try Macy's first.

///

It was nearly six o'clock when Jennifer trudged up the stairs to their apartment. When she opened the door, she was surprised to find Adam on the couch. He usually wasn't home this early. Then she realized he must have taken the rest of the day off after seeing his father.

"How did the meeting go?" she asked, making an effort to be pleasant. "Was your father helpful?"

"He was a delight," snapped Adam. "He gave me a valuable lecture about responsibility and consistency."

Jennifer hung up her coat and went over and sat next to Adam. His eyes were red with dark circles. "Was it that bad?"

"Worse," said Adam. "Now he believes I'm the cause of my mother's depression."

"But her depression started with your brother's death."

"He seems to have forgotten that."

"What did he say when you told him that we are going to have a child?"

"I didn't," said Adam. "I never had a chance. He made it very clear that I was on my own before I could even broach the subject."

"I'm sorry," said Jennifer.

Jennifer examined Adam's face. She didn't like what she saw. He seemed distant and cold. She wanted to ask him about Dr. Lawrence Foley but decided to put it off. "I think I'll take a shower," she said with a sigh as she stood up and walked into the bedroom.

At first, Adam sat and brooded. Gradually, he realized that he was acting like an adolescent. Getting up, he went into the bedroom and stripped off his clothes. Then he opened the door to the bathroom. "Leave the water on," he shouted over the sound of the shower. While he was brushing his teeth, Jennifer got out of the shower and, without looking at him, took her towel and went into the bedroom. Although she left the water going as he requested, it was obvious that she was irritated.

Adam had always found it difficult to apologize. Maybe they should do something crazy, like go out to dinner. Stepping into the shower, he decided to take Jennifer to a restaurant called One by Land, Two by Sea. It was close enough so they could walk. They'd never eaten there, but one of Adam's classmates had gone with his parents and had said it was fantastic and expensive. What the hell, thought Adam. He was going to have a real job soon and they needed to celebrate.

"Got a great idea," said Adam when he came into the bedroom. "How about going out for dinner?"

Jennifer looked away from the TV and gloomily shook her head.

"What do you mean, no?" said Adam. "Come on. We need to get out. It will be a real treat."

"We can't afford it," said Jennifer. She returned to the TV as if the matter were closed.

Adam towel-dried his hair while he considered this unexpected negative response. Jennifer was usually ready to try most anything. He sat down next to her and turned her head from the screen. "Hello," he said. "I'm trying to talk with you."

Jennifer raised her face, and he noticed that she looked as exhausted as he did.

"I hear you," she said. "I bought groceries. As soon as the news is over, I'll make dinner."

"Tonight I want something different than Hamburger Helper," said Adam.

"I didn't get Hamburger Helper," said Jennifer irritably.

"I meant that as a figure of speech," said Adam. "Come on. Let's go out for dinner. I think we need a break. I went to see the dean this

afternoon and made sure we can't borrow any more money. So I told
him I'm taking a leave of absence."

"You don't have to leave school," said Jennifer. "I already got
another job."

"What kind of job?" asked Adam.

"At Macy's. In the shoe section. The only problem is that I will have
to work alternate weekends, but hopefully we can coordinate that
with your on-call schedule. Surprisingly, I'll be making the same
salary as I did dancing. Anyway, you don't have to drop out of
school."

Adam stood up from the bed. "You're not working at Macy's and
that's final."

"Oh," said Jennifer, widening her eyes in mock surprise. "Has the
king spoken?"

"Jennifer, this is hardly the time for sarcasm."

"Isn't it?" said Jennifer. "Seems to me you were being sarcastic just
a few moments ago. It's OK for you but not for me?"

"I'm in no mood for an argument," said Adam, as he went to the
bureau for clean underwear. "You are not going to work at Macy's. I
don't want you standing for long hours while you're pregnant. Subject's closed."

"You are forgetting that this is *my* body," said Jennifer.

"That's true," said Adam. "But it is also true that it is *our* child."

Jennifer felt the blood rise into her face.

"In any case, I've made up my mind," said Adam. "I'm taking a
leave of absence so that I can work for a year or two. Your job will be
to take care of yourself and the baby, and that doesn't mean standing
around in a department store." Hoping to end the dialogue, Adam
stepped into the living room. Because of the small size of the bedroom closet, his clothes were in the hall closet.

"Why can't you stay here and discuss this?" Jennifer called out.

Adam came back into the bedroom. "There's nothing more to
discuss."

"Oh yes there is," said Jennifer, giving vent to her anger. "I have as
much to say about all this as you do. No one agrees with you about
leaving medical school and the reason is simple: you shouldn't. I'm
perfectly capable of working right up until the last month, even the
last week. Why do both of us have to interrupt our careers? Since I
obviously can't continue dancing, it's only sensible that I get the new

job. Your staying in school will be best for all of us in the long run. Besides, I already have a position and you don't have any idea of what you could do."

"Oh yes I have," snapped Adam. "I'm going to Arolen Pharmaceuticals in New Jersey. I called this afternoon and they are eager to see me. I have an interview tomorrow."

"Why are you being so bullheaded about this?" said Jennifer. "You don't have to leave school. I can work."

"If you call bullheadedness my desire to keep you healthy and keep your parents from interfering in our life, then, yes, I'm bullheaded. One way or the other, the issue is closed, the discussion is over. I'm leaving school and you are not working at Macy's. Any questions?" Adam knew he was taunting Jennifer, but he felt she deserved it.

"I've got plenty of questions," said Jennifer. "But I realize that it is useless to ask them. I wonder if you realize how much like your father you are."

"Just shut up about my father," shouted Adam. "If anybody around here is going to criticize my father, I'll do it. Besides, I'm not like my father in the slightest."

He kicked the bedroom door shut with a bang. For a moment he stood in the middle of the living room, wondering what he could break. Then, instead of doing something stupid, he finished dressing and drying his hair. Calmer, he decided to try and make peace with Jennifer. He started to open the bedroom door and was shocked to find it locked.

"Jennifer," he called over the sound of the TV. "I'm going to go out and get something to eat. I'd like you to go with me."

"You go ahead," called Jennifer. "I want to stay by myself for a while."

Adam could tell that she'd been crying and he felt guilty.

"Jennifer, open the door," he begged. The TV played on. "Jennifer, open the door."

Still no answer. Adam felt his anger return in a rush. Stepping back, he eyed the door. For a second it seemed symbolic of all his problems. Without thinking, he raised his right foot and kicked with all his strength. The wood around the latch gave, and the door flew open, crashing against the bedroom wall. Jennifer drew herself up in a tight ball against the headboard.

Adam could tell that she was terrified, and he immediately felt stupid. "They don't make doors the way they used to," he said lamely and tried to laugh. Jennifer didn't say anything. Adam pulled the door away from the wall. Where the doorknob had struck, there was a hole in the plaster.

"Well, that was stupid," he said, trying to sound cheerful. "Anyway, as I was saying. Let's go out and get something to eat."

Jennifer shook her head no.

Adam looked around self-consciously, embarrassed by his tantrum. "OK," he said meekly. "I'll be back later."

Jennifer nodded but didn't speak. She watched Adam leave and heard the door to the hall close and lock. What was happening to them, she wondered. Adam seemed like a different person. He'd never been violent, and violence terrified her. Was this pregnancy going to change everything?

Climbing the third and final flight of stairs in Cheryl Tedesco's apartment building, Jennifer was appalled. She'd thought her own building was bad, but Cheryl's made it seem like the Helmsley Palace. A couple of winos—Jennifer hoped they were not residents—had camped in the lobby.

Checking the number on Cheryl's apartment, Jennifer hesitated before knocking. Then she had to wait while there was a number of clicks and finally the sound of the chain being moved before the door swung open.

"Hi! Come on in," said Cheryl. "Sorry it took me so long. My dad insisted on putting on all sorts of locks."

"I think it's a good idea," said Jennifer, quickly stepping inside. Cheryl went into the bathroom to finish dressing while Jennifer looked about the unkempt apartment.

"I hope you followed doctor's orders," she called, knowing that Cheryl had been advised not to have food or drink save for a small amount of water when she first woke up.

"I haven't eaten a thing," yelled Cheryl.

Jennifer shifted her weight from one foot to another. Sensing that the entire building was filthy, she didn't want to sit down. The whole idea of accompanying Cheryl was beginning to upset her, but she couldn't let her go alone. At least she'd get to see the fabulous Dr. Foley, though she wasn't about to challenge Adam about obstetricians just yet. They had half made up the night before, but Jennifer was still distraught at the thought of Adam leaving medical school. She had her fingers crossed that this interview at Arolen would be unsuccessful.

"Ready," said Cheryl, emerging from the bedroom. She had an overnight bag slung over her shoulder. "Let's get the show on the road."

The hardest part of the trip to the Julian Clinic was climbing down Cheryl's stairs without falling and then getting by the winos. Cheryl was unconcerned about the bums, saying that when the super got up he'd send them packing.

They walked to the Lexington Avenue subway and caught the No. 6 train to 110th Street. It wasn't the greatest neighborhood, but it quickly improved the closer they got to the clinic. In fact, an entire city block had been leveled to accommodate the new health-care center. The building was a fifteen-story contemporary structure of mirrored glass, reflecting the image of the surrounding early nineteenth-century tenements. For a block in all directions, the old buildings had been renovated, sandblasted, and refurbished so that they shone with quaint splendor. And for another block beyond that, many of the buildings were fronted by scaffolding, indicating that they too were being repaired. It appeared as if the clinic was taking over a whole section of the city.

Jennifer went through the front entrance expecting the usual hospital furnishings but was pleasantly surprised by a lobby that reminded her more of a luxury hotel. Everything was new and spotlessly clean. The large reception area was so well staffed that Jennifer and Cheryl did not have to wait long before a pretty black secretary said, "May I help you?" She was dressed in a white blouse and blue jumper and wore a name tag that said "Hi! I'm Louise."

Cheryl's answer was barely audible. "I'm to see Dr. Foley. I'm to have an abortion."

Louise's face clouded over with concern. "Are you all right, Ms.
. . ."

"Tedesco," said Jennifer. "Cheryl Tedesco."

"I'm fine," insisted Cheryl. "Really I am."

"We have psychologists on call for admitting if you'd like to talk to one now. We'd like to make you as comfortable as possible."

"Thank you," said Cheryl. "But I have my friend here." She pointed to Jennifer. "I wanted to ask if she will be permitted to go upstairs with me."

"Absolutely," said Louise. "We encourage patients to have company. But first let me call up your record on my computer and then alert the admitting people. Why don't you two go over to the lounge and relax. We'll be with you in just a few minutes."

As Cheryl and Jennifer walked around to the comfortable sitting area, Jennifer said, "I'm beginning to understand why you and Candy are so high on this place. If Louise is any example of how they treat you here, I'm truly impressed."

They barely had time to slip out of their coats when an elderly gentleman approached them, pushing a cart with a coffee and tea dispenser. He was dressed in a pink jacket, which he proudly stated was worn by volunteers.

"Are the nurses this friendly, too?" asked Jennifer.

"Everybody is friendly here," said Cheryl, but despite her smile, Jennifer could tell that she was anxious.

"How are you doing?" she asked, reaching over and squeezing Cheryl's hand.

"Fine," said Cheryl, nodding her head up and down as if trying to convince herself.

"Excuse me, are you Cheryl Tedesco?" asked another pleasant-looking young woman dressed in a white shirt with a blue jumper. Her name tag said "Hi! I'm Karen."

"I'm Karen Krinitz," she said, offering a hand which Cheryl shook uncertainly. "I've been assigned to coordinate your case and to make sure everything runs smoothly. If you have any problems, just page me." She patted a small plastic device clipped over a blue belt that matched her jumper. "We want your stay here to be as pleasant as possible."

"Are all the patients assigned a coordinator?" asked Jennifer.

"They certainly are," said Karen proudly. "The whole idea here is that the patient comes first. We don't want to leave anything to chance. There is too much opportunity for misunderstanding, especially now that medicine has become so highly technical. Doctors can sometimes become so engrossed in the treatment that the patient is momentarily forgotten. It's our job to keep that from happening."

Jennifer watched as the woman said good-bye and disappeared around a planter. There was something about her that Jennifer found strange, but she couldn't put her finger on it.

"Did her speech seem odd to you?" she asked Cheryl.

"I didn't understand what she was talking about. Is that what you mean?"

"No," said Jennifer, turning to see if she could catch sight of the woman again. "I just thought there was something odd about the way she talked. But it must be me. I think morning sickness is affecting my brain."

"At least she was friendly," said Cheryl. "Wait until you meet Dr. Foley."

A few minutes later a man came by and introduced himself as Rodney Murray. He was wearing a blue jacket made of the same heavy cotton as Karen's jumper with an identical tag announcing his name. His voice also had an odd flat quality, and as Jennifer stared at him, she realized that his eyes did not seem to blink.

"Everything is ready for you, Ms. Tedesco," he said, fastening a plastic ID bracelet around Cheryl's wrist. "I'll be accompanying you upstairs, but first we have to go to the lab for your blood work and a few other tests."

"Can Jennifer come with us?" asked Cheryl.

"Absolutely," said Rodney.

The man was extraordinarily attentive to Cheryl, and after a few minutes Jennifer dismissed her initial impression as the working of an overwrought imagination.

The lab was expecting Cheryl, so they didn't have to wait. Again, Jennifer was impressed. She'd never been to a doctor's office or a hospital where she didn't have to wait for everything. Cheryl was finished in minutes.

As they rode up in the elevator, Rodney explained that Cheryl was going to a special area the hospital had for "pregnancy termination." Jennifer noted that everyone at the Julian Clinic studiously avoided the word "abortion." She felt it was a good idea. Abortion was an ugly word.

They got off at the sixth floor. Again, nothing about the floor resembled the average hospital. Instead of slick vinyl, the floor was covered with carpeting. The walls were painted a pale blue and hung with attractive framed prints.

Rodney took them to a central area that was carefully decorated not to look like a nurses' station. In front of the central station was a tastefully appointed lounge where five people dressed in what Jennifer assumed was the Julian uniform were waiting. Three of the women wore name tags indicating that they were RNs. Jennifer liked the fact that they were not dressed in the traditional starched white. She had the feeling that Karen was right: the Julian Clinic had thought of everything. She began to wonder if Dr. Vandermer had admitting privileges, since she was sure the delivery floor reflected the same attention to comfort.

"Ms. Tedesco, your room is right over here," said one of the nurses who had introduced herself as Marlene Polaski. She was a broad, big-boned woman with short blond hair who looked around Cheryl's room as if she were checking every detail. She even opened the door to the toilet. Satisfied, she patted the bed and told Cheryl to slip out of her clothes and make herself comfortable.

The room, like the corridor, was as pleasantly furnished as one in a good hotel, except for the standard hospital bed. A television was set into the ceiling at an angle so that it could be viewed comfortably from either the bed or the easy chair. The walls were light green with lots of built-in cabinets. The floor was covered with green carpet.

After changing into her own pajamas, Cheryl climbed into the bed. Marlene whisked back into the room, pushing an IV cart. She explained to Cheryl that they needed an IV just for safety's sake. She started one deftly in Cheryl's left arm, carefully attaching a small arm board. Jennifer and Cheryl watched the drops falling in the millipore chamber. All at once it didn't seem so much like a hotel room.

"So," said Marlene, putting on the last strips of tape. "We'll be taking you down to the treatment room in a few moments." Then, turning to Jennifer, she said, "You are welcome to come along. That is, of course, if Cheryl will permit it. She's the boss."

"Oh, yes!" said Cheryl, her face brightening. "Jennifer, you will come, won't you?"

The room seemed to spin momentarily. Jennifer felt as if she'd expected to go wading but instead was being thrown into the deep end of the pool. Both Marlene and Cheryl were looking at her expectantly.

"All right, I'll come," she said finally.

Another nurse swept in with a syringe.

"Here's a little tranquilizer for you," she said brightly as she pulled down Cheryl's sheet.

Jennifer turned to the window, vaguely studying the rooftop scene that she could see through the slats of the blinds. When she turned back, the nurse with the syringe was gone.

"Gangway," called another voice as a gowned and hooded nurse pushed a gurney into the room and positioned it alongside Cheryl's bed.

"My name is Gale Schelin," she said to Cheryl. "I know you don't really need this gurney and that you could walk down to the treatment room, but it's standard procedure for you to ride."

Before Jennifer had time to think, she was helping to move Cheryl onto the gurney and then push her out of the room.

"All the way to the end of the hall," directed Gale.

Outside the treatment room several orderlies took over the gurney. After the doors closed behind Cheryl, Jennifer felt relieved. Then Gale took her arm, saying, "You'll have to enter this way."

"I don't think it's a good idea . . ." began Jennifer.

"Nonsense," interrupted Gale. "I know what you're going to say. But this part of the procedure is nothing. The most important thing is Cheryl's outlook. It's important for her to have the kind of support that family can bring."

"But I'm not family," said Jennifer, wondering if she should add "and I'm pregnant myself."

"Family or friend," said Gale, "your presence is crucial. Here. Put this over your clothes and this over your hair. Make sure that all your hair is tucked in." She handed Jennifer a sterile gown and hood. "Then come on in." Gale disappeared through a connecting door.

Damn, thought Jennifer. She was in a storeroom filled with linens and a large stainless-steel machine that looked like a boiler. Jennifer guessed it was a sterilizer. Reluctantly, she put on a hood, tucking in her hair as she was advised. Then she put on the gown and tied it across her abdomen.

The connecting door opened and Gale returned, eyeing Jennifer as she opened the latch on the sterilizer. "You're fine. Go right in and stand to the left. If you feel faint or anything, just come back in here." There was a hiss as steam escaped from the machine.

Taking a deep breath, Jennifer went into the treatment room.

It looked just like she had imagined it would. The walls were white tile and the floor some sort of white vinyl. There was a white porcelain sink mounted on the wall and glass-fronted cabinets filled with medical paraphernalia along one side of the room.

Cheryl had been transferred to an examination table that stood in the center of the room. Next to it was a stand that supported a tray with a collection of stainless-steel bowls and plastic tubing. Against the far wall was an anesthesia cart with the usual cylinders of gas attached.

There were two nurses in the room. One of them was washing Cheryl's abdomen, while the other was busy opening various packets and dropping the contents onto the instrument tray.

The door to the treatment room opened and a gowned and gloved doctor came in. He immediately went to the instrument tray and arranged the instruments to his liking. Cheryl, who had been calmly resting, pushed herself up on one elbow.

"Ms. Tedesco," said one of the nurses, "you must lie back for the doctor."

"That's not Dr. Foley," said Cheryl. "Where is Dr. Foley?"

For a moment no one moved in the room. The doctor and the nurses exchanged glances.

"I'm not going through with this unless Dr. Foley is here," said Cheryl, her voice cracking.

"I'm Dr. Stephenson," said the man. "Dr. Foley cannot be here, but the Julian Clinic has authorized me to take his place. The procedure is very easy."

"I don't care," pouted Cheryl. "I won't have the abortion unless he does it."

"Dr. Stephenson is one of our best surgeons," said a nurse. "Please lie back and let us get on with this." She put her hand on Cheryl's shoulder and started to push her down.

"Just a minute," said Jennifer, surprised at her own assertiveness. "It is obvious that Cheryl wants Dr. Foley. I don't think you should try to force her to accept someone else."

Everyone in the room turned to Jennifer as if they'd just realized she was standing there. Dr. Stephenson came over and started to lead her out of the room.

"Just a minute," said Jennifer. "I'm not going to leave. Cheryl says she doesn't want the procedure unless Dr. Foley does it."

"We understand," said Dr. Stephenson. "If that is the way Miss Tedesco feels, then of course we will respect her wishes. At the Julian Clinic the patient always comes first. If you'll just go back to Miss Tedesco's room, she will be right along."

Jennifer glanced at Cheryl, who was now sitting on the edge of the examination table. "Don't worry," she said to Jennifer. "I won't let them do anything until Dr. Foley comes."

Bewildered, Jennifer let herself be led out of the treatment room. The gurney that had brought Cheryl was being rolled back inside, which made Jennifer feel more comfortable. Removing the hood and gown, she deposited them in a hamper in the corridor.

Almost immediately Marlene Polaski appeared. "I just heard what happened," she said to Jennifer. "I'm terribly sorry. No matter how hard you try in a large institution, sometimes things go wrong. It's been chaotic here for twenty-four hours. We thought that you knew about poor Dr. Foley."

"What are you talking about?" asked Jennifer.

"Dr. Foley committed suicide the night before last," said Marlene. "He shot his wife and then himself. It was in all the papers. We thought you knew."

Jennifer stepped into the corridor. Cheryl rolled past her. Jennifer sighed, glad she was with Dr. Vandermer after all.

/ / /

As Adam got off the bus in Montclair, New Jersey, he thanked the driver who looked at him as if he were crazy. Adam was in fact in an oddly jazzed-up mood, a combination of anxiety about the upcoming job interview and guilt about his behavior the previous evening. He'd attempted to apologize to Jennifer, but the best he'd been able to do was say he was sorry that he'd broken the door. He hadn't changed his mind about her standing up all day throughout her pregnancy selling shoes.

Adam spotted the Arolen car right where the secretary had said it would be: in front of the Montclair National Bank. Adam crossed the busy commercial street and tapped on the driver's window. The man was reading the New York *Daily News*. He reached over his shoulder and unlocked the rear door.

It was a short ride from the town to the newly constructed Arolen headquarters. Adam sat with his hands pressed between his knees, taking everything in. They stopped at a security gate, and a uniformed guard with a clipboard bent down and stared at Adam through the window. The driver said, "Schonberg," and the guard, apparently satisfied, lifted the white-and-black-striped gate.

As they went up the sloping drive, Adam was amazed by the opulence. There was a reflecting pool in the center of the well-tended grounds surrounded by trees. The main building was a huge bronzed structure whose surface acted like a mirror. The sides of the building tapered as they soared up into the sky. There were two smaller buildings on either side, connected to the main building by transparent bridges.

The driver skirted the reflecting pool and stopped directly in front of the main entrance. Adam thanked the man and walked up toward the door. As he drew closer, he checked his appearance in the mirror-like surface. He had on his best clothes, a blue blazer, white shirt, striped tie, and gray slacks. The only problem was that there were two buttons missing from the left sleeve of the jacket.

Inside the front door he was issued a special badge and told to take the elevator to the twelfth floor. Riding up in solitary splendor, he noticed a TV camera that slowly moved back and forth, and he wondered if he were being observed. When the doors opened, he was greeted by a man about his own age.

"Mr. McGuire?" asked Adam.

"No, I'm Tad, Mr. McGuire's secretary. Would you follow me, please."

He led Adam to an outer office, told him to wait, and disappeared through a door that said "District Sales Manager, Northeast."

Adam glanced around. The furniture was reproduction Chippendale, the wall-to-wall carpet a luxurious beige. Adam couldn't help but compare the environment to the decaying medical center he'd recently left, and recalled the dean's warning. He didn't have time for second thoughts before Clarence McGuire opened the door and motioned Adam inside. He walked over to a couch and sat down as McGuire gave Tad a few final orders before dismissing him.

McGuire was a youthful, stocky man an inch or so shorter than

Adam. His face had a satisfied air about it, and his eyes almost closed when he smiled.

"Would you care for something to drink?" he asked.

Adam shook his head.

"Then I think we should begin," said Mr. McGuire. "What made you interested in Arolen?"

Adam nervously cleared his throat. "I decided to leave medical school, and I thought that the pharmaceutical industry would find use for my training. Arolen gave my class their black bags and the name stuck in my mind."

Mr. McGuire smiled. "I appreciate your candor. OK, tell me why you are interested in pharmaceuticals."

Adam fidgeted a little. He was reluctant to give the real, humbling reasons for his interest: Jennifer's pregnancy and his desperate need for cash. Instead, he tried out the line he had practiced on the bus. "I was influenced to a large degree by my gradual disillusionment with the practice of medicine. It seems to me that doctors no longer consider the patient their prime responsibility. Technology and research have become more rewarding intellectually and financially, and medicine has become more of a trade than a profession." Adam wasn't sure what he meant by that phrase, but it had a nice ring to it so he let it stand. Besides, Mr. McGuire seemed to buy it.

"Over the last two and a half years I've come to believe the pharmaceutical companies have more to offer the patient than the individual doctor has. I think I can do more for people if I work for Arolen than if I stay in medicine."

Adam leaned back on the sofa. He thought what he had said sounded pretty good.

"Interesting," said McGuire. "It sounds as if you have given this a lot of thought. However, I must tell you that our usual method of starting people like yourself is in our sales force. What the medical professional likes to call 'detail men.' But I don't know if that would give you the sense of service you are seeking."

Adam leaned forward. "I assumed that I would start in sales, and I know it would be a number of years before I could really make a contribution." He watched McGuire for signs of skepticism, but the man continued to smile.

"One thing that I particularly wanted to ask . . ." said McGuire. "Is your father with the Food and Drug Administration?"

Adam felt the muscles of his neck tighten. "My father is David Schonberg of the FDA," he said, "but that has no bearing on my interest in Arolen. In fact, I am barely on speaking terms with my father, so I certainly couldn't influence his decisions in any way."

"I see," said Mr. McGuire. "But I can assure you that we are interested in you and not your father. Now, I would like to hear about your schooling and work experience."

Crossing his legs, Adam began from the beginning, starting with grammar school and leading up to medical school. He described all his summer jobs. It took about fifteen minutes.

"Very good," said Mr. McGuire when Adam had finished. "If you'll wait outside for a few minutes, I'll be out shortly." As soon as the door closed, McGuire picked up the phone and called his boss, William Shelly. Shelly's secretary answered, and McGuire told Joyce to put the VP on the line.

"What is it?" asked Bill Shelly, his voice crisp and commanding.

"I just finished interviewing Adam Schonberg," said Mr. McGuire, "and you were right. He is David Schonberg's son, and he's also one of the best candidates I've seen in five years. He's perfect Arolen executive material, right down to his philosophies about current medical practice."

"Sounds good," agreed Bill. "If he works out, you'll get a bonus."

"I'm afraid I can't take credit for finding him," said Clarence. "The kid called me."

"You'll get the bonus just the same," said Bill. "Give him some lunch and then bring him up to my office. I'd like to talk with him myself."

Clarence hung up the phone and returned to the waiting area outside his office. "I just spoke with the vice-president in charge of marketing who is my boss and he'd like to talk with you after lunch. What do you say?"

"I'm flattered," said Adam.

/ / /

Jennifer turned away from the window in Cheryl's room and looked at her friend. She seemed almost angelic with her white skin and freshly washed blond hair. The tranquilizer that she'd been given had obviously taken effect. Cheryl was asleep, her head comfortably elevated on a pillow.

Jennifer didn't know what to do. Cheryl had been brought back from the treatment room and told about Dr. Foley's death. Marlene Polaski had tried to convince Cheryl that Dr. Stephenson was as good a doctor as Dr. Foley and that Cheryl should go ahead and have the procedure done. She reminded Cheryl that every day that passed made the abortion more risky.

Jennifer eventually had agreed with Marlene and had tried to change Cheryl's mind, but the girl continued to insist that no one was going to touch her except Dr. Foley. It was as if she refused to believe the man had committed suicide.

Staring at the still form on the bed, Jennifer noticed that her friend's eyes were slowly opening.

"How do you feel?"

"Fine," said Cheryl sleepily.

"I think I should be going," said Jennifer. "I've got to get dinner ready before Adam gets home. I'll give you a call later. I can come back tomorrow if you'd like. Are you sure you don't want Dr. Stephenson to do the procedure?"

Cheryl's head lolled to the side. When she spoke, her words were slurred. "What did you say? I didn't hear you exactly."

"I said I think I'll be going," said Jennifer, smiling in spite of herself. "Did they give you some champagne before they brought you back here? You sound drunk."

"No champagne," murmured Cheryl as she fumbled with the bed covers. "I'll walk you to the elevator." Cheryl threw back the blanket, inadvertently jerking the IV line that was still attached to her left arm.

"I think you'd better stay where you are," said Jennifer. Her smile disappeared, and she felt the initial stirring of fear. She reached out to restrain Cheryl.

But Cheryl already had her legs over the side of the bed and was pushing herself up into a shaky sitting position. At that point she noticed that she had pulled out her IV and was bleeding from the spot where the tube had entered her arm.

"Look what I did," Cheryl said. She pointed to the IV and in doing so, lost her balance.

Jennifer tried to grab her shoulders, but in a limp, fluid movement,

Cheryl slipped off the bed onto the floor. All Jennifer could do was to ease her down. She ended up bent double, her face resting on her knees.

Jennifer didn't know what to do: call for help or lift Cheryl. Since Cheryl was in such an unnatural position, she decided to help her back to bed and then get the nurses, but when she raised Cheryl's arms, all she saw was blood.

"Oh God!" she cried. Blood was pouring from Cheryl's nose and mouth. Jennifer turned her on her back and noted that the skin around her eyes was black and blue, as if she'd been beaten. There was more blood on her legs, coming from beneath the hospital gown.

For a few seconds Jennifer was paralyzed. Then she lunged for the nurse's call button and pressed it repeatedly. Cheryl still had not moved. Abandoning the call button, Jennifer dashed to the door and frantically called for help. Marlene appeared almost immediately and pushed past Jennifer, who flattened herself against the wall of the corridor, her hands pressed to her mouth. Several other hospital nurses rushed into the room. Then someone ran out and issued an emergency page over the previously silent PA system.

Jennifer felt someone take her arm. "Mrs. Schonberg. Can you tell us what happened?"

Jennifer turned to face Marlene. There was blood on the side of the nurse's cheek. Jennifer peered into the room. They were giving Cheryl mouth-to-mouth resuscitation.

"We were talking," said Jennifer. "She didn't complain about anything. She just sounded drunk. When she tried to get out of bed, she collapsed and then there was all that blood."

Several doctors, including Dr. Stephenson, ran down the hallway and into Cheryl's room. Soon another doctor arrived with what looked like an anesthesia machine. Marlene helped him maneuver it into the room, leaving Jennifer alone. Jennifer leaned against the wall, feeling dizzy. She was vaguely aware of other patients standing in the doorways of their rooms.

Two orderlies appeared with a gurney. A moment later Jennifer saw Cheryl for the last time as she was taken back to the treatment room. She had a black anesthesia mask clasped over her shockingly pale face. At least a dozen people were grouped around her shouting orders.

"Are you all right?" asked Marlene, suddenly appearing in front of Jennifer.

"I think so," said Jennifer. Her voice was flat, like Dr. Stephenson's. "What's wrong with Cheryl?"

"I don't think anybody knows yet," said Marlene.

"She'll be all right," said Jennifer, more as a statement than a question.

"Dr. Stephenson is one of the very best," said Marlene. "Why don't you come to the lounge across from the nurses' station. I don't want you sitting by yourself."

"My bag is in Cheryl's room," said Jennifer.

"You wait here. I'll get it," said Marlene.

After retrieving it, Marlene took Jennifer to the lounge and offered her something to drink, but Jennifer assured her that she was fine.

"Do you know what they're going to do?" asked Jennifer, not certain she wanted to hear the answer.

"That's up to the doctors," said Marlene. "They'll certainly take out the fetus. Other than that, I don't know."

"Is the baby causing this bleeding?"

"Most likely. Both the bleeding and the shock. That's why they have to get it out."

Making Jennifer promise to call if she needed anything, Marlene went back to work. Every few minutes, though, she would wave to Jennifer and Jennifer would wave back.

Jennifer had never liked hospitals, and this present experience confirmed her long-standing aversion. She checked her watch. It was three-twenty.

Almost an hour passed before Dr. Stephenson reappeared. His hair was matted across his forehead, his face drawn. Jennifer's heart skipped a beat.

"We did the best we could," he said, sitting opposite her.

"Is she . . ." began Jennifer, feeling as if she were watching a soap opera.

Dr. Stephenson nodded. "She's dead. We couldn't save her. She had DIC, or diffuse intravascular coagulation. It's a condition that we don't really understand too well, but it is occasionally associated with abortions. We've only had one other case here at the Julian, and fortunately the patient did well. With Cheryl, however, the situation was complicated by uncontrollable hemorrhaging. Even if we had been able to resuscitate her, I'm afraid she would have lost her kidney function."

Jennifer nodded, but she didn't understand in the slightest. It was all too unbelievable.

"Do you know the family?" asked Dr. Stephenson.

"No," said Jennifer.

"That's too bad," he said. "Cheryl was not willing to give their address or phone number. It's going to make it difficult to track them down."

Marlene and Gale appeared in front of Jennifer. Both had been crying. Jennifer was astounded. She'd never heard of nurses crying.

"We're all very upset about this," said Dr. Stephenson. "That's the trouble with practicing medicine. You do your best, but sometimes it is just not enough. Losing a young, vibrant girl like Cheryl is a tragedy. Here at the Julian Clinic we take this kind of failure very personally."

Fifteen minutes later Jennifer left the clinic by the same door she'd entered with Cheryl only hours before. She could not quite grasp the fact that her friend was dead. She turned and looked up at the mirrored façade of the Julian Clinic. Despite what had happened, she still had a good feeling about the hospital. It was a place where people counted.

/ / /

Following McGuire off the elevator on the nineteenth floor after lunch, Adam paused. He was again both impressed and appalled by the costly furnishings. The appointments were so lavish they made McGuire's floor seem utilitarian by comparison.

Quickening his step, Adam caught up with McGuire just as he was entering the most spectacular office Adam had ever seen. One entire wall was glass, and beyond it the Jersey countryside unrolled in winter majesty.

"You like the view?" asked a voice. Adam turned. "I'm Bill Shelly," the man said, walking around his desk. "Glad you could come out and see us."

"My pleasure," said Adam, surprised at Mr. Shelly's youthfulness. Adam had expected someone at least fifty years of age as a senior executive. Mr. Shelly did not appear to be more than thirty. He was

Adam's height with closely cut blond hair combed with a razor-sharp part. His eyes were a startlingly bright blue. He was dressed in a white shirt with the sleeves rolled up, pink tie, and tan slacks.

Mr. Shelly gestured out the window. "Those buildings in the distance are Newark. Even Newark looks good from a distance." Behind Adam, McGuire chuckled.

Looking out the window, Adam realized he could also see the lower part of Manhattan. There were lots of clouds, and shafts of sunlight slanted down, illuminating some of the New York skyscrapers while leaving others in blue shadow.

"How about some refreshment," said Mr. Shelly, moving over to a coffee table that supported a silver service. "We've got coffee, tea, and just about anything else."

The three men sat down. McGuire and Adam asked for coffee. Bill Shelly poured himself a cup of tea.

"McGuire has told me a little about you," said Shelly, sizing up Adam as he talked.

Adam began to speak, repeating essentially the same things he had told McGuire earlier. The two Arolen executives exchanged glances, nodding imperceptibly. Bill had no doubt that McGuire's assessment had been accurate. The content of the personality profile that Bill had ordered drawn up during lunch confirmed Bill's sense that Adam was a particularly good choice for their managerial training program. Finding candidates was a high priority, since the company was expanding so rapidly. The only reservation Bill had was that the boy might go back to medical school, but that could be handled too.

When Adam finished, Bill put down his teacup and said, "We find your attitude about the medical profession sympathetic with our own. We too are aware of doctors' lack of social responsibility. I think you've come to the right place. Arolen could very well be a perfect home for you. Do you have any questions for us?"

"If I am hired, I would like to stay in the New York area," said Adam. He was reluctant to move away from the medical school and wanted Jennifer delivered at the center.

Bill turned to McGuire. "I think we could find an opening, don't you, Clarence?"

"Indeed," agreed Clarence quickly.

"Any other questions?" asked Mr. Shelly.

"Not that I can come up with at the moment," said Adam. Thinking the meeting over, he started to rise, but Bill leaned over to stop him. "Wait just a little longer." Dismissing his colleague, he said, "Clarence, I'll send him down to your office shortly." As the door closed behind McGuire, Bill rose to his feet.

"First, let me tell you that we are very interested in you. Your medical background is first-rate. Second, I want to assure you that we would be hiring you on your own merits, not because of any influence that you may or may not have with your father."

"I appreciate your saying that," said Adam, impressed by Mr. Shelly's frankness.

Lifting the personality profile that McGuire had put together, Shelly added, "You'd be amazed to know that we have already a complete report on you."

Adam felt a moment's outrage that Arolen would dare invade his privacy, but before he could protest, Bill was saying, "Everything in this report encourages me not only to hire you but to offer you a spot in our managerial training program. What do you say?"

Dazed, Adam tried to regain his composure. Things were moving faster than he'd ever expected. "Is the managerial training done here as well?" he asked.

"No," said Mr. Shelly. "Sales training is located here, but the management program is held at our main research center in Puerto Rico."

Puerto Rico! thought Adam. And he had been worried about leaving Manhattan. "That's a very generous offer," he said at last. "But I think I'd prefer to start out a little slower. My original idea was to begin as a sales rep so that I could learn about the business world."

"I can appreciate that," said Mr. Shelly. "But the offer remains. I should tell you that Arolen is planning to reduce its sales force starting next year. You might want to keep that in mind."

"Does this mean I have been offered a sales job?" asked Adam.

"Yes, indeed," said Bill. "And there's one more person in our organization that I'd like you to meet." He flipped on his intercom and asked his secretary to ask Dr. Nachman if he could come down and meet the new recruit they had discussed earlier.

"Dr. Heinrich Nachman is head of our research center in Puerto Rico. He's in town for our board meeting, which was held this morning. I'd like you to meet him. He's a renowned neurosurgeon and a fascinating individual. Talking with him might make you consider the Puerto Rico offer more seriously."

Adam nodded, then asked, "When would you like me to start? I'm ready now."

"I do like your attitude," said Shelly. "I'll have you enrolled in our next sales representative course, which I believe starts in a week. You'll have to spend a day with a sales rep before then, but I'm sure Clarence McGuire can set that up for you. As for salary, you'll go on the payroll immediately. Also, after reading your file, I guess you would like to know about our maternity benefits."

Adam could feel his face redden. He was saved from replying by Dr. Heinrich Nachman's entrance.

The neurosurgeon was exceptionally tall and thin. He had shaggy dark hair and eyes that appeared to miss very little. He greeted Adam with a broad smile and stared intensely at him for several minutes. Adam was about to squirm under the unwavering gaze when the doctor said, "Are we going to see this young man in Puerto Rico?"

"Unfortunately, not just yet," said Shelly. "Adam feels he'd like to learn a bit about the business before committing to managerial training."

"I see," said Dr. Nachman. "From what Bill's told me you'd be a real asset to our organization. Our research is moving ahead faster than we had anticipated. It would be a fantastic opportunity for you. You have no idea."

"What area does the research involve?" asked Adam.

"Psychotropic drugs and fetology," said Dr. Nachman.

There was a pause. Adam looked from one man to the other. They were both staring at him. "That's very interesting," he said self-consciously.

"At any rate," said Dr. Nachman, "welcome to Arolen Pharmaceuticals." The researcher stuck out his hand, and Adam shook it.

///

On the bus ride back to the city Adam felt some misgivings. He remembered Dr. Markowitz's statement about deserting to the enemy. The idea that a company could make so much money selling drugs to people who were ill seemed contrary to all his ideals. He realized that doctors did essentially the same thing. But there was something else that bothered Adam about Arolen, something he couldn't quite define. Perhaps it had to do with the fact that they had done a "complete report" on him.

In any case, he hadn't made a lifetime commitment and for the moment he needed the money. If he and Jennifer saved carefully, there was no reason he couldn't be back in medical school in eighteen months.

As the bus entered the Lincoln Tunnel, Adam pulled out his worn wallet and surreptitiously glanced into it. There they were, ten crisp hundred-dollar bills nestled against the half-dozen ragged singles. Adam had never seen so much money in cash. Bill had insisted Adam take an advance, pointing out he might need some new clothes. He wouldn't be wearing whites to work.

But a thousand dollars! Adam still could not believe it.

/ / /

Struggling with two Bloomingdale's bags containing shirts and a jacket for himself and a gift-wrapped new dress for Jennifer, Adam took the Lexington Avenue subway to Fourteenth Street and walked to the apartment.

As soon as he opened the door he heard Jennifer on the phone, talking to her mother. He glanced into the kitchen and saw no preparations for dinner. In fact, he saw no signs of groceries, either. Promising himself that he was not going to get upset that evening, he walked into the bedroom where Jennifer was just saying good-bye. She hung up the phone and turned to face him.

She looked terrible. Her cheeks were streaked and her eyes were red from crying. Her hair was half in a bun, half out, hanging limply over her shoulders.

"Don't tell me," said Adam. "Your parents are moving to Bangladesh."

Large tears welled up in her eyes, and Adam wished he'd kept his big mouth shut. He sat down next to her and put his arm around her shoulders.

"I tried to call you earlier," said Adam. "The phone was busy."

Jennifer let her hands drop into her lap. "Why were you calling?"

"Just to tell you I was going to be a little late. I got you a little surprise. Interested?"

Jennifer nodded. Adam went out and got the package. She opened it slowly. Finally, after carefully refolding the paper, she opened the box.

Expecting delight, Adam was upset when Jennifer just sat holding the pretty Belle France chemise, the tears continuing to roll down her cheeks.

"Don't you like it?" he asked.

Jennifer wiped her eyes and pulled the dress out of the box, stood up and held it under her chin so she could see herself in the mirror. "It's gorgeous," she said. "But where did you get the money?"

Adam shrugged his shoulders. "If you don't like it, I'm sure you can exchange it."

Jennifer walked back to Adam and, with the dress still pressed against her chest, kissed him on the mouth. "I love it. It's one of the prettiest dresses I've ever seen."

"Then why are you crying?"

"Because I had such an awful day. Did you ever meet Cheryl, Jason's secretary?"

"I don't think so," said Adam.

"It doesn't matter," said Jennifer. "But she was only nineteen or twenty. Today I went with her to a place called the Julian Clinic . . ."

"I know of it," interrupted Adam. "A huge, new HMO organization, kind of like the Mayo Clinic. Some of the students that have gone there for various rotations say it's a bit weird."

"It wasn't the place that was strange," said Jennifer. "It was what happened. Cheryl went there to have an abortion."

Adam cringed. "Wonderful!" he said with sarcasm. "You went with someone to have an abortion? Jennifer, are you crazy?"

"She didn't have anybody else," explained Jennifer. "I couldn't let her go alone."

"Of course not," said Adam. "But if you don't mind my asking, where was her family or her boyfriend? Why did it have to be you, Jennifer?"

"I don't know," admitted Jennifer. "But I went. And then she died!"

"Died!" repeated Adam with horror. "What did she die of? Was she sick?"

Jennifer shook her head. "She was apparently quite healthy. They were just about to do the abortion when Cheryl realized her own doctor wasn't present, and she refused to go ahead with the procedure. She expected a Dr. Foley, but the man is dead. He'd committed suicide. So another doctor was going to do the abortion."

"In some group practices the patient can't choose which physician they see," said Adam.

"That may be true," said Jennifer, "but it seems to me that the patient should be informed in advance if the doctor she expected is not going to be there."

"I can't argue with that," said Adam. "But if she refused the abortion, how did she die?"

"They said it was diffuse intravascular coagulation. She died right in front of me. One minute she was all right, and the next minute she fell on the floor bleeding. It was awful." Jennifer pulled her lower lip into her mouth and bit on it. Her eyes filled with tears.

Adam put both arms around her and patted her back.

Neither spoke for a few moments. Adam let Jennifer calm down while he puzzled over the story. How could Cheryl have died of DIC if the abortion had been canceled? He guessed that it had been a saline induced abortion and the solution had already been started. He was tempted to ask more but thought it best if Jennifer weren't made to dwell on the experience.

But Jennifer was unwilling to drop the subject. "What is diffuse intravascular coagulation?" she asked. "Is it common?"

"No, no," assured Adam. "It's very rare. I don't know too much about it. I don't think anybody does. Something starts the clotting process inside the blood vessels. I think it's associated with extensive trauma or bad burns and occasionally with abortions. But in any case, it is rare."

"It doesn't happen to people who are just pregnant?" asked Jennifer.

"Absolutely not!" said Adam. "Now I don't want you to get medical-schoolitis and think you're going to come down with every exotic disease you hear about. Right now I want you to take a shower, try on this new dress, and then we'll eat."

"I didn't get groceries," said Jennifer.

"I noticed," said Adam. "No matter. I have a wallet full of money
and I'm dying to tell you how I got it. You take a shower and we'll go
out to a fancy restaurant and celebrate, OK?"

Jennifer got a tissue and blew her nose. "OK," she managed. "I
hope I'll be good company. I'm so upset."

While Jennifer showered, Adam stepped into the living room and
looked up DIC. As he expected, the condition was not related to
pregnancy. Putting the medical text back on the shelf, he noticed the
PDR. His curiosity piqued, he slipped the volume out of the bookcase
and turned to the section for Arolen Pharmaceuticals. Except for an
extensive list of generic antibiotics, Arolen did not have many exclu-
sive products in the patented prescription drug category. There
were several tranquilizers that Adam did not recognize as well as
some anti-nausea preparations, including one for pregnant women,
called pregdolen.

Adam wondered how Arolen managed to do so well with such a
small list of new products. They had to sell a lot of drugs to pay for the
impressive headquarters. He put the book back, deciding Arolen's
financial base was none of his business. At least not as long as they
continued to pay his generous salary.

CHAPTER 7

Two days later, Adam was waiting on the street in front of his apartment house for the Arolen rep to pick him up. McGuire had called the preceding evening and said that a Percy Harmon would meet Adam at eight-thirty and take him on a round of sales calls.

Adam had been standing outside for nearly twenty minutes, but despite the cold drizzle he was glad to be out of the apartment. Although he and Jennifer had patched up their quarrel, she was still upset that he had dropped out of medical school and taken a job at a drug company. He knew part of the reason her reaction bothered him so much was his own ambivalence about working for Arolen. Still, it wasn't forever and it did solve their financial problems. Maybe his in-laws would even tell her he'd done the right thing when she went out to visit today, but he doubted it.

A blue Chevy was slowing in front of him. The driver stopped and rolled down the window. "Can you tell me where 514 is?"

"Percy Harmon?" called Adam.

"You betcha," answered the driver as he leaned over and opened the passenger-side door.

Closing his jacket against the rain, Adam ran down the steps and ducked into the car.

Percy apologized for being late, explaining that traffic on the FDR

Drive had been murderous due to an accident at the Forty-ninth Street exit.

Adam liked Percy immediately, appreciating his friendliness. He was a little older than Adam and was dressed in a dark blue suit with a red polka-dot tie and matching handkerchief. He looked businesslike and successful.

They turned north on Park Avenue and headed uptown.

"Clarence McGuire was pretty enthusiastic about you on the telephone," said Percy. "What's your secret?"

"I don't know for sure," said Adam, "but I suppose it's because I was a third-year medical student at the medical center."

"Good God, of course that's it!" said Percy. "No wonder they loved you. With your background, you'll be way ahead of us laymen."

Adam was far from convinced. He'd learned a lot of facts about bones and enzymes, and the function of T-lymphocytes. But how useful was that information to Arolen? Besides, such facts had a disturbing way of dropping out of Adam's mind after a particular test was over. He glanced around the inside of Percy's car. There were pamphlets in boxes on the back seat. Next to the boxes were looseleaf notebooks, computer printouts, and a pile of order forms. Printed memoranda were stuck into the recesses on the dash. The car had the look of a busy office. Adam was not convinced that his medical-school background would be of any use in his new job. He glanced over at Percy, who was busy navigating the New York City traffic. The man looked relaxed and confident and Adam felt envious.

"How'd you get involved with Arolen?" asked Adam.

"I was recruited straight out of business school," said Percy. "I'd taken some health economics courses in college and was interested in the health field. Somehow Arolen found out and contacted me for an interview. I researched the company and was impressed. Being a sales rep has been fun, but I'm looking forward to the next step. And thanks to you, I'm heading off for the managerial training in Puerto Rico."

"What do you mean 'thanks to me'?"

"Clarence told me that you were going to be my replacement. I've been trying to go to Puerto Rico for a year."

"They offered me the same opportunity," said Adam.

"To go straight to Puerto Rico?" exclaimed Percy. "My God, man, take them up on it. I don't know if you know it but Arolen is owned by an extremely fast-growing financial group. About ten years ago some clever guys started an organization called MTIC to invest in the health industry. Arolen was one of their first acquisitions. When they got control of the company, it was an inconsequential drug house. Now it is challenging the biggies like Lilly and Merck. Joining now, you'll still be getting in on the ground floor. Who did you meet out at Arolen besides Clarence McGuire?"

"Bill Shelly and Dr. Nachman."

Percy whistled and took his eyes off the traffic long enough to give Adam an appraising glance. "You got to meet two of the original MTIC founders. Both are rumored to be on the board of directors of MTIC as well as having executive positions with Arolen. And how did you meet Nachman? He is the head of research down in Puerto Rico."

"He was here for some meeting," explained Adam curtly. Percy's response made him wonder anew if Arolen was interested in him or, despite their assurances, his father.

"The other thing about Puerto Rico," Percy was saying, "is that the center there is as luxurious as a resort. I've only been there once, but it is out of this world. I'm looking forward to training there. It's going to seem like a paid vacation."

Watching the rain beat on the windshield, Adam wondered what kind of maternity facilities they had in Puerto Rico. The idea of bright sun as well as the chance to get Jennifer away from her parents had certain appeal. He sighed. It was nice to daydream, but the fact of the matter was that he wanted to stay as near to the medical center as possible. Puerto Rico was out of the question.

"Here we are," said Percy, guiding the car over to the curb in front of a typical midtown New York City apartment building. He parked in a "No Standing" tow zone, opened the glove compartment and took out a small sign that read: "Visiting Physician." "This represents a slight distortion of the usual meaning of this phrase, but it's none-theless true," he said, smiling at Adam. "Now let's plan the attack. The idea here is for you to get some idea of what it's like to call on a typical physician. This fellow's name is Dr. Jerry Smith. He happens to be a very successful Park Avenue obstetrician. He's also a horse's ass. He thinks of himself as some intellectual giant, so it will be extremely easy to butter him up. He also likes free samples, a predi-

lection which we will be happy to indulge. Any questions before we
go to battle?"

Adam said no, but Dr. Markowitz's comment about defecting to
the enemy haunted him as he got out of the car. Percy opened the
trunk and gave Adam a large umbrella to hold while he got out a
bunch of drug samples.

"Smith's favorites are tranquilizers," said Percy. "Whatever he
does with them all, I have no idea." Percy loaded a small cardboard
box with a variety of drugs, then closed the trunk.

Dr. Smith's office was packed with women. The air was close and
smelled of damp wool.

Adam hurried after Percy, who went straight to the receptionist.
Reluctantly, Adam glanced around and saw many pairs of eyes re-
garding him over the tops of magazines.

"Hello, Carol," Percy was saying. "What a stunning outfit. And
your hair! There's something different. Don't tell me. Let me guess.
You got a perm. God, it looks terrific. And how's that little boy of
yours? Good, huh. Well, let me introduce you to Adam Schonberg.
He's going to be taking over my customers. Now, would you mind if
he looked at that dynamite photo you have of your boy? The one on
the bear rug."

Adam found himself holding a cube of plexiglass with different
photos on each side. Percy adjusted it in his hand so that he was
looking at a chubby baby lying on a bath towel.

"And Carol, what about your father?" asked Percy, taking the
picture cube out of Adam's hands and putting it back down on the
desk. "Is he out of the hospital yet?"

Two minutes later Percy and Adam were standing in the doctor's
consultation room, waiting for Smith to appear. "That was an amazing performance," whispered Adam.

"Piece of cake," said Percy with a wave of his hand. "But I'll tell
you something. The receptionist or nurse is the person you have to
impress in the doctor's office. She controls access to the physician and
if you don't handle her properly, you'll die of old age waiting to get
in."

"But you acted like you were good friends with that woman," said
Adam. "How did you know all those things about her personal life?"

"Arolen provides you with that kind of information," said Percy
simply. "Arolen keeps a complete record on every member of each

physician's staff as well as the doctor himself. You feed it into the computer. Then when you have questions, you can get the answers. Nothing mysterious about it. It's just attention to detail."

Adam glanced around Smith's office. It was elegantly furnished, composed of dark lacquered cabinets and floor-to-ceiling bookshelves. Facing into the room was a large mahogany desk, piled high with journals. Adam glanced at the date on the top issue of the *American Journal of Obstetrics and Gynecology*. It was more than a year old. A paper mailing binder was still around the magazine. It had never been opened.

The door opened. Dr. Smith stopped on the threshold and called down the hall. "Put the next patients into rooms six and seven."

A voice answered, but it was too far away to hear.

"I know I'm behind schedule," shouted Dr. Smith. "So what else is new? Tell them I've got an important conference." He came into the office and kicked the door shut behind him. "Nurses, shit!" He was a big man with an impressive paunch. His heavy jowls made him look like an old bulldog.

"Dr. Smith, how are you?" beamed Percy. Smith allowed the rep to shake his hand and then quickly retreated behind his desk, where he brought out a pack of filter-tipped Camels. He lit one and blew the smoke out through his nostrils.

"I'd like you to meet Adam Schonberg," continued Percy, gesturing toward Adam. "He's started training for Arolen and I'm taking him around to meet a few of my more prestigious clients."

The doctor smiled and said, "Well, what do you boys have for me this morning?"

"All sorts of samples," said Percy, putting the cardboard box on the edge of the desk and opening it. Dr. Smith eagerly moved forward on his chair.

"I know how much you like Marlium, Arolen's top-selling tranquilizer, so I brought you a good supply. You'll notice that the packaging has been improved. Patients love these new bright yellow bottles. I also have a reprint for you. Studies just completed at the Julian Clinic here in New York indicate that Marlium has the fewest side effects of any tranquilizer on the market today. But I don't have to tell you that. You've been telling us the same thing for as long as I can remember."

"Damn right," said Dr. Smith.

Percy lined up the other drug samples in neat rows on Dr. Smith's desk, all the time maintaining a running commentary on the proven excellence of the various products. At every possible juncture he complimented Dr. Smith's perspicacity in prescribing Arolen drugs for his patients.

"And last but not least," said Percy, "I've brought you fifty starter samples of pregdolen. I know I don't have to convince you of the virtues of this drug for morning sickness. You were one of the first to recognize its value. However, I do have a reprint of a recent article that I'd like you to read when you get a chance. It compares pregdolen with other similar drugs on the market and shows that pregdolen is cleared by the liver faster than anything put out by the competition."

Percy put a glossy reprint on top of one of the piles on Dr. Smith's desk.

"By the way, how is that boy of yours, David? Isn't he a junior now up at Boston University? Adam, you should meet this kid. Looks like Tom Selleck, only better."

"He's doing very well, thanks," beamed Dr. Smith. He took one last drag on his cigarette before crushing it in a beanbag ashtray. "The kid is premed, you know."

"I know," said Percy. "He's not going to have any trouble getting into medical school."

Fifteen minutes later Adam found himself climbing back into the passenger side of the Chevy Celebrity. Percy slid the umbrella in on the floor of the back seat and then got behind the wheel. There was a parking ticket under the windshield wiper.

"Oh, well," said Percy. "That sign of mine doesn't always work." He turned on the wipers and the ticket disappeared. "Ta-da!" he said, raising his hands as if he'd just done a magic trick. "The car is registered to Arolen and the legal department takes care of that sort of thing. Now, let's see who's next." He picked up the clipboard and turned to the next computer printout.

The morning passed quickly as Adam watched Percy expertly handle receptionists and push Arolen products onto busy practitioners. Adam was amazed at how effective Percy was with the physicians. Having talked with Percy all morning, he was aware of how little scientific information Percy had to draw on. Yet it didn't seem to matter. Percy knew just enough to make it sound as if he knew a great deal, and armed with a lot of current drug information, he was able to snow the physician. Adam began to appreciate the low regard that Arolen had for the intelligence of the average doctor.

Around eleven-thirty, after leaving the office of an internist on Sutton Place South, Percy got into the car and rested his head on the steering wheel. "I think I'm having a hypoglycemic crisis. I gotta get something to eat. Is it too early for you?"

"It's never too early for me," said Adam.

"Great!" said Percy. "Since Arolen is paying, we're going to do it right."

Adam had joked in the past about the Four Seasons restaurant as being a symbol of the rich, though he'd never been in the place. When Percy had suggested they go there, Adam thought he was joking. When he led the way into the Grill Room, Adam almost passed out.

Putting his linen napkin on his lap, Adam tried to remember what it was like in the crowded hospital cafeteria. It seemed a million miles away. A waiter asked Adam if he wanted a drink. Not sure of himself, he looked over at Percy who calmly ordered a martini. What the hell, thought Adam, who quickly said he'd have the same.

"So what is your impression of the business now that you've gotten your feet wet?"

"It's interesting," said Adam evasively. "Do you eat here every day?"

"No, to tell you the truth. But McGuire said to impress you."

Adam laughed. He liked Percy's candor. "I'm impressed enough with your abilities. You're very good."

Percy shook his head. "It's easy. Like catching fish at a trout farm. For some inexplicable reason, doctors know very little about drugs. Maybe you can tell me the reason."

Adam thought for a moment. He'd had courses in pharmacology like everyone else, but it was true that he knew very little about the actual use of the drugs. He'd only been taught about their action on a cellular level. What little he knew about prescribing he'd picked up on the wards. Before he could answer Percy's question, their drinks arrived.

"Here's to your career with Arolen," said Percy, holding up his glass.

"What about this pregdolen you've been pushing?" asked Adam, remembering Jennifer's recent complaints. "My wife has been having some trouble with morning sickness. Maybe I should take a couple of those starter samples."

"I wouldn't if I were you," said Percy, suddenly serious. "I know Arolen sells a ton of it, and a lot of people think it's the best thing since sliced bread, but I don't think the drug works and there's a possibility it's toxic."

"What do you mean?" asked Adam.

"It's been written up in several of the more important medical journals," said Percy, taking another sip of his drink. "Of course, I don't refer to those articles when I call on the doctors. Obviously the doctors haven't read them because they keep prescribing the stuff like crazy. It sure explodes the myth that doctors get their drug information from the medical journals. For most practitioners that's bullshit. They get their drug information, what little they get, from the likes of me, and I only tell them what I want to tell them."

Percy shrugged when he noticed Adam's shocked expression. "You more than anyone must know that doctors prescribe out of hunch and habit. Our job is to try to make Arolen part of that habit."

Adam slowly turned his glass and watched the olive revolve. He was beginning to realize what he'd have to close his eyes to in this line of work.

Sensing Adam's misgivings, Percy added, "To tell you the honest truth, it will be a relief to get away from the sales end of the business."

"Why?" asked Adam.

Percy sighed. "I don't know how much of this I should be telling you. I don't want to dampen your enthusiasm. But some weird things have been going on in my area. For instance, a number of doctors that I'd been seeing on a regular basis have been taken off my sales list. At first I thought that they'd moved away or died, but then I found out that most of them had gone on an Arolen Conference Cruise, come back, and given up their practices to go to the Julian Clinic."

"Julian Clinic" evoked a strange response in the pit of Adam's stomach, as he remembered the name from Jennifer's story.

"Some of those doctors I'd gotten to know pretty well," continued Percy, "so I went to see them even though the Julian Clinic isn't part of my territory. What struck me was that they had all changed some-

how. A good example was a Dr. Lawrence Foley I'd been seeing since
I began working for Arolen. He didn't have much use for Arolen
products, but I saw him because I liked the man. In fact, we played
tennis about twice a month."

"The Lawrence Foley who just committed suicide?" asked Adam.

"That's the one," said Percy. "And his suicide is part of the kind of
change I'm talking about. I really felt I knew the man. He was a
partner in one of the busiest OB-GYN practices in town. Then he
went away on an Arolen cruise, came back, and gave up everything
to work at the Julian Clinic. When I went to see him, he was a
different man. He was so preoccupied with work, he couldn't take
the time to play tennis. And he was not the suicidal type. The man
had never been depressed a day in his life, and he loved his work and
his wife. When I heard what happened, I couldn't believe it. After
shooting his wife he put the shotgun in his mouth and . . ."

"I get the picture," said Adam quickly. "What's the story about
these Arolen Conference Cruises?"

"They are very popular medical seminars that are given on a cruise
ship in the Caribbean. The lecturers are the most famous professors
and researchers in their various fields. The meetings have the best
reputation of any medical conventions in the country," said Percy.
"But that's all I know. Being curious, I asked Clarence McGuire
about them, but he said he didn't know much more except that they
were organized by MTIC."

"If you're really curious," said Adam, "why not ask Bill Shelly? If
what you told me is true about Arolen liking information about doctors, it seems to me they'd be fascinated by your observations. Besides, I can tell you that Bill Shelly is a surprisingly young and person-
able guy."

"No kidding," said Percy. "Maybe you're right. Maybe I'll go over
there this afternoon. I've always wanted to meet Mr. Shelly and this
could be my chance."

///

When Adam asked Percy to drop him off at the medical center late
that afternoon, he had the feeling he was not going to be the same
doctor after working for Arolen. They had visited sixteen physicians'
offices and had, according to Percy, dispensed over five hundred

bottles of sample drugs. Most of the doctors had been like Smith: eager to get the samples, quick to accept Percy's pitch.

Adam went into the hospital through the medical school entrance and headed up to the periodical room at the library. He wanted to look up pregdolen in the recent journals. Percy's comments had made him curious, and he did not like the idea of selling a drug with really bad side effects.

He found what he wanted in a ten-month-old issue of the *New England Journal of Medicine.* It would have been hard for a practicing OB man to have missed it.

Just as Percy had suggested, pregdolen had proved inefficacious when tested against a placebo. In fact, in all but three cases the placebo had done a better job in controlling morning sickness. More importantly, the studies showed that pregdolen was often teratogenic, causing severe developmental abnormalities in fetuses.

Turning to the *Journal of Applied Pharmacology,* Adam found that despite the adverse publicity, pregdolen's sales had shown a steady increase over the years, with an especially impressive surge in the last year. Adam closed the journal, wondering if he were more awed by Arolen's marketing abilities or the average obstetrician's ignorance.

Putting the magazine back, he decided it was a toss-up.

///

Percy Harmon felt like he was on top of the world as he drove out of the parking area of his favorite Japanese restaurant with a fabulous meal of steak sukiyaki under his belt. The restaurant was located in, of all places, Fort Lee, New Jersey, but at that hour of the night, ten-thirty, it wouldn't take more than twenty minutes to return to his apartment in Manhattan.

He did not notice the nondescript man in a blue blazer and tan slacks who'd stayed at the bar the entire time Percy had been in the restaurant. The man watched until the blue Chevy disappeared from sight, then made for the nearby phone booth. "He's left the restaurant. Should be at the garage in fifteen minutes. I'll call the airport."

Without waiting for an answer, the man cut the connection and dropped in two more coins. He pushed the buttons slowly, almost mechanically.

Driving down the Harlem River Drive, Percy wondered why he had never thought of going to Bill Shelly before. Not only had the man welcomed Percy's observations, he'd been downright friendly. In fact, he'd taken Percy to meet the executive vice-president, and making those kinds of contacts within an organization like Arolen was invaluable. Percy felt that his future had never looked so promising.

Percy stopped in front of the garage Arolen had found for him just four blocks from his Seventy-fourth Street apartment. The only time it was inconvenient was when it was raining. It was in a huge warehouselike structure that dominated the potholed street. The entrance was barred by an imposing metal grate. Percy pressed the remote control device that he kept in the glove compartment and the grate lifted. Above the entrance was a single sign that said simply "Parking, day, week, or month," followed by a local telephone number.

After Percy had driven inside, the metal grille reactivated and with a terrible screeching closed with a definitive thud. There were no assigned spots, and Percy made a hopeful swing around before heading down the ramp to the next level. He preferred to park on the ground floor; the ill-lit spaces of the substreet levels always made him nervous.

Because of the late hour, Percy had to descend three levels before finding a spot. He locked the car and walked toward the stairwell, whistling to keep his spirits up. His heels echoed against the oil-stained cement floor and in the distance he could hear water dripping. Reaching the stairs, he yanked open the door and almost fainted with shock. Two men with old-fashioned crew cuts and wearing plain blue blazers faced him. They didn't move, they didn't speak. They just stood blocking his way.

Fear spread through Percy's body like a bolt of electricity. He let go of the door and stepped backward. One of the men reached out and with a bang sent the door crashing against the wall. Percy turned and fled, racing for the stairwell at the opposite end of the garage. His leather-soled shoes skidded on the concrete, making it hard for him to keep his balance.

Looking over his shoulder, he was relieved to see that neither of the two men was in pursuit. He reached the door of the far exit and tried to pull it open. The handle didn't budge. His heart sank. The door was locked!

All he could hear was the rasping sound of his own breath and the constant drip of water. The only other way out was the ramp and he started toward it. He was almost there when he saw one of the men standing immobile at the base of the sloping driveway, his arms at his side. Percy ducked behind a parked car and tried to think what to do. Obviously the men had split up; one was watching the stairwell, the other the ramp. It was then that Percy remembered the old automobile elevator in the center.

Keeping low, he moved toward it stealthily. When he reached it, he raised the wooden gate, ducked under, then lowered it after himself. The other three walls of the elevator were enclosed with a heavy wire mesh. The only light came from a bare overhead bulb. Percy's shaking finger pushed the button marked "1."

The elevator activated with a snapping noise, followed by the high-pitched whine of an electric motor. To Percy's relief, the platform jolted, then slowly started to rise.

The elevator moved at an agonizingly slow rate, and Percy was no more than six feet from street level when the two men materialized beneath him.

Without haste, one of them walked over to the elevator control and, to Percy's horror, reversed its direction. Panic-stricken, Percy repeatedly pushed the button, but the elevator relentlessly continued its descent. Gradually, he realized that they had planned for him to use the elevator. That was why they had not chased him. They wanted to trap him.

"What do you want?" he shouted. "You can have my money." Desperately, he pulled out his wallet and tossed it through the wooden lattice to the garage floor. One of the men bent and picked it up. Without looking through it, he pocketed it. The other man had pulled out what Percy first thought was a gun. But as he drew closer he realized it was a syringe.

Percy backed to the rear of the elevator, feeling like a trapped animal. As the machinery ground to a stop, one of the men reached out and raised the wooden gate. Percy screamed in terror and slid to the floor.

Just over an hour later, a blue van pulled onto the tarmac at Teterboro Airport and rolled to a stop in front of a Gulf Stream jet. Two men got out, walked to the rear of the van, and hefted out a sizable wooden crate. Silently, the cargo door on the plane slid open.

CHAPTER 8

There must have been more than a hundred people in the conference room. All had come to watch their friends and relatives graduate the Arolen sales course. Arnold Wiseman, the man who'd been in charge of the course, sat in the front of the podium next to Bill Shelly. To their right was a large limp American flag.

Adam was somewhat embarrassed by the ceremony, aware that Arolen was making more of a production than the four weeks of classes deserved. Yet it was fitting, since Adam had learned that nine-tenths of what the drug rep sold was pure show.

When he thought about it, Adam was amazed at how quickly those four weeks had gone. From the first day, he had realized that his two and a half years of medical school put him ahead of everyone else. Half of the other twenty students had degrees in pharmacology, five had master's degrees in business administration, and the rest were from various departments of Arolen Pharmaceuticals.

Adam searched the crowd for Jennifer, thinking she might have changed her mind at the last minute and come, but even as he searched he realized it was a vain hope. She'd been against his working for Arolen from the beginning, and even if she had overcome her distaste for his new job, her morning sickness had become so severe that she could rarely leave the apartment before noon. Still, he couldn't keep himself from staring at all the dark-haired women in the audience in case by some miracle she had arrived.

Suddenly his roving gaze stopped short at a small man with dark curly hair dressed in a black raincoat. He was standing by the entrance with his hands thrust into his pockets. Plain, wire-rimmed eyeglasses rested on his aquiline nose.

Adam turned away, thinking his eyes were playing a trick on him. Then he slowly turned to look at the man again. There was no doubt. It was his father.

Adam spent the rest of the ceremony in a state of shock. When the formalities were concluded and the reception had begun, he pushed his way toward the door where the man was standing. It was his father all right.

"Dad?" said Adam.

Dr. Schonberg turned around. He was holding a shrimp on the end of a toothpick. There was no smile on his lips or in his eyes.

"What a surprise," said Adam, unsure how to act. He was flattered that his father had come, but nervous too.

"So it is true," said Dr. Schonberg sternly. "You're working for Arolen Pharmaceuticals!"

Adam nodded.

"What happened to medical school?" asked Dr. Schonberg angrily. "What am I going to say to your mother? And after I went to such lengths to be sure you would be admitted!"

"I think my A average had something to do with that," said Adam. "Besides, I'll go back. I've just taken a leave of absence."

"Why?" demanded Dr. Schonberg.

"Because we need the money," said Adam. "We are going to have a child."

For a moment Adam thought he saw a softening in his father's expression. Then Dr. Schonberg was looking about the room with distaste. "So you have allied yourself with this . . ." He gestured at the sumptuously appointed hall. "Don't tell me you are unaware that business interests are trying to take over the medical profession."

"Arolen provides a public service," said Adam defensively.

"Spare me," said Dr. Schonberg. "I'm not interested in their propaganda. The drug houses and the holding companies that control them are out to make money like any other industry, yet they waste millions of PR dollars trying to convince the public otherwise. Well, it is a lie. And to think that my own son has become a part of it and because of that girl he married . . ."

"Her name is Jennifer," snapped Adam, feeling the blood rise to his face.

"Dr. David Schonberg." Bill Shelly had come up behind Adam, champagne glass in hand. "Welcome to Arolen. I'm sure you are as proud of your son as we are. My name is Bill Shelly."

Dr. Schonberg ignored the hand. "I know who you are," he said. "And to be perfectly honest, I am appalled rather than proud to see my son here. The only reason I responded to your invitation was to make certain that Arolen is not expecting any special considerations because Adam here has joined your organization."

"Dad," sputtered Adam.

"I've always appreciated honesty," said Bill, withdrawing his hand, "and I can assure you that we did not hire Adam because his father is with the FDA."

"I hope that is true," said Dr. Schonberg. "I wouldn't want you to think that Arolen will have an easier time getting new drugs approved."

Without waiting for a reply, Dr. Schonberg tossed his shrimp into a wastebasket and pushed through the crowd toward the door.

Adam shook his head in disbelief. "I'm terribly sorry," he said to Bill Shelly.

"There is no need to apologize," interrupted Bill. "You're not responsible for your father's beliefs. He's had lots of experience with the less honest companies in our field. I'm only sorry that he's not had enough contact with Arolen to appreciate the difference."

"That may be true," said Adam, "but it still does not excuse his behavior."

"Maybe someday we could convince your father to take one of the Arolen Conference Cruises. Have you heard of them?"

Adam nodded, remembering Percy Harmon. He had not thought about the man for over a month, but now Adam wondered why the genial rep had not kept in touch as he'd promised.

"We've invited your father many times," continued Bill. "Not only on the cruise, but also to visit our research facilities in Puerto Rico. Perhaps you might be able to talk him into accepting our invitation. I'm certain that if he did, his opinion about Arolen would change."

Adam forced a laugh. "At this point in my life I couldn't talk my father into accepting a free Rembrandt painting. We're barely on speaking terms. Frankly, I was shocked to see him here today."

"That's a shame," said Bill. "We'd love your father to be one of our featured lecturers. You know that the seminars have the best reputation in the country. And, of course, all your father's expenses would be paid if he agreed to speak."

"Sounds like you should try to appeal to my mother," laughed Adam.

"Spouses are not invited," said Bill as he guided Adam toward the champagne table.

"Why not?" asked Adam, taking a drink.

"The cruises are strictly academic," said Bill.

"Yeah, sure," said Adam.

"I mean it," said Bill. "The cruises are sponsored by Arolen, but they are run by MTIC. The only reason the company chose a ship was to keep the doctors from their usual interruptions: no telephone, no patients, and no stockbrokers. Each cruise concentrates on a particular clinical or research topic, and we invite the top men in each field to lecture. The quality of the seminars is really superb."

"So the ship just goes out to sea and anchors?" asked Adam.

"Oh, no," said Bill. "The ship leaves from Miami, travels to the Virgin Islands, then to Puerto Rico, then back to Miami. Some of the guests, usually the lecturers, disembark in Puerto Rico to visit our research institute."

"So it's all work and no play. Not even any gambling?"

"Well, just a little gambling," admitted Bill with a smile. "Anyway, your father would enjoy the experience, so if you have any influence as far as that might be concerned, you might try to use it."

Adam nodded, but he was still thinking about Percy Harmon. He'd seemed so sincere that Adam was surprised that he'd not called. He was about to ask Shelly when the rep had left Manhattan, but Bill was saying, "Have you given any more thought to our managerial training offer?"

"To tell the truth," said Adam, "I've been completely absorbed by the sales course. But I promise to think about it."

"Do that," said Bill, his eyes gleaming over the rim of his champagne glass.

Later that afternoon Adam was in McGuire's office, going over his sales territory. "You'll be taking over Percy Harmon's area," said McGuire. "Normally we'd assign a more experienced rep, but as you know we have great confidence in you. Here, let me show you."

Clarence opened up a map of Manhattan with a large portion of the east side outlined in yellow marking pencil. It started at Thirty-fourth Street and ran north, bounded on the west by Fifth Avenue and on the east by the river. Adam was disappointed that it did not include his medical center, but New York Hospital, Mount Sinai, and the Julian Clinic were within the border.

As if reading Adam's mind, Clarence said, "Of course you understand that you are not responsible for hospitals or large health maintenance organizations like the Julian Clinic."

"Why not?" questioned Adam.

"You are eager!" Clarence laughed. "But I can assure you that you will be busy enough with the private MDs in your area. All hospitals are handled by the main office."

"The Julian Clinic is more than a hospital," said Adam.

"That's true," said Clarence. "In fact, there is a special relationship between Arolen and the Julian, since both are controlled by MTIC. Consequently, the Julian provides Arolen with direct access to clinical information, and Arolen provides the Julian with special educational opportunities."

Leaning forward, Clarence picked up a computer printout and put it on Adam's lap. "If you have any concern about not being busy enough, just take a quick glance at this list of your clients."

The weight of the material in Adam's lap was considerable. The front page said: "Upper East Side Manhattan MD Listing." Under that was written: "Property of Arolen Pharmaceuticals, Montclair, New Jersey"; and in the lower right-hand corner was the single word "Confidential."

Adam flipped through the sheets and saw an alphabetical list of physicians followed by their addresses and phone numbers. The first name on the last page was Clark Vandermer, 67 East 36th Street.

As Adam considered what it would be like calling on Jennifer's obstetrician, McGuire launched into a long description of the kinds of doctors Adam would be seeing.

"Any questions?" he said at last.

"Yes," said Adam, remembering the one he'd forgotten to ask

Shelly that morning. "Do you know what happened to Percy Harmon?"

Clarence shook his head. "I'd heard that he was to take the managerial course in Puerto Rico, but I don't know if he actually did. I have no idea. Why do you ask?"

"No particular reason," said Adam.

"Well, if you don't have any other questions, you can be on your way. We're always available if you need us, and don't let me forget, here are the keys to your Arolen car. It's a Buick Century."

Adam took the keys.

"And here is the address of a parking garage. It's as near to your apartment as my staff could arrange. We pick up the rent."

Adam took the paper, again awed by his company's generosity. A parking place in the city was worth as much as a car.

"And last but not least, here's your computer access code, as was explained to you during the sales course. Your personal computer is in the trunk of the car. Good luck to you."

Adam took the final envelope and shook hands once again with the district sales manager. He was now officially an Arolen detail man.

/ / /

After tuning the radio to an FM rock station, Adam rolled down the window and jauntily stuck out an elbow. Traveling at fifty miles an hour, he felt unaccountably light-headed. Then he recalled his father's sneering disbelief and his smile faded.

"We need the money!" he said out loud. "If you'd helped us, I'd still be in medical school."

His mood did not improve when he reached the apartment only to find it empty, a short note taped to the refrigerator: "Gone home." Adam tore it off and threw it across the room.

He pulled open the refrigerator door and looked inside. There was a little leftover roast chicken. He took it out along with a jar of mayonnaise and two pieces of rye. After making a sandwich, he went into the living room and set up his personal computer. Turning it on, he keyed in his access code. What doctor should he look up? Hesitating a moment, he keyed in Vandermer's name. Then he took the telephone off the cradle and hooked it up to the modem. When everything was ready, he pushed the execute button, leaned back, and took a hefty bite from his sandwich. Small red lights appeared on the modem, indicating that he was attached to the Arolen mainframe.

The screen in front of Adam shimmered, then some text appeared. Adam stopped chewing for a moment and leaned forward to read.

CLARK VANDERMER, M.D., F.A.C.O.G.
——Biographical data
——Personal data
——Economic data
——Professional data
——Pharmaceutical usage data
(press space bar to select)

His interest aroused, Adam pressed the space bar until the cursor was next to "Personal Data." Then he pressed the execute key. Again he got an index:

PERSONAL DATA:
——Family history (past) includes parents and siblings
——Family history (present) includes wife and children
——Interests and hobbies
——Likes and dislikes
——Social history (includes education)
——Health history
——Personality profile
(press space bar to select)

My God, thought Adam, this is Orwell's *1984.* He moved the cursor to "Family history (present)" and again pushed the execute button. Immediately the screen filled with extensive text. For the next ten minutes Adam read about Clark Vandermer's wife and children. It was mostly insignificant detail, but there were some important things as well. Adam learned that Vandermer's wife had been hospitalized on three occasions for depression following the birth of their third child. He also discovered that his middle child, a female, was diagnosed as having anorexia nervosa.

Adam looked up from the screen, appalled. There was no reason for a drug firm like Arolen to have such a complete file on a doctor. He suspected everything they could use was summarized under the single category "Pharmaceutical usage data." To prove his point, Adam called up that category and got what he expected, namely an analysis of Vandermer's prescribing habits, including the amounts of each type of drug he prescribed each year.

Returning to the index, Adam asked the computer to print out on the high-speed dot-matrix printer a full report on Dr. Vandermer. The printer sprang to life, and Adam went back to the kitchen for a Coke.

It was thirty-two minutes before the printer fell silent. Adam tore off the last sheet and gathered the long train of paper that had formed behind the computer. There were almost fifty pages. Adam wondered if the good doctor had any idea of the amount of material Arolen had amassed on him.

The content of the report was dry and tediously complete. It even included Vandermer's investments. Adam skimmed until he got to a description of Vandermer's practice. He learned the doctor was a co-founder of GYN Associates along with Lawrence Foley! Lawrence Foley, the doctor who had committed suicide so unexpectedly. Adam wondered if Jennifer knew Foley had once been in partnership with her own doctor.

Reading on, Adam discovered that Vandermer's current associates were Dr. John Stens and Dr. June Baumgarten.

His curiosity piqued, Adam decided that Dr. Vandermer would be his first customer. Remembering Percy Harmon's advice that the way to the doctor was through his receptionist, Adam punched her up on the computer. Her name was Christine Morgan. She was twenty-seven, married to David Morgan, a painter, and had one male child, David Junior, nicknamed DJ.

Trying to conjure up Percy Harmon's confident air, he dialed GYN Associates. When Christine answered, he explained that he was taking over for Harmon. He mentioned in passing that the rep had spoken so warmly of her handsome son. He must have done something right because Christine told him to come right down. She'd try and get him in.

Five minutes later Adam was heading north on Park Avenue, trying to remember which Arolen drugs he was supposed to push on OB-GYNs. He decided he'd concentrate on the generic line of vitamins that Arolen advertised for pregnancy.

In the neighborhood of Thirty-sixth Street and Park Avenue even unoccupied tow zones were hard to come by. Adam had to be content with a fire hydrant space between Park and Lexington. After locking the car, he went around the back and opened the trunk. It was outfitted with a full complement of Arolen samples, reprints, and other paraphernalia. There were a dozen Cross pens emblazoned with the Arolen insignia. Adam was to give them out at his discretion.

Adam selected an appropriate sample of the drugs and reprints and tossed them into his briefcase. He slipped one of the Cross pens into the side pocket of his jacket. Locking the trunk, he set off at a brisk pace for Vandermer's office.

Christine Morgan was a tightly permed woman with frightened-birdlike mannerisms. She slid back the glass and asked if she could help him.

"I'm Adam Schonberg from Arolen," he said with as big a smile as he could muster as he gave out his first Arolen business card. She returned the smile and motioned for him to come into the reception area. After he'd admired her most recent photos of DJ, Christine led him back to one of the empty examining rooms, promising that she would let the head nurse know that he was there.

Adam sat down on the stool in front of the small white desk. He eyed the examination table with its stainless-steel stirrups. It was hard to imagine Jennifer there as a patient.

Several moments later the door burst open and Dr. Clark Vandermer walked in. To pass the time Adam had pulled out a desk drawer and was casually looking at the collection of pens, prescription pads, and lab slips. Now flushing a deep crimson, he shut the drawer and stood up.

"Was there something in particular you were looking for?" asked Dr. Vandermer sarcastically. He was holding Adam's business card and glanced back and forth between the card and Adam's embarrassed face. "Who the hell let you in here?"

"Your staff," managed Adam, purposefully vague.

"I'll have to talk to them," said Dr. Vandermer as he turned to leave. "I'll have someone show you out. I have patients to see."

"I have some samples for you," said Adam quickly. "Also a Cross pen." Hastily he fished out the pen and held it toward Vandermer who was about to tear Adam's business card in half.

"Are you by chance related to Jennifer Schonberg?" asked Dr. Vandermer.

"She's my wife," said Adam eagerly, adding, "and a patient of yours."

"I thought you were a medical student," said Dr. Vandermer.

"That's true," said Adam.

"Then what the hell kind of nonsense is this?" Vandermer said, waving the business card.

"I've taken a leave from medical school," said Adam defensively. "With Jennifer pregnant, we needed the money."

"This is not the time for you people to be having a baby," said Vandermer pedantically. "But if you are foolish enough to do so, your wife can still work."

"She's a dancer," said Adam. Remembering Vandermer's own personal problems, Adam didn't think it fair for the doctor to offer easy solutions.

"Well, it's a crime for you to leave medical school. And working as a detail man for a drug firm. My God, what a waste!"

Adam bit his lip. Vandermer was beginning to remind him of his father. Hoping to end the lecture, he asked Vandermer if there wasn't something that could be done for Jennifer's morning sickness.

"Fifty percent of my patients get morning sickness," said Dr. Vandermer with a wave of his hand. "Unless it causes nutritional problems, it is best to treat it symptomatically. I don't like to use drugs if I can avoid it, especially not Arolen's pregdolen. And don't you start playing doctor and give her any of that crap. It's not safe, despite its popularity."

Adam's opinion of Dr. Clark Vandermer rose a little. He might be unpleasantly brusque, but at least he was up-to-date in his medical reading.

"As long as you are here," said Dr. Vandermer, "you can save me a phone call. I'm scheduled to lecture next week on the Arolen Conference Cruise. What's the latest I can board the ship in Miami?"

"I don't have the slightest idea," admitted Adam.

"Wonderful," said Dr. Vandermer, reassuming his sarcastic tone. "Now would you come with me."

Grabbing his briefcase, Adam followed the man out of the examination room and down the narrow corridor. After about twenty steps Vandermer stopped, opened a door, and stepped aside to allow Adam to pass. As he did, Vandermer unceremoniously thrust the Arolen business card into Adam's hand, then closed the door behind him. Blinking, Adam found himself back in the crowded waiting room.

"Did you see the doctor?" asked Christine.

"I did indeed," said Adam, wondering why in hell they hadn't discussed the Arolen cruises during the sales course. If he had known the answer to Vandermer's question, he might have been able to make his pitch.

"I told you I could get you in," said Christine proudly.

Adam was about to ask if he could see either of the other doctors in the group, when he noticed the nameplates on the wall behind the receptionist. In addition to Vandermer, Baumgarten, and Stens, Dr. Lawrence Foley and Dr. Stuart Smyth were also listed. Adam didn't remember seeing a Dr. Smyth in Vandermer's file.

Reaching into his pocket, Adam pulled out the Cross pen. "Got a little surprise for you," he said, handing it to Christine. Brushing off her thanks, he pointed to Dr. Smyth's name. "Is he a new associate?"

"Oh, no," said Christine. "Dr. Smyth has been an associate for fifteen years. Unfortunately, he's very sick. But I never did see too much of him. He scheduled most of his patients at the Julian Clinic."

Adam looked back at the nameplates. "Is this the Dr. Foley who committed suicide?"

"Yes. What a tragedy," said Christine. "He was my favorite doctor. But we didn't see too much of him either during the last six months. He also began scheduling his patients at the clinic."

Christine's comment jogged Adam's memory. Percy Harmon had been upset that so many doctors, including Foley, were abandoning their practices to go to the Julian Clinic.

"Were you here when Dr. Foley left?" asked Adam.

"Unfortunately," admitted Christine. "It was a nightmare because all of his patients had to be called and rescheduled."

"Had he been on a trip before he moved?" asked Adam.

"I think so," said Christine. "If I remember correctly he'd been to some kind of medical meeting. I think it was a cruise."

"What about Dr. Baumgarten and Dr. Stens?" asked Adam. "Are they here today?"

"Sorry," said Christine. "They're both in surgery."

/ / /

"I don't understand," Adam said two hours later, waving his chop-sticks at Jennifer. "How come you were too sick to drive out to Arolen this morning, but well enough to go shopping with your mother all afternoon?"

Jennifer lowered her eyes, pushing her stir-fried vegetables around on her plate. Earlier she had tried to explain to Adam why it was important for her to talk with her mother. But Adam had shrugged off her explanation, and now, rather than say anything nasty, she decided to say nothing at all.

Adam drummed his fingers on the Formica tabletop. Ever since Jennifer had learned she was pregnant, they seemed unable to talk rationally about anything. Adam was afraid that if he criticized her further, she would start to cry.

"Look," he said, "forget about today. Let's just enjoy dinner. You look beautiful. Is that a new dress?"

She nodded, and he guessed it was a present from her mother.

"It's sure pretty," he said diplomatically, but Jennifer was not to be soothed.

"The dress may be OK, but I look awful. I thought being pregnant would make me glow with femininity, but I just feel fat and unattrac-tive." When Adam didn't answer, she added, "I think a lot of it has to do with this awful nausea. I don't know why they call it morning sickness when it seems to last all day."

Adam reached across the table and squeezed her hand. Hoping to cheer her up, he began telling her about his disastrous visit to Dr. Vandermer. While he talked, her face began to relax.

"I told you he had a dreadful bedside manner," laughed Jennifer. "Did he say anything useful about the nausea?"

"No, just that it would go away and you were doing fine."

Jennifer sighed. As they walked back from the restaurant, she said little and as soon as they got home she got into bed and turned on *Dynasty*.

Depressed by his first day as a rep and upset by his wife's silence,

Adam restlessly turned on his computer. Idly he called up GYN Associates, thinking he would add Dr. Smyth's name. To his surprise, it was already there. Wondering if he had made a mistake that afternoon, he went back to the printout on Vandermer. Smyth's name was not listed. To cross-check, Adam called up the other associates, Stens and Baumgarten. Neither Smyth nor Foley appeared in their files.

Adam bit his lower lip. There had to be checks in the program that would catch such an omission. Or maybe the programmers forgot to put in a cross-check. If that were the case, Adam felt he should probably tell Arolen.

Wondering which associates appeared in Smyth's file, Adam punched the doctor's name. The monitor blinked, then displayed a curt message: "OB-GYN Cruise Course 9/9/83. Refresher course scheduled 6/5/84 with planned visit to Puerto Rico Research Center." Adam rubbed the corners of his mouth. The computer obviously knew about Smyth but apparently had no file on him. Adam couldn't understand it.

He opened his list of customers and ran his finger down the list. Smyth wasn't mentioned. Adam decided that Arolen serviced Smyth at the Julian Clinic, even though he was technically a member of GYN Associates. Still, it all seemed very peculiar.

Puzzled, Adam decided to retrieve Lawrence Foley's file. The machine printed out a single word: "Terminated."

Pretty sick humor on the part of some programmer, thought Adam.

///

Over the next three weeks Adam's proficiency as a salesman improved significantly. As long as he loaded the doctors on his list with samples, most of them were pleased to hear him extol the virtues of Arolen Pharmaceuticals. They rarely questioned his claims or inquired about possible side effects. Adam cheerfully pushed Arolen's full line of drugs with one exception: pregdolen. The journal article and Vandermer's warning had impressed him, and he did not want to be responsible for encouraging the use of such a potentially dangerous drug.

In the evenings he would look up on the computer the doctors he planned to see next, but just for information to help sales. He decided not to worry about any possible omissions or inaccuracies like the one involving GYN Associates.

Then, just when he was relaxing into his new routine, something happened that aroused his misgivings. He had an appointment to see a group of busy internists, but when he reached the office, the receptionist told him they all had to cancel. One of the partners had just returned from an Arolen cruise and announced he was quitting the practice and going to work at the Julian Clinic. The other doctors were furious and at their wits' end trying to accommodate his patients.

Adam walked away remembering how Percy Harmon had described a similar incident. And that reminded him that he had never learned why Percy had failed to call him. When he'd asked in New Jersey, no one had seemed sure where Harmon was, though he apparently had not gone as planned to Puerto Rico. Knowing how excited Percy had been about the management program, Adam found this extremely disturbing.

One afternoon when he finished his rounds early, he decided to run out to headquarters and see if Bill Shelly could answer some of his questions. He'd become increasingly curious about the mysterious Arolen cruises. While he wasn't ready to move to Puerto Rico, he thought a five-day medical seminar at sea might be fascinating. It would make him feel as if he were back in medical school. And maybe a little vacation would put his marriage back in perspective. Jennifer's nausea had worsened, and she was spending more and more time at her parents'. When Adam tried to interest her in his new job or to persuade her to call some of her friends, she just put him off.

It was nearly three-thirty when Adam pulled into the Arolen parking lot. Shelly had said on the plane that he'd be available until four. A uniformed guard checked with Shelly's office before buzzing Adam through. When Adam reached the executive floor, Bill's secretary Joyce was waiting by the receptionist.

"Good to see you, Mr. Schonberg," she said. "Bill is upstairs. Would you follow me?"

At the end of the hall, Joyce unlocked the door to a small elevator. She stepped inside and, using the same key, selected the twenty-first floor. Adam was startled to find himself riding up the outside of the building in a glass cage. It was not a pleasant sensation, and he closed his eyes to the Jersey countryside until the elevator came to a stop.

He was greeted by a heavily muscled man in a tee shirt and khaki trousers.

"Adam Schonberg?" he asked before leading Adam down a sun-drenched corridor. The entire exterior wall was glass, and Adam edged as far away from it as possible. He wasn't exactly afraid of heights, but he didn't enjoy them. He felt better when they entered an empty lounge. A television screen was turned to the news. Beyond the lounge was a Nautilus room and beyond that, a locker room lined with massage cubicles. A wide door at the opposite end led to the pool.

The man in the tee shirt held the door but did not follow Adam through it. For a moment the light was so strong, Adam could barely see. One entire wall was glass, rising for two stories and curving back to form a portion of the roof. The floor was made of glistening white marble, and the pool itself was constructed of white tile with blue markings.

A lone swimmer was vigorously doing laps. As he turned, he caught sight of Adam and swam over to the edge. He was wearing tiny goggles that just covered his eyes and a black rubber racing cap.

"How about a swim?" said Bill Shelly.

Adam shook his head. "Sorry, but I forgot my bathing suit."

"No need for a suit right now. It's the men's hour. Come on, give it a try. I'm sure Paul can rustle up a towel."

Adam wavered. There really was no reason to refuse, and the chance to swim twenty-some stories off the ground did not come along every day.

"OK," said Adam. "How do I find Paul?"

"Go back into the locker room. You'll see a buzzer on the wall. Push it and Paul will appear like a genie."

Adam did as he was told. Paul showed him to a locker and supplied him with an enormous towel and a white terry-cloth robe.

Adam stripped off his clothes and put on the robe. Walking back outside, he was acutely aware of his winter white body, and he wondered again how Shelly maintained his tan. Feeling extremely self-conscious, Adam dropped the protective robe and dove in. The water was ice cold.

"We keep the pool cool so that it is stimulating," explained Bill when he caught the pained expression on Adam's face.

After he began swimming, Adam felt better, but when he tried to emulate Bill's tumbling turns, he only succeeded in getting a nose full of water. He came up coughing and sputtering.

Bill took pity on him and led him back to the locker room, suggesting they both have a short massage.

"What is it you wanted to see me about?" Bill asked when they were settled on adjoining tables.

Adam hesitated. Even though Bill had always been nice to Adam, he never dropped his cool executive manner.

"I wanted to learn more about the Conference Cruises," said Adam as Paul indicated he should roll on his back. "My customers always ask about them."

"What do they want to know?"

"Who can go. How you schedule the various specialties. Whether there's someone at Arolen they can call for information."

"They can call the toll-free MTIC number," said Bill stiffly. "I was hoping you were going to tell me you'd decided to take the managerial training course."

"Not just yet," said Adam as Paul continued to knead his shoulders. "But I was wondering if you would consider sending me on one of the cruises. Do any of the sales reps go?"

"I'm afraid not," said Bill, getting up and starting to dress. "There are a lot of people here who would like to go. Unfortunately, the *Fjord* is not that big a ship. Anyway, you'd find it boring. Since the purpose of the program is to supply continuing education to the practicing physician, most of the entertainment areas of the ship have been converted into lecture halls."

"I'd still like to go."

"I'm sorry," said Bill, who was obviously losing interest in the subject. He went to a mirror to put on his tie. "I think it would be smart for you to concentrate on the work that you are supposed to be doing."

Adam decided this was not the moment to ask about the doctors who had given up their practices after going on a cruise. It was obvious that Bill Shelly was becoming irritated by Adam's questions. As he dressed and followed Bill to the elevator Adam was careful to answer questions, not ask them. But later, driving back to New York,

Adam continued to ponder some of the strange occurrences he now associated with the Arolen cruise. Percy Harmon's disappearance in particular was disturbing. When Adam had learned Percy had not gone to Puerto Rico, he'd tried calling him but no one ever answered. As he drove into the city through the Lincoln Tunnel, Adam decided to stop by Percy's apartment. Maybe one of his neighbors knew where he was.

Percy lived in a rundown brownstone four doors in from Second Avenue. Adam found Percy Harmon's name next to the button for 3C. He pushed it and waited.

Diagonally across the street, a man in a rumpled blue suit threw down a cigarette and ground it under the heel of his shoe. Looking in both directions, he started across to the brownstone, his hand moving toward his breast pocket.

Adam shifted his weight and pushed the button for the superintendent. Almost immediately the small foyer filled with a raucous buzz and Adam opened the door. The interior was dilapidated but much cleaner than in Adam's building. On the floor below, Adam heard a door open. He walked to the head of the stairs and looked down. An unshaven man in a sleeveless undershirt was on his way up.

"Whaddaya want?" said the super.

"I'm looking for Percy Harmon," said Adam.

"You and everybody else," said the super, obviously unimpressed. "He ain't here, and I haven't seen him for more than a month."

"Sorry to bother you," said Adam as the super went back down. Turning to leave, Adam hesitated by the stairs. He heard the super's door close and on a sudden impulse quietly climbed to the third floor. He knocked on 3C, but there was no answer. He tried the door, but it was locked. He was debating leaving a note when he noticed a window at the end of the corridor leading to the fire escape.

Although he had never done anything like this in his life, Adam opened the window and climbed out. He had an intuitive feeling something had happened to Percy. He wanted to look into Harmon's apartment to see if there was any sign of how long he'd been away.

The fire escape was old and rusted, and Adam tried not to look down through the metal grate at the concrete courtyard below. After inching along with his hands pressed against the building, Adam finally reached Percy's window. It was ajar about two inches. Hoping no one would see him and call the cops, Adam raised the window.

Having come this far, he figured he had nothing to lose and climbed inside Percy's musty bedroom.

Heart pounding, Adam walked around the unmade bed and opened the closet door. It was filled with clothes. Turning, he looked inside the bathroom. The water level in the toilet was low, suggesting that it had not been used for some time.

Adam walked back through the bedroom and into the living room. There was a newspaper on the coffee table with a seven-week-old date. Moving into the kitchen, Adam saw that the dishes in the sink were covered with a fuzzy black mold. Obviously, Percy Harmon had planned to return. And that was exactly what Adam had feared. Something unexpected must have happened to the man.

Adam decided to get out and call the police. Before he could leave the kitchen, a soft noise made him freeze. It was the distinctive sound of a door closing.

Adam waited. There was only silence. He peered out into the living room. The security chain on the front door was slowly swinging back and forth.

Adam almost passed out. If it had been Percy who'd come in, why was he hiding? Adam stayed glued to his spot in the kitchen, straining to hear additional noise. When the refrigerator kicked on next to him, he moaned with fright. Finally, deciding that at least ten minutes had passed, that maybe it was all his imagination, he walked into the living room and glanced into the bedroom. He could see the open window to the fire escape. The curtains were slowly billowing in the draft. Adam estimated that it would only take a second to cross the room and climb out.

He never made it. As he ran for the window, a figure appeared from the closet. Before Adam could respond, a fist slammed into his abdomen, sending him sprawling to the floor.

CHAPTER 9

When Jennifer arrived at GYN Associates for her monthly checkup, she noticed there were fewer people waiting than on any of her previous visits. Sitting on one of the couches, which she had all to herself, she took out a magazine to read but couldn't concentrate. Instead, she marveled that nothing untoward had happened to her or her unborn child while Dr. Vandermer had been out of town attending his convention. She'd been sure that she'd start bleeding while he was away, and even though she still was not reconciled to his gruff manner, she didn't want to have to see a new doctor.

In less than fifteen minutes, Jennifer was taken to an examination room. As she took off her street clothes and put on the paper robe, she asked the nurse if Dr. Vandermer had enjoyed his vacation.

"I guess so," said Nancy without enthusiasm. She handed Jennifer the urine container and motioned toward the lavatory door.

Something in her tone bothered Jennifer, but when she came out of the bathroom, Dr. Vandermer was waiting.

"I haven't finished with Mrs. Schonberg," said Nancy. "Please, give me another few minutes. I still have to draw her hematocrit and weigh her."

"I just wanted to say hello." His voice was unusually soft, without his normally brusque overtone. "How are you, Jennifer? You look well."

"I'm fine," said Jennifer, surprised.

"Well, I'll be back as soon as Nancy's done." He closed the door, and Nancy stood for a moment staring after him. "God!" she said. "If I didn't know him better, I'd swear he was on something. Ever since he came back, he's been weird. He's much nicer to his patients, but he's made my job ten times more difficult. Oh well . . ." Nancy turned back to Jennifer. "Let's get your blood and weight."

She had just finished when Dr. Vandermer returned. "I'll take over," he said in the same flat voice. "Your weight is fine. How have you been feeling in general?"

"I haven't examined her yet," interrupted Nancy.

"That's all right," said Dr. Vandermer. "Why don't you run the hematocrit while I talk to Jennifer."

With an audible sigh, Nancy took the hematocrit tubes and left the room.

"So how have you been feeling?" asked Dr. Vandermer again.

Jennifer stared at the man facing her. He had the same polished good looks, but his face was slack, as if he were exhausted. His hair was also a little different. It seemed bushier, and instead of his usual hurried manner, he gave Jennifer the impression that he actually wanted to know what was on her mind.

"I guess I've been feeling pretty good," she said.

"You don't sound very enthusiastic."

"Well . . . ," said Jennifer, "I'm less tired, but the morning sickness has gotten worse, no matter what I do about diet."

"How do you feel about this pregnancy?" asked Dr. Vandermer. "Sometimes emotions play a role in our well-being."

Jennifer looked at Dr. Vandermer's face. He seemed genuinely concerned. "To tell the truth," she said, "I feel very ambivalent about being pregnant." Up until that moment she'd been unwilling to admit it, even to her mother. But Dr. Vandermer did not seem disapproving.

"Second thoughts are very common," he said gently. "Why don't you tell me how you really feel."

Encouraged by his attitude, Jennifer found herself telling him all of her fears about her career and her relationship with Adam. She admitted that Vandermer had been right; it wasn't the proper time for them to have a child. She talked for nearly ten minutes, saved from tears only by an odd lack of affect in Vandermer's expression. He was concerned but in some way remote.

When she finished, he said softly, "I appreciate your confiding in me. It's not healthy to bottle up your feelings. In fact, they may be related to your continued morning sickness, which should have abated by now. I think that we will have to try you on some medication." Turning to Nancy, who had just returned to the room, he said, "Would you go down to the supply room and bring back a handful of pregdolen samples?"

Nancy left without a word.

"Now then," said Dr. Vandermer, "let's get a good look at you."

The examination included ultrasonography, which Dr. Vandermer described as a method by which images were produced as ultrasonic waves echoed off the baby's tissues. Jennifer wasn't sure she understood, but Dr. Vandermer assured her it was both painless and harmless to mother and fetus alike, and indeed it was. Although a technician came in to run the unit, Dr. Vandermer insisted on doing the test himself. On a screen much like a television's Jennifer saw the outline of her baby.

"Do you care to know the sex of the child?" asked Dr. Vandermer, straightening up.

"I guess," said Jennifer, not having given the matter much thought.

"I can't be sure," said Dr. Vandermer, "but if I had to guess it looks like a boy."

Jennifer nodded. For the moment it didn't make any difference if it were a boy or a girl, but she wondered how Adam felt.

Back in the examination room, Dr. Vandermer sat down at the small desk and began to write up his findings. He dismissed Nancy, who left without a word, obviously displeased to have had her job curtailed.

Jennifer sat on the table, wondering whether she should dress. Finally, Dr. Vandermer turned to face her. "Aside from the morning sickness, you're doing fine, and maybe this will stop the nausea." He stacked the samples next to her and wrote out a prescription as well. "Take one pill three times a day."

Jennifer nodded. She was willing to try anything.

"Now," said Dr. Vandermer in his new monotone voice, "there are two things I want to discuss with you. First, the next time I see you it will be at the Julian Clinic."

Jennifer felt her heart skip a beat. The image of Cheryl slumping to the floor flashed before her. She could see the blood and feel the icy panic.

"Jennifer, are you all right?" asked Dr. Vandermer.

"Maybe I should lie down," said Jennifer, feeling suddenly dizzy.

Dr. Vandermer helped her to lie back.

"I'm terribly sorry," said Jennifer. "I'm all right now. Why will I be seeing you at the Julian Clinic?"

"Because I've decided to join their staff," said Dr. Vandermer, checking her pulse. "I'm no longer interested in private practice. And I can assure you that as a patient you will get better care at the Julian Clinic. Now, do you feel all right?"

Jennifer nodded.

"Is this the first time in your pregnancy you've felt faint like this?"

"Yes," said Jennifer and went on to describe Cheryl's unexpected death.

"What an awful experience for you," Dr. Vandermer said. "Especially being pregnant. Fortunately, such a clotting disorder is extremely rare, and I hope you don't blame the Julian Clinic. I heard about that case and I happen to know that Miss Tedesco had withheld certain aspects of her medical history. Her extensive drug usage had caused hematologic problems that did not show up in routine lab work. Had Miss Tedesco been more forthright, she'd undoubtedly be alive today. I'm only telling you this so you won't have any doubts about the clinic."

"I'd heard good things about it before I went with Cheryl. And I must admit I was impressed with the staff's caring attitude."

"That's one of the reasons I'm going there. The doctors aren't involved with any of the competitive nonsense associated with private practice."

Jennifer sat up, relieved to find that the dizziness had completely passed.

"Are you going to be all right now?" asked Dr. Vandermer.

"I think so," said Jennifer.

"The second thing I wanted to discuss with you is the possibility of doing amniocentesis."

Jennifer felt another rush of light-headedness, but this time it passed quickly. "You've changed your mind," she said. It was a statement, not a question.

"That is true," said Dr. Vandermer. "Initially, I was convinced that your brother's problem had been congenital, meaning a chromosomal change after conception. But I got the slides from the hospital where your brother died, and the lab thinks the problem may be hereditary. Given that possibility, it would be a mistake not to take advantage of all the technology at our disposal."

"Would the test show if my child had the same problem?" asked Jennifer.

"Absolutely," said Dr. Vandermer. "But we should do it soon, since it takes several weeks to get the results. If we wait too long, it will be difficult to do anything if the result is positive."

"By 'doing anything' you mean an abortion?" said Jennifer.

"Yes," said Dr. Vandermer. "The chances of a problem are very small, but with the ambivalence you've voiced, I think that you would be able to handle such an eventuality."

"I'll have to talk with my husband and my parents," said Jennifer.

She left the office nervous about the prospect of amniocentesis but glad she had a doctor as caring as Vandermer. She'd have to tell Adam that she'd totally reversed her original impression of the man.

///

Adam never quite lost consciousness. He was vaguely aware of being dragged into Percy's living room and unceremoniously dumped onto the couch. He felt his wallet being removed, and then replaced. That little sequence didn't jibe with his expectations, and puzzling it over, he shook off his stupor.

The first thing he did was search for his glasses, which were suddenly thrust into his hand. He put them on and the room came into focus. Sitting in front of him was a heavyset man in a blue suit and a white shirt open at the collar.

"Good morning," said the man. "Welcome back."

Adam moved. Nothing hurt, which was surprising.

"Unless you want to ride down to the police station, Mr. Schonberg, you'd better tell me what you were doing in this apartment."

"Nothing," croaked Adam. He cleared his throat.

"You're going to have to do better than that," said the man, lighting a cigarette and blowing smoke toward the ceiling.

"I could say the same for you," said Adam.

The stranger reached over and grabbed Adam's shirt front, almost lifting him off the couch. "I'm not in the mood for wisecracks," he snarled.

Adam nodded.

As suddenly as he'd grabbed him, the man let him go. "OK," said the stranger. "Let's start again. What were you doing in this apartment?"

"I am a friend of Percy Harmon," said Adam quickly. "Well, sort of a friend. I was starting work for Arolen Pharmaceuticals and he took me around to teach me the routine."

The man nodded slightly, as if he accepted the story so far.

"Percy was supposed to call me," Adam said. "He never did and he never answered his phone. So I came over to see if he was here."

"That doesn't explain why you broke into the apartment," said the stranger.

"It was an impulse," said Adam meekly. "I wanted to see if he was all right."

The man didn't say anything. The silence and the tension quickly began to wear on Adam. "I liked Percy," he said. "I was worried about him. He was supposed to go to Puerto Rico for a training course, but he never got there."

The man remained silent.

"That's all I know," said Adam. "I never saw him again."

"I believe you," said the man, after a pause.

"Thank you," said Adam, relieved to the point he could have cried.

The man stubbed out his cigarette. Reaching into his breast pocket, he pulled out a card and extended it to Adam. It said "Robert Marlow, Private Investigator." In the lower right-hand corner was a telephone number.

"About six weeks ago Percy Harmon left a Japanese restaurant in Fort Lee, New Jersey. He never got home. I've been hired by the family to see what I can find out. I've been watching the apartment. Aside from a couple of young ladies, you're the only one to show up."

"Do you have any idea of what could have happened to him?" asked Adam.

"Not the foggiest," said Mr. Marlow. "But if you happen to hear anything, I'd appreciate a call."

/ / /

Adam still felt shell-shocked when he got back to his empty apartment. Jennifer's absence irritated him. He was upset and he wanted to talk to her, but he guessed she was off with her mother again. He flung himself down on the bed and turned on the news. Slowly he began to unwind.

The next thing Adam knew, he heard the front door close and for a moment thought he was back in Harmon's apartment.

"Well, well," teased Jennifer. "Lying down on the job."

Adam didn't answer.

"What's the matter?" she asked.

"I suppose you've been to Englewood," Adam snapped unreasonably.

Jennifer stared at him. She wasn't up to one of Adam's moods. She resented having to apologize for seeing her parents. Putting her hands on her hips, she said, "Yes, I did go home."

"I guessed as much," said Adam, turning to the television.

"What is that supposed to mean?" asked Jennifer.

"Nothing in particular," said Adam.

"Look," said Jennifer, sitting on the edge of the bed, "I had good reason to go home. Dr. Vandermer suggested I have amniocentesis. I went home to discuss whether or not to do it."

"That's nice," said Adam sarcastically. "You discuss it with your parents even though it is our child."

"I knew I couldn't get hold of you during the day," explained Jennifer, trying to be reasonable. "Of course I planned to discuss it with you. But I wanted to talk to my mother because she experienced the trauma of giving birth to a Down's baby."

"I still think the decision is ours alone," said Adam.

He rolled over and put his feet on the floor, knowing he was being unfair. "Besides, I thought Vandermer said you didn't need amniocentesis."

"That's true," said Jennifer. "But today he told me that after checking the slides on my brother, he thinks I should have it."

Adam got to his feet and stretched. From the little he knew about genetics, he didn't think that Jennifer needed amniocentesis. "Maybe you should get a second opinion. When I initially asked around for an OB man, people also recommended Herbert Wickelman."

Jennifer shook her head. "I don't need to see anyone else. Another opinion would just confuse the issue further. I'm happy with Dr. Vandermer and I have confidence in him, particularly since his manner has improved so much."

"What do you mean?" asked Adam.

"Since he returned from his medical conference, he seems to have more time and interest," said Jennifer. "He isn't so rushed."

Adam forgot his anger. "Has he changed in any other way?" he asked.

"He says he's tired of private practice," said Jennifer, taking off her dress and heading into the bathroom. "He's decided to go to the Julian Clinic, and I'm to see him there from now on."

Adam slowly sank back on the bed.

"I never thought I'd go back to the Julian after Cheryl died," Jennifer called out, "but Dr. Vandermer has convinced me of its excellence. And you know I was impressed by the staff."

Adam heard the sound of water in the bathroom sink. He didn't know what to say. He hadn't mentioned anything to Jennifer about Percy Harmon's disappearance or any of his other suspicions about Arolen, but now that it seemed as if Vandermer was involved, Adam knew he had to do something.

Adam walked to the bathroom, where Jennifer was washing her face. "I'm going to insist that you see Dr. Wickelman. I don't like the idea of Vandermer going to the Julian Clinic."

Jennifer looked up, surprised. There were times lately when Adam acted very strangely.

"I'm serious," he began, but stopped in midsentence, glimpsing a familiar bottle on the edge of the sink.

"What the hell is this?" he demanded, grabbing it.

Jennifer glanced from his face to the small bottle he held in his hand. Then she turned and silently hung up her towel.

"I asked you a question," yelled Adam.

"I think the answer is obvious. It's pregdolen. For my morning sickness. Now if you'll excuse me." She started for the bedroom. Adam grabbed her arm.

"Where did you get this?" he demanded, holding the bottle directly in front of her.

Jennifer pushed it away. "If you must know, from Dr. Vandermer."

"That's impossible," said Adam. "Vandermer would never prescribe this stuff."

Jennifer pulled her arm free. "Are you suggesting that I'm lying?"

Adam returned to the bathroom and poured some of the blue-and-yellow capsules into his hand. It was pregdolen all right.

"Did you hear me?" demanded Jennifer.

"I don't want you taking this drug," he said. "Do you have any more of it?"

"I'm going to follow my doctor's orders," said Jennifer. "Since I started taking these pills, I've had the first nausea-free day in months. And remember, you are the one who sent me to Dr. Vandermer in the first place."

"Well, you're definitely not going back," said Adam. He lifted Jennifer's tote bag from the shelf above the toilet and looked inside. The additional packages of pregdolen were right on top.

Trying to grab the purse, Jennifer shouted, "I like Dr. Vandermer and I trust him. Give me my bag!"

Adam fished out the other samples before letting it go. "Listen!" he said. "I don't want you taking this stuff. It's dangerous."

"Dr. Vandermer wouldn't give it to me if it were dangerous," said Jennifer. "And I intend to take it. After all, I'm the one who is suffering, not you. And I think that you should remember that you are not a doctor. In fact, all you are right now is a drug salesman."

Adam opened the sample packages while he lifted the lid of the toilet with his foot.

"Give me my medicine!" yelled Jennifer, realizing what he was doing.

Adam dumped the contents of the first bottle into the toilet.

Desperately, Jennifer snatched a bottle from Adam's hand and ran into the bedroom. Stunned, Adam hesitated, then ran after her. For a minute they stood face to face. Then Jennifer dashed back into the bathroom and tried to lock the door. But she wasn't fast enough. Adam got his foot beyond the door, and a brief shoving match ensued. Slowly the door inched open until Jennifer gave way. She backed up against the shower stall, hiding the bottle behind her.

"Give me the pregdolen," ordered Adam.

Jennifer shook her head. Her breath was coming in short gasps.

"OK!" snapped Adam as he reached out and roughly pulled her hands from behind her back.

"No!" shouted Jennifer.

One by one he peeled back her fingers, took the bottle, and emptied it into the toilet. Jennifer began pounding his back. To protect himself, Adam threw up his right hand, accidentally hitting the side of her head. The blow sent her reeling against the wall, momentarily stunned.

Adam dumped the remaining samples into the bowl and flushed them away. Then he turned to apologize to Jennifer, but she was so furious she wouldn't listen.

"You're not my doctor," she screamed. "I'm tired of being sick every day, and if he gives me medication to feel better, I'm going to take it."

She tore into the bedroom and pulled her suitcase down from the top of the closet.

"Jennifer, what are you doing?" asked Adam, though it was pretty clear what she had in mind. Jennifer didn't answer but began rolling up clothes and throwing them into the case.

"Jennifer, we can have disagreements without your running away," said Adam.

Jennifer turned to face him, her cheeks flushed.

"I'm going home. I'm tired, I don't feel well, and I can't stand this bickering."

"Jennifer, I love you. The only reason I took those pills away is to protect our child."

"I don't care why you did it. I have to get away for a few days." She picked up the phone and Adam listened while she called her father and made arrangements to take a cab to his office so he could drive her home.

"Jennifer, please don't do this," he begged as she went back to her packing, but she refused to look at him while she closed the case, picked up her purse, and stalked out of the apartment.

Alone, it took Adam a few minutes to believe she had actually gone. Dazed, he wandered into the living room and sat down at the computer. Turning it on, he connected with the Arolen mainframe and tried to call up Vandermer's file. He intended to see if Dr. Vandermer's prescribing habits had changed, but the screen remained blank save for the stark message: "Transferred to Julian Clinic."

Shocked, Adam wondered if any other files had been erased from the computer. He pulled the printout McGuire had given him and then asked the machine to relist the doctors in his assigned territory. Not only had the computer dropped Vandermer's file, but six other doctors had been taken off the list.

Frantically, Adam began calling up each of the expunged doctors' names. None of them had files! Four had entries like Dr. Smyth's— "Refresher course scheduled . . ."—suggesting that if a doctor went on an Arolen cruise, he didn't have to be detailed any longer. Two had entries like Vandermer's: "Transferred to Julian Clinic." Adam wondered if the Cruise Conferences pitched the Julian Clinic as well as Arolen products.

More confused than ever, Adam asked the computer to list all the physicians on staff at the Julian Clinic. Dutifully the dot-matrix printer sprang to life and spewed out a sizable roster. Adam ran his eyes over the list of names and stopped short at an entry halfway down the sheet: Dr. Thayer Norton! What the hell was Norton doing at the Julian Clinic? He was chief of Internal Medicine at the university.

Slowly Adam typed Thayer Norton's name into the computer and requested his file. All he got was "Transferred to Julian Clinic"!

The idea that the old battle-ax would give up his coveted medical chair at the university was unthinkable. Adam wondered if Norton had recently taken a Conference Cruise.

Going back to the computer, Adam tried to access statistical data about the Julian. He discovered that of the six doctors who had transferred, four were OB-GYN specialists. Maybe that proved something. For another half hour Adam fed questions into the computer, but most of his requests were returned with the message that his access code was not recognized for the material he was requesting. Switching tactics, he asked for the number of times amniocentesis was done at the Julian in the previous calendar year. He got the number: 7,112. When he asked how many had shown an abnormality in the fetus, the computer again refused his access code. Adam finally asked how many therapeutic abortions had been performed during that time period: 1,217.

Totally mystified, Adam turned off the computer and went to bed, where he spent the night confronting an outraged Jennifer in his dreams.

The next morning Adam was so upset to wake up and find Jennifer's side of the bed empty, that he left the apartment without even bothering to have a cup of coffee. By eight-thirty he was pacing restlessly outside GYN Associates, waiting for the office to open. The moment he saw Christine he began pressing the bell.

"Hello, Adam Schonberg."

Adam thought it was propitious that she'd remembered his name. He adjusted his dark blue knit tie and said with the sincerest smile he could muster, "I was in the neighborhood so I thought I'd drop by and get an update on DJ's batting average."

"He's doing terrific," said Christine. "Better than even I anticipated. In fact, last Friday . . ."

Adam tuned out as he tried to organize his thoughts. When Christine paused for breath, he said, "What are the chances that you can get me in to see Dr. Vandermer?"

"Dr. Vandermer is at the Julian Clinic," she said.

"He's gone already?"

"Yup. The whole office is a disaster. Yesterday was his last day here, even though he has hundreds of patients scheduled for the next six months. I'll be on the phone from now until Christmas."

"So it wasn't expected?" asked Adam.

"Hardly," said Christine. "He came back from his cruise and told Dr. Stens and Dr. Baumgarten that he was leaving. He said he'd had it with private practice."

That was exactly what Percy had said about Foley, thought Adam, as Christine turned away to answer the phone.

"What a mess," she said once she'd hung up. "And all the patients are mad at me."

"Did Dr. Vandermer behave strangely when he got back from the cruise?" asked Adam.

"I'll say," laughed Christine. "Nothing we did was good enough for him. He drove us all crazy, though in some ways he was a lot more considerate. Before, he'd always been pretty abrupt."

Remembering his own meeting with the doctor, Adam felt that "abrupt" was a generous description of the man's manner.

"The strangest thing about the affair," continued Christine, "is that Dr. Vandermer's partner, Dr. Foley, did the very same thing. And at the time it made Dr. Vandermer furious. But it wasn't so bad when Dr. Foley left because there were four doctors to take up the slack. Now there are only two because poor Dr. Smyth is still in the hospital with his weird disease."

"What kind of disease?" asked Adam.

"I don't know the name," she said. "It's some kind of trouble with his nerves. I remember when it started." She lowered her voice as if what she was saying were a secret. "One moment he was normal, the next he was making strange faces. It was grotesque. And very embarrassing."

A woman entered the office and came up to the reception desk, and Adam stepped out of the way, thinking that Smyth's problem was similar to the case of tardive dyskinesia that he had discussed in his presentation at the medical school. In that case the cause was an unexpected reaction to tranquilizers.

"Do you know if Dr. Smyth had any psychiatric problems?" Adam asked once the patient was seated.

"I don't think so," said Christine. "He was one of the nicest young men. Looks a little bit like you. Dark, curly hair."

"What hospital is he in?" asked Adam.

"He was admitted to University, but I heard one of the nurses say that he was going to be transferred to the Julian Clinic."

The phone rang again, and Christine reached for it.

"One last question," said Adam. "Did Foley or Smyth go on a Conference Cruise like Dr. Vandermer?"

"I think they both did," said Christine, lifting the phone. "GYN Associates, could you please hold?" Turning back to Adam, she asked, "Would you like to see either Dr. Stens or Dr. Baumgarten?"

"Not today," said Adam. "Another time, when things aren't quite so hectic. Give my best to DJ."

Christine gave Adam a thumbs-up sign and pushed the blinking button on the telephone.

Leaving the office, Adam felt he could no longer ignore the strange coincidences relating to the Julian Clinic. Why had so many doctors abruptly left their practices to work there? And why, after doing so, had Vandermer suddenly decided to prescribe pregdolen to Jennifer? As unpleasant as this last interview would be, Adam felt he had no choice but to confront the obstetrician. He had to convince him either to treat Jennifer without medication or to relinquish her as a patient. Adam knew he couldn't persuade his wife to change physicians on his own.

As he approached the southern limits of Harlem, he saw the clinic towering over the surrounding tenements. Admiring its mirrored surface, Adam realized that it must have been designed by the same architects who had built Arolen headquarters. The office building was better suited to its surroundings. The clinic struck Adam as a twenty-first-century vision flung into a two-hundred-year-old setting.

A half block away Adam found a parking spot and backed into it. Taking his briefcase in case he needed to disguise his visit as a sales call, he jogged up the broad steps to the clinic's entrance.

The moment he walked inside his suspicions dissipated. He had intended to march through the lobby to the OB-GYN section as if he were a member of the staff. From his experience as a medical student he knew that if someone acted as if he belonged, he could go anywhere in a hospital. But the relaxed atmosphere of the Julian changed his mind. He walked directly up to the large information booth and said he wished to speak with Dr. Vandermer.

"Certainly," said the receptionist. She picked up a phone and relayed Adam's request. "The doctor is in," she said, smiling broadly. "Do you know how to get to the GYN clinic?"

"Maybe I should ask the doctor if he has time to see me. I want to talk to him about my wife."

"Of course he'll see you," she said, as if Adam had lost his senses. "Let me call one of the orderlies." She pressed a small bell on the counter and a young man in blue shirt and white chino pants appeared. The receptionist gave him instructions.

He led Adam down a long central hallway, past a flower shop, a bookstore, a pleasant-looking cafeteria.

"This is an impressive place," said Adam.

"Yes," said the young man mechanically.

Adam glanced at him as they walked. He had a broad, expressionless face. Looking more carefully, Adam thought he seemed drugged; he was probably a psychiatric case. A lot of the chronic patients worked in hospitals. It made them feel more confident.

The man left Adam in a lounge that resembled a private living room rather than a hospital waiting room. There was a couch, two chairs, and a small desk. Strange clinic, thought Adam as he walked to the window. The darkened glass gave a peculiar cast to the row houses across the street. He felt as if he were looking at an old photograph.

He wandered back to the couch and began leafing through one of the magazines. A few minutes later the door opened and Dr. Vandermer came in. Adam got hastily to his feet.

The man was imposing, especially in his starched white coat. But he seemed less hostile than at their first meeting.

"Adam Schonberg, welcome to the Julian," he said.

"Thank you," said Adam, relieved and at the same time taken aback by Vandermer's cordiality. "I'm surprised to find you here. I thought you were very happy in your practice."

"I was at one time," said Dr. Vandermer. "But fee-for-service medicine is a thing of the past. Here we try to keep people well, instead of just trying to cure them when they are sick."

Adam noticed that Vandermer's voice had an oddly flat inflection, as if he were reciting from memory. "I wanted to talk about Jennifer," he said.

"I assumed as much," said Dr. Vandermer. "I asked the geneticist to come by."

"Fine. But first I want to discuss the pregdolen."

"Has it helped your wife's nausea?" asked Dr. Vandermer.

"She thinks so," said Adam. "But I suspect it is simply a placebo effect. What surprises me is that you gave it to her."

"There are a number of drugs on the market," said Dr. Vandermer, "but I think pregdolen is the best. Normally, I don't like to use drugs for morning sickness, but your wife's had gone on too long."

"But why pregdolen?" said Adam tactfully. "Especially after the negative report in the *New England Journal.*"

"That was a poorly designed study," said Dr. Vandermer. "They didn't use the proper controls."

Unwilling to confront Vandermer directly, Adam finally said, "But you told me the last time we spoke that pregdolen was dangerous. What's made you change your mind?"

Dr. Vandermer shook his head, puzzled. "I've never said the drug was dangerous. I've been using it for years."

"I distinctly remember . . ." began Adam as two other doctors entered the lounge. One was a tall, thin man with gray hair. He was introduced as Dr. Benjamin Starr, the Julian Clinic's geneticist.

"Dr. Starr and I were just discussing your wife's case this morning," said Dr. Vandermer.

"Indeed," said Dr. Starr, launching into a detailed description of the case. His voice had the same flat inflection as Vandermer's, making Adam wonder if all the doctors at the Julian Clinic worked themselves to death.

Adam tried to understand what Starr was saying, but the man seemed to be speaking deliberately over Adam's head. After trying to make sense out of the reasons given for Jennifer's amniocentesis, Adam decided he was wasting his time. It was as if both Vandermer and Starr were trying to confuse him. As soon as he could, Adam said he had to leave. Dr. Vandermer offered to buy him lunch in the cafeteria, but Adam insisted he had to go.

Walking down the hall, he decided Jennifer was right. Dr. Vandermer was a changed man, and it made Adam nervous. In fact, the whole clinic struck a false note. Looking at the beautifully decorated rooms, he could understand why the Julian had such appeal. It seemed the ideal hospital environment. At the same time, it was almost too nice and, to Adam's mind, slightly sinister.

Back in the car, Adam hesitated before turning on the ignition. There was no doubt in his mind that Vandermer had originally proclaimed pregdolen dangerous and all that super-scientific rhetoric about Jennifer needing amniocentesis alarmed him. With his wife sequestered at her parents', his hands were tied. The only thing he was sure of was that he did not want Jennifer taking pregdolen, which meant that he didn't want her to keep seeing Vandermer. The problem was that she obviously trusted Vandermer and didn't want to change doctors.

Pulling out into the street, Adam realized that Jennifer was right on two counts: he wasn't a doctor and he knew nothing about obstetrics. He realized that if he hoped to change Jennifer's mind, he'd better study up on the subject.

There were no parking places within blocks of the university hospital, so Adam pulled the Buick into the hospital parking garage. After he'd found a space, he went down to the medical center. The Irish fellow at the information booth recognized him and lent him a white jacket.

In the library, he selected several recent textbooks on obstetrics and began looking up both morning sickness and amniocentesis. When he was finished, he turned to a chapter on fetoscopy—the visualization of the fetus within the uterus—and stared in wonder at the photos of what his child must look like at this stage in its development.

Returning the books to the desk, Adam made his way to the hospital. After the soft carpets and gleaming paint at the Julian, the university medical center looked like a set for Dante's Inferno. It was uniformly drab with peeling paint and stained floors. The nurses and staff appeared rushed, and their expressions indicated that their patients' psychological well-being was not high priority.

Adam took the main elevator to Neurology on the tenth floor. Pretending that he was still a student, he marched to the nurses' station and positioned himself squarely in front of the chart rack. There were three nurses, two ward clerks, and a resident standing about talking, but none of them so much as looked at Adam.

Dr. Stuart Smyth's chart was in the slot for room 1066. After a furtive glance at the nurses, Adam grasped the metal-backed record, pulled it out of the rack, and stepped back into the relative quiet of the chart room. There was a doctor there, but he was on the phone making a tennis date. Adam sat down at the desk.

Curiously, Smyth was diagnosed as having tardive dyskinesia. Reading over the history, Adam learned that Dr. Smyth had no past record of psychotropic drugs. The cause of his illness was still listed as unknown, and most of the workup involved sophisticated attempts to isolate a virus.

The only positive test Adam found was the EEG, but the resident had written that the results, though slightly abnormal, were nonspecific. In short, Dr. Smyth had been poked, prodded, and bled for a myriad of tests, yet the source of his troubles still had not been discovered. He'd been in and out of the hospital for two and a half months. On a happier note, he had started to improve, though no one knew why.

Adam returned the chart and walked down the hall to room 1066. Unlike the other rooms, the door was shut. Adam knocked. After hearing what sounded like "Come in," he pushed open the door and stepped into the room.

Stuart Smyth was seated near the window, surrounded by books and periodicals. As Adam entered, he looked up and adjusted rimless glasses.

Adam immediately saw that Christine's observation that he and Smyth looked alike was true, and it pleased Adam because Stuart was a handsome man.

Adam introduced himself as a medical student, and Smyth, whose face was periodically contorted by a grimace, asked Adam to sit down and explained that he was making the best of his confinement by reviewing the entire field of OB-GYN. His speech was difficult to understand because his lips and tongue were also affected by distorting spasms.

Despite his impediment, Dr. Smyth was eager for company and not at all shy about his illness. Adam waited patiently as he slowly recounted the details, most of which Adam had already gleaned from the chart. He did not mention the Arolen cruise, and Adam got around to the subject by first mentioning that Dr. Vandermer was taking care of Jennifer.

"Vandermer is a great obstetrician," said Dr. Smyth.

"He was recommended by one of the OB residents," said Adam. "Apparently he handles a lot of the house staff."

Dr. Smyth nodded.

"I suppose you've heard that he's just returned from an Arolen cruise?"

Dr. Smyth nodded as his face bunched in a spasm.

"Did you ever go on one of the cruises?" asked Adam.

The book Smyth had been reading slid from his lap and thumped on the floor. He reached down and picked it up, but when he started to answer, his tongue wouldn't cooperate and he ended up just nodding his head.

Adam was afraid of tiring Smyth with more questions, but when he stood to go the doctor waved him back to his seat, making it clear that he wanted to talk.

"The cruises are wonderful," Smyth managed at last. "I went on one six months ago and was scheduled to go again this week. This time I was invited to stop in Puerto Rico. I was looking forward to it, but obviously I'm not going to make it."

"When you are discharged," said Adam, "I'm sure you'll be able to reschedule."

"Maybe," said Smyth. "But it is difficult to get a reservation, especially for Puerto Rico."

Adam next asked about the Julian Clinic. Smyth offered a few superlatives, but then was taken by a series of contortions so severe he finally motioned Adam to leave.

Adam thought about returning in a few minutes, but was so far behind in his Arolen calls that he decided he'd better get to work. Even if he were suspicious about the drug company, he didn't want to get fired.

/ / /

When he got home slightly after six, he found the apartment in the same disorder in which he'd left it. His note, which said "Welcome home. I'm sorry. I love you," was still on the floor by the door where he'd left it.

Glancing in the refrigerator, he remembered there was nothing in it, and he'd have to go out to eat. Before doing so, he dialed Jennifer's parents' number, hoping she'd answer.

Unfortunately, her mother answered the call. "Adam! So nice of you to call," she said icily.

"Is Jennifer there?" asked Adam as politely as he could.

"She is," said Mrs. Carson. "She's been trying to call you since early this morning."

"I've been working," explained Adam, pleased that she wanted to reach him.

"Good for you," said Mrs. Carson. "I should tell you that Jennifer had an amniocentesis test this morning. Everything went smoothly."

Adam almost dropped the phone. "Oh my God, how is she?"

"Fine, no thanks to you."

"Please put her on the phone," said Adam.

"I'm sorry," said Mrs. Carson in a voice that suggested she wasn't sorry at all, "but Jennifer is sleeping at the moment. When she awakens, I'll mention that you called."

There was a click as Mrs. Carson hung up.

Adam eyed the receiver for a moment as if it were responsible for his frustration. Controlling himself, he calmly replaced the instrument in its cradle, but the nervousness and fear that he'd felt after leaving the Julian came back in a rush. Why on earth hadn't Vandermer mentioned Jennifer was in the clinic that morning?

CHAPTER 11

Jennifer never called, and the next morning Adam awoke still filled with anxiety. After shaving, he found himself pacing the bedroom floor. What was going on at the clinic? He was terrified at the thought of the strangely mechanical Vandermer continuing to treat Jennifer but didn't know how to stop his wife from seeing him. If only he could figure out why the doctors changed so much after the cruises. If only he could go on one himself, maybe he'd be able to figure out a way of persuading Jennifer that Vandermer was dangerous.

Smyth had said his cruise was scheduled to leave from Miami this week. Adam wondered what would happen if he showed up instead.

"They'd tell me to get my ass off the boat," he said out loud.

Suddenly he stopped pacing, went into the living room, and turned on the computer. By the time he got the phone hooked up to the modem, he was sure he was right.

In his usual two-fingered style, he called up Dr. Stuart Smyth's file and was told again that the doctor was scheduled for a refresher course, a second cruise, that was to leave that very day.

Dressing quickly, Adam made up his mind. Christine had said he looked like Smyth, and he had seen the resemblance himself. He picked up the phone and dialed Miami information. When the operator answered, he requested the number for Arolen Cruises. The operator said in a nasal voice, "Sorry, but there is nothing listed under that name."

Adam replaced the phone. Then he had another idea. This time he asked for a listing for the *Fjord*. No luck. There was a Fjord Travel Agency, but that didn't sound promising.

Adam picked up his seersucker jacket and took it into the kitchen. The iron was on top of the refrigerator and he plugged it into the wall socket next to the sink. Folding a bath towel lengthwise, he put it on the kitchen card table and pressed out the jacket's worst wrinkles. That was when he got the inspiration to call MTIC.

"There is no MTIC in the directory," said the Miami operator, "but there is MTIC Cruise Lines."

Elated, Adam took the number and tried to call. When a woman answered, he introduced himself as Dr. Stuart Smyth and asked if he were still expected on today's cruise. His secretary had failed to confirm his reservation.

"Just one moment please," said the woman. Adam could hear the faint sounds of a computer keyboard.

"Here it is," she said. "Stuart Smyth of New York City. You're expected with today's OB-GYN group. You should be on board no later than 6:00 P.M."

"Thank you," said Adam. "Can you tell me one other thing? Do I need a passport or anything?"

"Any type of identification is fine," said the woman. "You just need proof of citizenship."

"Thanks," said Adam, hanging up. How the hell was he going to get proof of Smyth's citizenship?

For ten minutes Adam sat on the edge of the bed trying to make a decision. Except for the passport problem, the idea of impersonating Smyth on the Arolen cruise had a lot of appeal. There was no doubt in Adam's mind that in order to change Jennifer's impression of Vandermer he'd have to have damn good evidence of the man's instability. Going on the cruise seemed the most promising course of action.

But could he impersonate a practicing OB man? And what if there were people on the cruise who were personal friends of Smyth? Impulsively, Adam decided he'd give it a try. What could he lose? If he ran into a personal friend of Smyth, he'd tell him that Smyth had sent him in his place. And if Arolen found him out, he'd simply say that he couldn't function as a rep without more information. The worst they could do was fire him.

With the decision made, Adam jumped into action. His first call was to Clarence McGuire, whom he told that a family crisis would take him out of town for a few days. Clarence was instantly sympathetic, hoping that things would work out.

Adam's next call was to the airlines to see what flight he could get to Miami. Between Delta and Eastern, he could go anytime he chose.

Finally, he worked up his courage to call Jennifer. His mouth went dry as he heard the connection go through. One ring. Another. Then Mrs. Carson picked up the phone.

Using all the graciousness he could muster, Adam said good morning and asked if he could talk with his wife.

"I'll see if she is awake," said Mrs. Carson coolly.

Adam was relieved when Jennifer said hello.

"I'm sorry if I woke you," said Adam.

"I wasn't asleep," said Jennifer.

"Jennifer," said Adam. "I'm sorry about the other night. I don't know what happened to me. But I want you to come home. The only trouble is that I have to go out of town for a few days for work."

"I see," said Jennifer.

"I'd prefer not to explain right now, but it is probably best for you to stay with your parents for a few more days."

"I suppose you're going down to Puerto Rico," said Jennifer icily.

"No, I'm not," said Adam.

"Where are you going?" asked Jennifer.

"I'd rather not say," said Adam.

"Fine," said Jennifer. "Have it your way. Incidentally, just in case you're interested, I had the amniocentesis yesterday."

"I know," said Adam.

"How did you know?" asked Jennifer. "I tried calling you from seven in the morning on. You were never in."

Adam realized that Mrs. Carson had not even told Jennifer that he'd phoned the previous evening. Getting his wife back was going to be an uphill battle.

"Well, you have a wonderful time on your trip," said Jennifer coldly, and she hung up before Adam could even tell her how much he loved her.

///

Jennifer put down the phone wondering what could be so important that Adam would leave her at this difficult time. It had to be Puerto Rico, and yet Adam had never lied to her before.

"Anything new?" questioned Mrs. Carson.

Jennifer turned to face her parents.

"Adam is going on some kind of trip," she said.

"How nice for him," said Mrs. Carson. "Where is he going?"

"I don't know," said Jennifer. "He wouldn't tell me."

"Could he be having an affair?" asked Mrs. Carson.

"By George, he better not be," said Mr. Carson, who lowered his *Wall Street Journal* and glared at the two women.

"He's not having an affair," said Jennifer irritably.

"Well, he's surely acting inappropriately," said her mother.

Jennifer got some Raisin Bran cereal and cut up a banana. Since she'd started the pregdolen, her nausea had all but disappeared. She carried her breakfast to the table and sat in front of the TV.

The phone rang again, and she leaped up, thinking it was Adam calling, having changed his mind about the trip. But when she picked up the phone, it was Dr. Vandermer on the other end.

"I'm sorry to be calling so early," he said, "but I wanted to be certain to get you."

"It's all right," said Jennifer, her stomach doing a flip-flop.

"I'd like you to come back to the clinic today," said Dr. Vandermer. "I need to talk to you. Could you make it this morning some time around ten? I'm afraid I have surgery this afternoon."

"Of course. I'll be there at ten," said Jennifer. She hung up the phone, afraid to ask what he wanted to talk about.

"Who was it, dear?" asked Mrs. Carson.

"Dr. Vandermer. He wants to see me this morning."

"What about?"

"He didn't say," said Jennifer softly.

"Well, at least it can't have anything to do with the amniocentesis," said Mrs. Carson. "He told us the results take about two weeks."

Jennifer dressed quickly, her mind trying to guess what Dr. Vandermer was going to tell her. Her mother's comment about the amniocentesis test made her feel a bit better. The only other thing she could think of was that one of the blood tests had shown she was low on iron or some vitamin.

Mrs. Carson insisted on driving Jennifer to the Julian Clinic and going in with her for her appointment. They were escorted immediately to Dr. Vandermer's new office, which smelled of fresh paint.

Dr. Vandermer stood when they entered and motioned for Jennifer and her mother to take the two chairs in front of his desk. Looking at his face, Jennifer knew that something was seriously wrong.

"I'm afraid I have some bad news," he said in a voice that betrayed no emotion.

Jennifer felt her heart leap. All at once the room felt intolerably hot.

"Normally it takes two weeks to get the results of an amniocentesis," said Dr. Vandermer. "The reason is that tissue cultures have to be made in order to see the nuclear material properly. Occasionally, however, the abnormality is so apparent that the free cells in the amniotic fluid tell the story. Jennifer, like your mother, you are carrying a baby with Down's syndrome. The karyotype is of the most severe type."

Jennifer was speechless. There had to be a mistake. She couldn't believe that her body would deceive her and produce some sort of monster.

"Does that mean that the child won't live more than a few weeks?" Mrs. Carson asked, struggling with her own memories.

"We believe that the infant wouldn't survive," said Dr. Vandermer. He walked over to Jennifer and put his arm on her shoulder. "I'm sorry to be the bearer of such news. I would have waited for the final results, but it is better for you to know now. It gives you more time to make a decision. It may not seem much consolation to you, but try to remember that you are a very young woman. You can have lots of other children and, as you mentioned yourself, this is not the best time for you and Adam to have a baby."

Jennifer listened in shocked silence. Dr. Vandermer turned and caught Mrs. Carson's eye.

"I think you should go home and discuss the situation with your family," Dr. Vandermer continued. "Believe me, it's better to come to a decision now than after a lengthy and difficult labor and delivery."

"I can vouch for that," said Mrs. Carson. "Dr. Vandermer's right, Jennifer. We'll go home and talk. Everything is going to work out fine."

Jennifer nodded and even managed a smile for Dr. Vandermer, whose face finally revealed a trace of emotion.

"Please call me whenever you want," he said as they left.

The two women passed through the clinic, descended into the parking garage, and retrieved their car in silence. As they drove up the ramp, Jennifer said, "I want to go home to my apartment."

"I thought we'd go right back to New Jersey," said Mrs. Carson. "I think your father should know about this."

"I'd like to see Adam," said Jennifer. "He didn't say what time he was leaving. Maybe I can catch him."

"Maybe we should call first," said Mrs. Carson.

"I'd prefer just to go," said Jennifer.

Deciding this was not the time to argue, Mrs. Carson drove her daughter downtown. When they went up to the apartment, Jennifer saw that Adam's two suitcases were still in the closet and none of his clothes seemed to be missing. She felt reasonably confident that he had not left.

"Well, what do you want to do?" asked her mother.

"Wait and talk to him," said Jennifer in a tone that brooked no further debate.

///

"I'm going to have to charge you a fee if this happens again," teased the porter at the university information booth.

Adam took the white coat and slipped it on.

"I just can't stay away from this place. I'm homesick." The sleeves were two inches too short and there was a big yellow stain on the pocket. "Is this the best you can do?" he joked.

Confident in his medical disguise, Adam took the elevator to Neurology, went directly to the nurses' station, smiled at the ward clerk, and again pulled Smyth's chart from the rack.

All he really wanted was the information on the front sheet. Turning his back to the clerk, Adam copied down all the personal information he could find on Smyth: health insurance information, social security number, wife's name, and birth date. That was a good start.

Returning the chart to the rack, Adam took the elevator back down to the library on the main floor. A research assistant directed him to a compendium of American physicians. Looking up Stuart Smyth, Adam checked the schools the man had attended from college through residency and was interested to note that he'd done a year of surgical training in Hawaii. Adam also memorized all of Smyth's professional associations.

His final act before leaving the medical center was to call Christine at GYN Associates under the pretext of setting up an appointment with Baumgarten and Stens the following week. He managed to learn that Smyth was an avid tennis player, a lover of classical music, and a movie buff.

Back in the Buick, Adam drove across town and turned right on Eighth Avenue. As he approached Forty-second Street, the city changed from office buildings and warehouses to garish movie theaters with harsh neon lights and adult bookstores advertising twenty-five-cent X-rated flicks. Streetwalkers in high-heeled sandals and miniskirts beckoned to him as he parked his car.

Adam wandered east, lingering in front of magazine stands. After many offers of drugs, he was approached by a thin man wearing one of those narrow mustaches that Adam remembered from thirties films.

"You interested in a real lady?" asked the man.

Adam wondered if a real lady was the opposite of the kind that you had to inflate. He was tempted to ask but wasn't sure if the thin man would appreciate his humor.

"I'm interested in some ID cards," said Adam.

"What kind?" asked the man as if it were an everyday request.

Adam shrugged. "I don't know. Maybe a driver's license and a voter's registration card."

"A voter's registration card?" repeated the thin man. "I never heard of somebody asking for that."

"No?" said Adam. "Well, I'm sort of new at this. I want to go on a cruise, and I don't want anyone to know who I really am."

"Then you want a friggin' passport," said the man. "When do you need it?"

"Right now," said Adam.

"I trust you got cash."

"Some," said Adam. He'd been careful to lock most of his money, plus his own identification cards, into the glove compartment of the car.

"It will cost you twenty-five for the driver's license and fifty for the passport," said the thin man.

"Wow," said Adam. "I only have fifty on me."

"Too bad," said the man. He turned and started toward Eighth Avenue.

Adam watched him for a moment, then continued walking toward Broadway. After a few steps he felt a hand on his shoulder.

"Sixty bucks for both," said the thin man.

Adam nodded.

Without another word the man led Adam back toward Eighth Avenue and into one of the many stores that were plastered with hand-lettered signs reading "Going Out of Business! Last Three Days! Everything Reduced!" Adam noticed that the "Last Three Days!" sign was brittle with age.

The store sold the usual assortment of cameras, calculators, and videotapes and a handful of "authentic Chinese ivories." A center table supported a line of miniature Empire State Buildings and Statues of Liberty, plus coffee mugs with "I Love New York" on the sides.

None of the salesmen even looked up as the thin man led Adam through the length of the store and out the rear door. In the back of the building was a hall with doors on either side. Adam hoped he wasn't getting himself into something he couldn't handle. The thin man knocked on the first door, then opened it and motioned Adam into a small, dark room.

In one corner was a Polaroid camera on a tripod. In another was a drafting table, set under a bright fluorescent light. A man with a shiny bald head sat at the table. He was wearing one of those green visors Adam remembered seeing on cardplayers in old westerns.

The thin man spoke. "This kid wants a driver's license and a passport for sixty bucks."

"What name?" asked the man with the green visor.

Adam quickly gave Smyth's name, address, birth date, and social security number.

There was no more talk. Adam was positioned behind the Polaroid camera and several pictures were taken. Next, the man with the green visor went over to the drafting table and began to work. The thin man leaned against the wall and lit a cigarette.

Ten minutes later Adam walked back through the store, clutching his phony IDs. He didn't open them until he reached the car, but when he did he found they looked entirely authentic. Pleased, he turned the car toward the Village. He had only an hour or so to pack.

When he reached the apartment, he was surprised to find the police lock unengaged. He pushed open the door and saw Jennifer and her mother.

"Hi," he said, quite amazed. "This is a nice surprise."

"I was hoping to catch you before you went to Puerto Rico," said Jennifer.

"I'm not going to Puerto Rico," said Adam.

"I don't think you should be going anyplace," said Mrs. Carson. "Jennifer has had a shock and she needs your support."

Adam put his things on the desk and turned to Jennifer. She did look pale.

"What's the matter?" asked Adam.

"Dr. Vandermer gave her some bad news," replied Mrs. Carson.

Adam did not take his eyes from Jennifer's face. He wanted to tell Mrs. Carson to shut up, but instead he stood directly in front of his wife. "What did Dr. Vandermer say?" he asked gently.

"The amniocentesis was positive. He said our baby is severely deformed. I'm so sorry, Adam. I think I'll have to have an abortion."

"That's impossible," said Adam, slamming his fist into his palm. "It takes weeks to do the tissue cultures after an amniocentesis. What the hell is wrong with this Vandermer?"

Adam strode to the phone.

Jennifer burst into tears. "It's not Dr. Vandermer's fault," she sobbed, explaining that the abnormality was so severe that tissue cultures weren't needed.

Adam hesitated, trying to remember what he'd read. He couldn't recall any cases where tissue culture wasn't needed.

"That's not good enough for me," he said, putting through a call to the Julian Clinic. When he asked for Dr. Vandermer, he was put on hold.

Mrs. Carson cleared her throat. "Adam, I think that you should be more concerned about Jennifer's feelings than about Dr. Vandermer."

Adam ignored her. The Julian Clinic operator came back on the line and told Adam that Dr. Vandermer was doing a procedure but

would call back. Adam gave his name and number and then dropped
the receiver into its cradle.

"This is crazy," he mumbled. "I had a strange feeling about the
Julian Clinic. And Vandermer . . ." He didn't finish the sentence.

"I think the Julian Clinic is one of the finest hospitals I've even
been in," said Mrs. Carson. "And except for my own doctor, I've
never met a more caring man than Dr. Vandermer."

"I'm going over there," said Adam, ignoring his mother-in-law. "I
want to talk to him in person." Picking up his keys, Adam strode
toward the door.

"What about your wife?" demanded Mrs. Carson.

"I'll be back." Then he left, slamming the door behind him.

Mrs. Carson was furious. She couldn't believe that she had originally favored the marriage. Hearing Jennifer weep, she decided it
was better not to say anything. She went over to her daughter,
murmuring, "We'll go home. Daddy will take care of everything."

Jennifer didn't object, but when she got to the door, she said, "I
want to leave Adam a note."

Mrs. Carson nodded and watched Jennifer write a short note at
Adam's desk, then put it on the floor by the door. It said simply:
"Gone home. Jennifer."

/ / /

Adam drove uptown like an aggressive New York City cabbie,
pulled directly in front of the Julian Clinic, and jumped out of the car.
A uniformed security guard tried to stop him, but Adam merely
called over his shoulder that he was Dr. Schonberg and it was an
emergency.

When he reached Gynecology, the receptionist acted as if he were
expected.

"Adam Schonberg," she said. "Dr. Vandermer said for you to wait
in his office." She pointed down another corridor. "It's the third door
on the left."

Adam thanked the girl and went to the office she'd indicated. The
room was impressive, the shelves filled with books and medical journals. Adam glanced at a row of model fetuses, feeling an uncharacter-
istic urge to vandalize the place. He wandered over to the desk. It

was a large, inlaid affair with claw feet. On top was a pile of typed operative notes awaiting signatures.

Dr. Vandermer came in almost immediately. He was carrying a manila folder under his arm.

"Won't you sit down?" he suggested.

"No, thank you," said Adam. "This won't take long. I just wanted to confirm my wife's diagnosis. I understand you believe she's carrying a chromosomally defective child."

"I'm afraid so," said Dr. Vandermer.

"I thought it took weeks to do tissue cultures," said Adam.

Dr. Vandermer looked Adam directly in the eye. "Normally, that is true," he said. "But in your wife's case there were plenty of cells for us to examine directly in the amniotic fluid. Adam, as a medical student, I'm sure you understand these things happen. But as I told your wife, you're both young. You can have other babies."

"I want to see the slides," said Adam, preparing himself for an argument. But Vandermer just nodded and said, "Why don't you follow me?"

Adam began to wonder if he'd been too hasty in his judgment. The man seemed genuinely sorry to be the bearer of such bad news.

On the fourth floor Vandermer led Adam to the cytology lab. Adam blinked as they went through the door. Everything was white: walls, floor, ceiling, and countertops. At the back of the room was a lab bench with four microscopes. Only one was in use, and a middle-aged brunette woman looked up as Dr. Vandermer approached.

"Cora," he asked, "I hate to bother you, but could you get us the slides on Jennifer Schonberg?"

Cora nodded and Vandermer motioned for Adam to sit down at a teaching microscope with dual viewing heads.

"I don't know if you wanted to see the B scan ultrasonography or not," said Dr. Vandermer, "but I brought it anyway." He opened the folder he'd been carrying and handed the images to Adam.

As a medical student, Adam had not had any experience with ultrasonography, and the pictures looked like inkblots to him. Dr. Vandermer took the photo that Adam was examining, turned it over, and outlined the developing fetus with the tip of his finger. "The technique is getting better and better," he said. "Here you can plainly see testicles. A lot of times at this age you can't tell the sex by ultrasound. Perhaps this little guy takes after his father."

Adam realized Vandermer was doing his best to be friendly.

The door swung open and Cora reappeared with a tray of slides. Each had a tiny cover glass over its center. Dr. Vandermer selected one that had been labeled with a grease pencil. He placed it under the optical head of the microscope, put a drop of oil on it, and lowered the oil-immersion lens. Adam sat up and looked through the eyepiece.

Dr. Vandermer explained that the specimens had been specially stained to make viewing of the chromatin material as easy as possible. He said they had to find a cell in the process of division. Finally, he gave up and asked for Cora's assistance.

"I should have let you do this in the first place," he said, changing seats with the woman.

It took Cora about thirty seconds to find an appropriate cell. By manipulating the hairline pointer, she showed Adam the chromosomal abnormality.

Adam was crushed. He had hoped the results would be ambiguous, but even to his inexperienced eye, the problem was clear. Cora continued pointing out other minor problems that had been noticed, including the fact that one of the X chromosomes also appeared slightly abnormal.

Finally, Cora asked if he would like to see another case that demonstrated a more common type of Down's syndrome.

Adam shook his head. "No, but thanks for your time." He put both hands on the lab bench and started to rise. Halfway up he stopped. Something was wrong. He leaned forward and peered into the microscope. "Show me that X chromosome abnormality again," said Adam.

Cora leaned forward and put her face to the eyepiece. Soon the hairline pointer moved to a pair of identical chromosomes. Cora started to explain the suspected abnormality, but Adam interrupted her.

"Are those X chromosomes?" asked Adam.

"Absolutely," said Cora. "But . . ."

Adam again interrupted her and asked Dr. Vandermer to take a look. "Do you see the X chromosomes?"

"I do," said Dr. Vandermer, "but like you, I can't appreciate the abnormality that Cora is talking about."

"I'm not concerned about the abnormality," said Adam. "I'm concerned about the two X chromosomes. Just a moment ago on the ultrasound image you pointed out that my child is a boy. This slide we are looking at is a girl."

Dr. Vandermer had straightened up when Adam had begun to talk. His face wiped clean of all expression.

Cora immediately turned to the microscope. "He's right," she said. "This slide is of a girl."

Slowly Dr. Vandermer raised his right hand to his face. Cora flipped over the edge of the slide tray and checked the number. Then she checked the number on the slide. They matched. Getting the main register, she checked the number there. The name was Jennifer Schonberg. Looking very pale, Dr. Vandermer told Adam to wait for a moment.

"Has anything like this ever happened before?" asked Adam when the doctor had gone.

"Never," said Cora.

Dr. Vandermer reappeared with a large man in tow. Like Dr. Vandermer, he was wearing a long white coat. Dr. Vandermer introduced him to Adam as Dr. Ridley Stanford. Adam recognized the name. He was the author of the textbook on pathology that Adam had used during his second year of medical school, and had been chief of pathology at University Hospital.

"This is a disaster," said Dr. Vandermer after Dr. Stanford had taken a look.

"I agree," said Dr. Stanford, his voice as emotionless as Vandermer's. "I can't imagine how this could have happened. Let me make some calls."

Within a few minutes there were ten other people crowded around the microscope.

"How many amniocenteses were done yesterday?" asked Dr. Vandermer.

Cora glanced at the book. "Twenty-one," she said.

"They all have to be repeated," said Dr. Vandermer.

"Absolutely," said Dr. Stanford.

Turning to Adam, Dr. Vandermer said, "We owe you a vote of thanks." The others echoed his sentiments.

Adam felt as if a huge black cloud had been lifted from over his head. His child was not some kind of genetic monster. The first thing he wanted to do was call Jennifer.

"We would be honored if you would stay for lunch," said Dr. Stanford. "There's a fabulous pathology lecture on retroperitoneal tumors which you might find interesting."

Adam excused himself and hurriedly descended to the main lobby. He couldn't believe that in the face of the current disaster they wanted him to stay for lunch and a lecture! There was no question but the place was weird. Passing the front door en route to the telephone, Adam was pleased to see that his car was still where he'd left it.

Adam first called the apartment, but there was no answer. Thinking that Jennifer might have gone home with her mother, he dialed the Englewood number, but there was no answer there, either.

After a moment's hesitation, Adam decided to go back to the apartment. He ran out of the Julian Clinic, got in his car, and started for home.

His excitement at the good news was beginning to give way to a heightened sense of uneasiness about the Julian Clinic and Dr. Vandermer. It had been only a lucky break that he'd noticed the discrepancy. What if he hadn't and Jennifer had had an abortion!

Adam felt all his anxieties return in a rush. He'd narrowly averted one catastrophe, but unless he could get Jennifer to switch from both Vandermer and the clinic, there might be more. For a while he'd abandoned the thought of the Arolen cruise. Now it looked again as if it might be the only way to get the evidence to prove Vandermer was dangerous. Adam looked at his watch. It was twelve-twenty. Still time to make the *Fjord* by six o'clock.

Reaching his apartment door, Adam was disappointed to find the police lock engaged. He found Jennifer's impersonal note and decided to call Englewood once again. He was pleased when Jennifer answered instead of her mother.

"I've got good news and bad."

"I'm in no mood to play games," said Jennifer.

"The good news is that they got your specimen mixed up at the clinic. Someone else's baby has the bad chromosomes. They mixed up the slides."

For a moment Jennifer was afraid to ask if Adam were telling the truth or if this were just some sort of plot to make her lose faith in Vandermer. The news seemed too good to be true.

"Jennifer, did you hear me?"

"Is it true?" asked Jennifer tentatively.

"Yes," said Adam, and he described how he'd noticed the discrepancy in relation to the sex of the cell.

"What did Dr. Vandermer say?" asked Jennifer.

"He said that all the amniocenteses done that day have to be repeated."

"Is that the bad news you were referring to?" asked Jennifer.

"No," said Adam. "The bad news is that I'm still going out of town, unless you promise me something."

"What do I have to promise?" asked Jennifer skeptically.

"Promise to see Dr. Wickelman for the remainder of your pregnancy and stop taking pregdolen."

"Adam . . ." said Jennifer, drawing out his name impatiently.

"I'm more convinced than ever that there is something strange about the Julian Clinic," said Adam. "If you agree to see Dr. Wickelman, I'll promise not to interfere with anything he suggests."

"Mistakes happen every day in hospitals," said Jennifer. "Just because one happened at the Julian Clinic doesn't mean I shouldn't go there. It seems like the ideal place to have my baby now that I've gotten over that episode with Cheryl Tedesco. I like the people there and the atmosphere."

"Well," said Adam. "I'll see you in a few days."

"Where are you going?" asked Jennifer.

"I'd rather not say," said Adam.

"Under the circumstances," said Jennifer, "don't you think that you should stay here? Adam, I need you."

"That's a little hard to believe with you at your parents' and me alone in the apartment. I'm sorry, but I have to run. I love you, Jennifer."

Adam hung up and called Eastern Airlines before he had time to have second thoughts. He booked a seat on a flight leaving for Miami from LaGuardia in forty-eight minutes.

Adam got his small Samsonite suitcase from the closet and began packing. Just as he was cramming in his toilet articles, the phone rang. Adam reached out his hand, but then, for once in his life, ignored the sound. Even a minute's delay would make him miss his flight.

Jennifer waited, letting the phone ring on and on. Finally, she hung up. Right after speaking with Adam, she'd decided that she'd be willing to see this Dr. Wickelman if it meant so much to Adam. She could at least give the man a chance, and if she didn't feel comfortable with him, she could always go back to Dr. Vandermer. But Adam had apparently left. Jennifer felt abandoned. Before she took her hand off the receiver, the phone rang again. Hoping it was Adam, she picked it up before the first ring was complete. It was Dr. Vandermer.

"I assume you have heard the good news."

"Yes, Adam just told me," said Jennifer.

"We are very grateful to your husband," said Dr. Vandermer. "It is unusual for someone to notice a secondary abnormality in the face of an overwhelmingly positive finding."

"So it is true that I am not carrying a defective child," said Jennifer.

"I'm afraid I can't go so far as to say that," said Dr. Vandermer. "Unfortunately, we have no idea of the result of your amniocentesis. We'll have to repeat the procedure. I'm terribly sorry this happened. There were twenty people besides yourself who had amniocentesis that day, and all of them have to be repeated. Obviously it will be done at the clinic's expense."

"When do you want to repeat the test?" asked Jennifer. She appreciated Dr. Vandermer's willingness to accept responsibility even though the error was undoubtedly made by someone in the lab.

"As soon as possible," said Dr. Vandermer. "Remember, we are up against a time constraint if there really is a problem."

"How about if I get back to you in the morning?" said Jennifer.

"That will be fine. There's no rush, but the sooner we do it, the better."

CHAPTER 12

The flight to Miami was uneventful. As soon as Adam was airborne, he removed his own driver's license from his billfold and replaced it with Smyth's. Then he studied the addresses in the passport. If someone asked him where he lived, he wanted to be able to rattle it off by heart.

The plane landed at five minutes after four, and since Adam had carried his luggage aboard, he was at the taxi stand by four-fifteen. The taxi was an old broken-down Dodge station wagon and the driver spoke only Spanish, but he recognized the name of the *Fjord* and understood that Adam was going on a cruise.

Adam stared at the tropical scenery. Miami was much more beautiful than he'd imagined. Soon they passed over a long causeway and Adam saw the harbor. The cruise ships were tied up in a line, with the *Fjord* the last in the row. Compared to the others, the *Fjord* seemed neither especially large nor particularly small. Like the others, it was painted white. It had one huge smokestack with an image of two intertwining arrows on the side. Adam wondered if that were MTIC's logo.

Adam's driver could not get close to the curb, so Adam paid him and got out in the middle of the street. Suitcase in hand, he made his way toward the entrance of the building. The din of car horns, voices, and idling motors was terrific, the air heavy with fumes. It was a relief to get inside.

Adam made his way to an information booth where the receptionists' uniforms reminded him of the staff's dress at the Julian Clinic. They, too, were dressed in white blouses and blue jumpers.

Adam had to shout to be heard. He asked how he should check in and was told to go up the escalator to the second level. Adam thanked the girl who'd directed him by mouthing the words.

Getting on the escalator was a trick, especially with the suitcase. While he rode up, he looked over the crowd. Although there were a few women, the majority of the people were men and they certainly looked like doctors—prosperous and self-satisfied. Most were dressed in business suits, though a few had on sport shirts and slacks.

On the second floor of the terminal was a long registration table, divided into alphabetical segments. Adam joined the line marked "N–Z."

Glancing around the room, he suddenly got cold feet. Maybe he should leave. No one would notice. He could just catch a cab to the airport and fly home. He began counting the number of people between him and the registration desk. At that moment, Adam's eye caught those of a man standing a few feet away in the neighboring line. Quickly looking away, Adam nervously tapped his foot. There was no reason for someone to be staring at him. Gradually, Adam allowed his eyes to return to the next line. Unfortunately, the man was still looking directly at him. When he saw Adam look up, he smiled. Self-consciously, Adam smiled back. Then, to his horror, the man came over.

"My name is Alan Jackson," he said, forcing Adam to put down his suitcase and shake hands. Nervously, Adam introduced himself as Stuart Smyth. Alan just nodded and smiled again.

He was at least ten years older than Adam and had broad shoulders and a narrow waist. His sandy hair was combed forward, probably to hide a bald spot.

"You look awfully familiar," said Alan. "Are you from New York?"

Adam felt the blood drain from his face. He hadn't even checked in yet and already he was in trouble.

At that moment the loudspeaker came to life: "Good afternoon, ladies and gentlemen. For those of you with boarding cards, the *Fjord* will be ready to receive you in just a few minutes. If you haven't received a boarding card, we recommend that you proceed to the registration desk immediately."

"Aren't you in orthopedics?" asked Alan as soon as the loudspeaker fell silent.

"No," said Adam, relieved. Obviously the man didn't know the real Smyth. "I'm OB-GYN. How about you?"

"Orthopedics. I'm with the University of California, San Diego. This your first Arolen cruise?"

"No," said Adam quickly. "How about you?"

"It's my second," said Alan, turning suddenly. "My God, there's Ned Janson. Hey, Ned, you old bastard. Over here!"

Adam saw a stocky, dark-haired man who was with one of the few women in the crowd look up. Seeing Alan, his face lit up with a smile. He took the woman by the arm and made his way over.

While Alan and Ned had a back-slapping reunion, Adam introduced himself to the woman. Her name was Clair Osborn. She was a handsome lady, about thirty, with a round, healthy face, and long, muscular legs. She was dressed in a short black-and-white skirt. Adam was enjoying himself until she told him she was a gynecologist.

"What's your specialty?" asked Clair. "Orthopedics or OB-GYN?"

"Why limit the choices to those two?" joked Adam, trying to change the subject.

"It's my brilliant intuition," said Clair. "Plus the fact that this cruise is for orthopods and obstetricians only."

Adam laughed nervously. "Well, I'm OB."

"Really?" said Clair with delight. "Then we'll be going to the same functions."

"That will be nice," said Adam. "Is this your first cruise?" Adam wanted to talk about anything other than OB-GYN. He didn't fool himself into thinking he could hold up his end of a professional conversation.

"Sure is," said Clair. "It's Ned's first time, too. Right, Ned?" Clair yanked on Ned's arm to get his attention. Hearing bits and pieces of their conversation, Adam understood that Alan and Ned had trained at the same hospital.

"Hey! This is great," said Ned after meeting Adam. "Why don't we all have dinner tonight?"

Alan shook his head. "The Arolen people do the seating. They consider meals an extension of the scientific sessions."

"Oh, bullshit," said Ned. "What is this supposed to be, summer camp?"

The man in front of Adam moved away with his boarding card in hand. Adam stepped up to the counter and faced a young man nattily dressed in a white blazer. On the breast pocket was the same logo Adam had seen painted on the side of the *Fjord*'s smokestack. On his lapel was a name tag that said "Juan." Below the name and in small letters was printed "MTIC."

"Your name, please?" asked Juan. His voice sounded as if he'd asked the question so often that he was speaking by rote.

"Stuart Smyth," said Adam and fumbled with his billfold to get out the driver's license. In the process his Arolen card dropped on the counter. Luckily, Juan was already busy entering Stuart Smyth into the computer so he didn't see it. Adam turned around to see if any of his new friends had noticed, but they were busy talking. Adam turned back to face Juan, thinking that by the time this cruise was over, he was going to be a nervous wreck. Furtively, he slipped the Arolen card into his jacket pocket.

"Passport?" asked Juan.

After a moment of panic Adam found the passport in his inside jacket pocket and handed it over. Juan opened it. Adam felt a stab of terror, but Juan just looked at it for two seconds and handed it back, saying, "Here's your boarding card. Please present it to the purser and he will assign you your stateroom. If you leave the ship during the cruise, be sure to have the card on your person. Next, please."

Adam stepped aside so the man behind him could approach the counter. So far so good.

After Alan had obtained his boarding card, he, Ned, and Clair accompanied Adam to the Arolen desk. There they were given a package of "goodies" as Ned called them. The process starts, thought Adam as he took the gift, a leather shoulder bag with the MTIC logo on the side. Inside the bag were a Cross pen and pencil set, a legal-sized, leatherbound note pad, and a lecture schedule for the cruise. There was also an array of Arolen products which comprised a small pharmacy. Adam glanced at the loot with interest, but knew that he'd have to wait to examine it in detail.

The loudspeaker crackled to life and it was announced that the ship was ready to board. A cheer rose from the crowd as Adam and his newly made friends slowly walked outside. A uniformed policeman checked their boarding cards at dockside, and they all trooped up the gangway.

Stepping off the ramp, Adam found himself on the main deck. It wasn't a new ship by any stretch of the imagination, but it appeared to be well cared for and certain sections seemed to have been recently renovated. The personnel were all dressed like the man at the registration desk, in white blazers and black slacks. Their uniforms were spotlessly clean and carefully pressed.

Adam was approached by one of the stewards who politely checked his boarding card and directed him to a desk to the right. Apparently, there were different colored boarding cards for those who had been on a previous cruise. Ned and Clair were sent to a different desk.

Adam was assigned stateroom 407 on A deck, which was the floor below the main deck. As he took his key, he noticed that the purser had the same monotonous inflection in his voice as the man at the registration desk.

Alan, who was right behind Adam, was assigned stateroom 409. As they walked away, Adam commented on the flat speech pattern.

"I suppose they say the same thing over and over again," said Alan.

A steward approached Adam and relieved him of his small suitcase and his new Arolen shoulder bag.

"Thank you," said Adam.

The man didn't respond except by indicating that Adam was to follow him.

"See you later, Stuart," called Alan.

It took Adam a moment to remember that that was his name. "Yes, of course," he called.

The steward was leading him past a gift shop filled with Gucci bags and Japanese cameras. At the back were wines, liquors, and tobaccos as well as a drug section. For the first time, Adam thought about the possibility of seasickness.

"Excuse me," he said. "When will the store be opened?"

"About an hour after departure."

"Do they sell Dramamine or those ear patches for motion sickness?" asked Adam.

The steward looked at him with a blank expression. "I don't know if they sell Dramamine or those ear patches." The way he echoed Adam's question didn't invite further conversation.

Staterooms 407 and 409 were adjacent on the port side of the ship. Alan was nowhere in sight. Adam's steward opened the door to 407 and led Adam inside.

To Adam, who'd never been on a luxury liner, the room seemed small. There was a single bed on the right with a night table. On the left were a small desk and a chair. The bathroom was a tiny affair with a shower, toilet, and sink crammed next to a narrow closet.

The steward stuck his head in the bathroom, entered, and reappeared a moment later with a glass of water, which he handed to Adam.

"For me?" asked Adam. He took the glass and sipped the water. It had a rather chemical taste.

The steward reached into his side pocket and pulled out a yellow capsule, which he extended toward Adam. "Welcome back," he said.

Adam smiled uneasily. "Sure is good to be here," he said, eyeing the yellow capsule. It became obvious that the steward expected him to take the pill.

Adam put out his hand and the steward dropped the capsule into his palm. It didn't look like Dramamine, but how was he to know?

"Is this for motion sickness?" he asked.

The steward said nothing, but his unblinking stare made Adam acutely uncomfortable.

"I'll bet it is for motion sickness," said Adam, tossing the pill into his mouth. After a swallow, he gave the water glass to the steward, who returned it to the bathroom. While he was out of the room, Adam took the yellow capsule out of his mouth and dropped it into his pocket.

The steward pulled down the covers on the bed as if he expected Adam to take a nap. Then he set Adam's suitcase on a stand and began to unpack.

Amazed at such service, Adam sat on the bed and watched the man silently go about his business. When the steward was finished, he thanked Adam and left.

For a moment Adam sat puzzling over the steward's behavior. Then he got up and upended his new Arolen shoulder bag. The drugs spilled onto the blanket.

Taking the yellow capsule out of his pocket, he checked to see if it matched any of the samples. It didn't. Adam wondered if he would be able to find a *PDR* on board. There should be a library with basic reference books. He was curious about the yellow capsule. It had to be for motion sickness. Adam glanced at it one last time, then put it into a small bottle of aspirin.

He picked up the lecture schedule and began to read. It was nearly twenty-five pages long. The first half dealt with orthopedics, the second with OB-GYN. Adam noted that most of the lectures were clinically oriented, which he thought accounted for the conferences' popularity.

Adam was convinced that if anything were done in the nature of brainwashing, it had to be done during the lectures. But what could they say to make a doctor like Vandermer change his mind about a drug? Could it be some kind of subliminal hypnosis? Adam tossed the schedule aside. He guessed he'd find out soon enough.

The blast of a horn made Adam jump. Then he heard the engines start. He decided to go on deck to watch.

Hanging up his seersucker jacket and removing his tie, Adam stepped into the corridor. He paused outside of room 409, realizing that although they shared a common wall, he'd heard nothing from Alan. Adam rapped on the door and waited, but there was no answer. Another steward came past, and Adam had to flatten himself against the wall. Then he knocked again. He was about to leave when he heard a thump from inside the room. With the heel of his hand, he pounded on the door, thinking perhaps Alan was in the bathroom. Still there was no answer. Reaching down, Adam tried the latch. The door was unlocked and swung inward.

Alan was sitting on the edge of the bed. At his feet was a water glass that had apparently just fallen to the floor.

"I beg your pardon," said Adam, embarrassed. Alan mumbled that it didn't matter, but Adam saw that he must have been asleep.

"Sorry to have disturbed you," said Adam. "I was going to watch the departure and thought that maybe you . . ." Adam didn't finish his sentence. Alan was slowly falling forward. Entering the room, Adam grabbed him before he hit the floor and eased him back onto the bed.

"Hey, are you OK?" asked Adam.

Sleepily, Alan nodded. "I'm just tired."

"I think you'd better have a snooze," laughed Adam, glancing around at the night table, suspecting that Alan might have taken a drink or two. But there was no liquor in evidence. He debated if he should cover the man, but since Alan was fully dressed, he just left him on top of the spread.

Back at the reception area there were still a few people waiting for room assignments. The gangplank, however, had been raised. Adam continued up two levels to what was called the promenade deck and went outside.

The change from air-conditioned coolness to the torpid Miami heat was a shock. Adam went to the railing and looked down at the quay. Stevedores were busy casting off the lines, freeing the ship from its mooring. The vibrations of the engines increased, and side thrusters moved the ship slowly away from the pier. From the stern Adam heard a cheer and then the noise of a Dixieland band.

Walking forward, Adam soon came to a teak barrier with a door leading to the bow. A sign cautioned: "Crew Only. Passengers Not Permitted Foward." Adam tried the door. It was unlocked, but he decided not to test his luck by going through.

The horn blared again and at the same time the vibration of the ship changed. Adam guessed that the main screws had started to turn. Slowly, the ship began to move forward.

Adam met other passengers exploring the ship. Everyone was friendly and outgoing. A vacation mood prevailed.

Adam descended a deck and found himself surrounded by conference rooms of all sizes, ranging from a full-fledged theater to seminar rooms for less than a dozen people. Almost all the rooms were equipped with blackboards and slide projectors.

Amidships, Adam came to a door marked "Library." He wanted to go in and look for a *PDR*, but the door was locked. Assuming that it would be open in the morning, he continued forward. Soon the central corridor ended at a locked door, which Adam guessed led to the crew's quarters.

Descending another level, Adam came out on the main deck. He wandered past the store and the reception area and stopped to look into the main dining room. It was huge, with crystal chandeliers and large picture windows. At one end was a raised platform with a podium for speakers. On either side of the platform were swinging doors which apparently led to the kitchen. Stewards busy laying the tables were going in and out of the doors with their trays. A sign near the entrance stated that dinner would be served at nine o'clock.

Adam descended another level to the A deck where his stateroom was located. A number of cabin doors were open, and Adam could see the doctors unpacking and going in and out of each other's rooms.

Walking down still another level, Adam found more conference rooms, a small gym, the ship's doctor's office, and an indoor swimming pool. Deciding he had explored the ship as much as he could, Adam made his way back to the promenade deck, where a noisy cocktail party was well under way.

Ned Janson spotted him and rushed him over to a group next to the pool. There was no way Adam could refuse, and soon he found himself drinking an ice-cold Heineken.

"Where the hell is Alan?" asked Ned over the babble of voices.

"In his room, sleeping," said Adam.

Ned nodded as if it were expected and then started slapping his thigh as the band struck up "When the Saints Come Marchin' In."

Adam smiled across the table at Clair, who seemed to be enjoying herself, and then glanced around the party. It seemed a typical gathering of MDs. It was boisterous, physical—with lots of backslapping, jokes, and booze. The minute Adam finished his beer, Ned thrust another into his hand.

Rather suddenly the ship began to pitch. Adam looked back and saw that the lights of Miami had vanished. The ship was now out into the Atlantic. His stomach did a flip-flop, and he hastily put down the beer.

The other doctors at the table seemed oblivious to the ship's motion, and Adam wished he'd been able to find an anti-nauseant. Once again he wondered if the yellow capsule were for seasickness. He was tempted to ask but then decided he couldn't stay in the loud, laughing group a minute longer.

He excused himself and quickly walked forward to a quiet spot by the rail. After a few minutes he felt better but decided to lie down for a while in his cabin. Closing his eyes, he felt OK, although the beer was still sloshing around in his stomach.

/ / /

Jennifer and her father had gone for a walk in the field behind their house. She knew he wanted to discuss her pregnancy, and for the last half hour she had held him off with a barrage of chatter. Finally, turning back to the house, Jennifer decided it was time to face the subject.

"What do you think I should do, Father?"

Mr. Carson put his arm around her. "Whatever you think is right."

"But what is your opinion?" asked Jennifer.

"That's a different question," said Mr. Carson. "Your mother really trusts this Dr. Vandermer. The mix-up with the amniocentesis samples was unfortunate, but I like the way he handled it. My feeling is that you should follow his recommendations."

"Dr. Vandermer wants me to repeat the amniocentesis immediately," said Jennifer.

"If he thinks there is a chance you might want to consider an abortion, then I think you should do it. Your mother and I don't believe that a severely defective child should be brought into this world. It's not fair to anyone, including the child. But that's just the way we feel."

"I suppose I feel the same way," said Jennifer. "It just makes me feel so bad."

Mr. Carson gave his daughter a squeeze. "Of course, honey. And your husband isn't making things any easier. I don't like to make judgments, but I don't appreciate the way he is acting. He should be here helping make these decisions, not gallivanting off on some mysterious trip."

They reached the screen door at the back of the house. They could hear Mrs. Carson in the kitchen, preparing dinner.

"You're probably right," said Jennifer, opening the door. "I'll call Dr. Vandermer and have the amniocentesis repeated tomorrow."

/ / /

"Good evening, ladies and gentlemen. Dinner is now being served."

Adam woke from a sound sleep, and it took him several minutes to realize that the voice was coming from a small speaker in the wall of the cabin. He looked at his watch. It was nine o'clock.

Struggling to his feet, Adam felt the ship rolling as well as pitching. The idea of dinner wasn't all that appealing. He took a quick shower, trying to maintain his balance, then dressed and left the cabin. He paused a minute and knocked on Alan's door, but there was no answer. Either the man was still asleep or he had already gone to dinner. In either case, it wasn't any of Adam's business.

He noticed the ship's store was open and went in to buy Dramamine, but the man behind the counter said they were out and would have to wait until morning to get more from the storeroom. Disappointed, Adam made his way to the dining room, where a steward asked if he was an obstetrician or an orthopedist. Adam told him OB and the steward led him to a table near the speaker's platform.

There were five other doctors already seated. Adam was so busy remembering that his name was Stuart, he only caught two of his companions' names during the introductions: Ted and Archibald.

The conversation was almost exclusively medical, although more about the profession's economics than its practice.

Adam said little, preoccupied with his queasy stomach. As soon as he could, he motioned for the steward to remove his plate, wondering how the others could ignore the rolling motion of the ship. After coffee was served, a tall, dark man mounted the speaker's platform.

"Hello, hello," he said, testing the microphone. "My name is Raymond Powell, and I am your official MTIC host. Welcome to the Arolen Pharmaceuticals Medical Conference Cruise."

Conversation ceased as people turned their attention to the podium. Powell gave a typical welcoming speech and then handed the microphone to Dr. Goddard, who was in charge of the actual medical program.

When Goddard finished speaking, Powell stepped back to the microphone and said, "And now we have a surprise. For your enjoyment, let me present the Caribbean Dancers."

Doors on either side of the speaker's platform burst open and a dozen scantily clad dancers swept into the room. Adam noticed only two men. The rest were unusually pretty young girls. Behind the dancers was a rock group with electric guitars. This band quickly set up speakers on the platform.

As the girls worked the audience, Adam saw that Powell and Goddard were standing to one side as if trying to assess the effect of the dancers on the usually restrained medical group. After a few minutes Adam found his attention held by a particularly attractive brunette. She had narrow hips and firm, upstanding breasts. She caught Adam's eye for just a moment and he could have sworn that she winked at him. Unfortunately, Adam's stomach was not cooperative, and in the middle of the performance, Adam reluctantly decided that he'd better visit the deck.

Excusing himself, he fought his way through the boisterous crowd in more and more of a hurry to get away. He barely reached the rail of the promenade deck before his stomach turned over and he vomited violently over the side. After a minute he glanced around to check if anyone had seen him. Thankfully, the deck was deserted. Lowering his eyes, he inspected the front of his shirt. It was clean. Relieved, Adam wandered forward into the wind. He wasn't ready to go below yet.

After a few minutes he felt a little better, and when he reached the door forbidden to passengers, he simply opened it and walked through. The lights were scarcer in this part of the ship and the deck was a plain unvarnished gray. Adam walked all the way to the bow and looked down on a tangle of ropes and chains. The sea leaped and twisted on either side. The starry sky stretched out above him.

A hand suddenly fell on Adam's shoulder.

"This is an unauthorized area," said a man with a Spanish accent.

"I'm sorry," said Adam nervously, trying to make out the man's face. "This is my first cruise and I was just wandering around. Any chance of visiting the bridge?" Adam remembered the adage that the best defense was offense.

"Are you stoned?" asked the man.

"Me?" said Adam, taken aback. "No. I'm fine."

"No offense," said the man, "but we've had some bad experiences with passengers in the past. The captain happens to be on the bridge. I'll see if he'll let you up."

After asking for Adam's name, the man disappeared as silently as he'd arrived. A moment later a voice shouted down, inviting him up. There was a ladder to starboard.

Adam walked around the side and found a stairway. He guessed that on a ship a ladder and a stairway were the same thing. At the top, the man with the Spanish accent was holding open the door to the bridge.

Inside, Adam saw that the instruments were illuminated by red lights, giving the room a surrealistic air. The man at the wheel ignored Adam's presence, but another man stood up and introduced himself as Captain Eric Nordstrom. He seemed younger than Adam would have expected and, at first, seemed rather wary of his guest.

"José said this is your first cruise, Dr. Smyth."

"That's right," said Adam uneasily, remembering that Smyth had already been on an Arolen cruise. The captain made no comment, and Adam asked, "Who owns the ship?"

"I'm not sure," said Nordstrom. "The crew works for a company called MTIC. Whether they own the ship or lease it, I don't really know."

"Is MTIC a good employer?"

Captain Nordstrom shrugged. "We get our paychecks on time. It's a bit boring running the same route over and over, and socializing with this crew has its limitations."

"Don't you get to meet the passengers?" asked Adam.

"Never," said Captain Nordstrom. "MTIC is strict about keeping the passengers and the ship's crew from fraternizing. You're the first person I've had on the bridge in a long time. We've had some unfortunate experiences with the passengers getting drunk."

Adam nodded. If the amount of alcohol that the doctors had consumed tonight was any indication, he wasn't surprised.

Away from the sea breeze, the pitching of the ship began to bother Adam again, and he decided to say good-bye.

"José, accompany Dr. Smyth back to the passenger section," said Captain Nordstrom.

José moved quickly, preceding Adam out the door. He went down the steep ladder, oblivious to the movement of the ship. Adam followed but much more cautiously.

"In a day or so you'll have your sea legs," said José with a laugh. Adam wondered.

As they walked aft, José offered some technical details about the ship. Adam nodded dutifully, but most of the terms went over his head. When they got to the barrier, José hesitated, shifting his weight from one foot to the other. In the better light Adam could see the man's face, which was dominated by a luxurious mustache.

"Dr. Smyth . . ." began José. "I was wondering if you would do me a favor."

"What do you have in mind?" asked Adam suspiciously. From what the captain had said, crew and passengers were not supposed to mix, and Adam was not interested in any trouble. On the other hand, the idea of having a friend among the crew was appealing and could come in handy.

"They sell cigarettes in the ship's store," said José. "If I gave you the money, would you buy some for me?"

"Why don't you get them yourself?" asked Adam.

"We're not allowed beyond this door."

Adam considered the request. It seemed sufficiently innocuous. "How many packs do you want?"

"As many as you can get for this." José reached into his pocket and pulled out a fifty-dollar bill.

Adam had the feeling that José's request wasn't so innocent after all. José was probably running a little shipboard black market.

"Let me start with ten dollars' worth," said Adam.

José quickly substituted a ten for the fifty.

Adam took the money and told José that he'd meet him at the same location the next day at eleven. He remembered from the lecture schedule there was a coffee break scheduled at that time. José smiled broadly, his teeth startlingly white against his mustache.

Taking a few deep breaths of sea air, Adam went inside and headed for his stateroom.

CHAPTER 13

Adam heard the voice calling Dr. Smyth but ignored it. The name had nothing to do with him, and he preferred remaining immobile. Then someone grasped his arm and with great effort he opened his eyes.

"My glasses," said Adam, surprised to find he was slurring his words.

Slowly and carefully he swung his feet over the side of the bunk and groped around on the night table. His hand hit the glasses and knocked them on the floor. Reaching over to pick them up, he suddenly remembered he was Dr. Smyth.

The steward handed him a glass of water.

"Thank you," said Adam, puzzled.

Then the steward held out another one of the yellow capsules. Without hesitating, Adam took it and put it into his mouth. But as he had done the day before, he didn't swallow it, taking a little water instead.

Satisfied, the steward took the glass into the bathroom. Adam slipped the capsule from his mouth.

"Excuse me," he said, his words much clearer. "What are these yellow pills?"

"They are to relax you," the steward said in his oddly mechanical voice.

"Hey," said Adam. "I am relaxed. A little seasick maybe, but relaxed. Wouldn't it be better if you gave me something for my stomach?"

"The yellow pills are to make you more relaxed and receptive," the steward said, opening the door.

"Receptive to what?" called Adam.

"To instructions," said the steward as he pulled the door closed.

Adam got up feeling unusually tired and weak. He'd had no idea that seasickness could be so debilitating. Forcing himself into the bathroom, he showered and dressed, still puzzling over the steward's comment.

On his way to breakfast, he decided to see if Alan were up. This time, instead of knocking, he just turned the knob and the door swung open.

Alan was still stretched out on the bed, his eyes closed, his breathing deep and even.

"Alan," called Adam. Slowly the man's eyes fluttered open, only to close again. Adam bent down and gently lifted Alan's eyelids. At first, all he saw was sclera, but then the corneas descended and seemed to focus.

"Wake up," said Adam. He took his hands from Alan's eyes and, grabbing his shoulders, pulled him into a sitting position.

"What's the matter with you?" he asked.

"Nothing," said Alan in a flat voice that reminded Adam of the steward's. "I'm just tired. Let me sleep." He started to sag backward, but Adam caught him.

"Tell me," demanded Adam. "What is your name?"

"Alan Jackson."

"Where are you?" asked Adam.

"I'm on an Arolen cruise." Alan spoke with no inflection whatsoever.

"What month is this?"

"June," said Alan.

"Raise your right hand," said Adam.

Dutifully, Alan raised his right hand. He was like an automaton or a patient under heavy sedation. In fact, he reminded Adam of his patient with tardive dyskinesia. When the man had first come into the hospital, he'd been so heavily medicated that he'd slept around the clock, although if aroused he'd been oriented to time and place.

Adam allowed Alan to slump back onto his bed. After watching him for a moment or two, he returned to his own stateroom. Closing the door, Adam felt really afraid for the first time. Alan had been drugged. There was little doubt of that.

Obviously, the yellow pills were some kind of tranquilizer. All at once Adam recalled how drowsy he'd felt when the steward had awakened him. He had attributed his condition to the aftermath of seasickness, but maybe he, too, had been drugged. Yet how could that have happened? He hadn't taken the yellow pills and what little dinner he'd eaten he'd vomited almost immediately. Maybe it was the water.

Adam went into the bathroom and filled his glass. It had no smell. Gingerly, he tasted it. It had a chemical flavor, but that could be from chlorination. Dumping it down the drain, Adam decided to go to breakfast.

The dining room held no trace of last night's raucous party. A buffet had been set up in the center of the room with an impressive array of food. People were lined up, patiently awaiting their turn. Adam strolled among the tables and looked for Ned and Clair but didn't see them.

His stomach not only felt better, he was actually hungry. The only trouble was, now that he had an appetite, he was terrified to eat. He eyed the buffet. There was the usual selection of scrambled eggs, bacon, sausage, and Danish. Then Adam saw something even better: a large bowl of fruit.

Thinking that unpeeled fruit had to be safe, he took several bananas, two oranges, and a grapefruit and made his way to an empty table. Just as he sat down, Ned and Clair appeared. Adam called out to them, and they came over to his table. They said they would join him.

Adam watched them go through the buffet line. They seemed tired, and when they came and sat down, Adam noticed that they hadn't taken much food. He was puzzled. If the drug were in the food and water, why weren't they and the other doctors in the room knocked out like Alan? Maybe it was the yellow pill. Maybe it was only given to guests on their second cruise. Maybe it was the combination of the capsule and whatever was put in the food . . .

"Quite an affair last night," said Ned interrupting Adam's thoughts.

Adam nodded.

"I'm exhausted," said Clair. "I didn't think I'd drunk as much as I must have. I slept like the dead."

"Same with me," said Ned. "Must be the salt air."

Trying to sound casual, Adam said, "Have you people been given any yellow capsules for seasickness?"

"I haven't," said Ned, sipping his coffee. He looked at Clair.

"Nor have I," she said. "Why do you ask?"

"Well, I'm looking for an anti-nauseant. I just wondered . . ." He let his voice trail off, not wanting to arouse their suspicion. If he mentioned anything about the doctors being drugged, they would think he was crazy. Ned and Clair drank their coffee in silence. Obviously, neither of them felt very well.

After breakfast Adam stopped at the ship's store. It had a new supply of Dramamine and anti-motion patches. Adam bought some of the patches, and before he left he remembered to pick up ten dollars' worth of Marlboros for José.

Back in his cabin he found another yellow capsule with a glass of water on his night table. This time he flushed both down the toilet.

The first lecture of the morning was scheduled for the large auditorium. Given by a Columbia pathologist, it was stultifyingly dull. Adam noticed that a number of the doctors were dozing and wondered whether it was because they were bored or drugged. The second lecture was given by Dr. Goddard and was far more interesting. Adam noticed a number of the doctors straightening up in their chairs. Goddard was summarizing a recent experiment that showed that fetal tissue that was injected into adults was not rejected. The guess was that the fetal tissue had not developed antigens strong enough to elicit an antibody response. The potential for the therapy was immense. Repopulating islet cells in the pancreases of diabetics was only one of the revolutionary possibilities.

At the coffee break, Adam went back to his stateroom, got the cartons of Marlboros, and headed up to the promenade deck. He waited until no one seemed to be around, then walked up to the barrier and stepped through the door. José was waiting. He had a canvas bag over his shoulder and the cartons disappeared into it in a flash. At least he's not drugged, thought Adam, and he handed back José's ten-dollar bill.

Confused, the sailor examined the bill, thinking something was wrong with it.

"I have a deal you can't refuse," said Adam. "I'll get you cigarettes if you get me food and water."

José raised his eyebrows. "What's the matter with the food back there? I thought it was pretty fancy."

"Part of the deal is no questions," said Adam. "I won't ask you what you do with so many cigarettes, and you don't ask me what I do with the food."

"Fine by me," said José. "When do you want to meet again?"

"At four this afternoon, but I'd like some food now."

José glanced over his shoulder, then told Adam to follow him. They walked forward to a bulkhead door, which José opened. Making sure they were alone, José led Adam down to his cabin in the bowels of the ship. It was like a jail cell. There was a shower and a toilet with no door and the air was heavy with the odor of sweat and stale cigarettes.

José told Adam to make himself comfortable, laughing at his own joke as he went out the door. Adam eyed the bunk and sat down on it.

Within five minutes José returned with a paper bag full of food, including bread, cheese, fruit and juice. He handed the parcel to Adam, who pointed at an empty container in the corner of the room which he asked José to fill at the sink.

"Do you have the same water as the rest of the ship?" asked Adam.

"I don't know," said José. "I'm not an engineer." He opened the door and peered out. "We have to be careful. There are some people who wouldn't like the fact that we are doing business."

Adam took the hint and scuttled back to his cabin, where he opened his suitcase and hid the food. He put the two juice containers into the closet and covered them with a soiled shirt. Checking his watch, he realized he was late for the third lecture and hurried back.

///

Stretched out on an examining table in the Julian Clinic, Jennifer was amazed at her own calm. Deciding whether or not to repeat the amniocentesis had been far harder than the actual return to the hospital. Dr. Vandermer had scheduled her for an early appointment, and she and her mother were waiting for his arrival. He didn't keep them long, but he looked so haggard, Jennifer decided the amniocentesis mix-up had worse ramifications for him than for herself. Vandermer's face was puffy and his speech brief and halting, yet he performed the procedure even more smoothly than the first time. The only problem for Jennifer was that she felt her child move soon after the needle had been placed. It frightened her, but Dr. Vandermer assured her that there was no cause for alarm.

Afterward, Jennifer sat up on the table and said, "I guess I don't have to tell you to contact me as soon as you learn anything."

"No, you don't," he said. "I'm taking personal interest in how the laboratory handles this. You try to relax, and don't worry."

"I'll try," said Jennifer. She appreciated the attention Dr. Vandermer was giving her, but she wished he didn't look so serious. It made her more nervous than she already was.

///

At lunch Adam bought another ten dollars' worth of cigarettes and took them back to his cabin. On his way out, he decided to check again on Alan.

The door was still unlocked, but when Adam opened it, Alan was gone! Adam checked the bathroom, thinking that perhaps the man had collapsed there, but the cabin was completely empty. Adam was certain that the man he'd seen before breakfast was in no shape to go for a walk. But it was possible he had improved, and Adam hoped that was the explanation. Yet it was also possible that he had been taken out, and the implications of that were frightening. One way or another, Adam felt it was important to find Alan.

He first checked the dining room, then the sun deck, where an outdoor grill had been set up for hamburgers and hot dogs. A number of passengers were stretched out on deck chairs, sleeping. Adam walked back through the empty conference rooms and made his way down to the gym and doctor's office. A sign on the door said: "For Emergency, See Steward."

Adam was getting more and more anxious. He had to calm down or someone would notice and become suspicious. He decided to go back to the dining room. He wouldn't eat, but he'd watch the other doctors.

As soon as he found his table, he realized that the girl on his right was the brunette dancer he'd admired the night before. She was dressed in a demure suit and could have been mistaken for a passenger.

Gazing around the room, Adam spotted a number of other dancers. Feeling a tug on his sleeve, he turned his attention to the brunette next to him.

"My name is Heather," she said in that oddly inflectionless voice Adam was beginning to associate with the cruise. She didn't offer her last name.

The other guests at the table seemed to be concentrating on their meal. A bowl of savory minestrone was placed in front of Adam. As he pretended to eat a little, Heather rewarded him with her undivided attention. Adam kept nodding and smiling until she finally said, "You're not eating much."

Adam, who had been toying with his food, said simply, "I'm afraid I've been seasick." It was the only excuse that came to mind.

"It's better to eat," said Heather. "Strangely enough, an empty stomach is more vulnerable."

"Really?" said Adam evasively. Then as an afterthought, he added, "You haven't eaten much yourself."

Heather laughed a high-pitched, grating laugh. "That's a problem of being a dancer. I always have to watch my weight."

Adam nodded. He knew from Jennifer that dancers were obsessed with their weight.

"Would you like me to come to your cabin tonight?" Heather asked as casually as she would if inquiring about the weather.

Adam was glad he hadn't been eating. If he'd had anything in his mouth, he would have choked. As it was, he coughed and glanced around to see if anyone else had heard, but his fellow guests just continued eating in their silent half-stupor. Adam turned to Heather. Although her voice was strange, she certainly didn't seem drugged. Adam decided to play along. She might be able to answer some questions about this increasingly odd cruise.

"Come after your last performance," he whispered.

"I'll be in your cabin at eleven," she agreed enthusiastically.

Adam turned beet red. Fortunately, the other diners seemed too out of it to notice. With a quick smile Adam nodded to her.

He went down to his cabin and hastily ate some of José's bread and cheese. At the afternoon lecture Adam noticed more and more empty seats. There was no sign of Alan, though later on Adam caught up with Ned and Clair. They smiled but hadn't seen Alan and had very little to say. Adam guessed they were receiving low dosages of tranquilizers. By the third lecture, a good number of people in the audience were asleep, and Adam was convinced it wasn't just because they were bored.

At four he left and went to meet José. Maybe the sailor would have an idea where Alan might be found.

"I'd like to talk," said Adam when José let him through the barrier.

"What's the matter?" asked José.

"Nothing," said Adam. "I'd just like to ask you some questions."

José led him back to his cabin and shut the door. From an upright locker he produced two glasses and a bottle of dark rum. Adam declined, but José filled both glasses anyway. "What's on your mind?" he said.

"Have you been around the entire ship?" asked Adam.

José downed his rum in a single gulp. "Nope," he said, wiping his mouth with the back of his hand. "Not all of it. I haven't seen where all those pricks with the white coats berth."

"I thought they lived up here with the crew," said Adam.

"What, are you crazy?" asked José. "We never see those weird guys. They have cabins on C deck."

"Where is that? I thought B was the lowest deck."

José lifted the second glass. "You sure you don't want some rum?" Adam shook his head.

"The stairs to the stewards' quarters are in the passengers' mess," said José, sipping the second drink. "The only reason I know that is because I went there looking for something to eat one day when we were in port. Unfortunately, I got caught and I almost lost my job. But what do you care about those guys?"

"The reason I'm asking these questions," explained Adam, "is because a passenger in the room next to mine seems to have disappeared. First he seemed ill, and now he's vanished."

"Did you try the sick bay?" asked José. "One of the crew told me they have a fully equipped hospital. He knew because he helped bring in the equipment."

"Where is it?" asked Adam.

"On B deck," said José. "Behind the doctor's office."

Adam picked up the food José had wrapped for him. The sick bay sounded like a promising place to find Alan.

"What about more cigarettes?" asked José.

"Sure," said Adam. "Tomorrow morning. Same time."

"Sounds good," said José. "Let me check the hall." He put down his empty glass and started to open the door.

"One more question," said Adam. "Do you know anything about the dancers?"

José looked back at Adam with a broad smile. "Not as much as I'd like to know."

"Are they prostitutes?" asked Adam, thinking it would be good to know for sure before Heather's visit.

José shook his head, laughing. "No, they're college girls working for extra credit. What kind of question is that?"

"Do you ever get to see them?" asked Adam.

"I wish," said José. "Listen, they never let us mingle with those weirdos who run the cruise. But I did see one of the girls on a beach in Puerto Rico about a year ago. I tried to get some action, but she wasn't interested. I was pretty drunk and tried to grab her. That's when I found out she was wearing a wig. It came off, and her head was shaved. On either temple there were big round scars. Now tell me that isn't weird."

"What had happened to her?" asked Adam.

"I never found out," said José. "She kneed me and suddenly I lost interest."

"What a cruise," said Adam, picking up his parcel.

"What's the matter?" asked José. "You're not enjoying yourself?"

/ / /

When the phone rang, Jennifer had a premonition it was Dr. Vandermer. She heard her mother answer and then a moment later give a little shriek. That was when Jennifer knew. She started downstairs before her mother could call her. When she reached the kitchen, Mrs. Carson wordlessly held out the receiver.

"Hello, Dr. Vandermer," Jennifer said, controlling her voice.

"Hello, Jennifer," he said. There was a long pause. "I'm afraid I have bad news."

"I expected it," she said. She could sense that Dr. Vandermer was struggling to find the right words.

"The amniocentesis is definitely positive," he said. "This time I supervised the straining of the amniotic fluid myself. There was no chance of error. The same major chromosomal abnormality is there. In fact, the specimens were never mixed up. I'm afraid that in addition to Down's syndrome, your fetus must have significant developmental abnormality of its sex organs."

"Oh God," said Jennifer. "That's terrible."

"It is," agreed Dr. Vandermer. "Look, if we are going to do something, I think we should act quickly."

"I agree. I've thought it over carefully, and I want to have an abortion. The sooner the better."

"In that case I'll try to arrange it for tomorrow."

"Thank you, Dr. Vandermer," said Jennifer. Then she hung up.

Mrs. Carson put her arms around her daughter and said, "I know how you must feel, but I believe you are doing the right thing."

"I know I am. I just want to talk to Adam."

Mrs. Carson's mouth tightened angrily.

"Mother, he's still my husband, and I don't want to do this without telling him."

"Well, dear, whatever you think best." Her mother left the kitchen and went upstairs, probably to complain about Adam to her husband on the other phone.

As soon as she was alone, Jennifer dialed the apartment just in case Adam had returned. She let it ring twenty times before hanging up and dialing information for Arolen Pharmaceuticals in Montclair, New Jersey. When the Arolen switchboard answered, she demanded to speak to Clarence McGuire. She wasn't put through until she'd had a shouting match with his secretary.

"How are you, Mrs. Schonberg?" McGuire said when he finally came on the line.

"Not very well," said Jennifer coldly. "I want to know where my husband is."

"I'm sorry, but I don't know myself. He called in and said he had to go out of town because of family problems."

"You wouldn't lie to me, would you?" asked Jennifer. "I thought you'd sent him to Puerto Rico."

"He turned down the offer," said McGuire. "And there's no reason for me to lie to you."

Jennifer hung up feeling confused. She'd been so certain that Adam was on a trip for Arolen and hadn't wanted to tell her, she had trouble conceiving of any other possibility. Impulsively, she placed a call to Adam's father.

"I'm sorry to bother you, Dr. Schonberg," said Jennifer, who'd never called the man before, "but I'm looking for Adam and I thought you might know where he is."

"I haven't the slightest idea," said Dr. Schonberg, "and you of all people should know that."

Jennifer hung up the phone as her mother came back into the kitchen. She must have overheard Jennifer's conversation with McGuire. "Better not tell your father this," she said. "He already thinks Adam is having an affair."

///

Adam was nervous. He'd been handed another yellow capsule about six o'clock, and the stewards were watching him carefully during dinner. Afraid that they were realizing he was avoiding their treatment, Adam resorted to hiding food in his napkin to make it look like he was eating. As soon as he could, he left the dining room. On the way back to his cabin he checked out the infirmary. It was an impressive setup with a full operating room and fancy radiological equipment. But there were no patients in the small ward.

As he passed Alan's room, he opened the door, expecting to see an empty cabin. To his surprise, Alan was in bed and in essentially the same condition as he'd been in before his disappearance. Adam roused him. Alan seemed to know where he was but insisted he had never left his room. Adam eased him back onto the bed and returned to his own cabin.

Coming on the cruise to discover why Vandermer had changed his position on pregdolen had seemed like a good idea in the safety of New York. Now Adam only wanted to get home safe and sound to his wife. He remembered someone explaining to him that the reason Arolen sent the doctors on a cruise was to get them away from their usual cares. But drugging them so they didn't know what they were doing was more than extreme. It was terrifying.

A knock on Adam's door sent his pulse racing. He hoped it wasn't the blank-faced steward with another pill.

"Oh God," said Adam when he saw it was Heather.

"I'm so glad they let me off the last set," she said, coming in and looking about the small cabin. She was wearing a see-through blouse and what must have been the shortest skirt Adam had ever seen. She did have a marvelous figure. I'm crazy, thought Adam, unable to take his eyes off her. How on earth would he go about explaining this scene to Jennifer?

"Heather, why don't you sit down so I can talk with you?"

Heather stopped the little dance she was doing about the room. "Sure," she said, dropping onto the bed next to Adam and pressing her bare thigh against his leg. With two dainty kicks she sent her high heels across the room.

"What would you like to talk about?"

"You," said Adam, finding it difficult not to look down at the curve of her breasts.

"I'd rather talk about you," said Heather, putting her arms around his neck.

"That's what you told me at lunch," said Adam, gently pushing her away, "but I really want to get to know you."

"There's not a whole lot to tell," insisted Heather.

"Look, this isn't a run-of-the-mill job for a young girl. How did you happen to end up here?"

Heather didn't answer. At first Adam believed she was thinking, but when he looked at her, she appeared to be in a trance.

"Heather?" said Adam, waving his hand in front of her eyes.

"Yes," she said, blinking.

"I asked you a question."

"Oh, yeah. How did I end up on the *Fjord?* Well, it's a long story. I was a secretary at Arolen Pharmaceuticals in New Jersey. They liked me and offered me a job with MTIC in Puerto Rico. I started as a secretary there, too, but then they found out I liked to dance, so I got this job."

That explained the dancing, thought Adam, but not the prostitution, if she actually was a prostitute. Adam was willing to give her the benefit of the doubt.

"Are you enjoying yourself on the cruise?" Heather asked, changing the subject.

"I'm having a wonderful time," said Adam.

"I'm going to make it even better," promised Heather. "But first I have a present for you."

"Really," said Adam.

"You wait right here." Getting up, she went over to the little purse she'd put on the desk. When she turned around, Adam saw she was holding out two more of the yellow capsules. He felt a twinge of panic.

"Could you get me some fruit juice from the closet?" he asked. "I can't stand the water."

"OK," said Heather agreeably. She put the pills down on the desk and fetched the juice. Removing the top of the container, she handed it to Adam, who palmed the pills and dropped them behind the bed when she put the juice back.

"Now I'm really going to make you enjoy this cruise," she said, sitting on his lap.

"Wait just a second," said Adam, avoiding her lips. "What were the capsules you just gave me?"

"It was for enjoyment," said Heather. "To make you relax and forget your troubles."

"Do you take them?" asked Adam.

"No," said Heather with her high-pitched laugh. "I don't have any troubles."

"What makes you think I do?" asked Adam.

"All the doctors have troubles," said Heather.

"Do you visit all the doctors?" asked Adam. "You and the other dancers?"

"No," said Heather. "Just the ones Mr. Powell and Dr. Goddard tell us to see."

"And they told you to see me?"

Heather nodded.

"Do you know why?"

"Because you haven't relaxed enough," said Heather petulantly. "Aren't you interested in me?"

"Yes, indeed," said Adam. He bent her head and kissed her, while his fingers probed her hairline to see if she was wearing a wig. She wasn't, but as he rubbed the skin above her temples he felt little ridged lines.

"Heather, I want to ask you a question. Are those scars?"

"I don't think so," said Heather, sounding annoyed. "Where?"

"Along your temples," said Adam. Gently, he turned her head to one side and separated her hair so he could see. There were small scars, about a centimeter long, just as José had described.

Heather raised her hand and felt the spot. Then she shrugged.

"Do you have any idea how you got those?" asked Adam.

"No," said Heather. "And what's more, I don't care."

"I'm sorry if I'm not much fun," said Adam. "I guess I'm just too relaxed."

Heather looked disappointed. "Maybe I should have waited to give you the capsules."

"Will Mr. Powell be pleased that I've finally forgotten my worries?" asked Adam.

Heather nodded, gently rubbing his shoulders.

"Why does Mr. Powell care if I'm relaxed?" asked Adam.

"So you can go to the instruction room," said Heather.

Adam stared at the girl. She caught his glance and said quickly, "Are you sure you're too relaxed?"

"Absolutely," said Adam. "Do you know where this instruction room is?"

"Of course. In fact I'm supposed to take you there. But not until you're ready."

"I've never been this relaxed before," said Adam, allowing his arms to go limp. "Why don't you take me now?"

Instead of answering, Heather seemed to go into another trance. A few minutes later she picked up the conversation as if she were unaware of the pause. "I could take you to the instruction room if you take another pill. I'm supposed to make sure you fall asleep."

"Give it to me," said Adam. "I can hardly keep my eyes open now."

It was curious how easy it was to fool Heather. Like the steward, she seemed almost childlike in her trust. After a while Adam lay back and closed his eyes. Ten minutes later, Heather helped him to his feet and guided him out the door. They went back to the central stairs, climbed to the main deck, and entered the dining room. Just beyond one of the doors to the side of the podium was a pantry with table-cloths, flatware, and trays. To the right was another door that opened onto a stairway that descended deep into the ship. Adam guessed it led to C deck.

As they went down, they passed several stewards coming up. Adam tried to avoid their eyes. He didn't want anyone to notice that he was faking his sedation.

When they reached the bottom of the stairs, they went down a long hall to a pair of double doors.

"Stuart Smyth," said Heather to the steward who was guarding the entrance. "He's a repeat."

"Bench 47," said the steward, handing Heather something that looked like a credit card. She and Adam went inside.

When Adam's eyes adjusted to the dark, he saw he was in what appeared to be the lobby of a theater. Peering over the chest-high wall, he saw a movie screen. There was no sound, but he thought he saw images of doctors flickering in the dark.

A steward took the card from Heather and without a word grasped Adam by the arm and pulled him into the theater. Even in the dark Adam could see that the seats were very different from those in a regular movie house. Each one looked like a miniature electric chair with a myriad of electrodes and straps. There were fifteen to twenty seats in each row and more than twenty rows.

Holding his arm in an uncomfortably firm grip, the steward led Adam down the center aisle. Adam was shocked to see that the doctors were stark naked and were restrained by leather straps. They all wore helmets fitted with earphones and surface electrodes for stimulation. They all seemed to be heavily drugged, like Alan, to a point between sleeping and wakefulness. More wires snaked around their bodies and were attached with needle electrodes to various nerve sites.

The steward stopped by an empty chair in the front row. Then he inserted the card into a slot on the side of the chair and started to adjust the wires.

Adam was almost afraid to breathe. He felt as if he'd been dropped into a horror movie. Glancing up at the huge screen, he saw the image of a doctor offering a patient a generic brand of medicine. The moment the name flashed on the screen, the doctor's face contorted in pain and he dropped the bottle. At the same time Adam heard an eerie wail rise from the doctors in the room. Then the doctor on the screen reached for an Arolen product and a broad smile crossed his face. Adam glanced at the doctor next to him and saw that he, too, was smiling blissfully.

Watching the steward position the straps, Adam realized he was seeing the very latest in mind-control techniques involving adverse conditioning and positive reinforcing. As more clinical situations were enacted on the screen, Adam saw the faces of the doctors near him contorting in either pain or pleasure, depending on the circumstances projected.

My God, thought Adam, I'm in a nightmare where the doctor has become the patient! No wonder Vandermer had changed his mind about pregdolen. And to think he is in charge of Jennifer!

The steward began unbuttoning Adam's shirt, and the touch of his fingers made Adam aware of his own vulnerability. He wasn't an observer. They meant to wire him up and subject him to the same treatment.

Studying the blank face of the steward as he awkwardly struggled with the buttons, Adam realized the man was drugged like the doctors, just less heavily. In fact, Adam decided, all the stewards must be drugged. Maybe some had even had psychosurgery, as Adam suspected Heather had.

A sequence that condemned unnecessary surgery came on the screen. Apparently, MTIC wanted to do more than simply brainwash the doctors into prescribing Arolen products.

The steward had taken off Adam's shirt and was fumbling with his belt.

"Do you know what you are doing?" rasped Adam, unable to remain silent any longer.

"We are helping the doctors learn," said the steward, taken aback by Adam's unexpected question.

"At what cost?" said Adam, grabbing the man's wrist.

Slowly but with great strength, the steward peeled Adam's fingers off his arm. Adam was amazed at the man's strength in light of the amount of drugs he'd undoubtedly been given.

"Please," said the steward. "You must cooperate." He lifted the helmet device with the intention of slipping it over the top of Adam's head.

Knowing surprise was his only weapon, Adam snatched the helmet and jammed it down on the steward's head. Grasping the mass of wires, Adam wrapped them around the man's neck, then turned and fled, hoping the steward would be unable to shout before Adam could get out of the room.

As Adam ran up the central aisle, the doctors issued another anguished wail, sending a new spike of terror down his spine. He rushed for the door, bursting into the hallway at full speed. As he shot by the guard in the booth, the man gave a shout.

Adam raced up the stairs to the main deck so quickly that he almost fell. A steward coming down reached out a hand to help, but he made no attempt to stop Adam.

In the dining room Adam had to choose whether or not to go farther up. He decided he would, since the areas below made him claustrophobic. Running past the lecture halls, he heard a series of bells. Then the ship's PA system crackled to life.

"Now hear this. Passenger Smyth is in distress and must be detained."

Pausing at the top of the stairs, Adam began to shake with fright. Desperately, he tried to control his panic and think of a place to hide. The various lockers and closets seemed to obvious. Besides, he'd be trapped. He continued up another flight of stairs. As he passed the promenade deck, he heard men shouting on the level below.

Gripped by terror, he emerged on the sun deck and ran by the swimming pool. Suddenly the imposing white smokestack loomed in front of him. He could see a metal ladder set into the near side. Without thinking, he grabbed the lowest rung and began climbing. As he rose from the shelter of the deck the wind buffeted his naked chest. He had gone about fifty feet when he heard his pursuers on the sun deck below. Imagining a spotlight pinning him against the white wall, Adam closed his eyes with fear.

After several seconds had passed with no shout of discovery, Adam hazarded a downward glance. Several stewards were methodically lifting the canvas covers of the lifeboats and opening the various lockers. At least they hadn't guessed his hiding spot, but seeing how high he was above the deck made him dizzy. When he looked up, it wasn't any better. The stars seemed to be careening back and forth across the sky.

After a few minutes Adam looked down again. Several stewards were milling about at the base of the stack. Despite his fear of heights, Adam began inching his way farther up the ladder. He estimated that he had another twenty-five feet or so before the top.

Just below the top on either side of the stack were two dark openings, each about the size of a man. He decided to see if he could hide in one. Trying to keep his mind off the possibility of falling, Adam reached the openings. Within each was a metal grate floor.

Knowing he couldn't remain in his exposed position any longer, he grasped the edge of the opening on the left and worked his foot over to the lip. Suspended between the ladder and the opening, he almost lost his nerve. It was a long drop to the deck. Marshaling his courage, he let go of the ladder and pulled himself inside the stack.

Adam walked around on the catwalk inside of the smokestack once he'd regained his balance. He had no idea what the space could be used for, but he was happy it was there. Feeling more secure now that no one could see him, he began trying to figure out what to do next. The image of those doctors moaning in pain haunted him. Now he understood what Vandermer and Foley had endured.

Remembering Dr. Goddard's lecture about Arolen's interest in fetology, he realized the company must have a growing need for fetal tissue. He suddenly knew why the Julian Clinic had such an active amniocentesis program. The mix-up with Jennifer's specimen was probably not an accident. Adam broke into a cold sweat. What if they talked Jennifer into repeating the amniocentesis before he got back to New York!

Adam sank to his knees. If he had only run forward, he might have gotten to the crew's quarters and somehow used the radio. No, he thought, that was pure fantasy. He was trying to think how he could get back to the deck when there was a thud against the outside of the stack.

Carefully Adam pulled himself to the edge of the opening and looked over the rim. About halfway up the ladder was a steward. Adam panicked again. He was trapped. Maybe the man would not climb into the opening, but that seemed unlikely.

Adam could hear the man's labored breathing, and a second later a hand gripped the rim, followed by a foot and then the steward himself. Adam waited until the man was silhouetted against the opening, his arms apart for balance. Lunging forward, Adam used both hands to grab the man's head and ram it as hard as he could against the steel plate of the chimney. Adam had to grab the steward's jacket to keep him from tumbling backward out of the opening.

He pulled him in and allowed the man to crumble onto the catwalk. He bent down to look at the man's head. At least there was no blood.

Pulling the steward into a sitting position, Adam struggled to remove the man's shirt and white jacket. The bow tie was easy to take off, since it was just a clip-on. Standing up, Adam tried on the clothes. They were big but serviceable. Buttoning the top button of the shirt, he put on the bow tie. Stepping over the man, Adam sighted down the ladder, deciding that he'd better leave before the man regained consciousness. Adam figured his best bet was to hide in the crew's quarters.

He was halfway down the ladder when a number of stewards appeared on the deck below. He'd just have to bluff his way through. When he got to the deck, he straightened his tie, smoothed his jacket, and started forward.

He had to fight the urge to run as he passed one of the stewards who was checking deck-chair lockers near the main stairs. Fortunately, the stairway itself was empty, and Adam reached the promenade deck otherwise unobserved. The rest of the stewards had dispersed, no doubt searching for him in other parts of the ship. Adam exited on the starboard side and walked forward. As he slipped through the door in the barricade, he realized his disguise might make him look suspicious in that part of the ship. Pulling off the jacket, he threw it overboard.

Moving quickly, Adam walked to the door that he'd entered with José. Opening the door, he looked down a corridor illuminated by bare light bulbs which threw grotesque shadows on the walls. From the far end of the hall, Adam heard voices and the clink of cutlery. He guessed it was the crew's mess.

Moving as silently as the metal floor would allow, Adam tiptoed to José's door and knocked. There was no answer. He tried the knob, which turned easily, then stepped inside, quickly closing the door behind him.

Unfortunately, there was no light in the room. He ran his fingers along the wall by the door but didn't encounter any switches. Cautiously, he advanced farther into the room, trying to recall the floor plan. He remembered there was a lamp fixed to the wall above the suspended bed.

Suddenly a hand came out of the blackness and grabbed Adam by the throat.

"José!" he gasped before the hand tightened its grip, cutting off his air. Adam was just about to pass out when the grip on his neck loosened. There was a click, and light filled the room. José was standing in front of Adam, looking at him with disgust.

"Are you trying to get yourself killed?" he asked, taking his hand away and sitting on the edge of the bed.

"I knocked," Adam managed to say, rubbing his throat. "You didn't answer."

"I was fucking asleep," said José.

"I'm sorry," said Adam, "but it was an emergency."

"One of the college girls after you?" asked José sarcastically.

"Not quite," said Adam. "It's the weirdos in the white jackets."

"What the hell do they want with you?" asked José.

"You wouldn't believe me if I told you. But there's a chance for you to make some money. Does that interest you?"

"Money always interests me," said José. "What do you have in mind?"

"When do we get to St. Thomas?"

"What time is it?"

Adam looked at his watch. "One-thirty."

"In four or five hours. Something like that."

"Well, I need to stay hidden until we dock, and then I'll have to sneak off the ship."

José wiped his face with the back of his hand. "What kind of money are we talking about?"

Adam took out his wallet and counted the cash. All told, he had close to three hundred dollars.

"I'll need some for a taxi, but two hundred seventy-five is yours," said Adam.

José raised his eyebrows. "I can't guarantee anything, but I'll give it a try. If you get caught, though, I'll swear we never met."

Adam handed over a hundred dollars. "You'll get the rest when I get ashore."

José nodded agreement and went over to his locker. He pulled out a pair of grease-stained khaki trousers and a torn flannel shirt. Tossing them to Adam, he said, "Put them on and you pass for crew. I got a couple of friends who hate the stewards as much as I do. Maybe they'll help. You stay here. No one should bother you."

Adam tried to tell José how much he appreciated his help, but José stopped him and said the money was all he wanted. Then he pulled on a pair of pants and left the room.

Adam put on the filthy clothes and stashed his own in the back of the locker. Then he looked at himself in the mirror above the sink. He looked terrible, but for once he appreciated his rapid-growing beard. He certainly no longer looked like one of the passengers.

The door opened again and Adam almost fainted, but it was only José.

"Next time, why don't you knock," Adam said.

"Hey, this is my fucking cabin," said José irritably.

Adam couldn't argue that point.

José sat back down on the bed. "I just talked to a friend of mine about getting you off the ship. He knows a way. Seems he used it himself one day when the crew wasn't supposed to go ashore in St. Thomas. The problem is that it requires all your money up front. I got to pay off two other guys."

Adam shook his head.

"Listen," said José, "if you're not happy with the arrangement, why don't you leave?"

Adam got the point. He didn't have any leverage at all. If José wanted to, he could take the money by force.

With a sigh of resignation, Adam pulled out his wallet. Keeping twenty-five dollars for himself, he handed the rest to José.

"You act as if you're doing me a favor," the sailor said, stuffing the notes into his pocket. "But let me tell you, we wouldn't be sticking our necks out for this kind of money except we hate those steward bastards."

"I appreciate it," said Adam, wondering what the chances were that José was just taking him for a ride.

"You can hide here for the rest of the night. In the morning, after we dock, I'll come and get you. Understand?"

Adam nodded. "Can you give me an idea of your plans?"

José smiled. "I'd rather let that be a surprise. You make yourself comfortable and don't worry about a thing."

Adam could hear José laughing as he closed the door.

Looking at his watch, Adam guessed that it was going to be a long night. He thought he was much too tense to sleep, but after a while he drifted off. He didn't know how many hours had passed when he was awakened by loud shouts in the corridor. Adam recognized the voice at once.

"In this part of the ship, I am in command, and no one is going to search without my permission." It was the captain speaking.

A deeper voice responded, "I'm in charge of the ship, so please let me through."

Adam thought it might have been Raymond Powell.

Other voices began shouting, and Adam could hear doors being opened and slammed shut.

In panic, Adam glanced around the tiny room for someplace to hide. There was nowhere. Even the locker was too narrow to squeeze into. Then he had an idea. He pulled his hair forward over his forehead and yanked the grease-stained pants down around his ankles. Hobbling over to the exposed toilet, he sat down. A *Penthouse* magazine was laying next to the toilet, and he picked it up and put it on his lap. In a couple of minutes he heard a key in the lock and the door swung open.

Adam looked up. A steward was standing in the doorway. Adam saw Mr. Powell right behind him and heard Captain Nordstrom, who was still protesting. Powell gave Adam a look of disgust and moved on. The steward slammed the door behind him.

For a moment, Adam didn't move. He could hear the group noisily moving farther down the corridor. Finally, he stood up and pulled up his pants. Taking the *Penthouse* over to the bunk, he tried to read but was too scared the search party would return. In the end, he fell back to sleep until a loud banging announced the ship had docked. It was five-fifteen.

The next hour and a quarter were the longest in Adam's life. People would occasionally pass in the passageway, and each time Adam was sure they were coming to find him.

At six-thirty José came back.

"Everything is ready," he said, going over to the locker and getting out the bottle of dark rum. "First, I think you better have a drink."

"Do you think I need it?"

"Yup," said José as he handed Adam a glass. "I would take it if I were you."

Adam took a small sip, but the liquor was rough and bitter. He shook his head and handed the glass back to José. Unconcerned, José tossed it down.

Returning the bottle to the locker, José rubbed his hands. "Your name's Angel in case someone asks. But I don't think you'll have to do much talking."

José opened the door to the corridor and motioned Adam to follow him.

CHAPTER **14**

Jennifer had a restless night and was in the kitchen when the phone rang at seven forty-five. She answered it quickly, thinking that her parents were still sleeping, but her mother had already picked up.

"I've got it, mother," said Jennifer when she heard Dr. Vander-mer's voice.

"Good morning, Jennifer," he said. "We're all set to take you at three-thirty. I'm sorry it's so late, but we're so busy we had trouble even fitting you in. Just stick to clear liquids and by tonight it will be all over and you can order whatever you want for dinner."

"OK," said Jennifer without much feeling. "How long will I be staying?"

"Probably just overnight. I'll explain things to you when you are here."

"What time should I check in?"

"Why not drive over later this morning? That way we can do the routine admission work. And if the surgical schedule lightens up, maybe we can take you earlier. Meanwhile, just relax and let me worry about the details."

Jennifer made herself some coffee and walked out into the garden. For a moment she had second thoughts, but then she decided she was doing the right thing. Both Dr. Vandermer and her parents felt she had no other choice. She just wished Adam was there to share in the decision.

/ / /

Adam followed José, trying to make himself as unobtrusive as possible. They walked the length of the passageway, passing the mess, and descended a steep flight of stairs. The crew members they encountered seemed to take Adam's presence for granted. Even so, it was a nerve-racking experience for Adam. He kept expecting someone to recognize him and sound the alarm.

When they reached the lowest level, they began to walk aft down a narrow corridor that was lined with pipes and smelled of diesel fuel. They passed rooms filled with machines, which Adam guessed were the generators. A number of men were working there, stripped to their waists, their bodies glistening with sweat. The noise was deafening.

They walked until they came to a large dark room filled with painted metal dumpsters on casters that stank from the garbage they contained. José went in and guided Adam to the far corner, where two men were sitting on the floor playing blackjack. As José approached, the larger fellow glanced up and then went back to his game.

"Hit me easylike," he said to the smaller man as José squatted down.

In the wall behind the player was a wide opening through which Adam could see a portion of the bustling pier. A swath of radiant sunlight, which looked heavenly in the hellish surroundings, slanted into the room.

"Hallelujah," he muttered as he moved over to the lower door, shielding his eyes from the intensity of the tropical sun. He felt so close to land—and freedom. Never mind that he still didn't see how he'd get there. He glanced outside at the concrete pier again and his elation vanished. To his immediate right was a passenger gangway carefully guarded by a brace of white-jacketed stewards who were carefully screening anyone leaving the ship.

"José, there's no way I can walk out there without being stopped," said Adam, trying to control his voice.

Without looking up from the card game, José said, "Just wait."

Adam stood there for a few minutes, wondering what to do.

"José," he said, "is this how you're getting me off the ship?" He nodded toward the gangway.

"Nope," said José, "the best is yet to come."

"What are you planning?" said Adam angrily.

José didn't answer. Going back to the opening, Adam stared longingly at the green hills rising gently from the harbor. They were dotted with small cottages. He was about to question José again when a line of yellow garbage trucks started down the pier, belching diesel smoke from vertical exhaust pipes. They came to a halt not far from the ship's side, one behind the other. Then there was a fearful blast of an air horn.

The cardplayers cursed, threw down their cards, and went over to the nearest dumpster. With the big fellow pushing and the other two pulling, they rolled it down the ramp and up to the lead truck. While the men returned for another dumpster, the truck went to work. Large hydraulic arms came forward and grabbed the dumpster, lifting it high over the truck's cab and dumping the contents in back. It was all done very neatly because the dumpster had a metal lid that did not open until the last moment. By the time the dumpster was slammed back onto the concrete, José and the others had the next one out on the quay. After a few more loads had been swallowed by the truck, José shouted to Adam, "OK, come over here."

Adam followed him to the next dumpster in line.

"You're going out with the trash," said José. The three men began to laugh.

"You want me to get into that?" asked Adam with horror.

"You've no time to argue," said José. "This is the last load for the first truck."

"Is this the only way off the ship?" asked Adam.

"The only way," said the huskier cardplayer. "I did it myself once. Not the fanciest way to ride around town, but it ain't crowded."

"Where will it take me?" asked Adam, considering what he should do if he went through with their plan.

"Right out to a landfill near the airport."

"Jesus," said Adam. "Why didn't you tell me you were going to send me out with the garbage."

"This ain't garbage," said the cardplayer. "We dump that into the ocean. This is trash."

The truck's air horn impatiently sounded.

"You have to go," said José. "You can't hang around my cabin forever. Put your foot here." He made a platform of his hands and, against his better judgment, Adam used it as a step. The big cardplayer lifted the dumpster's lid, and with a swift movement José tossed Adam headfirst into the mess of boxes, paper, waxed containers, and other debris. And contrary to what the cardplayer had said, there was garbage, too. The lid banged down, and Adam was plunged into darkness. He felt the dumpster roll down the ramp onto the pier. Then there was a violent jolt and Adam visualized his rise from the ground. The dumpster shook, tilted upside down, and with a flash of light Adam screamed and flew into the back of the truck. He ended up on his hands and knees, covered with trash.

Almost at once the truck began to roll. It was well away from the pier before Adam worked his head clear of the trash. The junk cushioned his ride, and he was not disturbed by the bumpy road. But after a few minutes the tropical sun turned the truck's metal shell into a broiling oven. Adam began to sweat, and by the time the truck got to the landfill he didn't care what happened to him as long as he could get out. He was dimly aware of a diesel whining beneath him as the back of the truck began to lift. A moment later he shot onto an enormous pile of trash. He got to his feet in time to see his truck lumber away.

No one had seen him leave the ship. He was safe. Looking about, he could see the tiny island airport two hundred yards to his right. To his left, the blue Caribbean stretched as far as he could see.

Dusting himself off as best he could, Adam started walking to the terminal.

The airport was a casual affair with an entrance crowded with colorfully painted taxis. As Adam started inside, he saw a group of tourists eyeing him nervously. It was clear that he could not casually buy a ticket unless he did something about his appearance. Ducking into a small store, he charged a pair of jeans and a tee shirt that cheerfully proclaimed: "Come to St. Thomas." In the crowded men's room Adam found an empty stall and changed his shirt and pants. On the way out, he tossed José's old clothes into the trash where they certainly belonged.

Looking about, Adam spotted the flight schedules, which were displayed on felt boards with white plastic letters. There were two

major carriers: American and Eastern. To his delight, Adam realized
that he could easily make American's nonstop flight to New York,
which would leave at nine-twenty. He got at the end of the line to
buy his ticket.

The line crept forward at a snail's pace, and Adam began to fear he
would miss the plane.

"One-way ticket to New York," he said when he finally reached the
counter.

The girl glared at him as if she thought his casual dress, unshaved
face, and lack of luggage a little odd, but all she said was, "How do
you plan to pay?"

"Credit card," said Adam as he pulled out his wallet, which had
somehow snagged a piece of lemon peel. Embarrassed, Adam flicked
it off and extracted his Visa card.

The girl looked at the card and requested some identification.
Adam went back to his wallet and pulled out his driver's license. The
girl checked it, then showed it to the heavyset clerk at the next
counter.

"The Visa card is for Schonberg, but the license reads Smyth," the
man said, coming over to Adam.

Beet red, Adam got out his real license plus his Arolen employ-
ment card that had his picture and handed them over. He tried to
explain that a friend had entrusted him with his license.

"Would you step to the side, please?" the man said, taking Adam's
cards and disappearing through a door. Adam tried not to appear
nervous as the girl continued to sell tickets to the rest of the people in
line, eyeing Adam from time to time to make sure he was not about
to leave.

It was nearly ten minutes before the clerk returned with an airline
agent who told Adam he was Baldwin Jacob, the supervisor. He was
holding Adam's cards.

"We'll issue you a ticket," he said, "but the flight is full. You'll have
to go standby."

Adam nodded. There was nothing else he could do. The clerk
made out the ticket and pointedly asked Adam if he had any luggage.

"No," said Adam. "I travel light when I'm on vacation."

He walked over to a cafeteria and bought a couple of donuts and a
cup of coffee, happy not to have to worry about the possibility of
being drugged. Then he put through a call to the Carsons'. Just as

he'd feared, Jennifer didn't answer the phone. Instead, Mr. Carson's baritone echoed over the wire.

"Hello," said Adam more cheerfully than he felt. "This is Adam. Is Jennifer awake yet?"

"Jennifer is not here," said Mr. Carson in a distinctly unfriendly voice.

"Where is she?"

"I don't think you can reach her."

"Look, I know you love your daughter," said Adam, "but the fact of the matter is that I am her husband, and it is urgent that I speak with her."

There was a pause as Mr. Carson apparently made up his mind. "She's not here. She and her mother just left for the Julian Clinic. They are admitting her this morning."

"Admitting her?" repeated Adam with alarm. "Why is she being admitted? Is she all right?"

"She's fine," said Mr. Carson. "And that's why I think you should leave her alone for a few days. After that, you two can iron out your differences. But frankly, Adam, your being away at this time is very upsetting."

"Why? What's going on?" said Adam, trying to control his fear.

"Jennifer had a repeat amniocentesis," said Mr. Carson, "and it was again positive. She's decided to have an abortion."

Adam felt something snap. "She doesn't need an abortion," he shouted.

"That's your opinion," said Mr. Carson calmly. "It is not ours or Jennifer's, and under the circumstances, there's not a lot you can do about it."

There was a click. The line was dead.

In a panic, Adam tried to call Jennifer at the clinic, only to learn that she had not been assigned a room yet and, no, patients could not be paged.

Adam slammed the phone down. There was still a half hour before flight time. He tried calling Vandermer, but was told he was in surgery.

Leaving the phone booth, Adam ran back to the American Airlines counter, which was now jammed with people trying to check in for the flight. Pushing and shoving, he managed to get to the front of the line and asked to speak to the supervisor.

It was several minutes before Mr. Jacob appeared. Not even trying to conceal his rising hysteria, Adam told the man he had to get to New York because his wife was going to have a baby.

The supervisor took Adam's ticket and without saying anything checked the computer. "We'll do the best we can, but, as I said, the flight is fully booked."

Adam didn't know what to do. Jacob obviously wasn't going to put out any extraordinary effort for his sake. Adam stood there, trying to think what he could do. Then he ran back to the telephone and put in a call to an old friend from college, Harvey Hatfield. Harvey had finished law school and was working at a big Wall Street firm. Without going into details, Adam told Harvey that his wife was going to have an abortion and he wanted to stop her.

Harvey seemed to think he was kidding. "So why are you calling a firm that specializes in corporate mergers?" he asked.

"Jesus, Harvey, I'm serious."

"Well, you'd better get someone who specializes in litigation. Try Emmet Redford. He's a friend of my father."

"Thanks," said Adam as his flight was announced over the loudspeaker, the flight he hoped to be on. He dropped the receiver and ran back to the counter, where he practically flung himself at the clerk he'd originally approached.

"Please, Miss, I've got to get on the plane. My wife is having a baby and it's going to die unless I get to New York."

For the first time, Adam had the feeling that someone was taking pity on him. The girl stared into his frantic eyes and said, "I'll put you on top of the standby list."

Adam allowed himself a little hope, but a few more passengers arrived breathlessly and were given boarding passes. Then a portly man showed up with a walkie-talkie. He went through the boarding gate and pulled it closed behind him.

"Mr. Schonberg," called Carol, the airline clerk.

Adam dashed back to the desk, but Carol was shaking her head. "Sorry, but the plane is completely full. No standbys at all."

Crushed, Adam collapsed into a seat. He could hear the whine of the jet engines starting up outside. Then the boarding door reopened and a stewardess appeared, holding up one finger.

The clerk turned to Adam. "Seems like there is one seat, but it is in smoking. Do you want it?"

/ / /

Unfortunately, the receptionist who greeted Jennifer at the Julian Clinic was the same girl who had helped admit Cheryl Tedesco. Seeing Karen Krinitz in her white blouse and blue jumper, Jennifer remembered the whole awful episode. Karen, however, acted as if they'd never met. She greeted Jennifer and her mother with the same mechanical smile.

"Hi! I'm Karen. I've been assigned to your case. I'm here to help if you have any questions or problems. We want your stay to be as pleasant as possible, so please call me if you need anything."

"Well, isn't that nice," said Mrs. Carson, but Jennifer had the strange feeling she had heard the entire speech before—word for word.

Karen went on, explaining the Julian philosophy. When she was done, Mrs. Carson thanked her enthusiastically, saying, "I'm not sure I'll ever be satisfied with Englewood Memorial after this. There is so much concern for the patient here."

Jennifer nodded. The clinic certainly cared about people. Yet Karen's speech bothered Jennifer. She had felt it was a little too pat the first time she'd heard it.

Jennifer sighed. She decided the experience with Cheryl was upsetting her. Who cared if a woman memorized a speech that she was required to give to all the patients?

"Are you all right, dear?" asked Mrs. Carson.

"I'm fine, mother," said Jennifer as she watched Karen recede down the hall. "Thanks for coming with me today. It means a lot to me."

Mrs. Carson reached over and gave her daughter a hug. She didn't want Jennifer to know how worried she really was.

/ / /

The moment Adam's plane landed at Kennedy he ran for the nearest phone booth. First, he called the Julian Clinic and asked to be put through to Jennifer's room. There was no answer. Then he dialed again and asked when Jennifer's procedure was scheduled. When the operator asked who wanted to know, he said Dr. Smyth. The operator seemed to accept his answer, and a moment later a nurse came on the line and said that Jennifer Schonberg was set for that afternoon.

"So she hasn't been done yet?" said Adam.

"Not yet, but she's been called for the OR. Dr. Vandermer is almost ready for her."

Adam fumbled with his coins and dialed the Julian Clinic a third time, this time asking to have Dr. Vandermer paged. An OR nurse picked up and said the doctor was unavailable, but should be done with his current case in thirty minutes.

With renewed panic, Adam called the lawyer that Harvey had recommended, Emmet Redford. Shouting that it was a life-or-death situation, he finally got put through. As briefly as possible, Adam told the lawyer that his wife was going to have an abortion and that he wanted to stop her.

"There's not much you can do, my friend," said Mr. Redford. "According to the Supreme Court, a husband cannot block his wife's abortion."

"That's incredible," said Adam. "It's my child, too. Isn't there anything you can do?"

"Well, I might be able to delay it."

"Do it!" shouted Adam. "Whatever you can!"

"Give me her name and all the particulars," said Mr. Redford.

Adam did so as quickly as he could.

"When is she scheduled to have the abortion?" asked Mr. Redford.

"In thirty minutes or so," said Adam desperately.

"Thirty minutes! What do you expect me to do in half an hour?"

"I've got to go," said Adam. "She's at the Julian Clinic. There's no time to lose."

Adam dropped the phone and ran through the terminal to the taxi stand. Leaping into the first cab in line, he yelled for the driver to take him to the Julian Clinic.

"You got money?" the cabbie asked, eyeing Adam's casual dress.

Adam pulled out his twenty, hoping it would be enough. Satisfied, the man put the car in gear and pulled away from the curb.

///

Jennifer was lying on a gurney just outside the treatment room. Her mother was standing beside her, and Jennifer was again forcibly reminded of her earlier visit to the Julian with Cheryl. Mrs. Carson was smiling, feigning confidence, but it was clear she was as nervous as her daughter.

"Why don't you go back to the lounge?" suggested Jennifer. "I'll be fine. From what Dr. Vandermer says, it's going to be easy."

Mrs. Carson glanced at her daughter, undecided as to what she should do.

"Please," said Jennifer. "Don't make a big deal out of this. Go back and read a magazine."

Relenting, Mrs. Carson bent down, kissed Jennifer on her forehead, and headed back toward the lounge. Jennifer watched her go with mixed emotions.

"OK," said the nurse, emerging from the treatment room. "We're all ready for you." She released the brake on the gurney and pushed Jennifer through the door. In contrast to the room where she'd had her amniocentesis, this room looked very much like an OR. Jennifer remembered the white floor and large white glass-fronted cabinets.

Two nurses were waiting. As they moved her to the table, one said, "It will all be over very soon, and you'll be able to forget the whole episode."

As she lay back, Jennifer thought she felt the child move. She struggled not to cry as one of the nurses prepped her lower abdomen.

The door to the corridor opened, and Dr. Vandermer came in, dressed in a surgical scrub suit. Jennifer felt better the moment she saw him.

"How are you doing?" he asked.

"OK, I guess," said Jennifer faintly.

Jennifer wanted him to say something else, but he just stared at her with unblinking eyes. She looked questioningly at the nurses, but they didn't seem to think there was anything odd about his silence. Then Vandermer seemed to come out of his trance and asked the nurses to hand him the anesthetic.

"You'll just feel a little sting now," said Dr. Vandermer flatly. With a deft jab he slipped the needle beneath Jennifer's skin.

Closing her eyes, Jennifer tried also to close her mind to what was about to happen.

/ / /

The cab ride from Kennedy Airport to the Julian Clinic was hair-raising. Once Adam had flashed his twenty, the driver acted as if he were in a race for his life. He screeched to a halt in front of the hospital in less than thirty minutes. Adam tossed him the twenty and dashed up the stairs without waiting for change.

Interrupting the girls chatting at the reception desk, he demanded to know where Vandermer was operating.

"He's performing an abortion on my wife," he gasped.

"Pregnancy terminations are done on the sixth floor, but . . ."

Adam didn't wait for her to finish. He ducked into an elevator just as the doors were closing, ignoring the receptionist who yelled after him that he was not allowed to go to six unaccompanied.

When the elevator stopped, Adam got out and made for the double doors at the end of the hall marked "Treatment Rooms." As he passed the nurses' station, he noticed the elaborate antique furniture and wondered what the Julian was trying to prove.

One of the nurses yelled for him to stop, but Adam kept running. He went through the double doors and opened the first treatment room door. It was empty. He went on to the next. A nurse tried to bar his way, but he was able to look over her shoulder at the patient's face. It wasn't Jennifer.

Adam crossed the hall and tried another door.

"Exactly what do you think you are doing?" asked a nurse with a German accent.

Adam rudely shoved the woman aside. He saw Dr. Vandermer bending over the table. He was holding a hypodermic whose needle sparkled under the overhead light.

"Jennifer!" shouted Adam, relieved that the surgery had proceeded no further than her being given the local anesthetic. "Don't do it, please. Don't have the abortion. Not without further tests."

Jennifer started to sit up as two orderlies rushed through the door and pinned Adam's arms behind his back. Adam saw that both men had the same unblinking stares as the stewards on the ship.

"OK, OK," said Adam. "You've made your point. You're stronger than I am. Now kindly let me go."

"Adam Schonberg?" said Dr. Vandermer. Until he'd heard Adam's voice, he'd thought they were dealing with a psychotic stranger. "What are you doing here? Jennifer just told me you were out of town."

"Please don't go ahead with the procedure. There's something I must tell you."

As if suddenly remembering the orderlies, Dr. Vandermer tapped the nearest on the shoulder and said, "I know this man. You can let go of him." He undid his mask and let it fall on his chest.

The orderlies released Adam as the door to the corridor opened and a number of clinic staff members peered in to see what was happening.

"Everything is under control," said Dr. Vandermer. Addressing the orderlies, he said, "Why don't you two wait outside."

As soon as they left, he guided Adam to a small anteroom, promising Jennifer they would both be back in a minute.

As soon as the door was closed, Adam blurted out, "I managed to get on one of the Arolen cruises."

Dr. Vandermer stared at him as if just noticing the jeans and St. Thomas tee shirt for the first time. If he knew what Adam was talking about, he gave no indication.

"I'm happy you got to go," was all he said. "We can compare notes later. Right now I need to take care of your wife. Why don't you go down to the lounge and wait for me? I won't be long."

"But you don't understand," said Adam. "The Arolen cruises are more than continuing education sessions. They're a cover for an elaborate behavior-modification scheme."

Dr. Vandermer debated what to do. Adam was obviously psychotic. Maybe he could persuade him to go over to Psychiatry, where someone with experience could help him. Taking a step forward, Dr. Vandermer put his arm around Adam's shoulder. "I think the person you should be talking with is Dr. Pace. Why don't we go downstairs and I'll introduce you to him?"

Adam pushed Dr. Vandermer's arm away. "I don't think you heard what I said. I'm talking about drug-induced behavior modification. Dr. Vandermer, you were a victim. You were drugged. Do you understand me?"

Dr. Vandermer sighed. "Adam, I know you believe what you are saying, but I was not drugged on my cruise. I gave lectures. It was a delightful time, as were the days I spent in Puerto Rico."

"I saw it all," said Adam. "I was on the *Fjord.* I saw how they drugged the doctors' food and kept giving them yellow pills. Then they were subjected to these films. It was mind control. Look, you've got to believe me. Think. Why did you change your mind about pregdolen? Before you went on the cruise, you thought the drug was unsafe. You told me you'd never prescribe it."

"I've never changed my mind about pregdolen," protested Dr. Vandermer. "I've always thought it was the best product on the market if one were forced to use medication for morning sickness."

Realizing he was making no headway, Adam grabbed Dr. Vandermer's hand. Looking directly into the doctor's eyes, he said, "Please, even if you don't believe me, please don't abort my child. I think the lab mix-up that occurred with the amniocentesis slides was deliberate. I think Arolen is trying to increase its supply of fetal tissue, and this is how it is done."

The door to the room opened.

"Dr. Vandermer," said the nurse in the doorway, "what are we to do?"

Dr. Vandermer waved her away.

"Adam," he said kindly, "I can appreciate how upset you must be with the way things have turned out."

"Don't be condescending," warned Adam as he rubbed his eyes. "All I want is to delay the abortion. That's all. I don't think that's asking too much."

"It depends from whose point of view you're talking about." He pointed toward the treatment room. "Jennifer might feel differently. To delay at this point would be cruel for her. She's already been through more than enough."

Adam realized he was losing the battle. Desperately, he sought some way to get through to the doctor.

"Now," Vandermer said firmly. "Why don't you go down to the lounge and wait. I'll be there shortly."

"No," shouted Adam, blocking the way. "You haven't heard everything."

"Adam!" shouted Dr. Vandermer. "Move out of my way or I'll be forced to have you removed."

"Listen, I think some of the people running the cruise have had psychosurgery. I'm telling you the truth. They had scars on the sides of their heads. Right here." Adam reached out to touch the spot he meant on Vandermer's head. When he did, he jumped back in horror. Tiny ridged lines were on either side of the doctor's skull. Adam could just see the healing incisions. Dr. Vandermer reacted angrily.

"This has gone far enough." He opened the door and motioned for the two orderlies to take Adam away. "Please show Mr. Schonberg down to the lounge. He can wait there if he behaves himself, but if he gives you any trouble, call Psychiatry."

Adam put up his hands. "I won't cause any trouble," he said softly. The last thing he wanted was to be given some kind of tranquilizer. He realized that if Vandermer had undergone some sort of psychosurgery, there was no way he could be persuaded of Arolen's treachery.

"May I speak to my wife?" he said.

Dr. Vandermer eyed Adam for a moment and then shook his head. "I don't think it is in Jennifer's best interests, but I will let her make the decision."

He opened the door to the treatment room and stepped inside. Jennifer pushed herself up on her elbow. "What is happening?" she asked anxiously.

Dr. Vandermer briefly described his scene with Adam, ending with Adam's request to talk with her. "He seems to have been unable to deal with the stress of your pregnancy" was the only thing Vandermer had to offer by way of an opinion.

"Well, he certainly hasn't made the situation any easier for me," said Jennifer. "I'm sorry he's caused you so much trouble."

"There's no need to apologize," said Dr. Vandermer. "I think we should get on with the procedure. You can deal with Adam when we are done."

Jennifer nodded. "Why did he have to come back? You're right. I don't think I can handle Adam just now. Why don't you just go ahead while I'm still in control?"

Dr. Vandermer smiled reassuringly and motioned for the nurse to begin setting up again. Then he returned to the anteroom and told Adam that Jennifer would speak to him afterward.

Adam realized there was no use in protesting further. Numbly, he followed the orderlies down the corridor.

Dr. Vandermer rescrubbed and went back into the treatment room. Picking up the hypodermic, he gave Jennifer the local anesthetic. He was just about to begin the procedure when the door opened again.

"Dr. Vandermer, I'm afraid you'll have to hold up on this case."

Jennifer opened her eyes. Standing at the door was a stocky

woman dressed in a scrub suit. Jennifer didn't recognize her, but Dr. Vandermer did. It was Helen Clark, director of the ORs at the Julian Clinic.

"We have just been served with an emergency restraining order. We cannot proceed with Jennifer Schonberg's abortion."

"On what grounds?" asked an astonished Dr. Vandermer.

"I don't know the details," said Mrs. Clark, "but it is signed by a New York Supreme Court judge."

Dr. Vandermer shrugged and turned back to Jennifer.

"Don't do anything foolish," warned Mrs. Clark. "Defying a court order would get us all in trouble."

"This is ridiculous," said Dr. Vandermer. "Litigation in the operating room." But he took off his mask and gloves.

Seeing that he was about to leave, Jennifer bit down on her lower lip to keep from screaming.

/ / /

After Vandermer had thrown him out of the treatment room, Adam had immediately phoned Emmet Redford. The lawyer told him that he'd called in an old favor and had gotten a restraining order. It was on its way to the clinic as they spoke. Adam went back to the lounge, praying that the papers would be served in time. Seeing Mrs. Carson bent over a magazine, he took a chair out of her line of vision.

Less than five minutes later a nurse hurried over to Mrs. Carson. She bent and whispered something to the older woman who then threw up her hands and cried, "Her abortion has been canceled!"

Adam felt like cheering until he heard Jennifer's sobs as she was wheeled down the corridor. He and Mrs. Carson both ran over to her and ended up standing on opposite sides of the gurney.

"Jennifer," said Adam, grasping her hand. "Everything is going to be all right."

She wrenched her hand away, crying hysterically, "Leave me alone. You've gone crazy. Leave me alone."

Adam stepped away and sadly watched the gurney continue down the corridor.

"Are you responsible for this disaster?" sputtered Mrs. Carson.

Adam was too upset to answer. Was it a disaster to prevent an unnecessary abortion? Close to tears himself, he turned and walked blindly to the elevator. Once out on the street, he checked his wallet. Only three dollars and some change left. He decided he'd better take the subway to Emmet Redford's Fifth Avenue office.

"Sorry about my clothes," said Adam when the secretary ushered him in. "I didn't want to waste any time going home to change."

Mr. Redford nodded, although he was disturbed by Adam's appearance. In fact, he was disturbed by the whole case. Though he'd arranged for the restraining order, he felt Adam's claims were dubious at best, especially in light of the information he'd just received from the assistant he had assigned the case to.

"I think I should be frank," Redford began. "I agreed to help out as a favor to Harvey, but there are a number of points that seriously trouble me."

"I couldn't agree more," said Adam. "I think the Julian Clinic is deliberately doing unnecessary abortions."

"I see," said Redford, taking in Adam's unkempt hair and unshaven face.

"But the real problem," continued Adam, "is that Arolen Pharmaceuticals and its parent company, MTIC, have an elaborate program involving drugs and even brain surgery to influence the way doctors practice medicine."

This man is nuts, thought Redford with dismay.

Adam's voice became more urgent. "But now that I've learned all this," he said, "I don't know what to do about it."

"I can understand your dilemma," said Redford, wondering if Adam were potentially violent. He certainly seemed excitable. Redford pressed a concealed button under his desk and said, "Mr. Schonberg, do you mind if I ask a personal question?"

"Not at all," said Adam.

"Have you ever sought professional help for your obsessions? I think that might be in everyone's best interest."

"What I'm telling you is true," protested Adam.

There was a soft knock on the door. Redford got up to open it and told his secretary to ask Mr. Stupenski to join them. "I'm afraid a grand jury wouldn't give much credence to your allegations," he said to Adam while they waited.

Adam searched the lawyer's face for some hint that the man believed him. There was none.

"I guess you're right," admitted Adam. "The only proof I have is what I saw."

The door opened again and a young man wearing a pin-striped suit identical to Redford's came into the room.

"This is my associate, Mr. Stupenski," said Redford.

Adam said hello and then tried once more to convince Redford that his story was true. "They drug the food on the cruises and supplement those doses with yellow pills that have to be some kind of tranquilizer."

"So you say, Mr. Schonberg, but the problem is you have no proof," repeated Redford.

The lawyers exchanged knowing glances. Adam stared at them in frustration.

"I think I should tell you that given the amniocentesis report that the clinic showed Mr. Stupenski, I'm sorry we went about getting the restraining order," said Redford. "As it is, it remains in force only until the emergency hearing three days from now, and since I'm certainly not going to argue for the motion, you can expect it will be rescinded at that time. Good day, Mr. Schonberg."

It took Adam a moment to realize that the interview was over.

///

Four hours later, washed and shaved and dressed in his best suit, Adam was sitting outside his father's office waiting for Dr. Schonberg to finish with his last appointment. It was after six o'clock.

When Dr. Schonberg was finally free, he listened with some impatience to what even Adam had to admit sounded farfetched.

"I simply can't believe this," he told Adam. "Look, if it will make you feel better, let me call Peter Davenport of the AMA. He's the guy who certifies the courses for CME credits. He's been on several of the cruises himself."

Dr. Schonberg dialed Davenport at home and jovially asked his opinion of the Arolen cruises. After listening for a few minutes, he thanked the man and hung up.

"Pete says the seminars on the *Fjord* are completely above board. Some of the evening entertainment was a little risqué, but otherwise the conferences were among the best he's attended."

"He was probably drugged like the rest of them," said Adam.

"Adam, please," said Dr. Schonberg. "You are being ridiculous. MTIC has been sponsoring seminars and medical conventions either under its own auspices or through Arolen Pharmaceuticals for over a decade. The cruises have been going on for five years."

"That may be," said Adam, losing hope of convincing even his own father, "but I swear to you they are drugging the doctors and subjecting them to rigorous behavior modification. They even operate on certain people. I saw the scars on Dr. Vandermer myself. I think they are controlling him through some kind of remote-control device."

Dr. Schonberg rolled his eyes. "Even given the small amount of psychiatry that you've had, Adam, I would think you would be able to recognize how paranoid your story sounds."

Adam abruptly stood up and started for the door.

"Wait," called Dr. Schonberg. "Come back here for a minute."

Adam hesitated, wondering if his father would relent.

Dr. Schonberg tilted back his chair. "Let's say for the sake of discussion that there is something to your story."

"That's gracious of you," said Adam.

"What would you have me do? I'm the director of new products for the FDA and I can't espouse a wild theory like yours. But seeing you are so upset, perhaps I should go on one of these cruises and see for myself."

"No," interrupted Adam. "Don't go on the cruise. Please."

"Well, what would you like me to do?"

"I guess I want you to start an investigation."

"I'll make you a deal," said Dr. Schonberg. "If you agree to see a psychiatrist and explore the possibility that you may be experiencing some sort of paranoid reaction, I'll make further explorations into Arolen."

Adam took off his glasses and rubbed his eyes. If one more person suggested that he see a shrink, he'd scream.

"Thanks, Dad," he said. "I'll give your offer some serious thought."

As he rode back to the airport, Adam wondered just what kind of treatment Arolen had given Pete Davenport of the AMA and how much of the medical profession was under MTIC's control.

///

Adam landed at LaGuardia around nine and took a cab back to the city. The thought of returning to his empty apartment was depressing, and he was very concerned about Jennifer. Although he dreaded having to drive out to Englewood and brave the Carsons' anger, he didn't feel he had much choice. He had to talk to Jennifer.

There were no lights on at the Carson house when he pulled into the drive. Cautiously, he walked up the front steps and pressed the doorbell. He was surprised when the door opened almost immediately.

"Your headlights shone right into our bedroom," Mr. Carson said angrily. "What on earth do you want at this hour?"

"I'm sorry if I woke you," said Adam, "but I need to speak to Jennifer."

Mr. Carson folded his sizable arms across his chest. "Well, you have some nerve. I'll give you credit for that, but my daughter refuses to speak to you. Maybe she'll change her mind after a few days, but for the moment . . ."

"I'm afraid that I must insist," said Adam. "You see, I don't believe she needs an abortion . . ."

Mr. Carson grabbed Adam's shirt and shouted, "You will insist on nothing!" He shoved Adam back from the doorway.

Adam regained his balance, cupped his hands over his mouth, and began calling, "Jennifer! Jennifer!"

"That's enough," yelled Mr. Carson. He grabbed Adam again, intending to march him to his car. But Adam sidestepped his father-in-law and ran inside. At the foot of the steps he shouted again for his wife. Jennifer appeared in her nightgown in the upstairs hall. She looked down at her husband with dismay.

"Listen to me," shouted Adam again, but before Jennifer could speak, Mr. Carson had grabbed Adam from behind and carried him back out the door. Unwilling to fight back, Adam tripped when he was shoved toward his car and fell off the porch into the bushes. He heard the door slam before he could scramble to his feet. He was beginning to get the message that Mr. Carson would never let him speak to Jennifer that night.

Climbing into his car, Adam tried to figure out what he could do to keep Jennifer from having the abortion, at least until she got a second opinion. He only had three days to persuade her.

He was halfway back across the George Washington Bridge before he knew what he had to do. Everyone wanted proof. Well, he'd go to Puerto Rico to get proof. He was certain everything he'd seen on the cruise would be replicated there in spades.

Bill Shelly rose from his desk and clasped Adam's hand. "Congratulations," he said. "You've probably just made the best decision of your life."

"I'm not saying I'll definitely take the position," cautioned Adam. "But I've been giving Puerto Rico a lot of thought, and I'd like to take you up on the offer to go down there and see the facility firsthand. Jennifer's not happy about the idea, but if I really want to go, she'll support me in the decision."

"That reminds me; Clarence left a message that he'd gotten a rather strange call from your wife. She thought you were away on Arolen business."

"In-law problems," said Adam with a wave of his hand. "She and my father have never gotten along."

Even Adam wasn't sure what he meant, but fortunately Shelly nodded understandingly and said, "Getting back to the matter at hand, I'm certain you will be thrilled with the Arolen research center. When would you like to go?"

"Immediately," said Adam brightly. "My bag is packed and in the car."

Mr. Shelly chuckled. "Your attitude has always been refreshing. Let me see if the Arolen plane is available."

While Shelly waited for his secretary to check, he asked Adam what had changed his mind about the management training program. "I was afraid I hadn't been convincing enough," he said.

"Quite the contrary," said Adam, "If it hadn't been for you, I never would have considered it." As he spoke, Adam eyed Bill Shelly's skull, resisting the urge to see if he, too, had been subjected to surgery. At this point Adam had no idea if anybody at Arolen could be trusted.

/ / /

There were two Arolen executives on the luxurious Gulf Stream jet. One had gotten on the plane with Adam, and the other came aboard in Atlanta. Though both offered friendly greetings, they spent the trip working, leaving Adam to distract himself with some old magazines.

When they landed in San Juan, the two executives headed for the Arolen minibus, which was waiting at the curb. Adam was wondering if he should join them when he was greeted by two men in blue blazers and white duck pants. Both had close-cropped hair: one blond, the other dark. Their MTIC name tags said "Rodman" and "Dunly."

"Good afternoon, Mr. Schonberg," said Rodman. "Welcome to Puerto Rico."

As Dunly relieved Adam of his shoulder bag, Adam felt gooseflesh form on his back and arms in spite of the tropical heat. Rodman's voice had the same inflectionless quality of the stewards on the *Fjord,* and as they walked to an awaiting limousine, Adam noticed that both men moved with the same mechanical step.

The limousine was not new, but it was a limousine nonetheless, and Adam felt self-conscious when they put him in the back seat by himself.

Leaning forward, he looked out at the rush-hour traffic. They drove out of the city, apparently paralleling the northern coast of the island, although Adam could not see the ocean. They passed shopping centers, gas stations, and automobile body shops. Everything appeared to be both beginning to decay and in the process of construction at the same time. It was a strange combination. Rusting rods stuck out of the concrete in various locations as if additional rooms or floors had been originally planned but the workers had failed to return. And there was litter everywhere. Adam wasn't impressed.

Gradually, the shabby commercial buildings gave way to equally shabby housing, although on occasion there was a well-appointed and cared-for home amid the general squalor. There was no separation between rich and poor, and goats and chickens ran free everywhere.

Eventually, the road narrowed from four lanes to two, and Adam caught glimpses of the ocean beyond the green hills. The air became fresh and clean.

Finally, after about an hour and a half, they turned off the main road onto a well-paved lane that twisted and turned through the lush vegetation. At one point there was a gap in the foliage, and Adam had a spectacular view of the Caribbean sea. The sky was shot with red, and Adam knew the sun was about to set.

The road plunged down a hill and tunneled beneath a dark canopy of exotic trees. About a quarter mile farther, the limousine slowed and then stopped. They had arrived at a gatehouse. On either side and extending off into the forest was an impressive chain link fence, topped with spirals of barbed wire. Resisters on the wire suggested the fence was electrified.

An armed guard came out of the house and approached the car. After taking a sheet of paper from the driver, he glanced at Adam and opened the gate. As the limousine drove onto the MTIC grounds, Adam twisted in his seat and watched the gate close. He wondered if the security was there to keep people out or to keep people in. He began to question what he was getting himself into. As when he was on the *Fjord*, he had no real plan and didn't delude himself that he had any talent as a detective. His only consolation was that in Puerto Rico he wasn't hiding behind an assumed name.

The car suddenly swept around a bend, and he was confronted by some of the most magnificent architecture he had ever seen, set against a background of rolling lawns and clear turquoise sea.

The main building was a hexagonally shaped glass structure of the same mirrored bronzed glass as Arolen headquarters. To the left and closer to the beach was another building, only two stories high, which appeared to be a club. Tennis courts and a generous swimming pool were off to one side. Beyond it was a white sand beach with a volleyball court and a row of Hobie Cats and surf sailers. Several of the craft were in use, and their colorful sails stood out sharply against the water. On the other side of the clearing were beachfront condominiums. All in all, the compound appeared like a world-class resort. Adam was impressed.

The limousine pulled up beneath a large awning at the front of the main building.

"Good evening, Mr. Schonberg," said the doorman. "Welcome to MTIC. This way, please."

Adam got out of the car and followed the man to a registration desk. It was like signing into a hotel. The chief difference was that there was no cashier.

After Adam signed in, another blue-jacketed clerk, whose name tag said "Craig," picked up his bag and led him to the elevator. They got out at the sixth floor and walked down a long corridor. At the very end was another elevator.

"Will you be with us long?" asked Craig in the now familiar inflectionless speech.

"Just a few days," said Adam evasively as Craig pulled out his key and opened one of the doors.

Adam didn't have a room; he had a suite. Craig went around like a bellhop, checking all the lighting, making sure the TV worked, glancing at the full bar, and opening the drapes. Adam tried to give him a tip, but he politely refused.

Adam was amazed by the accommodations. He had a magnificent view of the ocean, which had darkened with the approaching night. On the distant islands pinpoint lights sparkled. Adam watched as a single Hobie Cat beat its way toward the shore. Hearing sounds of Caribbean music, he stepped out onto the terrace. A band seemed to be playing in the building Adam thought was a club. The weather was perfect, and Adam wished Jennifer was with him. Even the honeymoon suite they'd had in the Poconos, with the heart-shaped bath, hadn't been so luxurious.

Adam decided to try to call her. To his delight, she answered the phone herself, but when she realized who it was, her voice became cool.

"Jennifer, please promise me one thing," said Adam. "Don't have the abortion until I get back."

"Get back?" questioned Jennifer. "Where are you?"

Adam hadn't meant to tell her where he was, but it was too late to think of a lie. "Puerto Rico," he said reluctantly.

"Adam," said Jennifer, making it obvious that she was furious, "if you want to tell me what to do, you can't keep running off. The moment the court gives me clearance, I intend to go back to the clinic."

"Please, Jennifer," said Adam.

"I hope you're enjoying yourself," said Jennifer, and she slammed down the receiver.

Adam sank back on the bed totally depressed. He only had two more days. The phone rang and Adam grabbed the receiver, thinking it might be Jennifer, but it was just the receptionist, telling him that dinner was in half an hour.

/ / /

The dining room was in the club overlooking the beach. The row of Hobie Cats stood in the sand just beyond the sliding doors. A full moon had risen, casting a glittering path along the surface of the water.

The room had dark green walls and matching carpet with pink tablecloths and pink upholstery. The waiters were dressed in white jackets with black pants.

Adam was seated at a round table for eight. To his immediate right was Dr. Heinrich Nachman, whom Adam had met the day he'd had his interview at Arolen. Next to Dr. Nachman was Dr. Sinclair Glover, a short, portly, red-faced man who said he supervised fetal research.

Next to Dr. Glover was Dr. Winfield Mitchell, a bearded but bald middle-aged man wearing wire-rimmed glasses. Nachman said Mitchell was in charge of psychotropic drug development. Adam had the distinct impression the man was a psychiatrist, judging by how calmly he listened to the conversation without contributing anything, yet at the same time maintaining a superior-than-thou attitude.

Beyond Dr. Mitchell was a business executive, a William somebody; Adam missed his last name. He was strictly Ivy League, with sandy blond hair and a boyish complexion. Also at the table were Brian Hopkins, who was in charge of management training, Ms. Linda Aronson, who handled PR, and a jovial older man named Harry Burkett, who was the manager of the Puerto Rican compound.

Remembering his experience on the *Fjord*, Adam was at first reluctant to try the food, but everyone else was eating with gusto, and none of them appeared to be drugged. Besides, Adam reasoned, if they had intended to drug him, they could have done so on the plane.

The atmosphere at the table was relaxed, and everyone made a point of making Adam feel welcome. Burkett explained the reason MTIC chose Puerto Rico for its research center was because the government offered excellent tax incentives as well as a policy of noninterference. It turned out that many drug firms had large installations on the island.

Adam asked about the heavy security.

"That's one of the prices we have to pay for living in this paradise," said Harry Burkett. "There's always a chance of terrorist activity from the small group championing Puerto Rican independence."

Adam wondered if that were the whole story, but he did not pursue the issue.

William, the MTIC executive, looked over at Adam and said, "MTIC has a certain philosophy about the medical profession. We feel that economic interests have supplanted service. I've heard that you agree with that premise."

Adam noticed that the rest of the table was listening. He swallowed a bite of dessert and said, "Yes, that's true. In the brief time I was at medical school I was dismayed by the lack of humanism. I felt that technology and research were considered more rewarding than patient care."

There were several doctors at the table and Adam hoped he wasn't offending them, but he did notice that Dr. Nachman was smiling. Adam was pleased, since he thought the more enthusiastic they were about him, the better his chance of learning what they were doing.

"Do you think your attitude would make dealing with doctors difficult?" asked Linda Aronson.

"Not at all," said Adam. "I think my understanding of medical reality makes it easier. As a sales rep I've been reasonably successful."

"From what Bill Shelly has reported," said Nachman, "I think that Mr. Schonberg is being modest."

"Adam, has anyone described our plans should you decide to enlist in our management training program?" asked Dr. Glover.

"Not specifically," said Adam.

Dr. Nachman folded his hands and leaned forward. "Arolen is

about to release a whole new generation of drugs or treatment modalities as a result of our fetal research. We are looking for someone to work with Linda to educate the medical profession in these new concepts. We feel that you have the perfect background and attitudes for the job."

"Precisely," said Linda. "But we don't mean to overwhelm you. At first, all you would be doing would be familiarizing yourself with Arolen's research."

Adam wished he had more than two days. The job they had in mind would undoubtedly put him in a position to learn what he needed.

"That's not quite true," said Brian Hopkins. "Mr. Schonberg must first take our management training course."

"Brian, we all know that Mr. Schonberg has to take your course first."

"Please," said Dr. Nachman. "Let's not display our departmental jealousies yet. There will be plenty of time for that."

Everyone laughed except Hopkins.

Adam finished his dessert and put down his spoon. Looking at Dr. Nachman, he said, "That was a wonderful dinner, but I'm eager to see the research facility."

"And we are eager to show it to you. Tomorrow we plan to . . ."

"Why not tonight?" interrupted Adam enthusiastically.

Dr. Nachman looked at Glover and Mitchell, who smiled and shrugged. "I suppose we could show you some of the facilities tonight," said Dr. Nachman. "Are you sure you are not too tired?"

"Not in the slightest," said Adam.

Dr. Nachman stood up, followed by Dr. Glover and Dr. Mitchell. The others excused themselves, preferring to remain at the table for more coffee and after-dinner drinks.

Dr. Nachman led Adam back to the main building, where guests signed in. Then the four went through another set of double doors to the research center. This part of the building was floored in white tile, the walls painted in bright primary colors.

"These are the administration offices," explained Dr. Nachman. A moment later Adam found himself crossing a glass-walled bridge. He could see palm trees waving on either side and realized that there were two concentric buildings, one nestled inside of the other, much like the Pentagon in Washington.

Turning down another hallway, Adam smelled the unmistakable odor of caged animals. Dr. Glover opened the first door and for the next half hour led Adam from room to room, explaining the complicated machinery and examining an endless number of rats and monkeys. This was where Arolen was doing its basic fetology research.

To Adam's surprise, white-gowned technicians were working in some of the labs, despite the late hour. Dr. Glover explained that ever since they'd begun to get positive results with fetal implants, they'd been working around the clock.

"Where do you get your material?" asked Adam, pausing by a cage of pink mice.

"Most of the research is done with animal systems," explained Dr. Glover, "and we breed our animals right here at the center."

"But surely you're doing some human implants. Where do you get your tissue?" persisted Adam.

"Very good question," said Dr. Glover. "We did run into a bit of a problem after restrictive laws were passed, but we've managed one way or another. Most of our material comes from the Julian Clinic."

Adam wanted to pound the glass cases in frustration. Why couldn't he get anyone to listen to him? Obviously, doctors like Vandermer were increasing the supply of fetal tissue by merely increasing the number of therapeutic abortions.

"Tomorrow," continued Dr. Glover, pleased that Adam was demonstrating such interest, "we will take you into our hospital wing. We've had some amazing results, particularly in treating diabetics with fetal pancreatic extracts."

"I know how interesting this is, but I think Dr. Mitchell would like to describe some of his work," said Nachman, smiling at Glover.

"Indeed," echoed Dr. Mitchell. "A year from now, when the sales figures are in, we'll see whose department accounts for the biggest increases."

Mitchell devoted the next thirty minutes to a non-stop monologue on psychotropic drugs, particularly a new brand of phenothiazine. "It's effective for every type of psychotic condition. It's essentially nontoxic, and it changes the most disturbed individual into an exemplary citizen. Of course, some spontaneity is sacrificed."

Adam started to protest, but thought better of it. He was certain that "some spontaneity is sacrificed" was the company's way of downplaying the drug's side effects. Certainly the stewards on the *Fjord* and the orderlies at the Julian had lacked "spontaneity."

"What's the name of this new drug?" Adam asked instead.

"Scientific, generic, or trade name?" asked Dr. Mitchell, out of breath from his monologue.

"Trade name."

"Conformin," said Dr. Mitchell.

"Would it be possible for me to get a sample?"

"You'll be able to get all the samples you want when the drug is released," said Dr. Mitchell. "We're waiting for FDA clearance."

"Just a small amount?" asked Adam. "I'd like to see how it's packaged. As a sales rep, I've learned how important that is."

Dr. Mitchell looked at Adam strangely. "Perhaps a small amount," he murmured.

Adam didn't push the issue, saying, "If the drug is close to being released, then you've started human testing."

"My word, yes," said Dr. Mitchell, brightening. "We've been using the drug on humans for several years, on patients with intractable psychiatric problems brought in from all over the world, in fact. The drug has proved one hundred percent effective."

"I'd like to visit the ward," said Adam.

"Tomorrow," said Dr. Mitchell. "Right now, I'd like to show you our main chemistry laboratory. It's one of the most advanced in the world."

There was no doubt in Adam's mind that Arolen's research facilities were superb, especially when compared with those at University Hospital, where money was so tight that every No. 2 Mongol pencil had to be included in grant requests. But after seeing so many labs, Adam became bored. He tried to look interested, but the longer the tour went on, the more difficult that became.

"I think that will be enough for tonight," said Dr. Nachman finally. "We don't want to exhaust Mr. Schonberg on his first evening with us."

"I'll second that," said Dr. Glover. "We only spent half an hour in my department."

"That's because there is more to see here," said Dr. Mitchell.

"Gentlemen!" interjected Dr. Nachman, lifting his hands.

"I've enjoyed all of it," protested Adam, careful to use the past tense so as not to encourage an encore from Dr. Mitchell.

They walked down the main corridor and crossed the connecting bridge to the outer building. Adam stopped to look behind him. He could see that the bridge continued beyond the corridor to a third interior building, which was blocked off by heavy steel doors.

"What's back there?" asked Adam.

"The clinical wards," said Dr. Nachman. "You'll see them tomorrow."

That must be where the psychiatric ward is located, thought Adam. He hesitated a minute, then followed Nachman out to the main lobby where they all said good night.

It was quarter to twelve, and even though Adam had had a busy day, he was not sleepy. A dull headache was beginning behind his eyes, and he could not forget he had only two more days to come up with convincing, concrete evidence. Even if he got a sample of Conformin, it would take time to have it analyzed, and then even more time to try to convince someone like Vandermer to have himself checked to see if he'd received it. Knowing sleep was out of the question, Adam opened his door and walked the length of the corridor to the far elevator. A small Formica sign said "Bathers' Elevator."

Descending to the ground floor, Adam found himself outside in a dense garden of palms, bamboo, and ferns. A curving pathway led through the lush vegetation. Following it, Adam arrived at the beach.

Taking off his shoes, he stepped onto the cool sand. The full moon made the night almost as bright as day. The sand was smooth and soft as powder. A slight wind rattled the rigging of the Hobie Cats so that they sounded like Japanese wind chimes. Adam could understand why people like Bill Shelly were so enchanted with the place.

Passing the club, Adam could see into the dining room. A few of the busboys were still laying the tables for the next meal.

About a hundred yards beyond the club Adam saw the condominiums. They were designed in a pseudo-Spanish style with stuccoed walls and red tile roofs. Lights were burning in some of the residences, and Adam caught glimpses of men and women watching television or reading. The whole scene was so peaceful it was hard to believe it could be the center of some gigantic conspiracy. Yet apparently it was. All drug firms spent millions of dollars attempting to influence the purchasing behavior of doctors, but MTIC wanted more. It wanted to control the doctors. It was no wonder that Arolen was planning to reduce its sales force.

Adam turned and retreated along the beach to where he'd left his shoes, then made his way back to the main building. Halfway down the hallway, he noticed an exit sign. He tried the door, which opened onto a staircase that wound up toward the roof. After making sure that he could get back in, Adam followed the steps to a door, which was also unlocked. Turning the knob, he found himself gazing out across the top of the main building. The wind was whipping in off the sea. Adam walked over to the four-foot-high wall that marked the edge of the roof. From this vantage point, he had a clear view of the compound. The residential structures ended at a small rocky hill, beyond which was dense forest. As large as the center was, Adam realized that there could well be more buildings hidden from sight.

Turning, he looked back at the first interior building. In the bright moonlight he could clearly see its outline, and he realized that it was an excellent architectural solution for eliminating windowless offices. Looking down, Adam could see that the space between the buildings had been carefully landscaped with pools, greenery, and palm trees. Both buildings were of equal height, and there was a bridge from one to the other on each floor.

The core building, which Dr. Nachman had said housed the hospital, was not visible. Adam crossed the bridge to the second building, walked to the inner edge, and looked down. Below him was the hospital. It was only three stories, which was why Adam had been unable to see it before. Directly below him was the connecting bridge that led to the steel doors he'd seen on his way out of the lab.

The roof bristled with antennae, wires, and satellite discs, which Adam guessed were related to some complicated communications center. There were a number of bubble skylights, the largest being in the exact center of the building. The roof also contained a cooling tower for air-conditioning and a shedlike access door similar to the one Adam had used to get to the roof of the outer building. Light from the central skylight gave the whole complex an alien, futuristic appearance.

For a few minutes Adam stood with his palms resting on the concrete wall, which was still warm from the day's sun. The night breeze tousled his hair. With a sigh he wondered what insane impulse had taken him to Puerto Rico. There was no way MTIC would let him leave with its secrets. Frustrated and depressed, he decided he might as well go to bed.

CHAPTER **16**

The next day, despite Adam's impatience to see the hospital, he found it wasn't on his schedule until the afternoon. Most of the morning was spent with Mr. Burkett, who showed Adam not only the condo where he and Jennifer would live, but also all the facilities MTIC offered employees' spouses and children. He wondered what Burkett's response would be if he suddenly confronted the man with the knowledge that MTIC was doing its best to see that Adam's child was never born. It took all of his willpower to smile admiringly as they walked about the compound. Adam was relieved when Burkett finally released him just outside of Linda Aronson's office.

Linda greeted Adam with enthusiasm and showed him the computer terminals that distributed Arolen's information all over the world in a matter of minutes. She also introduced Adam to Mr. Crawford, who organized the Arolen cruises. Adam thought the man a dead ringer for the con artist who'd provided Smyth's fake passport.

Crawford showed Adam a graph analyzing where the doctors who took the cruise practiced. Most came from the New York City area, though in recent months there had been a number of doctors from Chicago and Los Angeles as well. Adam noted that a good ten percent of the doctors who'd been on more than one cruise now worked at the Julian Clinic.

"The cruises have certainly become popular," said Adam, concealing his dismay.

"Popular isn't the word," said Crawford proudly. "With our present facilities, there is no way that we can keep up with the demand. MTIC has already purchased a second cruise ship on the west coast. We estimate it will be in service within the year. The eventual plan is to have five ships in operation, which will mean we will be able to accommodate the entire medical profession."

Mr. Crawford folded his arms across his chest and gave Adam a what-do-you-think-of-that look, a proud parent describing his child's accomplishments. Adam felt sick. An entire generation of doctors programmed to be unknowing representatives of a pharmaceutical house.

Dr. Nachman met Adam for lunch and afterward led him down to Dr. Glover's office, where Glover and Mitchell were arguing over who should show Adam around first.

"It's getting so I can't leave the two of you in the same room," said Nachman irritably.

Adam wondered if the center's isolation was responsible for their bickering. The competition between the two doctors had a neurotic quality. But Adam was pleased that he would at last be seeing the hospital. He didn't relish another hour of Mitchell's commentary, though, and hoped to escape it.

When they reached the double doors to the innermost building, Dr. Nachman opened them by gently pressing his thumb against a small electronic scanner. Beyond the doors, the covered bridge was glassed on both sides, and Adam saw the attractive landscaping he'd appreciated from the roof the night before.

There was a second set of double doors at the end of the walkway, which Dr. Nachman again opened with his thumb. The minute the men went through, Adam recognized the familiar smell of a hospital. After passing through a three-story foyer illuminated by some of the bubble skylights Adam had seen the night before, they walked past a series of small operating rooms to a nurses' station that boasted all the latest telemetry equipment. One of the nurses showed them into the locked ward beyond. Dr. Glover introduced Adam to several of the patients.

The doctor presented each case, impressing Adam with the amount of information he had committed to memory. The few details he couldn't remember, he was able to call up on one of the computer terminals that were in each room.

There were several diabetics who had received fetal islet-cell infusions and who were now completely off insulin. Adam was impressed in spite of himself, though he knew the ends could never justify the means.

On the far side of the ward were the patients with central nervous system implants. Adam met a young woman whose spinal cord had been severed in an automobile accident. After having been a paraplegic for over a year, she now was able to move her legs, thanks to infusions of fetal central nervous system tissue. Her movement was uncoordinated as yet, but the results were astounding when compared with the hopelessness of traditional treatment.

She greeted Dr. Glover with a hug. "Thank you for giving me hope," she said.

"You're welcome," said Glover, beaming with pride, while Dr. Mitchell glanced through the chart.

"Bacteria count is going up in the urine," Mitchell criticized.

"We are quite aware of that," said Dr. Glover.

"Let's move on," said Dr. Nachman.

They saw another ten or fifteen patients before Dr. Nachman led them back to the foyer, where they took the elevator to the next level. This was the psychiatric floor, and the minute they walked down the hall Dr. Mitchell seemed to come alive. Stroking his beard, running his hand over the smooth crown of his head, he described his patients with the enthusiasm of a born teacher.

"Our main treatment modality is psychopharmacology," he stated. "Once therapeutic psychotropic drug levels are achieved, we then use a type of behavior modification."

They came to a set of double doors similar to those that blocked access to the hospital proper. Dr. Mitchell pressed his thumb against the scanner.

"This, of course, is the nurses' station," said Dr. Mitchell as he waved to two middle-aged women dressed in white blouses and blue jumpers. They just nodded, but two orderlies in blue blazers jumped to their feet. Adam immediately noticed their stiff smiles and unblinking stares.

"Some spontaneity is sacrificed," thought Adam wryly.

As they continued down the hall, Mitchell described all the technical devices, until Dr. Glover interrupted, saying, "Adam understands all this, for God's sake. He's been to medical school."

But Dr. Mitchell didn't even pause in his narrative. Using his thumb, he opened the double doors leading to the ward, and Adam and the others filed in.

For such a modern hospital facility, Adam was surprised to find the ward laid out identically to the one at University Hospital. But aside from the floor plan, everything else was different. At University Hospital the beds, the nightstands, and even the ceilings were about to collapse from lack of maintenance. In sharp contrast, the ward at MTIC was so spotlessly clean that it looked as if it had just opened. Even the patients were lying well cared for in their beds, their covers uniformly pulled up to their chests. They were awake but immobile. Only their eyes moved as they followed the visitors' progress down the ward. Adam had never seen such a peaceful ward and certainly not such a peaceful psychiatric one.

Adam's eyes roved over the blank faces. Dr. Mitchell had begun another of his interminable lectures. Adam was wondering how long he'd have to listen when his eyes fell on the patient in the second bed to the right. It was Alan Jackson! Adam's heart began to pound. He was horrified that Alan might recognize him. He turned quickly to hide his face, but when he glanced back, Alan's expression had not changed. He was obviously heavily sedated. Adam permitted himself a closer look. Alan's head was swathed in bandages, and there was an IV dripping clear fluid into his right arm. Adam realized that the *Fjord* must have stopped in Puerto Rico the day before. No wonder they had kept Alan so heavily sedated. They had scheduled him for involuntary surgery all along.

When Mitchell paused in his patient survey, Adam pointed to Alan and asked, "What was this man's problem?"

Dr. Mitchell looked at Dr. Nachman, who nodded. Mitchell picked up the chart at the foot of Alan's bed and read the summary out loud. " 'Robert Iseman of Sandusky, Ohio; admitted for intractable temporal lobe epilepsy with criminally violent episodes; unresponsive to traditional treatment.' Iseman had been committed to a psychiatric prison without hope of parole. He volunteered to participate in the

Arolen treatment series." Dr. Mitchell placed the chart back in its rack.

"Has he been here long?" asked Adam.

"A few days," said Dr. Mitchell vaguely. "Why don't we . . ."

"Excuse me," said Adam, interrupting, "but sometimes it's easier to learn from a specific case than from generalities. What kind of treatment has this man had? It would seem from his bandages that he's had some form of brain surgery."

"He has indeed," said Mitchell after another quick glance at Dr. Nachman. "We know from his history that he was a particularly intractable case, and after a course of Conformin we implanted microelectrodes into the limbic system of his brain. That was his only hope for a lasting cure. You remember the classic experiments in which electrodes were imbedded in a bull's head and used to stop it from charging? Well, we've perfected the technique. We can do a lot more than merely stop a bull from charging."

Adam nodded slowly, as if trying to understand, but his mind recoiled in horror.

"Keep in mind that Mr. Iseman's treatment has just begun," Dr. Nachman said. "After he's more fully recovered from the operation, he will undergo conditioning."

"Absolutely," echoed Dr. Mitchell. "In fact, treatment will begin tomorrow, and he can anticipate discharge in about four days. Why don't we go down to the conditioning rooms so you can see exactly what we do."

Adam took a final glance at Alan's expressionless face and followed the doctors through the ward.

"Mr. Iseman will be given a combination of reinforced operant conditioning and adversive conditioning," Dr. Mitchell was saying. "A computer-guided program will be able to detect undesirable mental processes and reverse them before they manifest themselves in outward behavior."

Adam's mind whirled. He wondered what Mitchell meant by "undesirable mental processes." It probably ranged from refusing to prescribe Arolen products to belief in fee-for-service medicine.

"Here is one of our conditioning rooms," said Mitchell, swinging open a door and allowing Adam to look inside. It was a miniature of the theater on the *Fjord*. There was a large projection screen on the far wall facing two chairs that were fully equipped with electrodes and straps. Adam turned away in horror, allowing the door to swing shut.

"Is there much effect on the personality?" he asked.

"Of course," said Dr. Mitchell. "That is part of the program. We select only the most desirable personality traits."

"What about intellect?" asked Adam.

"Very little adverse effect," said Dr. Mitchell, leading the way back through the ward. "We've been able to document some minor decrease in creativity, but memory retention is normal. In fact, in some regards memory is enhanced, particularly for technical information."

Adam looked at Alan as they passed. The man's expression still hadn't changed. He had been reduced to some kind of zombie.

"The research is progressing well," said Dr. Nachman as he let them through the steel doors. "Of course, application is limited."

"The fetology work certainly can be put to more general use," said Dr. Glover.

"That's a matter of opinion," said Dr. Mitchell. "With the behavior-modification techniques we are perfecting, there will eventually be no locked wards either in hospitals or in prisons. In fact, both the National Institute of Mental Health and the Prisons Administration Board are funding our experiments."

They emerged into the three-story lobby with the bubble skylights. Dr. Glover was not about to let Mitchell get in the last word. He began to enumerate the various government agencies that were funding fetology.

Adam was in a state of shock. MTIC planned the ultimate destruction of an independent medical profession. Doctors would no longer be free-thinking professionals. They would be employees of the MTIC-Arolen medical empire.

"Adam," said Dr. Nachman, trying to get Adam's attention. "Are you still with us?"

"Yes, of course," said Adam quickly. "I'm just overwhelmed."

"Quite understandable," said Dr. Nachman. "And I think that we should give you some time to enjoy our recreational facilities. A few hours at the beach will do you a world of good. Shall we meet for dinner at eight?"

"What about visiting the operating rooms for psychosurgery? If possible, I'd like to see them."

"I'm afraid that is out of the question," said Dr. Nachman. "They're getting ready for a case this evening."

"Could I watch?" asked Adam.

Dr. Nachman shook his head. "We appreciate your interest, but unfortunately there is no viewing gallery. If you decide to take the job down here, though, I'm certain we can get you into the OR."

As Adam went back to his room to change, he realized that he'd better figure out some way of smuggling tangible evidence out of the center. But what evidence? What could he bring back to New York that not only would convince Jennifer not to have an abortion, but would cause the medical profession to put MTIC out of business?

After several hours of lying in the sun, Adam thought he had an idea. It was wild, and probably impossible to execute, but if successful, Adam knew he would have no trouble convincing anyone to take his warnings seriously.

Cocktails and dinner were an ordeal for Adam. Dr. Nachman seemed to want to introduce him to as many people as possible, and it was almost eleven before he could escape to his room after pleading fatigue.

He had decided he could not start to put his plan into effect until midnight. Too restless to lie down in the meantime, he took off his suit and dressed in a dark blue shirt and jeans, then carefully opened his shoulder bag and checked the supplies he'd organized that afternoon.

At eleven fifty-five he could stand the suspense no longer. He left his room and took the stairway to the roof. The moonlight was again almost as bright as day. He quickly crossed the bridge to the first inner building and then walked across to look down at the second. The skylights blazed, but Adam wasn't certain that indicated any special activity inside.

Setting his bag on the roof, Adam opened it and pulled out the rope he'd stolen that afternoon from one of the sailboats. Then he searched for an appropriate ventilation pipe. After testing to see if it were securely fastened to the roof, he tied the rope to it and dropped the free end down three floors onto the bridge to the innermost building.

Unaccustomed to climbing and terrified of heights, Adam summoned all his fortitude to climb up on the four-foot wall and lower his legs over the side. After a short prayer, Adam grasped the rope and let go of the wall. Hanging on for dear life, he inched his way down until his feet touched the roof of the bridge. He dropped to his hands and knees and scrambled to the roof of the hospital building, where he made his way over to the large central skylight. A movement below made him hold up.

Slowly, he inched to the edge and looked down. Below him was a scene straight out of a science fiction horror film. The area under the skylight was an enormous operating room, but instead of being staffed with doctors and nurses, it was fully automated. Two patients were being worked on at once by robotlike machines with long flexible arms.

On the far side of the room several patients were lying on a conveyor-beltlike system, their heads locked into stereotaxic vises. At present, there were only four, but Adam could see that the system was designed to accommodate at least a dozen at a time.

Adam remained glued to the skylight, mesmerized by the sheer scope of the horror. One of the patients on the belt began to move forward and was fed into a large CAT scanner, which started to rotate around the patient's head. When the rotation was complete, the machine paused while robotlike arms extended and incised the patient's head at the same points at which Vandermer's scars were made. A small amount of blood appeared and pooled below the patient's head. Other arms appeared and smoothly bored into the patient's skull. Adam could hear the whine of the drill through the skylight. Then the scanner began to function again, while a third set of arms extended and pushed into the patient's brain. Adam guessed that the system was inserting the controlling electrodes into the patients' brains using the CAT scanner to ensure proper placement.

A movement at the left of the room caught Adam's eye and he pulled back. Behind a leaded-glass partition, a group of people were seated at a control panel. They would have had a clear view of Adam if they cared to look up. Adam lay down. He could see in by peeking over the edge of the skylight, but was pretty sure now that he couldn't be seen.

He saw Dr. Nachman reach out and slap Dr. Mitchell on the back. One of the patients had been completed and was being moved off in preparation for the next. Adam thought he was going to be sick. MTIC-Arolen was definitely planning psychosurgery on a massive scale.

After ducking away from the skylight, Adam climbed to his feet and crossed the roof to the access door. Luckily, it was not locked. He entered a stairwell similar to the one he had used to reach the roof of his building. Except for a steady hum of the automated machinery from the OR, everything was quiet. Moving quickly, he descended to the second floor and carefully opened the door. As he had expected, he was just beyond the conditioning room. He looked down the hall into the darkened ward. The only light came from the glass-enclosed nurses' station on the opposite side of the ward. The nurse on duty appeared to be eating. Beyond her were two immobile orderlies sitting in straightback chairs.

Staying close to the wall, Adam moved into the ward and ducked down behind the first bed. In the half light he caught a glimpse of the patient's face. To his surprise, the man was awake. Adam waited, wondering if the patient would sound an alarm, but he just lay still, his unblinking gaze fixed on Adam.

Taking a deep breath, Adam began to crawl the length of the ward under the beds. When he got to the second from the end, he raised his head to look at the nurses' station. He was surprised how close he was to it. The nurse was still working on her sandwich, and the two orderlies hadn't moved.

It was now or never for his plan. Adam turned to the patient on the bed above him. Alan gave no sign of recognition.

"Alan, I want to take you out of here," Adam whispered. "Can you make it?"

There was no response. Adam might as well have been talking to the IV pole. Alan didn't even blink as Adam carefully undid the tape that held the IV in place and pulled out the catheter.

"If I get you up, do you think you can walk?"

Again, there was no response.

Grasping Alan's covers, Adam was about to yank them back when he saw a flashlight beam dance across the ceiling of the ward. Looking at the double entry doors, Adam saw the nurse pressing her thumb against the scanner. As the doors hissed open, Adam slid to the floor and ducked under the bed.

The nurse walked up the center aisle, shining her flashlight at each patient. Adam held his breath as she passed Alan's bed, hoping she wouldn't spot the detached IV. She didn't pause. Adam could see her feet move to the end of the ward, pivot, then return. The double doors hissed open, and the nurse went back outside.

Guessing she wouldn't be back for a while, Adam felt it was an opportune time to make his move. Pulling back Alan's covers, Adam grabbed him by the arms and eased him over to the side of the bed. Then, as gently as he could, he lifted Alan's torso and lowered the man to the floor. There was a slight thud when his legs hit the floor, but no one at the nurses' station seemed to hear.

"Can you crawl along the floor?" Adam whispered in Alan's ear. There was no response.

Refusing to give up, he grasped Alan's hand and began to pull him along the floor. To his surprise, Alan responded and soon began to crawl on his own. It was as if he couldn't act unless he were shown what to do.

They made it to the end of the ward. When Adam looked back, all was quiet at the nurses' station. The next fifty feet were going to be the most dangerous. Leaving the protection of the beds, they crawled down the hall toward the stairs. If anyone looked in their direction, they would be seen. When they reached the door, Adam opened it a few inches and was alarmed when light spilled out from the stairwell. Holding his breath, he opened the door wider and urged Alan through. A moment later they were safe.

Adam stood up and stretched. Then he bent over and lifted Alan to his feet. He was unsteady at first but regained his balance after a few seconds.

"Can you understand me?" asked Adam. There was a suggestion of a nod, but Adam wasn't sure. "We're getting out of here!" Taking Alan by the hand, Adam led the way up the stairs. Alan walked as if he had no idea where his feet were, but by the time they reached the third floor his movements became smoother. It seemed that the more he had to do, the easier it became. By the time they got to the roof, Alan seemed to be operating under his own power. Such rapid improvement made Adam think that Alan had been receiving a small but constant dose of tranquilizer through the IV. When they emerged onto the roof, Alan seemed almost awake, and Adam noticed that the pupils of his eyes were no longer fully dilated. But there still seemed no way Alan would be able to climb the rope three stories to the outer building. Adam wasn't sure he could even do it himself and cursed his lack of foresight in not planning better for their escape.

Looking at the landscaped space between the hospital and the next building he knew they could probably go down easier than up, but he suspected there was no way of escaping from the enclosed garden.

Afraid Alan's absence would be noticed, Adam realized he had to act. For lack of a better idea, he took the end of the rope and tied it under Alan's arms. Then, grasping the rope, Adam began to pull himself up the side of the building. The most difficult part was at the top when Adam had to let go of the rope and grasp the top of the wall. His feet flailed in the air as he tried to get purchase on the sheer concrete. Finally, he made it onto the roof.

After catching his breath, he bent over the wall. Alan was still standing with his back against the side of the building.

Adam tensed the rope but was only able to lift Alan a few inches. He realized he needed more leverage. Suddenly, he remembered seeing pictures of Egyptian slaves hauling stones up the pyramids. They'd held the ropes over their shoulders like beasts of burden. Adam decided to do the same. Straining forward with all his might, he staggered back to the far wall and quickly tied the slack onto the same pipe where the rope had initially been fastened. When he ran back to the side, he saw Alan dangling about a third of the way up.

Adam repeated his maneuver three more times. On the fourth tug the rope stuck, and when Adam looked, he saw Alan was caught directly under the lip of the wall surrounding the roof. Reaching down, he pulled the doctor sideways and got hold of his legs, and with great effort, he heaved him over. The two men fell onto the roof.

When Adam got his breath back, he untied the rope and stuffed it into his shoulder bag. Then he helped Alan up. There was an angry abrasion on the man's right cheek, but otherwise he seemed to have weathered the ordeal admirably.

Slinging his bag over his shoulder, Adam led Alan across the roof to the outer building and then down the stairwell. At that point Adam was stumbling more than Alan. His arms felt limp, his thighs quivered from exertion, and the palms of his hands were raw. When they reached Adam's room, he dropped the doctor on the bed and collapsed beside him.

Adam was out of shape for such rigorous physical activity. He would have liked to have rested, but he knew the danger of discovery increased with every minute that passed. He helped Alan out of his hospital gown and quickly dressed him. Fortunately, the two men were approximately the same size. Then he tucked Alan into bed and prayed that he was still sufficiently drugged to go back to sleep. As a precaution, Adam locked the door behind him when he left the room to see if he could find a car. As he hurried down the hall, he wished once again that he had made better plans for escape.

///

Selma Parkman yawned and glanced at the clock over the medication locker. It was only one-fifteen. She had over five hours' more duty, and she was already bored to death. Glancing over at the two orderlies, she wished she had a little of their patience. From the moment she had arrived at the center she had been amazed at the staff's placid acceptance of the dull routine.

"I think I'll take a walk," she said, flipping closed her Robert Ludlum novel. The orderlies didn't answer.

"Did you hear me?" she asked petulantly.

"We'll watch the ward," said one of them at last.

"You do that," said Selma, working her feet into her shoes. She knew that nothing would happen while she was gone. Nothing ever happened. When she'd taken the job, she'd expected a bit more excitement than babysitting a bunch of automatons. She'd left a good job in Philadelphia at the Hobart Psychiatric Institute to come down to Puerto Rico, and she was beginning to wonder if she had made a mistake.

Selma left the nurses' station and, desperate for some conversation, took the elevator to the OR floor and entered the gallery. Dr. Nachman smiled when he saw her. "Bored?" he said. "I can see we'll have to get you a more exciting schedule." In reality, he was irritated by her restlessness and had put her on the list for a course of Conformin treatment.

Selma watched the computer-generated images appearing on the screen in front of the operators, but she had no idea what she was seeing and soon became as bored as she'd been downstairs. She said good-bye, but no one responded. Shrugging her shoulders, she left the gallery, descended a floor, and retraced her steps to the nurses' station. The orderlies were as she'd left them. It wasn't time for her rounds, but since she was already up, she got the flashlight and went into the ward.

The job wasn't demanding to say the least. About half of the patients were on IVs, and she was supposed to check them at least twice during her shift. Otherwise all she had to do was shine her flashlight into the face of each patient to make sure he was still alive.

Selma stopped, her light playing on an empty pillow. Bending down, she looked along the floor. Once a patient had fallen out of bed, but that did not seem to be the case here. She moved over to the chart and read the name: Iseman.

Still thinking that the patient must be nearby, she went back to the nurses' station and flipped on the ward's overhead lights. A harsh fluorescent glare flooded the room. Summoning the orderlies, Selma quickly checked the room herself. There was no doubt about it: Iseman had vanished.

Selma began to worry. Nothing like this had ever happened. Telling the orderlies to keep searching, she hurried back up to the OR.

"A patient is missing," she said, spotting Nachman and Mitchell as they were about to leave.

"That's impossible," said Dr. Mitchell.

"It may be impossible," said Selma, "but Mr. Iseman's bed is empty, and he's nowhere in sight. I think that you'd better come down and see for yourselves."

"That's the patient that was operated on yesterday," said Dr. Nachman. "Wasn't he on a continuous Conformin drip?"

Without waiting for Mitchell's answer, he hurried off downstairs. As they entered the ward, Selma gestured triumphantly toward the empty bed.

Dr. Mitchell picked up the IV line and looked at the catheter. It was still slowly dripping. "Well, he can't be far."

After exhausting all possible hiding places on the floor, Dr. Nachman and Dr. Mitchell tried the fetology floor, then the roof, and finally the garden.

"I think we'd better call out all the orderlies," said Dr. Nachman. "We have to find Iseman immediately."

"This is incredible," said Dr. Mitchell with disbelief. "I'm surprised the man could even walk."

"If we don't find him right away," asked Dr. Nachman, "what

would happen if we were to activate his implanted electrodes?" Would that let us hone in on him?"

Dr. Mitchell shrugged. "The patient has not started conditioning. If we activate him, the signals could cause either pain or pleasure but without any specific control on behavior. It could be dangerous."

"Dangerous to whom?" asked Dr. Nachman. "The patient or people around him?"

"That I can't answer," admitted Dr. Mitchell.

"Well, that's a worst-case scenario," said Dr. Nachman. "I hope he'll be found in short order. Maybe the dosage in his IV was wrong. In any case, let's alert all the orderlies. Tell them to carry full hypodermics of Conformin so that when he is found there's no trouble."

/ / /

Adam was beginning to get desperate. There were plenty of cars in the parking lot opposite the main building, but no keys. Adam had assumed that with the tight security, people would be careless. But unfortunately, that was not the case. He cursed himself again for his casual planning.

Not quite sure what he might find, he made his way down the secluded walk to the beach and over to the club. A handful of cars were in the parking lot behind the clubhouse, and Adam went from one to another without luck. Then he noticed a good-sized Ford truck parked at the delivery entrance.

The door was open and Adam swung himself into the cab. He started to search for the ignition, but before he could find it, an alarm went off with an ear-piercing wail. Adam fumbled for the door and leapt out in panic.

The club door opened and Adam ran around the building to the shelter of a stand of pines. The alarm was turned off, but the sound of approaching voices made Adam realize he would have to keep moving. Seeing the masts of the Hobie Cats, Adam raced to the beach and slid under the nearest one.

He could hear the men returning to the club. They had obviously decided it was a false alarm, but Adam knew he only had a few hours before daylight to figure out how to get Alan out of the compound. He wondered if anyone had noticed the patient was missing.

///

Dr. Nachman's face appeared more haggard than usual. His eyes seemed to have visibly sunk into their sockets.

"He has to be here," said Dr. Mitchell.

"If he's here, then he should have been found," said Dr. Nachman humorlessly.

"Perhaps he's in the garden. It's the only place left."

"We have twenty orderlies searching," snapped Dr. Nachman. "If he were there, they would have found him by now."

"He'll be found," said Mitchell, more to convince himself than anyone else. "Maybe we'll have to wait until it gets light."

"I'm wondering if he could have gotten out of the hospital," said Dr. Nachman. "He's not the kind of patient we'd like to have found on the outside."

"He can't have escaped, even if he'd wanted to," said Dr. Mitchell. "He couldn't have opened the security doors. And besides, Ms. Parkman has been here. She said she definitely saw the patient when she made her earlier rounds."

"She wasn't here when she came up to the OR," said Dr. Nachman.

"But that was just for a few minutes," said Selma. "And the two orderlies on duty said that everything was quiet."

"I want the search extended to the main building," said Dr. Nachman, ignoring Selma. "I'm beginning to fear that someone else is involved, someone with access to the ward. If that is the case, I think we should try to activate the patient's electrodes. That might allow us to trace the man via the transmitter."

"I don't know if it will work," said Dr. Mitchell. "We've never tried to activate from a distance."

"Well, try it now," ordered Dr. Nachman. "Also, call security and tell them that no one goes through the main gate."

Dr. Mitchell went to the telephone and called Security. Then he called the head of programming, Edgar Hofstra, telling him that there was an emergency and he was needed in the control room. Then he and Nachman went upstairs.

The control room was on the same floor as the automated operating room. At one end, protected by a glass wall, was the MTIC mainframe computer. About a half dozen white-coated technicians were in evidence, performing a wide range of operational and maintenance procedures.

Hofstra arrived about ten minutes later, his eyes still puffy with sleep.

Not even bothering to apologize, Mitchell outlined the problem. "If we can activate the patient's electrodes, I think security can trace the patient by the transmitter. Do you think you can activate him from long range?"

"I'm not certain," said Hofstra, seating himself at the terminal. As soon as he punched in Iseman's name, the computer responded by saying that there was an error and that the patient was not engaged. Hofstra overrode the signal.

Everyone in the room watched anxiously. After a minute the screen flashed "electrodes activated," followed in another minute by the word "proceed."

"So far, so good," said Hofstra. "Now let's see if his battery has any power." He entered the command for Iseman's electrodes to transmit. The result was a very weak signal that was unintelligible to the computer.

Hofstra swung around in his chair. "Well, the electrodes activated, but the signal is so weak, I doubt we can trace the location."

/ / /

Adam never knew where he found the courage to go back into the main building, particularly when he saw that most of the lights had been turned on and that groups of men in blue blazers, carrying hypodermic syringes, were swarming over the ground floor. Only the thought of Jennifer and her impending abortion had forced him to risk the comparative safety of the outdoors. Now he simply walked through the main building lobby as if nothing was wrong. When he got out of the elevator on six, the hall was quiet and Adam guessed that they hadn't begun to search the guests' rooms.

He turned on the light when he got to his room and was relieved to find Alan still sleeping peacefully.

"I don't know if you can understand me," said Adam tensely, "but we have to get the hell out of here."

He pulled Alan to a sitting position and checked the rolls of gauze covering his head. Once he'd carefully unwound them, he was pleased to see that the automated surgery had only shaved a small area on either side of the man's head. Adam grabbed his comb and carefully covered the bald patches with Alan's remaining hair.

With his heart pounding, he helped Alan to his feet and quietly opened the door. Three orderlies were entering a suite at the end of the corridor. Adam knew that if he hesitated he wouldn't get a second chance. The moment they disappeared into the suite he grabbed Alan's hand and hurried him down to the bathers' elevator. As the doors closed, Adam heard voices, but no one seemed to be shouting alarm.

He pressed the ground-floor button. To his horror, after descending briefly, the elevator stopped on three!

Adam glanced at Alan. He looked better without his bandage, but his face still had that telltale drugged blankness.

The doors opened and a scarfaced orderly stepped into the elevator. Glancing mechanically at Adam and Alan, he turned to face the closing doors. He was so close, Adam could see the individual hairs on his neck. Adam held his breath as the elevator recommenced its descent.

They were just passing two when the orderly seemed to recognize their presence. He made a slow turn. In his left hand he held a hypodermic syringe without its protective plastic cap.

Adam reacted by reflex with speed that surprised him. He went for the syringe, wresting it from the orderly's grip with a quick twist, and then pushed the orderly forward into Alan. As the men collided, Adam jammed the needle into the man's back just to the side of the spine, depressing the plunger with the heel of his hand.

All three of them fell against the wall of the elevator and collapsed in a heap with Alan on the bottom. The orderly arched his back, rolled to the side, and opened his mouth to scream. Adam clamped his hand over the man's mouth to muffle the cry. The elevator stopped and the doors opened.

The orderly grabbed Adam's arm in a tight grip and began to pry his hand from his face. Adam strained to keep the man's mouth covered. Then he saw the man's eyes cross. Abruptly, the man's grip loosened and his body went limp.

Adam removed his hand and then recoiled in horror. He pushed himself away and stared at the man, whose eyes had now rolled up into his head. Although he appeared to have had some kind of plastic

surgery to mar his facial features, Adam still recognized him. It was
Percy Harmon!

For a second Adam was too startled to react. Then the elevator
doors started to close, and Adam knew he had to keep moving.
Wedging Alan against the door to keep it ajar, he dragged Harmon
outside and dropped him behind the dense ferns. He had a moment's
hope of taking him along, then realized it would be hard enough just
handling Alan. He led the doctor out the back door to the path that
led to the beach. His vague plan was to head over to the condominiums and see if he could find a car there.

The moon was now partially concealed, and the beach was not the
bright landscape it had been before. The palms and pine trees provided deep concealing shadow.

Halfway to the club, Adam and Alan came upon the Hobie Cat
Adam had hidden under. Adam halted. An idea stirred in the back of
his mind. He looked out at the ocean and wondered. He wasn't a
good sailor by any stretch of the imagination, but he knew a little
about small boats. And he was pleased to note that the last person to
use the Hobie Cat had beached it without taking off the sails.

The sound of a man's shout from the area of the main building
made him decide for sure. Time was running out. First, Adam
dragged the boat to the water. Next, he led Alan to it and helped him
climb on, forcing him to lie down on the canvas. With the bowline,
Adam tied Alan loosely to the mast. Wading into the water, Adam
pulled the Hobie off the sand and into the surf. The waves were only
two or three feet high, but they made it hard to control the boat.
When he was waist-deep, he hauled himself aboard.

His original idea was to paddle the boat out of sight around the
point, but he saw that was going to be impossible. He would have to
raise the sail. As quickly as he could, he hauled up the mainsail. He
winced in pain from his raw palms, but he kept at it. Finally the sail
billowed out, and the boom lifted with a clatter. To his relief, the boat
stabilized the moment it was under sail. Turning around, he snapped
the rudders into position, then pushed the tiller to the right.

For an agonizing minute, the boat seemed to drift back toward the
beach. Then, falling off the wind, it shot forward, smacking the in-
coming waves as it headed away from the beach. There was little
Adam could do but grab Alan with one hand and hold the tiller with
the other.

The boat passed directly in front of the club, but Adam was afraid to try to change his course. He heaved a sigh of relief when they got beyond the breakers. Soon after, they were around the point and safely out of sight.

Relaxing to a degree, Adam looked up at the parabolic curve of the sail contrasted against the star-strewn tropical sky. Glancing to the west, he saw the moon intermittently veiled with small, scudding clouds. Below the moon was the dark silhouette of Puerto Rico's craggy mountains. The beauty was overwhelming. Then the boat hit the long Atlantic swells and Adam had to turn his full attention to the tiller. Cleating the mainsheet securely, he raised the jib and the Hobie Cat shot through the water at even greater speed. He started to feel optimistic that within a few hours he'd be far enough up the coast to find help.

/ / /

Dr. Nachman turned from the computer in a rage. Harry Burkett had come to update the research director on the search, but Nachman wasn't content with false assurances.

"Are you telling me that all you've learned with forty men and a million dollars' worth of security equipment is that one of the orderlies has been found unconscious and one of our guests, Mr. Schonberg, is missing from his room?"

"That's correct," said Mr. Burkett.

"And the orderly," continued Dr. Nachman, "was presumably injected in the back with his own syringe of Conformin?"

"Exactly," said Mr. Burkett. "He was injected with such force that the needle broke off and is imbedded in the man's skin." Mr. Burkett wanted to impress the research director with the completeness of his investigation, but Nachman wasn't having any of it. He found it inconceivable that Mr. Burkett, with his huge staff and sophisticated resources, could not locate a heavily sedated patient. Thanks to Burkett's inefficiency, what had started as an inconvenience was rapidly becoming a serious affair.

Dr. Nachman angrily lit his pipe, which had gone out for the tenth time. He couldn't decide whether or not he should inform the inner circle of MTIC. If the problem got worse, the earlier he reported it, the better off he'd be. But if the problem resolved itself, it would be best to remain silent.

"Has there been any evidence of anyone touching the perimeter fence?" he asked.

"Absolutely not," said Burkett. "And no one has been allowed out of the main gate since Dr. Mitchell called." He glanced at the psychiatrist, who was nervously examining his cuticles.

Dr. Nachman nodded. He was certain the patient was still on the grounds and that the electrified fence was an insurmountable barrier, but he still worried about the competence of Burkett's security force. There was no reason to take chances.

"I want you to send someone to the airport to check the departing flights," he ordered.

"I think that's going a bit far," said Burkett. "The patient won't get off the compound."

"I don't care what you think," interrupted Dr. Nachman. "Everyone told me the patient couldn't have left the hospital, and obviously he has. So cover the airport."

"OK," said Burkett with an exasperated sigh.

Dr. Mitchell, who was well aware that he was the man who had insisted the patient couldn't have left the hospital, stood up, saying, "Even if the transmitter is too weak to use to trace the patient, maybe if we stimulate his electrodes, he'll reveal himself."

Dr. Nachman looked at Mr. Hofstra. "Could we do that?"

"I don't know," said Hofstra. "The position of his electrodes hasn't been neurophysiologically mapped. I don't know what would happen if we stimulated him. It might kill him."

"But could we stimulate him?" asked Dr. Nachman again.

"Maybe," said Hofstra. "But it will take some time. The present program has been written with the expectation that the patient would be initially present."

"What kind of time are you talking about?"

Hofstra spread his hands apart. "I should know if I'll be able to do it in an hour or so."

"But you didn't have any trouble activating the electrodes."

"That's true," said Hofstra. "But actual stimulation is much more complicated."

"Try it," said Dr. Nachman wearily. Then, gesturing with his hands toward Mr. Burkett, who was still on the phone, he said, "I'd like to have some kind of backup for his Keystone Kops."

/ / /

Looking at his watch, Adam realized that they'd been sailing for nearly two hours. Once they'd rounded the point north of the MTIC-Arolen beach, they'd encountered increasingly high swells that occasionally crested and broke over the canvas trampoline. A couple of times when they were in the rough of a particularly high wave, Adam was afraid they would be buried by tons of seawater. But each time the boat had bobbed up and ridden like a cork over the top of the wave.

They headed due west along the northern coast. Unsure if there were any reefs or not, Adam stayed about two or three hundred yards offshore. By far the hardest part of the adventure was dealing with his imagination. Each minute, his concern grew about sharks lurking beneath them in the dark swirling water. Every time he glanced down, he expected to see a huge black fin break the surface.

Certain that they had long since passed the limits of the MTIC-Arolen compound, Adam began to aim the Hobie Cat toward land. In the past fifteen minutes or so he'd begun to see occasional lights along the shore. He now could hear the waves pounding on the beach. He tried not to think about what that might mean.

A scream shattered the silence. All at once Alan grabbed his head with both hands and shrieked into the night. Adam was caught totally off guard. A large bolus of adrenaline shot into his system.

Alan's screams increased to full lung capacity, and he tried to stand up, straining against the rope that secured him to the mast. He began to throw himself from side to side, threatening to capsize the boat. Adam abandoned the tiller and the mainsail sheet and tried to restrain the crazed man. The boat immediately fell off the wind and the mainsail luffed.

"Alan!" yelled Adam above the sound of the wind. "What's the matter?" He grabbed Alan by the shoulders and shook him as hard as he could. Alan was still clasping his head with his hands with such force that his face was distorted. His shrieks came amid gasps for breath.

"What's the matter?" shouted Adam again.

Alan let go of his head, and for a second Adam could see his face. The man's previously blank expression had twisted into one of pain and rage. Like a mad dog, Alan lunged for Adam's throat.

Shocked at Alan's strength, Adam tried to scramble out of his reach, but there was little room on the Hobie Cat's trampoline. Alan twisted within his bonds and flailed his arms, catching Adam in the face with a forceful punch. Screaming himself, Adam teetered on the edge of the Hobie Cat, his hands frantically grabbing for a purchase. His fingers found the uncoiled mainsail halyard, but it did not provide any support. In a kind of agonizing slow motion Adam toppled into the forbidding ocean.

He plunged beneath the surface of the icy water. Desperately clawing at the water, Adam fought back up to the air, terrified that at any moment he would be bitten by a sea monster. His leg brushed the rope in his hand and he screamed.

Although the sails were luffing, the strong trade wind continued to push the boat through the water. Adam held on to the mainsail halyard and was dragged behind like bait on the end of a fish line. He could feel his right eyelid swelling, but worst of all, there was trailing warmth from his nose, which he guessed was blood. He expected his legs to be snapped off at any moment. Hand over hand, he frantically pulled himself back to the boat. On the trampoline Alan was still shrieking in pain. Adam grabbed a pontoon and started to scramble out of the water.

The snapping of the uncleated mainsail sounded like rifle shots. The boat had rotated to windward, and suddenly the boom wildly traversed the back of the boat, slamming into the side of Alan's head and pitching him face downward onto the trampoline.

Adam hauled himself out of the water and, watching out for the swinging boom, approached the man uneasily, half expecting him to explode anew. But Alan was unconscious and breathing deeply. Steadying himself on the bobbing boat, Adam felt Alan's head for a fracture. All he found was an actively swelling egg-shaped lump.

Carefully Adam rolled Alan over, wondering what had possessed the man. He'd been so peaceful until that terrifying moment. Adam noticed that one of the sutured incisions had pulled open, and suddenly he guessed what might have happened.

Scrambling back to the stern, Adam grabbed the tiller and then pulled in on the mainsail tackle. The boat responded and the sails filled. Falling off the wind, Adam headed for the shore. He now had another, unanticipated problem. He had no idea what Alan could be made to do. Adam shivered, more from fear than from the chill of his damp clothes.

/ / /

Edgar Hofstra glanced up at Dr. Nachman, whose eyes had become blood red. The man's lower lids hung away from his globes while he bent over Hofstra's shoulder, staring at the computer screen.

"I can't be one hundred percent sure that the electrodes responded," said Hofstra, "but that was the strongest signal I could send at the moment. If you give me a couple of hours, I will be able to increase the power."

"Well, see if you can speed things up," said Dr. Nachman. "And maybe you can remember if any of our early experiments with monkeys gave us clues as to how the subject will respond."

"I hate to tell you," said Mitchell, "but in addition to destroying everything around them, the monkeys in such situations ended up killing themselves."

Dr. Nachman got up and stretched. "Listen, that may be the good news."

"I'll have to take the whole system off line while we work on it," said Hofstra.

"That's OK," said Dr. Nachman. "At this hour I can't imagine anybody wanting to send instructions to any of the 'controlled' doctors."

"Too bad the patient hadn't at least been conditioned for the self-destruct mode," said Dr. Mitchell.

"Yeah, too bad," agreed Dr. Nachman.

/ / /

By the time Adam got within a hundred feet of shore, the night had become significantly darker. He turned the boat to the west and paralleled the island while he listened carefully to the waves crashing on the shore. He hoped that the type of sound would enable him to guess the composition of the beach. With the heavy surf, he was afraid of coral.

Alan had moaned a few times but had not tried to get up. Adam thought that he was either still unconscious from the blow to his head or in some kind of post-ictic state from what had been a seizure of sorts. In any case, Adam hoped that he'd stay quiet until they reached the shore.

The sound of a dog barking against the noise of the ocean caught Adam's attention, and he strained his eyes shoreward. He could make out, nestled among the graceful trunks of a forest of coconut palms, a group of dark houses. Thinking that they were a good indication of a sand beach, Adam shoved the tiller over, ducked under the jibing mainsail, and headed the boat toward land.

Although Adam let the sail out and was spilling the wind, the boat seemed to be flying. Holding the tiller with his leg, he reached up and let loose the jib, which began to flap angrily in the wind. Ahead, he could see where the waves were cresting, a white line of foam against the blackness of the island.

The closer they got, the louder was the noise of the breakers pounding the shoreline. Adam prayed silently for a sand beach, although at that speed even sand would be trouble. A huge wave passed under the boat, then a larger one built behind. The Hobie rode up the face of the wave, and with terror, Adam thought they were about to flip end over end. But the boat righted itself as the wave rolled under. Looking behind again, Adam saw another wave bearing down on them. It looked as big as a house. Its upper edge feathered against the sky, suggesting it was about to break. Adam saw the top begin to curl. Holding the tiller with one hand and the side of the trampoline with the other, he closed his eyes and braced himself for submersion.

But the tons of water that Adam expected didn't come. Instead, the Hobie Cat shot forward with an exhilarating burst of speed. Adam opened his eyes and saw that they were racing toward shore in front of the torrent of white water.

Before he knew what was happening, the speeding boat hit the backwash of the previous wave and bounced into the air, throwing him over the side into the water. He came up sputtering, but happily surprised that the water was only waist deep. Alan had remained on the boat's trampoline, secured by the line around his chest, but he had rotated around the mast and his legs dangled over the side. Adam grabbed the boat and pulled it toward shore, straining against the undertow. The pontoons finally hit the bottom, and Adam waited for the next wave before running the boat up onto dry land.

He immediately collapsed onto the sand to catch his breath, then fished out his glasses and slipped them on. Looking around, he saw that they had landed on a narrow and rather steep sand beach that was strewn with all sorts of debris. A number of old wood-planked boats were drawn up from the water's edge and secured around the trunks of nearby coconut palms. Within the darkness of the trees was a village of ramshackle houses.

A welcoming committee of two scraggy dogs appeared at the edge of the beach and began to bark loudly. A light went on in the nearest house. When Adam struggled to his feet, the dogs dashed out of sight for a moment, only to reappear and bark more insistently. Adam ignored them. He untied Alan and got the man standing.

Alan held his head as Adam led him up the beach. Just within the shelter of the palms, they came upon a ramshackle house with a beaten-up half-ton pickup parked outside. Adam peered hungrily inside the cab. No keys were dangling from the ignition. He decided to knock on the door of the house and take his chances. The dogs were barking wildly now, nipping at his legs.

As he walked up the steps, a light went on and a face appeared at the window. Adam checked his back pocket to make sure his wallet was safe. A moment later the door opened. The man who opened it was stripped to the waist and barefoot. He had a gun in his hand, an old revolver with a mother-of-pearl handle.

"No hablo much español," said Adam, trying to smile. The man did not smile back.

"Me puede dar un ride al aeropuerto," said Adam, turning slightly and pointing toward the truck.

The man looked at Adam as if he were crazy. Then he made a waving motion of dismissal with the pistol and started to close the door.

"Por favor," pleaded Adam. Then, in a combination of Spanish and English, he rapidly tried to explain how he'd been lost at sea on a sailboat with a sick friend and that they had to get to the airport immediately. Pulling out his wallet, he began counting out soggy bills. That finally perked the man's interest. He put the gun into his pocket and allowed Adam to lead him down to the beach.

In the midst of his frantic attempts to capture the man's interest, Adam had had an idea. When he got to the beach, he picked up the bowline of the Hobie Cat and put it into the Puerto Rican's hand. At the same time he struggled to explain to the man that the boat was his if he took them to the airport.

The Puerto Rican finally seemed to comprehend. A broad smile appeared on his face. Gleefully, he pulled the boat higher on the beach and lashed it to one of the coconut palms. Then he went back to the house, presumably to dress.

Adam lost no time in getting Alan into the cab of the truck. Almost immediately the Puerto Rican reappeared, swinging his keys. He started up the truck, glancing warily at Alan, who was slumped in his seat, and at the point of drifting off to sleep again. Adam tried to explain that his friend was sick, but he soon gave up, deciding it was easier to pretend that he, too, had fallen asleep. He sat with his eyes closed until they reached the airport. Indicating that he wanted to be dropped at the Eastern departure area, he began to worry how on earth he could explain Alan's and his appearance to the ticket clerk.

The truck came to a stop, and Adam touched Alan's shoulder. This time it was easier to wake him up.

"Muchas gracias," Adam said as they got out.

"De nada," called the driver, and roared away.

"OK," said Adam, taking Alan by the arm. "This is the last lap." He walked into the almost empty terminal. A few taxis and an ambulance idled by the entrance, but it was too early for many departing tourists. Adam surveyed the old-fashioned building and seated Alan at an empty shoeshine stand. Then he went over to the ticket counter.

Looking up at the schedule, he saw that the next Eastern flight to Miami was in two hours. A small sign said "For After Hours, Use Phone." Adam picked up the receiver next to the sign. When the agent answered, he told Adam that he'd be right out. Sure enough, by the time Adam hung up, a man in a clean and pressed brown uniform emerged from a door behind the counter. When he saw Adam, his smile faltered.

Adam was acutely conscious of his ragged appearance. The ride in the truck had almost dried his clothes, but seeing the agent's reac-

tion, he decided he'd better come up with a good story. Hesitating
only a moment, he launched into a long explanation that featured an
end-of-vacation party with lots of booze and a last-minute sail. He
and his friend had washed up on a beach miles from their hotel and
then had hitched a ride to the airport. Adam said they had to be at
work the next day and that their luggage would follow when the rest
of their group flew back.

"It's been a hell of a vacation," he added.

The agent nodded as if he understood and said there was plenty of
space available. Adam asked if there were any earlier flights to the
States and was told that Delta had a flight to Atlanta in an hour.

As far as Adam was concerned, the sooner they got off the island
the better. He asked for directions to Delta and was told to go to the
next building. Deciding Alan was best off where he was, Adam hurried to the next terminal, where there were a number of travelers
waiting to check in.

Adam joined the end of the line. When he got to the counter, the
agent eyed him uneasily, but Adam repeated his now practiced story.
Again, the agent seemed to believe him.

"First-class or coach?" he asked.

Adam looked at the man, wondering if he were trying to be funny.
But then, remembering that Arolen paid his Visa card charges, he
said, "First-class, of course."

Adam scanned the terminal nervously as the man wrote up the
tickets, but he didn't spot anyone who appeared to have been sent by
MTIC.

When the agent had finished, Adam said, "We could use a wheelchair. My friend really got banged up when we tipped over in the
surf."

"Oh my gosh," said the agent. "I'll see what I can do."

In less than five minutes he was back with the wheelchair.

Adam thanked him and set off for the other building to get Alan.

///

From a vantage point on the mezzanine overlooking the Delta
ticket counter, two ambulance attendants dressed in white uniforms
watched as Adam disappeared from sight. The fact that he was pushing a wheelchair suggested that Iseman could not be far away.

The two men quickly descended to the terminal floor and hurried outside to the ambulance, where they told the driver to radio Mr. Burkett that the subjects had been spotted. The taller of the attendants, a burly man with a blond crew cut, pulled two collapsible gurneys from the back of the ambulance, while his partner stuffed a number of syringes into a medical bag.

Back in the terminal, they checked the gate number for the Delta flight to Atlanta and set out for Concourse B.

When Adam got back to the shoeshine stand, he was horrified to find the bench empty. Frantically, he ran the wheelchair back toward the Eastern counter, where he spotted Alan trying to talk to the agent, who was telling him that he was in Puerto Rico, not Miami, but that he could give him a reservation to Miami if he wanted one.

"He's with me," explained Adam, helping Alan into the chair.

"The man thinks he's in Miami," said the agent.

"He's been through a lot," said Adam. "You know, the shipwreck . . ." He let his voice trail off and started back to Delta.

"What am I doing in Puerto Rico?" asked Alan. Although his diction was still slurred, he was the most alert he'd been since Adam had talked to him at the *Fjord* departure terminal.

With only twenty minutes before flight time, Adam pushed Alan at a rapid pace. A tour group with gaudy shirts was noisily assembled in front of the Delta counter. Having the people around gave Adam a sense of safety. Going through security before boarding the plane, Adam helped Alan out of the wheelchair so he could go through the metal detector. The guard eyed them suspiciously but didn't say a word. Once they were through and on their way to the gate, Adam felt a growing sense of excitement. He'd done it. In a few hours they'd be landing in the States.

The floor of the concourse angled downward and Adam now had to restrain the wheelchair from rolling forward on its own accord. Ahead was a water fountain and rest rooms, and Adam considered stopping; they had nearly twenty minutes to spare. He noticed a small sign on the floor next to the men's room door, indicating that the rest rooms were being cleaned. Adam decided to do his drinking and peeing on the plane.

He had slowed to a normal walk and was about to continue on when out of the corner of his eye he caught a sudden movement. Just as he began to turn his head, someone grabbed him from behind, crushing his arms against his torso. Before Adam could respond, he was lifted off the floor.

Adam tried to twist as he cried out, but he was rammed directly against the closed door of the men's room, hitting it with his chest and forehead. The impact threw open the door, and both Adam and his attacker fell headfirst onto the tile floor.

The force of the fall released the man's stranglehold on Adam. Although dazed, Adam got his arms free and scrambled to his feet, only to be tripped again when the man grabbed him around the ankles. Again Adam fell, his head narrowly missing the edge of the sink, but this time his hands were free to cushion the fall.

Behind him, Adam was dimly aware of Alan in the wheelchair being propelled by a second man in white. Alan had been pushed against the men's room door as Adam had, his head snapping forward on impact. When the door had opened, he was forcibly shoved forward, his head hyperextending. The unguided wheelchair now sped through, arcing to the left and then colliding with the bank of urinals, spilling Alan out of the chair.

The second man turned and locked the door behind him, then came to the aid of his partner. Together, the two men bore down on Adam, quickly overwhelming him and pinning him to the floor.

Marshaling his strength, Adam gave a powerful kick with his legs and succeeded in getting one arm free. Swinging widely, he connected with the lower jaw of the larger of his two attackers. The man cried out. His partner snapped back and, in a fit of anger, punched Adam solidly in the stomach.

Adam's breath left him with an audible whoosh, making him gag and leaving him momentarily helpless. The two men held Adam on the floor with their combined weight. The smaller medic pulled a syringe from his pocket. Using his teeth, he removed the plastic cover from the needle. With one hand he smoothed out the cloth covering Adam's thigh and then plunged the needle into Adam's flesh, all the way to the hilt.

Adam tried to move but without success. The medic pulled back on the plunger to make certain that the needle was not in a blood vessel, then, regrasping the syringe, prepared to inject.

Suddenly, a fearsome shriek reverberated around the tiled room. The unworldly sound momentarily paralyzed the two men holding Adam to the floor.

Alan grabbed his head as he'd done on the Hobie Cat and leapt to his feet. His eyes snapped open and his lips rolled back to expose his teeth. With a ripping sound, his hands came away from his head, clutching tufts of hair from his scalp. Like a rabid animal, he sprang from the urinals toward the threesome sprawled on the floor. He grasped his hands together to form a club and after swinging them in a great arc, pounded the man who had just inserted the syringe into Adam. The blow caught the man on the side of the head with such force that he was propelled from astride Adam into the mouth of an open toilet stall, ramming into the divider with a sickening crunch.

The smaller medic stood up in shock, his eyes reflecting the horror of having witnessed the materialization of a monster. He took a step backward and raised his hands, but Alan was on him in a flash, biting off most of the man's ear with a snap of his jaws. The medic's terror made it impossible for him to defend himself. Alan grabbed his head and began to beat it against one of the mirrors above the sinks, whipping frothy spirals of blood onto the glass in graceful arcs. The mirror cracked, splintered, and then shattered in a cascade of shards.

Adam had also been initially transfixed by the unexpected transformation of Alan, but having seen it once before, he was better able to recover. He yanked the syringe from his thigh and, scrambling to his feet, quickly assessed the chances of being able to pass Alan, who continued to smash the medic's head against the mirror. Unfortunately, at that moment the medic's body went limp and he fell to the floor. Alan immediately lost interest in him. Throwing his head back and shrieking again, Alan now came after Adam.

Adam's only recourse was to dash into a toilet stall and try to close the door behind him. Alan got his hand around the edge of the door though, and began to prevail in the shoving match that ensued. As Adam sensed that he was losing the test of strength, he lifted his legs against the door. With his back against the wall, he thrust the door closed, catching Alan's fingers in the jamb. Alan shrieked anew and pulled his hand free.

Adam latched the door and backed against the wall, the toilet between his legs. His mind raced as to what he could do next.

Alan began to throw his body against the door repeatedly. Each time the latch bent a little more. Finally it snapped, and the door burst open.

Adam screamed Alan's name, but Alan came at him like a locomotive, his pupils pinpoints and his eyes crazed. More out of pure defense than thought, Adam held out the syringe which he had been clutching. Alan ran directly onto the needle, which pierced his abdomen. The force of his charge depressed the plunger, sending the contents into his flesh.

Alan did not even feel the needle. He grabbed Adam's head with seemingly superhuman strength and practically lifted Adam off the floor. But then, as Adam watched, his crazed eyes fluttered and his pupils dilated. His right eye wandered like a child's lazy eye, and his left one assumed a questioning look. His grip relaxed and he slowly sagged to his knees. Finally, he collapsed backward and flopped out of the stall onto the floor in front of one of the sinks.

For a moment Adam could not move. He felt he'd come close to death. Slowly he lowered his eyes to look at the tip of the needle that was still in his hand. A drop of fluid had collected there and now dropped off. Adam let go of the syringe, and it clattered to the floor.

Stepping out of the stall and pushing aside two gurneys that were at the back of the room, Adam knelt beside Alan and felt his pulse. It was strong and normal. To Adam's surprise, the man's eyes fluttered open. In a very slurred voice he complained that his hands hurt.

///

"At that level of energy, there is no doubt that our patient's electrodes were stimulated to maximum," said Hofstra. "The result has to have been devastating."

"But now we may have a new problem," said Dr. Nachman. "If the patient is dead, no one can examine the body. We can't let anyone find the implants. We must find him at once."

The phone rang, and Dr. Mitchell answered. After listening and saying "good" several times, he turned to Nachman with a thumbs-up sign.

"Your idea of covering the airport was a good one," he said. "Burkett says the patient and Mr. Schonberg were sighted and are being picked up by the ambulance medics."

"What if they were already in the ambulance when the stimulus was given?" asked Nachman.

"It could have been big trouble. I think we'd better search the road between here and the airport."

Dr. Nachman threw up his hands. "When is this going to end?"

/ / /

Adam had no doubt that Alan's psychotic episodes were due to remote stimulation, and he prayed that once they were airborne Alan would be out of range. Their one hope was to get aboard, but Adam was now afraid they both looked so bad that the Delta agents might turn them away. There were only five more minutes until their flight was due to take off.

Adam washed his face quickly and tried to wipe Alan's hands, which were coated with blood. Worse still, there were several raw patches on his head, where Alan had torn out clumps of his hair. Adam mopped at them with little result. Well, there was nothing more he could do. He lifted Alan onto the wheelchair and was about to push him out the door when he spotted a full hypodermic lying on the floor. He picked it up, deciding it would be useful if Alan had another fit.

As he approached the gate, Adam saw the plane was in the final boarding process.

"Hold it," he yelled. Two Delta agents eyed him curiously. Then one of them said, "Are you the two who were stranded on the sail-boat?"

"That's right," said Adam, handing over the tickets.

"The agent at the ticket counter said to expect you. We thought that perhaps you'd changed your minds."

"Heavens, no," said Adam. "It's just been hard getting my friend motivated."

The agent looked at Alan, whose head was lolling sideways. "He's not drunk, is he?"

"Hell, no," said Adam. "He got pretty scraped up when we capsized. They had to give him a painkiller, and it seems to have knocked him out."

"Oh, I see," said the agent, handing Adam the boarding cards. "Seats 2A and 2B. Will you need a wheelchair in Atlanta?"

"That would be nice," said Adam. "Actually, we'll be going on to Washington. Could you make those arrangements for us?"

"Absolutely," said the agent.

Adam wheeled Alan down the jetway with a sense of relief. The stewardesses were less than enthusiastic when they saw the pair board, but they helped Alan out of the wheelchair and listened politely as Adam ran through his shipwreck story one more time. The plane was only half full, and most of the other passengers were asleep. Adam decided to close his eyes too and slept all the way to Atlanta except for the few minutes when he woke to wolf down breakfast.

Adam dreaded the transfer, thinking that there might be trouble. But a Delta agent had a wheelchair waiting and ticketed them straight through to Washington. The layover was only forty minutes, but it gave Adam a chance to call Jennifer. Luckily, she answered herself.

"Jennifer, everything is going to be all right. I can explain everything."

"Oh," she said vaguely.

"Just promise me you won't have the abortion until I get there."

"The hearing is this morning," said Jennifer, "and I won't do anything today, but if you're not here by tomorrow . . ." Her voice trailed off.

"Jennifer, I love you. I have to get to the plane now. We're just taking off from Atlanta."

"Atlanta?" said Jennifer, completely confused. "And who's 'we'?"

/ / /

"Adam?" asked Margaret Weintrob, her nimble fingers coming to an abrupt halt on her typewriter. "Is that you?"

Arm in arm, like drunken buddies, Adam and Alan staggered past the startled secretary's desk.

"Adam!" shouted Mrs. Weintrob, starting to rise. "You can't go in your father's office. He has . . ."

But Adam had already opened the door.

The two well-dressed men sitting across from Dr. Schonberg turned in surprise. Momentarily speechless, Dr. Schonberg sat helplessly as Adam asked the two men to wait outside.

"Adam," said Dr. Schonberg finally, "what on earth is the meaning of this?"

"Did you take any action on the charges we discussed the last time I was here?" asked Adam.

"No, not yet."

"I'm not surprised," said Adam. "You said that you needed more evidence. Well, I've brought all the proof you'll ever want. Come over here and meet Dr. Alan Jackson of the University of California. He has just come from one of the famous Arolen cruises. And made a short stop at the research center in Puerto Rico."

"Is the man drunk?" asked Dr. Schonberg.

"No," said Adam. "Drugged and a victim of psychosurgery. Come over here. I'll show you."

Dr. Schonberg approached Alan cautiously, as if he expected the man to leap suddenly out of his chair.

Adam gently tilted Alan's head so his father could see the small incisions where the electrodes had been implanted.

"They implanted some kind of remote-control device there," said Adam, his voice softer and shaded with compassion. "But I got Alan out before they 'conditioned' him. As soon as his drug wears off, he'll be able to tell you at least some of what happened. And I know he will agree to have the electrodes removed and examined."

Dr. Schonberg looked up at his son after examining the incisions on the sides of Alan's head. He was silent for a moment and then turned on the intercom and said, "Margaret, I want you to call Bernard Niepold at the Justice Department. Tell him it is urgent that I see him immediately. And call the Bethesda Naval Hospital and tell them to expect a confidential patient under my signature. And I want a twenty-four-hour guard."

EPILOGUE

Jennifer was exhausted. Despite all of the childbirth classes she'd attended, she'd not been prepared for the real thing. Giving birth was both better and worse than she'd expected. No amount of reading or hearing about other women's experiences could have readied her for this unique and passionate event.

The pain of labor had been intense yet strangely thrilling, but as the hours had gone by, she had felt progressively drained. She wondered if she would find the strength. Then the pain came more often and for longer periods until finally, from somewhere deep in her being, came a new burst of energy. She felt an irresistible urge, half voluntary, half involuntary, to push and bear down. A crescendo of pressure made her feel she was stretched to her limit, yet still she pushed and held her breath.

Suddenly, there was an almost sensuous release, accompanied by a gush of fluid and the thrilling squeal of a newborn infant exercising its vocal cords for the first time.

Opening her eyes, Jennifer gripped Adam's hand with what little strength she had remaining. Looking up into his face, she could see that his attention was directed down between her outstretched legs. With a terrible feeling of dread, she watched him. No test had been able to dispel the worry she had about the health and well-being of the child within her. Doctors at University Hospital had repeated the amniocentesis and had reported that the baby was normal, but with all that had happened, Jennifer had had trouble believing it.

She watched Adam to see what glimpse of disaster would register on his face. She wanted to know how their child was from him, not from seeing for herself. As she expected, he didn't smile and didn't blink. After what seemed too long a time, he lowered his eyes to meet hers, cradling her head with his hands as he did so. He spoke softly, sensitive to her feelings. First he told her he loved her!

Jennifer's heart seemed to stop. She held her breath, although the physical pain had ceased, and waited for the inevitable, dreaded news. In her heart she had known all along. She shouldn't have listened to anyone, she told herself. She'd had a bad feeling ever since the mix-up at the Julian lab, never mind that it had been done on purpose.

Adam wetted his dry lips with the tip of his tongue. "We have a beautiful, healthy boy, Jennifer. Luckily, he looks like you."

It took a moment for Adam's words to sink in. When she finally comprehended, tears of happiness and thanksgiving welled in her eyes. She tried to speak but couldn't. She swallowed. Then she reached up and pulled Adam down and hugged his head as hard as she could. His laugh gave voice to the joy and relief in her heart. All she could think to do was thank God.

/ / /

Adam collected himself, smoothed out his surgical scrub suit, and stepped from the delivery area into University Hospital's obstetrical waiting room. One glance was enough. It was hard to believe, but the message he'd gotten during the last stages of Jennifer's labor had been correct. Sitting among a group of expectant fathers was his own, Dr. David Schonberg.

Dr. Schonberg met his son as soon as he entered the room.

"Hello, Adam," he said in his usual cool manner.

"Hello, father," said Adam.

Dr. Schonberg adjusted his glasses higher on his nose. "What's it like being back in medical school?"

"Just fine," said Adam. "I'm so glad to be back. I've hardly minded the catch-up work."

"That's good to hear," said Dr. Schonberg. "How's Jennifer?"

Adam stared at his father. It was the first time the man had ever called Jennifer by name.

"She's just fine," answered Adam.

"And what about the baby?"

"The baby's a healthy, beautiful boy," said Adam.

To Adam's utter astonishment he saw something he'd never seen before: tears in his father's eyes. Before the shock could register, his father's arms were around him, hugging him. Another first. Adam hugged back. Tears formed in Adam's eyes as well, and the two men stood there, holding each other for so long that some of the soon-to-be fathers began to stare.

Finally, a somewhat embarrassed Dr. Schonberg pushed Adam back, but lovingly held onto his arms. Each looked at the other's tears, then both laughed.

"I wasn't crying," said Dr. Schonberg.

"Neither was I," said Adam.

"You know what I think?" said Dr. Schonberg.

"What?" asked Adam.

"I think we're both lousy liars."

"I think I'd have to agree."

AUTHOR'S NOTE

Since I graduated from medical school in 1966, I have heard the term "crisis in medicine" so often that it conjures up the allegory of the shepherd boy who cried wolf too many times. But until now the crises have all been voiced by particular interest groups and were often contradictory: too few hospital beds, too many hospital beds; not enough physicians, too many physicians. It was enough to make anyone confused and apathetic.

But now I have come to believe that "crisis in medicine" is applicable in a truly general sense. Unfortunately, because so many people have cried wolf in the past, the media have only just begun to take note of this very real crisis. What we are witnessing today is the gradual but quickening pace of the intrusion of business into medicine. It must be understood that the corporate mentality of the balance sheet is diametrically opposed to the traditional aspects of altruism that have formed the foundation of the practice of medicine, and this dichotomy augers disaster for the moral and ethical foundations of the profession. Big Business views the medical field as a high—cash-flow, high-profit, low-risk, and low-capital investment industry that is now particularly ripe for takeover.

Evidence of this shift toward business interests in the medical field is reflected in the newly interlocking ownership of proprietary (for profit) hospitals and nursing home chains, medical suppliers, and a deluge of other health-care organizations like dialysis centers, surgicenters, etc. Even research has gone in the direction of business as evidenced by the new biotech companies.

Response to this activity has been surprisingly slight, despite the insidious effect it has on the practice of medicine. Professional journals have viewed the process with curious academic disinterest, doctors have either joined the entrepreneurial bandwagon or ignored it, the public has remained silent, and the media have only just begun to run articles sounding the alarm. It is my hope that *Mindbend* will help focus public attention. By couching the problem in an emotional framework, it brings the process into personal perspective and allows the reader to understand the implications of the situation through identification with the main character, which I believe is one of the key values of fiction.

For me, the realization of the intrusion of business into medicine came with a letter I received from a hospital, informing me that its census was low and that I should admit more patients for surgery, as if I had a group of people in the wings who were being denied appropriate operations. That letter, more than any other experience, made me realize that our medical system had inadvertently been constructed to depend upon and reward overutilization of facilities and services, thereby fostering its own rising costs. No wonder businessmen became interested.

For *Mindbend* I chose the drug industry as the focal point not because it has been any worse than any other group, but because it has been around longer than most businesses associated with medicine and it exerts a powerful and growing influence. The important point is that the drug firms are corporations which do not exist for the public weal, no matter how much they try to convince the public otherwise. Their goal is to provide a return on their investors' capital.

The overriding commercial interest of the drug firms is underlined by the ungodly amount of money (billions of dollars per year) that they spend on promotion of their products, primarily attempting to influence the physician, who unfortunately is rather easy prey. There are very few doctors who have not accepted some gift or service from the drug industry. I still have the black bag given to me as a third-year medical student, and I have attended a number of symposia sponsored by a drug company. The drug industry currently spends more on promotion and advertising each year than it does on research! According to *Pills, Profits, and Politics*, the amount is also more than the total spent on all educational activities conducted by all the medical schools in the United States to train medical students. It would be unfair to suggest that the pharmaceutical industry has not contributed to society. But this has been the by-product, not the goal. And there have been cases in which the public good has been ignored. One need only to mention the thalidomide disaster or the DES calamity to recognize that the record is variegated and that commercial interests can have unfortunate consequences. Drug companies have marketed products that they knew might be dangerous or ineffective or both merely to turn a profit.

Medical practice as it has been known in this country for the last thirty years or so is changing. The doctor-patient relationship used to be the fulcrum, but it is losing ground to economic and business interests. The American public has a right and an obligation to know what kind of system is evolving.

For those people interested in pursuing the issue, I recommend the following books:

Ainsworth, T. H., M.D., *Live or Die* (Macmillan, 1983). Written by a physician who looks at the problem from the vantage point of having been both a practitioner and a hospital medical director, this book is particularly poignant in its appeal for physicians to recognize what is happening to the profession and to reexert their leadership.

Silverman, Milton, et al., *Pills, Profits, and Politics* (University of California Press, 1974). This book gives an overall view of the pharmaceutical industry, and it makes for interesting reading. I'm confident it will arouse some unexpected emotions. Although it was written over ten years ago, it is still strikingly relevant.

Starr, Paul, *The Social Transformation of American Medicine* (Basic Books, 1982). This book provides an impressive overview of the history of medicine in America and gives one a realistic comprehension of how the current situation has developed.

Wohl, Stanley, M.D., *The Medical Industrial Complex* (Harmony Books, 1984). This readable, concise book discusses the issues with few embellishments.